PRAISE FOR *IN THE CARDS*

"Infused with . . . fresh detail. Between the sweetness of the relationship and the summery beach setting, romance fans will find this a warming winter read."

—*Publishers Weekly*

"Fans will love the frank honesty of her characters. [Beck's] scenery is richly detailed and the story engaging."

—*RT Book Reviews*

"[A] realistic and heartwarming story of redemption and love . . . Beck's understanding of interpersonal relationships and her flawless prose make for a believable romance and an entertaining read."

—*Booklist*

PRAISE FOR *WORTH THE WAIT*

"[A] poignant and heartwarming story of young love and redemption and will literally make your heart ache . . . Jamie Beck has a real talent for making the reader feel the sorrow, regret, and yearning of this young character."

—*Fresh Fiction*

PRAISE FOR *WORTH THE TROUBLE*

"Beck takes readers on a journey of self-reinvention and risky investments, in love and in life . . . With strong family ties, loyalty, playful banter, and sexual tension, Beck has crafted a beautiful second-chances story."

—*Publishers Weekly* (starred review)

PRAISE FOR *SECRETLY HERS*

"[I]n Beck's ambitious, uplifting second Sterling Canyon contemporary . . . [c]onflicting views and family drama lay the foundation for emotional development in this strong Colorado-set contemporary."

—*Publishers Weekly*

"Witty banter and the deepening of the characters and their relationship, along with some unexpected plot twists and a lovable supporting cast . . . will keep the reader hooked . . . A smart, fun, sexy, and very contemporary romance."

—*Kirkus Reviews*

PRAISE FOR *WORTH THE RISK*

"An emotional read that will leave you reeling at times and hopeful at others."

—*Books and Boys Book Blog*

PRAISE FOR *UNEXPECTEDLY HERS*

"Character-driven, sweet, and chock-full of interesting secondary characters."

—*Kirkus Reviews*

PRAISE FOR *BEFORE I KNEW*

"A tender romance rises from the tragedy of two families—a must read!"

—Robyn Carr, #1 *New York Times* bestselling author

"Jamie Beck's deeply felt novel hits all the right notes, celebrating the power of forgiveness, the sweetness of second chances, and the heady joy of reaching for a dream. Don't miss this one!"

—Susan Wiggs, #1 *New York Times* bestselling author

"*Before I Knew* kept me totally enthralled as two compassionate, relatable characters, each in search of forgiveness and fulfillment, turn a recipe for heartache into a story of love, hope, and some really good menus!"

—Shelley Noble, *New York Times* bestselling author of *Whisper Beach*

PRAISE FOR *ALL WE KNEW*

"A moving story about the flux of life and the steadfastness of family."

—*Publishers Weekly*

"An impressively crafted and deftly entertaining read from first page to last."

—*Midwest Book Review*

"*All We Knew* is compelling, heartbreaking, and emotional."

—*Harlequin Junkie*

PRAISE FOR *JOYFULLY HIS*

"A quick and sweet read that is perfect for the holidays."

—*Harlequin Junkie*

PRAISE FOR *WHEN YOU KNEW*

"[A]n opposites-attract romance with heart."

—*Harlequin Junkie*

PRAISE FOR *THE MEMORY OF YOU*

"[Beck] deepens a typical story about first loves reuniting by exploring the aftermath of a violent act. Readers will root for an ending that repairs this couple's past hurt."

—*Booklist*

"Beck's portrayals of divorce and trauma are keen . . . Readers will be caught up in their journey toward healing and romance."

—*Publishers Weekly*

"*The Memory of You* is heartbreaking, emotional, entertaining, and a unique second-chance romance."

—*Harlequin Junkie*

PRAISE FOR *THE PROMISE OF US*

"Beck's depiction of trauma, loss, friendship, and family resonates deeply. A low-key small-town romance unflinching in its portrayal of the complexities of friendship and family, and the joys and sorrows they bring."

—*Kirkus Reviews*

"A fully absorbing and unfailingly entertaining read."

—*Midwest Book Review*

PRAISE FOR *THE WONDER OF NOW*

"*The Wonder of Now* is emotional, it is uplifting, it is heartbreaking, but ultimately shows the reader the best of humanity in a heartfelt story."

—*Midwest Book Review*

PRAISE FOR *IF YOU MUST KNOW*

"Beck expertly captures the bickering between sisters, the pain of regret, and the thorny path to forgiveness. With well-realized secondary characters . . . and believable surprises peppered throughout, Beck's emotional tale rings true."

—*Publishers Weekly*

Truth
of the
Matter

ALSO BY JAMIE BECK

In the Cards

The St. James Novels

Worth the Wait

Worth the Trouble

Worth the Risk

The Sterling Canyon Novels

Accidentally Hers

Secretly Hers

Unexpectedly Hers

Joyfully His

The Cabot Novels

Before I Knew

All We Knew

When You Knew

The Sanctuary Sound Novels

The Memory of You

The Promise of Us

The Wonder of Now

The Potomac Point Novels

If You Must Know

Truth of the Matter

A Potomac Point Novel

JAMIE BECK

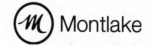 Montlake

Text copyright © 2020 by Write Ideas, LLC

Published by Montlake, Seattle

www.apub.com

Amazon, the Amazon logo, and Montlake are trademarks of Amazon.com, Inc., or its affiliates.

ISBN-13: 9781542008730
ISBN-10: 1542008735

Cover design by David Drummond

Printed in the United States of America

For Ford and Kayla, with all the love in my heart.

CHAPTER ONE

ANNE SULLIVAN CHASE

Ten more minutes—fifteen, tops. I can stick this closing out for that long without falling apart. A revenge plan of some kind might've cushioned the blow, but payback won't put my family back together. I've survived losses before. The only new ground this time will be helping my daughter, Katy, cope with the fallout. I have a plan for that, but at present I'm best served by relaxing my shoulders, sipping my water, and maintaining my carefully blank expression.

Hiding my feelings would be easier if I hadn't left our home for the last time less than an hour ago. Without drapes and carpets, the McMansion had felt cooler than the inside of its Sub-Zero refrigerator. A fitting end.

Recollections of those final moments spent in the foyer bombard me. On the wall, unfaded squares where my original paintings had hung. The faint echoes of the shrill bell on the pink bike Katy used to pedal across the floor, and of the futile marital arguments about missed soccer games and inconsiderate in-laws that replaced laughter and "I love yous." The aroma of cocoa on rainy mornings spent seated in the family room's window bench, where I'd stared past the pool to the wooded perimeter, wondering how I could be a mother and wife yet so lonesome.

Like shadows, my memories record the history of a family that will no longer live under one roof. Of the atrophied dreams and broken promises flayed by the sharp blade of divorce. But the worst part of my morning was the look on Katy's tear-streaked face before she jumped into the yellow Jeep that Richard bought her on her sixteenth birthday, and sped away from me like a canary freed of its cage.

Now, while the brokers leave the conference room to confirm the wire transfer and the buyers exchange a celebratory kiss at the other end of the table, Richard turns to me. "Jim will be in touch to finalize the transfer of stocks and other things before the end of the week."

It's not surprising that my husband of seventeen years treats the end of our marriage as nothing more than another negotiation. His emotional IQ has dipped in direct inverse relation to his legal career's spike. He's probably quite self-satisfied for being so "generous" with our divorce settlement, but, honestly, I'd prefer less money in exchange for seeing even an ounce of regret in his eyes.

I say nothing about the stocks because "Thank you" seems unwarranted for something I earned in exchange for years of waiting patiently—raising our daughter largely on my own while supporting him as he built his practice—on the promise of the life we would one day share. Surprise! Instead of planning empty-nest vacation weekends in Bermuda, he dumped me to bestow those perks on Lauren, the interloper.

I hate Lauren. A blow-up-pictures-of-her-face-and-toss-darts, stopping-barely-short-of-wishing-harm-on-her kind of hate. And I've never hated anyone in my life, so I haven't mastered control over the crippling surges of vengeance. It's frightening, to be honest, so I redirect my thoughts and ask Richard about his plans with our daughter.

"Where are you taking Katy for lunch?" At the first hint of his confused expression, I grip my purse to keep from pounding my fists on the table. "Don't tell me you forgot."

Sorry *not* sorry about my irked tone.

"I did." He proceeds to scrub his face with both hands in one deliberate motion. God, that annoys me. Each gesture, word, and outfit is chosen with care. "I promised Lauren—"

"You cannot blow off Katy for your girlfriend today of all days." Technically Lauren's his new fiancée, but I won't give her that respect. Three and a half months ago, Richard confessed his affair and asked for this divorce. Nine weeks ago, he moved out. His eagerness to move on is driving his acquiescence on financial and custody matters. Still, Richard's already put a ring on Lauren's finger although technically our divorce isn't finalized. "Lauren sees you plenty. Katy needs your reassurance today. She's having a rough time with the changes. Please be there for her, Richard."

Ah, finally. The tiniest trace of guilt disrupts the cool surface of those Pacific-blue eyes. "I'll have lunch with Katy."

Again, "Thank you" seems unfitting. I settle on "Good."

"But don't act like I'm abandoning her. *You're* taking her out of town." He drums his fingers on the table, glowering.

He probably doesn't expect me to smile in response, but I can't help it. Purchasing my gram's old Cape Cod–style home in the sleepy bayside town of Potomac Point has been my only silver lining in this situation.

Yes, part of me is fleeing Arlington to avoid both the pitying whispers of "friends" and bumping into Richard and Lauren. But my childhood summers on the water were a salve after I lost my mother, and living there should help Katy deal with *this* loss. Plus, I want to spend more time with Gram before her dementia erases every shared memory.

Katy and I deserve something good in our lives, so I won't apologize for it.

Still, Richard knows me well enough to suspect I wrestle doubts, mostly because of Katy's intensifying anxiety about leaving her friends and changing schools. Yet every parenting book promises she'll gain new confidence from learning to adapt. Real confidence, not the false kind she gets from tap-dancing to her father's tune for praise. Once we get through these rocky first weeks, the change of pace will be good for us both.

"Please let me live with Dad," Katy had pleaded before driving off. Each of those words had whistled through the air to pierce my heart like poison-tipped darts, and not only because I've devoted myself to parenting her. Richard hasn't and won't.

From the moment we accidentally conceived her in college, he's loved the *idea* of his mini-me—our gorgeous, intelligent daughter—yet, over time, his priorities have undermined her bit by bit, pecking away at her like a crow.

Despite this act he's putting on now, he doesn't want Katy disturbing his next family, but of course he won't tell her that. Once again he's left the black hat on the table for me to wear while I flounder for some way not to devastate her—exactly like he did when he dropped the divorce bomb on me in early May and then took off for New York for a few weeks to work some big deal.

Frankly, I expected him to do or say something to reset the balance of power today. For once, control is something *I* can deny *him* for a change. He leans forward, hands stretched out on the table, wedding band already removed. I cover my wedding rings before pulling both hands onto my lap.

"Anne, you'll be better off once you admit that you weren't any happier in our marriage than I've been lately. Trust me, there's someone out there who's more capable of meeting your needs than I ever was. You deserve that, too."

Blandishments? My temperature is steadily climbing. At this rate, I could blow like Vesuvius before the brokers return. All these years I've set aside my own ambitions and managed our home and daughter while he focused on his career, and this is how he repays me? In any case, the last thing I want now is another man in my life after having spent my entire adulthood with this one.

"Gee, thanks." I refuse to look away although something uncomfortable slithers through me—perhaps an acknowledgment of my willingness over time to settle for a B-minus marriage instead of striving for an A-plus one.

Our passion had begun to ebb once he'd graduated from law school and gone to work. Truth be told, Richard practically lived at his office while building his practice, which then left me little opportunity to be either an outstanding or a poor wife.

Then Katy started showing signs of extreme sensitivities around four—a hyperawareness of others' opinions, banging her head against a wall when she made a mistake, crying too easily over every little thing. Richard called them tantrums, but I worried she might have deeper issues. Managing her behavior and schedule required more and more of my attention, exhausting me.

Between Richard's long hours, my volunteerism, and Katy's needs, it seemed as if sex became scheduled like every other obligation, and our conversations veered toward efficiency rather than intimacy. But we'd had Katy to connect us, and I thought we'd rediscover each other and spontaneity once she went to college.

The actual result? Richard now enjoys a thriving practice and new family while I'm living in a chronic state of confusion with a teen who constantly misconstrues me.

He's still handsome, though: thick dark hair with hints of silver, cheekbones I envy, and a gorgeous mouth. Vital, too, thanks to vigorous exercise and boundless energy. Most things come easily to him, as with Katy. Maybe that's why neither of them is patient with how hard the rest of us work for the things that matter.

"Seems I can't do anything right today." He sits back. It saddens me that this exchange has probably reaffirmed his relief to be ditching me. I bury every bit of grief beneath the thick seams of resentment and righteous indignation his adultery has handed me.

To look at him now, I wouldn't recognize the man who pursued me during our junior year at the University of Richmond. He'd been relentless, coming around the studio where I'd painted, or bringing his books along to the James River Park's green spaces where I'd sketched. Like my gram, he'd encouraged my wildest artistic dreams. That praise, the belly kisses and hushed whispers as we lay naked and spent, the love notes stuck in my backpack, the flowers he'd bring for no reason—all his ardor tricked me into believing that, despite being twenty, naive, and pregnant, we could build a happy life together—a family like the one I'd lost when my mother died.

Since then, I've come to call that zeal his "acquisition mode," as he's wooed new clients with the same intensity. His surname suits him, because he much prefers the chase to maintenance.

Lauren will be in my shoes soon enough. The day some major new client or other woman crosses his radar, I'll have the last laugh. Of course, I'll feel bad for her two young children, who'll be casualties of his whims. Like Katy.

If Richard and I were alone now, I might literally reach across the table to slap that self-pitying look off his face. Look at him sitting there as if everything is about *him*. He doesn't get it and never will. My mood—the *root* of my concern—is about Katy.

Yes, I'm a woman in my prime. A woman of some means. A woman with talent, some might even say. But first and foremost I am a mother.

"What'd you do with the furniture? It can't all fit in Marie's old house." Richard's question temporarily throws me.

"Severed Ties took what we didn't need." The high-end consignment store pays the original owner 50 percent of its profit on sales. "Whatever I make will be put toward Katy's college fund."

"Keep it." His full lips bend into a conciliatory smile. "I can pay her tuition."

Here he goes again, sounding generous when really he's trying to buy me off so he can boast to others about how fair he's been. He's never understood this about me: I don't care about hoarding money or things. Never did and never will. "And I can afford to contribute."

Some might consider me lucky because, along with my suitcases, I take a comfortable nest egg and alimony—enough that I'm not panicked about establishing a career after all these years at home. But he's still gotten off pretty cheaply for betraying me and our old dreams. Naturally, I don't share my feelings or let him see my pain.

"Fine, Anne." He rolls his eyes and checks his watch. "Jesus, I'm trying to be a decent guy."

Too little, too late.

A laundry list of insults cycles through my mind like ticker tape, but I literally bite my tongue when another image of Katy's splotchy face from this morning flickers through my mind. All the time spent filling her life with love and opportunity means very little in light of one inescapable reality: by letting our family fall apart, Richard and I have fundamentally failed our daughter.

Condemning my husband is pointless. However we got here, the result is the same.

The brokers return, confirm the payments, congratulate us all, and quickly show us out. Even though I never loved that house, the finality of what's happening hits me like a board to the face. My married life and home are truly lost to me. There will be no going back. No fixing what broke. I'm starting over at thirty-seven. That prospect festers like an ulcer. All I know is how to be a wife and mother.

My hands tremble for a split second as I grapple with my purse strap. Please, God, don't let Richard see my strength falter. His affair humiliated me. He can never know how badly he's hurt me, too.

The buyers walk ahead of us, holding hands. The woman is decked out in a Trina Turk "Vanah" dress, diamonds and sapphires in her ears and around her neck and wrists, and cute platform espadrilles. Her husband is attractive in a Tom Hardy way and carries his success like Richard does—chin up, shoulders proud.

I can picture him—much like my soon-to-be ex—proudly moving into that home that has three times more space than any family needs. What he doesn't yet know is that four stories and a dozen rooms make it too easy to slink away from each other for entire evenings. Bit by bit that disconnect—the physical space between each person—becomes the sort of emotional distance that loosens family bonds. Not that you see it happening in the moment.

I've often wondered whether Richard and I might've stayed together if we'd remained in the two-thousand-square-foot home we'd previously owned. Questions like that keep me up nights.

A decade ago, we were excited. Happy. A young family on our way up. The problem with rising so high so fast? When you fall—and that fall will come, usually when you least expect it—you smack the ground so hard a part of you dies.

Once reanimated, you feel more like a roamer on *The Walking Dead* than a person.

Richard leans in as if he might kiss my cheek, but stops short when I flinch. "Good luck, Anne. Hope you don't die of boredom in that small town."

His condescension pricks the ugly bitterness that has blistered beneath my skin since his May confessional.

"Well, I survived life with you, so how bad can Potomac Point be?" I pat his shoulder twice. "Don't worry about me. Save your energy for staying sane while Lauren has you stuck at home raising her young kids. I'll be sure to send postcards from Paris and Prague to give you goals to look forward to in another twelve or fourteen years."

I turn away and walk to my car without looking back so he can't see my brave face slip. The truth is I'd wanted more kids but, after the agony of a late-term miscarriage, chose to focus all my love on Katy and her anxieties. Once she'd turned six, Richard no longer wanted to bring an infant into our lives. Another decision to regret, I suppose, because both Katy and I might be better off if we had another person in our shrinking family.

By the time my car door closes, fresh tears blur my vision. Contrary to my goal, I did not escape that closing with my dignity intact—behaving no better than my teen daughter.

It takes a bunch of tugging and a good lick to wrench my wedding rings from my finger. In the sunlight their dazzling sparkle is full of false promise, so I drop them into my purse. I stretch the fingers of my bare left hand, which now looks as unfamiliar as everything else about my undone life.

Richard wasn't the husband I'd hoped he'd be, and ours hadn't been the perfect marriage. But I've given so much of myself to that life that I can't stand the way it's ending. He's skipping forward as if our years together meant nothing, leaving me behind on an uncertain path. Seeing him quickly—and happily—replace our family stings like an ice-cold shower.

I've been telling myself I'm not running. Telling myself that this move will be for the best.

Please, God, let me be right.

CHAPTER TWO

KATY

I tuck my dab pen back in my purse before asking the Uber driver to drop me off on Connecticut Avenue, less than a block from the front door of my dad's office building in DC. A quick glance in the mirror on the back of my phone reflects my bright-red eyes.

I shouldn't have taken that second hit. Haven't quite got the hang of this yet, but after my dad moved out in June, my friend Jen saved me with this little gift.

"I'll tip you on the app." I wave at the Uber dude before exiting his ancient Honda.

"Thanks!"

He pulls away from the curb as soon as I close the door. His car putters off, leaving me in the shadow of the multistory building that is basically my dad's second home. It's near Nordstrom Rack and GW University, so there are actually a lot of people close to my age in the vicinity.

The first time I remember coming here was for a Bring Your Daughter to Work Day. Fourth grade. Mom had dressed me in a blue velvet dress from Crewcuts, a sparkle headband, tights, and gray suede ankle boots. She'd stuffed my backpack with a sketch pad, colored pencils that smelled like cherries and grapes and lemons, and a copy of *Wonderstruck*.

Dad had let me sit at his desk and explained to me what he did. Reading and writing those contracts every day sounded boring, but I saw the same buzz in his eyes then that he got whenever I made him proud. I've tried to make him proud all the time so he'd make it home for dinner or spend more time with me on the weekends than just our Sunday-morning runs. Now, we don't even have those.

When I yank on the heavy glass door, the lobby I've entered less than a dozen times since that first day is pretty much the same: shiny cream-colored marble tile floors inlaid inside a hideous rose-colored border, mirrors and brass on the walls, the scuffle of shoes coming and going, the bell tones from the elevator banks behind the security desk.

Normally I get really nervous here, but my muscles are finally loosening thanks to that second hit. Things move in slow motion as I cross to the security desk, sign in, stick a little badge on my shirt, and head to the elevator. Top floor. My dad's corner office has a pretty sweet view.

When I get off the elevator, I stop at the reception desk rather than risk catching my dad in his office with Lauren. She works here, too. High as I am, if I see her, I might do or say something nobody will like—like the first time I met her, right after Dad moved out. He'd brought her to lunch without warning me, so I ignored her the entire time.

My mom might hover too much, but she'd never blindside me.

The receptionist looks maybe five years older than me. Blonde—like Lauren. Big boobs—also like Lauren. My mom isn't sexy. She's just a mom. Brown, curly hair that she pulls into a ponytail most days. Hardly wears makeup. Smiles way too much for any normal person most of the time—but not so much this summer.

Didn't she know that all the gold diggers in this office would go after him? I mean, he's loaded, he's nice-looking for an old guy, and he's so smart. Everybody wants his attention. Mom was careless to let her guard down. But Dad didn't just leave her. He left me, too. If he really thought I was so special, he wouldn't do that.

"Hi. Can you let my dad know I'm here—Richard Chase, I mean." I clear my throat and try to pull myself together so he can't tell that I vaped. "I'm Katy."

The cheap-looking version of Lauren smiles at me. "Sure, Katy. Go ahead and take a seat."

While she connects to my dad's office, I plop onto the leather sofa. This area reminds me a little of home. Our *old* home. The Tibetan carpet. The reds and golds and burnished brown decor, with glossy wood tables. Classic. Like Dad and his navy blue suits.

My eyes water, so I close them and swallow the lump in my throat. Round and round I twine a long strand of hair until there is almost no feeling left in my fingertip.

"Katy." My eyes pop open to catch my dad crossing the small reception area, his arms open for me, with a book in one hand.

I untangle my hair and push off the sofa. For the few seconds I'm smooshed against his chest, there is hope. "Hey, Dad."

He eases away and tips my chin up with his fingers. "Have you been crying?"

At least it's an excuse for my red eyes. I don't lie, exactly. Just shrug my shoulders and let him draw his own conclusion. That earns me another hug and a kiss on the top of my head.

"I'm sorry," he says. Is he, though? Because he could change his mind if he really was sorry. Mom might take him back if I begged.

"Yeah." My stomach tenses. We have to leave before Lauren appears. "Can we go eat?"

"Yes." He glances over his shoulder at Big Boobs. "Gretchen, I'll be out for ninety minutes."

Ninety minutes. I'm lucky he gave me *any* time on a workday. Normally he wouldn't. Still, now every time I see him will be a "visit" reduced to some kind of time frame. Forty-eight-hour weekends. Two-week vacations. Wednesday-night dinners.

My lungs turn to ash. I almost kick his shin and run out on him the way he's run out on me. But that will only convince him that he's better off with Lauren.

On the elevator, he hands me Malcolm Gladwell's book *Talking to Strangers*. "I just finished this and thought you might like it. I don't agree with all his conclusions, but there are some really interesting insights about reading people—or misreading them. In our multicultural world, I think it's important to better understand this so you can communicate well. Bottom line, we jump to conclusions about strangers based on very little information, though we shouldn't, because they are as nuanced and complicated as we are."

"Cool." I smile and take the book although it's the last thing I care about right now. He should worry more about reading me than reading strangers.

"KAZ?" he asks as we exit the building.

"Sure." KAZ Sushi Bistro is a short walk, and we both like sushi.

When we get to the restaurant, I slide onto the tan suede bench seat against the wall and let my dad have the chair at our small table so he won't be distracted by things going on around us. He orders himself a hot sake and me an iced tea—my usual.

"So, how are you handling everything?" He folds his hands on his lap.

Gripping the sides of the small table, I drop a big hint about what I want from him. "I don't want to leave my friends and school."

"I know that's hard, but try to focus on the positive, like living near a beach. Your mom loves it there, so you probably will, too." His weak smile proves he doesn't believe that. I'm more like him than her. Why is he acting like his leaving Mom and me is no big deal?

"Seriously, Dad? She keeps talking about how we can go draw by the bay." Two years ago I overheard him arguing with Mom when I thought about taking a line-drawing class. *"Anne, you know as well as anyone how impossible it is to make a living in art. Katy can be anything she wants—except a starving artist."* If he cares so much about my future, then he shouldn't let Mom take me to public school. "*Nobody* takes their kids *out* of Whitman Prep. You guys are ruining my life."

A notification ping snags my attention, but I don't look. Jen or Mom, probably. Neither matters as much as this conversation right now. Dad's focused on folding the paper napkin like an accordion, as if he hasn't spent the past sixteen years priming me for valedictorian glory.

The waitress brings our drinks, so Dad puts me off longer by ordering lunch. We're down to sixty-seven minutes.

"I'll have the Chirashi." He gestures to me.

I glance at the waitress. "May I please have the Temaki Special—salmon and avocado, spicy tuna, and crunchy shrimp?"

She nods, takes our menus, and disappears. It takes a beat or two before I accept the fact that he's going to ignore my hints. I'm used to my mom skirting around things, but not so much my dad.

My history as the result of an unplanned pregnancy isn't a secret. Mom says that it was the happiest of accidents, but if that were true, Dad wouldn't be leaving me. My arms and legs buzz with heat and electricity, but I blurt, "Can't I stay with you?"

I hold my breath until I'm dizzy.

He tugs at his shirtsleeve cuffs. "Honey, Lauren and I have just moved in to a new house with her children. It's not the best time for another change."

I absorb that blow like a prizefighter. It's almost verbatim what my mom said when I begged her to let me stay in Arlington with Dad. That conversation probably gutted her as much as his answer just did me, which means I made her even sadder than she already is. Sometimes I really suck, but I never see it until it's too late.

Another reason why my own dad would rather live with Lauren and her little brats, Zoe and Brody, than with me.

"So you don't care that I'll be shipped off to Podunk Point." I slump back against my seat.

He twists his lips and raises an index finger. "Come on, Katy. That's not a fair characterization. I'm not thrilled about the school stuff, but at the end of the day, your mother's in a better position to take care of you. Lauren and I work full-time. You've got two big years ahead. SATs, college applications—your mom's the best person to get you through all of that." Then he makes this sympathetic face. "Besides, neither of us wants to see her living alone right now, do we?"

Holy shit. He's giving *me* a guilt trip? I check my phone. Less than an hour remaining.

"Katy," he says, but I keep staring at my iced tea. "Be honest. You don't really want to live with Lauren."

I snap my head up. "You're right. And I still don't know why you do. What did Mom and I do so wrong that made you want to leave?" I cross my arms to keep from knocking over my water glass.

Dad's face pales. He leans forward to answer, but then the waitress returns and sets our food down. It takes forever—or so it seems.

Once she leaves us, Dad says, "What's happened has nothing to do with anything you did or didn't do, Katy. I've told you that."

"Why don't you love Mom anymore?" My nose tingles. She's a worrywart, but she's always there for us, doing little things like making meals I like or putting fresh flowers from the yard in vases around the house. She's nice—nicer than my dad or me.

He rubs his face with both hands. "Your mom and I aren't the same people we were when you were born. Lots has changed, and we grew apart. That's all. There's no one to blame."

"Except Lauren."

"No." He shakes his head. "She didn't cause this."

She took advantage, though.

My leg is bouncing out of control beneath the table while my head clogs with ugly thoughts. The kind of things I could shout at my mom if she made me this mad, because she'd never stop loving me or leave me. But my dad might, just like he's done with my mom.

I dig the heel of my sandal into the big toe of my other foot while I drink some of my soup. Dad's already eating, obviously finished discussing my living arrangements. Does he think he's made me believe he actually cares about my mom's feelings or what's best for me? 'Cause if he *really* cared, he wouldn't have moved on with Lauren already.

He looks up and smiles. "We forgot to have Gretchen validate your parking stub."

"I did it before you came out of your office." The lie doesn't even bother me now.

I left my car at Jen's because I wasn't sober. Would Dad trust Mom to take care of me if he knew *that*?

He winks and stuffs another bite of yellowtail in his mouth.

Last time I got high, I ate a whole box of cereal, but my stomach is like a stone today. I peek over at Dad again while picking up one of my hand rolls. I'm invisible while sitting right across the table. So much for him actually learning anything from the book he gave me. I think I'll burn it rather than read it.

I love him, but right now I sort of hate him.

CHAPTER THREE

Before driving across town to check out the remodeling progress on my new house, I drop my luggage at the Kentwood Inn, where Katy and I will spend the weekend. After years of letting Richard be in charge, making decisions on my own—let alone tough ones—is much harder than it should be. But the invisible baggage that has followed me to Potomac Point temporarily disappears when I pull down Autumn Lane and into the driveway of the first home I've ever owned by myself.

The town has developed a lot since my teens. Our house sits in the original residential section. The old-growth sycamores, red maples, and Eastern redbud trees crowd the landscape and lend charm to the spaghetti streets on this old side of town. It's a more pleasing aesthetic than that of the newer planned developments on the west side.

Happy tears—a welcome change today—form upon seeing the sloped roof and dormers of Gram's old Cape Cod. The home dates back to the midthirties. When Gram's father, Dr. Lewis Robson, built it, it was one of the grander homes in the hamlet. The vivid peacock-blue paint I chose for the front door and shutters contrasts nicely against the newly whitewashed brick exterior. Words like "cute," "cozy," and "homey" spring to mind. Pretty phlox, ornamental grasses, and pink oxalis soften the lines of the home and improve its curb appeal.

It'd be perfect if not for the silver Foley Construction pickup truck parked in the driveway. A quick glance at the clock in my car confirms it's after five o'clock. At this hour I should've been in the clear.

I need time to myself in the empty space. Time to visualize, to dream, to stamp out my misgivings. To prepare for my first steps in this new life. Instead, I face another round of strained conversation with the contractor. Shoving my car fob into my shorts pocket, I dawdle, checking the flower beds for weeds on the way up the walkway.

Years ago, Dan Foley made my teen heart flutter from his perch on the lifeguard chair at the public beach. Brown curls sun-kissed by honey highlights. Tan skin stretched tight across a chest that looked more like a man's than a boy's with its tuft of hair. Cool sunglasses and a whistle that he'd twirled around his fingers over and over.

Not that he'd ever noticed me. He's four or five years older and had been surrounded by plenty of girls his own age who competed for his attention.

In July, when the broker handed me a list of contractors for the planned renovations, Dan's name had jumped out like a shot of confetti. I remembered him as an affable guy beloved by many, and assumed he'd be the type to help someone new integrate into town. But from our first meeting, it became clear he wouldn't be part of my welcome wagon.

Perhaps it was foolish to expect him to be that perfectly laid-back, pleasant boy from the beach. Decades of life's disappointments weather us all and expose our jagged, broken pieces. Jaded I can handle, but judgmental is trickier. It's clear from our many exchanges and my several requested change orders that he considers me a persnickety outsider. I might be both, but this house is the foundation of my and Katy's fresh start, so it needs to be flawless.

"Hello!" My voice echoes throughout the empty space.

Dan peeks out from the kitchen. "Hey, there. Didn't expect to see you today."

He forces a polite smile, but not quickly enough to convince me that he's actually pleased to see me.

"I dropped my bags at the hotel but couldn't resist checking out the progress." I crouch to stroke the refinished hardwood floors, admiring the rich espresso stain warmed by golden sunrays streaming through the large picture window behind me. "These old boards look amazing."

Being here also brings back fond memories of my grandpa. This is where he taught me the jitterbug to old Elvis Presley songs. Rock step, slow-slow, rock step, cuddle, send you across . . .

After I lost my mom when I was eight years old, my father shipped me to Gram and Grandpa that summer and the ones that followed so he wouldn't need to hire a sitter while he was at work. I didn't mind because it was cold living in the shadow of my father's grief. I almost dreaded the weekends he would come down to visit, sorrow rolling in with him like thunderclouds. Not to mention the thin tension between him and Gram. Thank God for her and Grandpa, who doted on me, which I so needed then—much like Katy will need now to help her cope with the loss of life as she knew it.

"Glad you're happy." Dan's voice wakes me from my reverie. He sounds relieved and a bit surprised, rubbing his chin while giving the floor another look. It may have taken seven attempts to formulate the precise blend of stains, but one can't argue with perfection. "I was concerned the color would close up the space, but the big windows bring in tons of light."

"The warm tone is comforting." I stand and begin to mentally place my furniture and artwork around the room, pleased by the way the new slate facing and live-edge mantel update the old fireplace.

"Are you sure you want to move in before we finish the kitchen and master bath?" He presses his lips into a firm line. I recognize that tone—like a parent trying to get a kid to rethink the decision not to wear a coat in December. "It'll be a few weeks until that work is completed. A short-term rental might be best until then."

After years of being micromanaged by Richard, I won't be second-guessed by another man who apparently can't credit me with a basic understanding of the pros and cons of my own choices.

"My daughter needs to be settled when school starts. She's . . . struggling with all the changes." My face is hot because, regardless of what Richard did, Dan knows that on some level I didn't satisfy my husband. In fact, Dan probably empathizes with my ex and is equally as eager to leave me behind.

"Guess that's one good thing about not having kids. My divorce was a clean break." His mouth pulls into a sort of lemon-faced frown, having apparently let that comment slip.

I had no idea he'd ever been married. Lucky for him, I'm not up for trading divorce stories today, so I revert to the conversation about the house. "We'll be fine here. I'll share the upstairs bathroom with Katy until the master is complete. We'll use the new patio and grill as our kitchen as long as the weather remains mild."

A dubious gaze clouds otherwise luminescent eyes the color of rich amber beer. His attitude is discouraging, but it's better than him being a charmer who tells me what I want to hear. In my vulnerable state, a flirt could mess with my head much worse than Dan's doubts do.

"Hopefully your crew can work fast to install the cabinets and appliances."

"Well, there's good news there. We've already got the kitchen down to the studs. Wanna see?" He waves me over.

Dan had initially tried to persuade me to knock down walls and create an open floor plan. That might be all the rage these days, but I still prefer a bit of separation between the kitchen and other spaces. We compromised by enlarging the archways to create a more open feel.

I also replaced the kitchen window above the sink with an oversize box bay. Not only does it offer a pretty view of the butterfly bushes separating my yard from my neighbor's, but it also doubles as a sunny ledge for potted herbs. Large-pane french doors now lead out to the patio and flood the relatively small kitchen with natural light.

"Oh, this will be fabulous." I hug myself to hold on to a moment of happiness.

"I hope so." Dan rests one hand high up along the arch, inadvertently showcasing his chest and biceps in that snug T-shirt. Sometimes the position of his eyebrows makes that scar on his forehead look like a lightning bolt.

For an irrational moment I wonder what I'd do if my curmudgeonly childhood crush hit on me. I'm not beautiful, but I'm attractive enough. Daily walks and weekly yoga have kept me trim, and I thank God for my mother's Italian skin. Not that I'm at all ready for a tour of the Tinder store.

My stomach sours as it dawns on me that, from now on, these are the reservations I'll have—the games I'll be playing—with men. Careless boys trampled my heart in my teens, and then Richard and I rushed into marriage so young because of Katy. I've got zero experience with normal dating, but I'd venture a guess that it isn't easier in one's thirties. That goes double with the serious trust issues Richard's betrayal left in its wake. It's a pointless worry, though, because I've got Katy to keep me occupied. She's the song in my heart and real love of my life. I don't want to miss a minute of what little time we have left together before she goes off to college.

"I'm surprised you didn't go with the white-and-gray palette," he says.

I've no interest in my home being a carbon copy of the taste du jour. For the first time in forever, I don't have to answer to Richard or fight for my taste. This house is like a canvas of a sort—a new medium of expression that I don't need to sell to others or impress them with. That is this woman's definition of heaven and a definite upside of divorce.

"Not my style." The space will be filled with modern, whitewashed-wood base cabinets, white quartzite counters, and black-and-glass upper cabinets, all of which will be set off with polished brass fixtures and drawer pulls. The glass cabinets' turquoise interiors will create an unexpected pop. "I'm sorry our living here will make finishing up a little harder on you, but I'm stubborn once my mind is set, so I'm sticking with my plan. Give me the weekend to unpack all the boxes; then your crew can come back on Monday and keep going."

"Sure." He shrugs and crosses his arms. "You realize that taping off areas with plastic sheeting will only keep so much of the dust down. And it won't buffer any of the noise."

"I'll dust every day to keep up with it if need be."

"Seems like a lot of extra work." He mumbles that one, almost to himself.

"That won't fall on your shoulders." My tone should signal the end of this debate.

He sighs, ushering the return of another of our standard awkward silences.

"While I'm here, let's take a quick look at the master bath and closet reconfigurations while that space is empty," Dan finally says as he walks out the back side of the kitchen. "Oh, and I have a surprise for you, too."

I shudder because "surprise" is usually a euphemism for unforeseen problems that increase the costs. "A good surprise?"

He glances over his shoulder while he walks. "Not sure. We found something when clearing out the crawl space behind the master closet."

Intrigued, I follow him to the bathroom, where I'm caught off guard by the transformation of the emptied room. Spinning on my heel, I gasp. "Oh! This is even more spacious than I imagined."

"Most women would prefer a huge closet to a bigger bathroom." His brows rise to emphasize his point.

22

You would think he's aware by now that I'm not most women. In fact, I've gladly downsized my humongous closet and wardrobe for something simpler. There's no need for so many things when there won't be balls and galas and client dinners to attend, or massive parties to throw for people I barely know.

A simple, quiet life in comfortable jeans, flip-flops, and cotton shirts suits me better. Most of my clothes had been paint stained until Katy hit kindergarten. "Been there, done that, and am all in on less laundry."

When he chuckles, the rich sound tickles my chest. He, too, looks surprised at himself. It might be the first time I've made him laugh since we started working together. When did I become the dour thirtysomething?

He reaches for something from the corner, then, stepping closer, hands me a dusty white tin box with red letters that read RECIPES. "Here's the surprise."

I open it expecting to find handwritten notecards with some of Gram's old favorites, including the delicious shortbread cookies she'd stocked in the cookie jar—the ones she'd always served with a side dish of strawberry ice cream. Nothing beat coming home from the beach to the buttery aroma they created in the kitchen.

Instead, the first thing I pull out is a man's handkerchief embroidered with *W. T.* in one corner. The box also contains a rusty nail, a yellowed Polaroid of a slender young man with slicked-back hair and a dimpled chin, and a vintage red silk scarf with a faint hand-painted outline of a mountain and what looks like a cherry tree sprig.

"I wonder whose stuff this is." The initials don't match any of my known relatives, nor does the man in the photograph look familiar.

Dan shrugs. "Not sure, but I like a good mystery. Maybe Mrs. Sullivan can fill in the blanks."

"Maybe," I say absently. A memory of a whispered conversation between Gram and Grandpa on a hot summer night, when their voices had drifted up from the back patio through my open window, resurfaces. *"You should tell Bobby what you went through, Marie. Maybe it could help him do better with Annie."*

I'd been mourning my mother—missing the way she'd brushed my hair, and played tea party, and cooked my favorite meals—so I hadn't thought much about the significance of those words. A little shudder ripples through me as I finger the items in the box. Might they be clues to whatever Grandpa had been referring to? I'll have to ask my dad the next time we talk.

My skin prickles with the sudden awareness of Dan's scrutiny.

I close the lid and tuck the box under my arm, returning to the matter of the remodel. "This bathroom will be a fabulous retreat. I can't wait for the soaker tub."

"We've hit a little snag—a delay—with that." Dan grimaces. "It's on back order for another couple of weeks, but it shouldn't hold up the rest of the rebuild."

Everything about his expression tells me he's bracing for me to complain or to blame him.

A few more weeks of this will be a long time to deal with each other if things between us don't improve.

"That tub is worth *any* delay. I'm already counting the days until I can soak in it with a lit candle and a good audiobook." Not the most romantic use for such a tub, but a true escape.

"Sounds nice." He clears his throat, eyes on his work boots.

"Mom?" Katy's voice from the other room interrupts us.

"Back here!" I make my way toward the living room, where I find my daughter.

Her puffy face doesn't look much better than when she zoomed away from me this morning. Lunch mustn't have gone as she'd planned. I'd hug her and ask if she's okay, but she'd be embarrassed in front of Dan.

"Katy, this is Dan Foley, the contractor doing all the work on the house. Dan, this is my daughter, Katy." I remove the tin box from under my arm and hold it at my side.

Katy's gaze flicks toward it, but then Dan steps forward with his hand extended.

"Nice to meet you, Katy."

She shakes his hand. "Nice to meet you, too. Guess we'll be seeing a lot of each other for a while."

"Yes, but you can hide out upstairs. I won't be offended." He winks. Dan's apparently better with kids than with grown-ups.

Out of nowhere, I recall him treating a young boy who'd been stung by a jellyfish. He'd calmed the hysterical kid by asking a dozen questions about Pokémon, all the while using tweezers to remove tentacles with the steady hand of a surgeon, then washing the sting in a saline-vinegar solution.

Makes me wonder why he never had children. Questions form, but I keep mum. It's not my business, although it seems a shame that an otherwise circumspect man like Dan never had a child, while a careless one like Richard takes his for granted.

Katy flashes a respectful smile similar to the ones she gives her dad's friends and clients. Afterward, her gaze lands on me. "Looks like we'll be eating out. Is there any good restaurant in this town?"

I bug my eyes from behind Dan's back. "Of course there are nice restaurants, honey. In fact, it's such a beautiful evening we should go to the East Beach Café. They have an outdoor seating area on a dock that extends over the bay. Good seafood, too."

"Fine." She makes a sort of raspberry sound. "What's in that box?"

I hold it up. "Old memorabilia. Dan found it when break-ing through the closet. We can ask Gram about it when we visit on Monday."

She lifts one shoulder, showing little enthusiasm for visiting with her great-grandmother—the woman who's been the closest thing I've had to an actual mother for most of my life.

Grandpa died before I graduated from high school. But when Katy was very young, I'd brought her to visit Gram every several weeks until school and sports obligations ate up our free time. These past two years we've seen Gram only for birthdays and holidays. Still, I call her at least twice a month.

"Well, I'll make myself scarce," Dan says. He takes a step toward the door, then pauses. "Katy, a lot of the teens around here spend summer days at the Bayshore Point beach. And I think Dante's is still the pizza joint of preference."

Although Katy and her friends frequent high-end coffee bars and health food restaurants instead of pizza shops, she offers him a courteous nod. "Thanks."

He casually salutes us. "See you ladies on Monday at eight a.m."

"Thanks, Dan." I walk him out and wave as he jogs to his truck. "Enjoy your weekend."

As the door clicks shut, I take a deep breath before spinning around. "Did you have a nice lunch with your father?"

"Don't worry. He didn't invite me to live with him."

I'm simultaneously relieved and furious. Mostly relieved, though. Even so, I would force Richard to take her if I believed living with him would be better for her in the long run. When he gives her his full attention, she comes alive. But two or three hours per week is not enough to sustain her without me there to make up for the rest.

Watching her struggle with our divorce reminds me of when my mother's death taught me that family could be cruelly snatched away. My dad didn't greet me with my mom's bright smile or tuck me in with a bedtime story, but I'd had Gram and Grandpa to cushion the blow. I don't want Katy to lose faith in—or struggle with—love because her father is currently too preoccupied with his own happiness to pay attention to hers.

Katy strolls the living room. "This whole house could fit in our old basement."

She's not wrong. This Cape is slightly more than two thousand square feet, which definitely would fit in our old basement.

"Less to clean and maintain, which means more time and money for travel or art lessons," I add hopefully. "Maybe we can plan a trip to Grand Cayman at Christmas, or Paris during spring break?"

Katy nods before bobbing her head from side to side. "Can we call the school and switch my digital engineering class to a photography elective? Screw Dad and his STEM bullshit."

"Let's watch the language."

She's acting tough, but her recent manicure is already a mess and she's plucking at her hair. Since she hit kindergarten, I've monitored her nails chewed to the quick, hair twisted and plucked, teary outbursts, and irritability in unfamiliar environments. Not that Richard shared my concerns. His Katy-bear was flawless or merely going through a phase. *"Let's not saddle her with mental illness labels like all these other parents do."*

Aware that my approval of her decision could cause her to reverse course, I choose my next words carefully. "I bet you'd enjoy photography, but you shouldn't use electives as weapons to irritate your father."

"Why do you care? He dumped you for another woman. You should be pissed."

The truth of that remark doesn't lessen the sting of her disdain. But my feelings are less important than making sure she doesn't feel pressured to choose sides. "No matter what happens between your father and me, he's your dad. He loves you and does his best by you."

"His best sucks." Her scowl can't mask the sadness in her voice.

"So does mine sometimes. Yours too. If you want to be forgiven for your mistakes, then you need to forgive us, too."

If ever a "do as I say, not as I do" parenting moment existed, this might be it, because I haven't forgiven Richard for cheating. The humiliation is the least of it. His behavior denigrates everything I held dear and built my life upon.

Katy's extraocular muscles get quite a workout. "Don't take this the wrong way, Mom, but when I'm older, I won't be anything like you."

My mouth falls open. "What's the 'right' way to take that insult, Katy?"

Another eye roll. "Even now, you won't yell. Why do you let people walk all over you?"

I hate when restraint is misread as weakness instead of strength. Really *hate* that. With an exaggerated howl, I stomp my feet a few times, then collect myself and smile. "Better?"

"You're so weird."

Maybe, but my weirdness wrests a brief grin on her end. Getting her to smile on a day like today makes it a little better.

"Screaming like a shrew and complaining don't change the facts. Better to look inward and control one's reactions than point the finger at others for causing them." Sure, I've blamed Richard for a lot lately, but not in front of Katy. And deep down I'm vaguely aware of my role in our divorce. I'm just not ready to embrace it.

"Whatever . . ." She exhales and gnaws her thumbnail. "Can we go eat?"

"How about a hug first?" I close the distance between us to comfort her. "I know you're not excited about this place, but please give it a chance. We can be happy here."

Katy doesn't reach for me, but she doesn't push me away, either. With my arms secured around her, her resolve melts as she absorbs all the love I can offer in an attempt to restore the reserves Richard depleted from her today.

If I close my eyes and inhale, I can transport myself back to those earliest days with my precious girl, when my heart was gooier than a molten lava cake, overflowing with awe and hope and warmth—back before the terrible twos, the middle school melodramas, and the teen rebellion. Even now, that uncomplicated, unconditional mother's love floods my veins.

I could hold her forever, but she breaks away.

"Can I see what's in that box?" she asks.

Happy to discuss something else, I hand it to her.

She picks through the items, sifting the scarf through her fingers and then staring at the photo. "Are these Grammy's things?"

"Maybe." They could've belonged to her younger sister, Lonna, or even her own mother. I have no idea when the Polaroid was invented. Again I'm intrigued by the unfamiliar initials on the hankie and by the photograph. The man is wearing some kind of work uniform beneath his jacket, but I can't make out the insignia. He looks a bit shy in the picture. "It's odd that she hid these things in a crawl space if they mattered enough to keep."

"It's probably just some old high school boyfriend's stuff that she forgot about." Katy returns the scarf and photo to the box before she hands it back to me, already uninterested.

"Probably." But Grandpa's whispered reference to whatever Gram had gone through rolls through my thoughts again as I study that rusty nail and those haunting round eyes in the photograph. Gram has been such an important figure in my life—a role model for how to prioritize family. It's odd to think she had some other life—a secret one—that she never shared with me. Instead of asking my dad, maybe I'll ask her about it when we visit.

I hope she's lucid enough to remember.

CHAPTER FOUR

ANNE

Following a frenzied forty-eight hours of unpacking and breaking down boxes, moving furniture, and hanging artwork, it's a second-cup-of-coffee kind of morning. I'm rubbing my sore shoulder when Dan knocks on the front door at eight o'clock sharp. Obscenely punctual, like Richard. It might be an ideal quality in a contractor, but I could've used an extra ten minutes this morning to turn into something resembling a human being.

The plush red-and-silver silk Tibetan rug cushions my bare feet as I cross the living room. Its threads change color depending on my position and the angle that the light hits them. Like all good art, it mirrors life that way. Richard and I bought this carpet on our tenth anniversary. The fact that I didn't toss it says a lot about its exquisite craftsmanship.

"Good morning." After forcing a welcoming expression past my exhaustion, I gesture toward the buffet in the dining room that temporarily hosts my coffee maker, toaster, and dorm-size refrigerator. The rest of my kitchenware remains stored in the basement for now. "There's a large pot of coffee if you'd like a cup."

Dan comes inside and stops dead, eyes wide, as if he's just stepped into the "after" part of an episode of *Fixer Upper*. "Wow."

Dan Foley is not easy to read, so that "wow" could be praise or derision.

Of course, "wow" also might have nothing to do with my taste and everything to do with the fact that—with the exception of the unfinished kitchen and bathroom—it already looks like we've lived here for weeks. In truth, my ultra efficiency has been a lifelong blessing and curse. My dad used to throw a long list of chores at me on Saturdays to buy himself some free time, but I always powered through them quickly.

In this instance, it helped that I'd already laid everything out on paper well before the movers arrived on Saturday morning. And let's not forget neither Katy nor I had anything better to do on Saturday night than unpack boxes and put away clothes.

For the first time in months, I'm finally building something new instead of tearing something down, so I labored straight through with few breaks. If only remodeling the rest of my future would be as easy.

Dan strolls through the living room toward the fireplace, drawn to the bold impastoed painting hanging above the mantel. "This is cool. Where'd you get it?"

"I painted it." The award that cityscape won in college marked the first time I seriously believed in my ability to make a living as an artist. Like Kandinsky, I'd used color to manipulate a viewer's soul. To this day its vibrancy stirs my optimism. I'd had my sights set on an MFA at Columbia and a loft in New York City, but then I got pregnant and married, and Richard started law school at Georgetown. "It's an abstract cityscape of Richmond, Virginia, viewed from the Manchester Floodwall Walk."

"No kidding." He turns on his heel, head tipped, looking at me as if meeting for the first time. "I didn't realize you were an artist."

Once upon a time, maybe.

"Thanks." Gram was my first fan, so it seems fitting for someone—even Dan—to be standing in this room, giving me a pep talk.

My cheeks are probably as red as the carpet. Compliments always make me itchy. Professor Agate used to say mettle was as crucial as talent. He'd urged us to extol our work and fiercely defend it against critics. Heeding his advice had been my biggest challenge. "It's been years since I've painted anything like that."

More than a decade, in fact. At the outset of my marriage, I didn't believe that I needed to stay at home like my mom and gram to be a good mother. Somehow I was sure I could juggle parenting Katy and becoming another Helen Frankenthaler without an MFA or the move to New York.

When I wasn't nursing or working part-time at Baby Gap for grocery money, I painted. Like many artists, I'd approached each canvas as a problem that couldn't be left unsolved. Luckily, problem-solving on canvas was always easier than doing so in real life. In any case, I was young and in love and a new mom, so happiness oozed from my pores and fingertips and into my work. I even sold a handful of pieces, although none made much money or achieved high acclaim.

But when Katy was four, she got into the turpentine after I turned my back for five minutes. Richard freaked—as did I. Then Katy's concerning behaviors appeared and escalated. Richard offered to pay for a sitter, but I didn't want to be like my dad, foisting a sad or troubled kid on someone else. Katy was my beloved child. I would be the one to get her through this life. Of all the mediums at my disposal, she would be my greatest creation, after all. My one lasting legacy.

As such, I hit pause on my unremarkable career to focus on parenting Katy. It wasn't a sacrifice. From the first time I'd held my daughter, I'd cherished her. But while the head banging stopped around the age of six, other things cropped up—extreme self-criticism, the hair twisting and pulling, and withdrawal. Before I knew it, reading parenting books and managing her life had gobbled up the years.

"Seems a shame to have given it up." Dan stares at me intently.

This is our first conversation that lacks a strong riptide of tension. Inexplicably, that throws me off-balance. I can't decide whether the final years of my marriage conditioned me to expect friction with all men or if I'm simply yearning for our established dynamic because I need something consistent in my life.

"I don't have regrets." Not serious ones, anyway. Rothko once said that an artist needs faith in his or her ability to produce miracles when needed, and given the recent upheaval in my life, my faith in miracles is at an all-time low. "Besides, I'm so rusty I can't imagine creating anything worthwhile right now."

"Huh." With his hands on his hips, he casts another glance over his shoulder to examine my piece again. The scrutiny feels like he's undressing me.

Restless from his nudging, I gulp down the rest of my coffee. "I'll go wake Katy so we can get out of your hair for a few hours."

Dan nods before turning toward the kitchen, but the melody of his whistling follows me up the stairs. Whistling is something cheerful, plucky people do, yet despite the slight thaw between us this morning, I wouldn't exactly liken Dan to Happy the Dwarf.

I rap on Katy's door before opening it. She hates her bedroom's sloped roofline, but these days she's primed to complain about everything. In time maybe she'll decide it's cozy.

Three of the room's four walls are painted the faintest seashell pink, and we glammed up her pink bedding with white, gray, and gold accents. I left the wall around the side window white in case she gets inspired to paint a mural or cover it in some kind of collage—her favorite.

Richard had wanted our old house to be a showcase. I'm determined to make *this* house a home.

Katy spent yesterday afternoon unpacking her clothes and pinning pictures of her friends to her oversize bulletin board. Her soccer cleats are set out, ready for the first round of tryouts this afternoon. She made the varsity team last year, but her old school was smaller and probably had less competition. Katy's used to winning, so my stomach is already tight with anticipation of how she'll react if she ends up on the JV team.

My daughter is sleeping on her stomach, wrapped around a pillow. Before touching her shoulder, I raise the blinds. Sunlight makes the pink walls glimmer like the horizon of the bay at sunrise. "Katy-bear, the workers are here. Let's pop out for breakfast and then visit Gram."

She groans and rolls onto her back as if she suddenly weighs five hundred pounds. "Do I have to go? School starts next week. Can't I sleep in?"

"Once the banging begins, you'll hardly sleep anyway. But tomorrow you can try. Deal?"

"Fine." She yawns with her entire body and groans before reaching for her phone to check her messages.

"I'll fix you a coffee with cream and sugar for the ride."

After a sleepy nod of approval, she whips her coverlet off and pushes up to a seated position before combing her hair away from her face with her fingers. "I'll meet you downstairs."

Her feet hit the floor, so I leave her alone and go tie my own curls into a ponytail and swipe on a bit of lipstick. By this point, two other men have arrived and are clambering around the kitchen and master bathroom with Dan.

While fixing Katy's to-go cup, I study the painting that Dan admired. Like me at that age, it's vibrant, brimming with life and hope. A subconscious kick in the pants, perhaps? The reminder of the woman buried somewhere beneath all these blues.

A drill shrieks from yonder, yanking me from my daze. If I had a job, I'd escape the dust and noise. But who would hire a housewife with a fine arts major and no marketable skills or work experience? Plus, Katy's not yet settled. I'm a pro at school volunteering, which will help me evade all this noise and meet other moms in this community.

Katy appears wearing running shorts and a hoodie.

"Is that how you want to look when you see your great-grand-mother?" Too late, I realize my brows have reached my hairline.

She narrows her gaze. "What's the difference? Even if she hates my outfit, she won't remember it for long."

Some battles aren't worth fighting, so I relent and save up for one that matters. Still, her attitude sucks. "That was rude. I hope this heart-lessness is a phase."

"Sorry." It's mumbled but, based on her flushed cheeks, sincere. Like her father, Katy doesn't like to be wrong, so she struggles with apologies.

Dan emerges from the kitchen and heads toward the master bedroom.

"We're leaving." I snatch the white tin box, which could come in handy if Gram doesn't remember us today, from the buffet. "You have my cell if you need me for anything."

He lifts his gaze from the box in my hand. "Hope you get some answers."

So do I.

———

The entrance to the Sandy Shores Care Center is protected by wrought iron gates and a guard. I roll down the window and show my ID before being waved through by a bored-looking young man who's probably watching YouTube in that guardhouse.

"Well, at least it's a *fancy* prison," Katy remarks, having briefly raised her eyes from her phone to survey the facility. "I'd rather off myself than have people wipe my butt and shove pills down my throat."

"Katy!" I scowl. "Needing a little help doesn't mean that you can't enjoy the sunrise, or a game of chess, or a pleasant conversation."

"Chess?" She grimaces. "Like I said, pass the pills."

Had I ever been that cynical? My mother probably wouldn't tell me the truth if she were alive. She preferred rose-colored glasses to reality. Even at death's door—having contracted Legionnaires' weeks after a hike to natural hot springs in Colorado—she'd refused to accept the truth about her prognosis.

What she and Dad had first considered the flu got diagnosed too late for antibiotics to save her. I close my eyes against the memory of the bloody sputum, the high fever, the pained moans and diarrhea. Those were the most terrifying weeks of my life . . . At least they were until Katy started banging her head against walls.

But Gram's present circumstances must be lonely. My dad made his regular excuses when I invited him to drive down to visit her with us this week. Gram's sister, Lonna, died years ago from breast cancer, but her girls keep in touch with Gram by phone. I doubt any of them have actually visited since Gram's eightieth birthday, though. Even I'd lapsed into substituting phone calls for real visits most of the year.

I sigh heavily enough to encompass my pity for everyone, including myself. Sliding a side-eye toward Katy, I say, "Please inform me when my real daughter reclaims her body."

"Ha ha." Another half-joking eye roll and then she's back to swiping and typing.

Grandpa once said that when kids are little, they step on your toes, but when they are older, they step on your heart. It wasn't until Katy turned fourteen—when the stakes of her choices rocketed to the stratosphere at the exact time she honed her ability to pinpoint my flaws and tender spots—that I fully understood his meaning.

I would ask if she's nervous about soccer tryouts, but she might read my question as pressure, like I'd be disappointed if she doesn't make varsity. Worse, my forcing her to think about it could increase her anxiety, which could make tryouts harder.

Instead, I read the wooden directional signs as we wind past the independent-living apartments to the assisted-living unit. This is my first time here. I hadn't been able to help with the move because my dad had scheduled it on the day of my first divorce mediation meeting with Richard.

The manicured campus—with lush, neatly trimmed flower beds, an octagonal gazebo, and gulls flying overhead—resembles a seaside resort more than a care facility. The backside of Gram's building probably offers distant views of the bay, too. As a child, I'd sometimes caught her sitting at the dining table, gazing out the window at the treetops and daydreaming. Today she might enjoy watching the sailboats from a quiet bench outside.

Katy misses all the scenery while staring at her phone, scrolling through a seemingly endless list of images, pausing only occasionally while her thumbs type at breakneck speed.

"Ready to ask Gram about the box?" I ask too brightly.

She twirls an index finger. "Woo-hoo."

"Come on, Katy-bear."

"I'm sixteen, Mom. Katy-bear went into lifelong hibernation at least eight years ago." She sticks her phone in her pocket.

"You'll always be my baby." I turn off the ignition, recalling that once-toothless grin and the sticky-fingered hugs of yesteryear as if they happened this morning. "What's got you so rapt by your Insta feed?"

"Snapchat . . . ," she intones, like I'm an alien who can't keep up with a single trend. Which, I suppose, is sort of true. "My friends are comparing what classes and teachers they got."

She begins to twist a section of her hair around her index finger until the tip turns white.

"They start tomorrow, right? At least you have an extra week of summer." I flash a hopeful smile.

She tucks her chin and shoots me a pleading look. "Please stop begging me to be happy. Your 'lemonade from lemons' speeches don't make me miss my friends and old school less. And I'll still be the 'weird girl' from the city when school starts here."

"Or the interesting, beautiful new girl in town."

"I just asked you to stop," she says.

"Sorry." I grab the tin box between us. "Do me a huge favor for the next thirty minutes: pretend to like me and be sweet to Gram. This is a scary time for her, and maybe we can make it a little easier."

As soon as those words slip past my lips, I brace for her to misread my comment as dismissive of *her* worries. She surprises me by not popping off with defensive remarks. "How much *does* she remember?"

"I'm not sure. She has good days and bad ones, but wanted to move out before she hurt herself or someone else."

Always responsible. She taught me the value of doing the right thing at a young age. *"Remember you aren't the only one who pays the consequences of bad choices—everyone who loves you will feel pain when you suffer."* I'll never forget the grave look on her face when she told me that—right after I'd singed all my eyelashes from pouring kerosene on hot charcoals—like it was the most important advice she would ever give me. It crosses my mind anytime I'm about to take a risk.

"So she'll remember us?" Katy asks.

"She should." Of course, it's been a couple of weeks since I've spoken with her. I have no idea what today might bring.

We sign in at the security desk and then are asked to wait in the reception area until we can be taken to her room.

"It smells funny," Katy whispers.

"Antiseptic," I agree. Although relatively new construction, it's all very generic—sand- and cream-colored paints, laminate flooring, cheap hollow doors and fixtures. Even so, it's nicer than the facility Richard's mother was in last year for a month of rehab following spinal surgery. One whiff of the putrid mush it served prompted me to bring her meals four days each week so she wouldn't lose weight. Lauren doesn't strike me as the overly attentive type, so his mother might be out of luck next time. I wonder if Richard will notice or care.

Shaking off that self-pity, I return to the present. Skylights brighten the reception area and keep the myriad potted plants alive. We sink onto the comfortable beige leather sofa. Katy kicks her feet a bit while half-heartedly leafing through a *People* magazine, reading gossip about celebrities I've never heard of.

I use the quiet moment to collect myself before facing Gram.

My summers in Potomac Point rush back. Grandpa, a chemistry teacher, had happily devoted his summers to taking me fishing and to drive-in movies. He and Gram indulged me with weekly visits to Dream Cream for banana splits. Most important, Gram had encouraged me to paint and draw, while Grandpa got me to read some of the classics, which we'd talk about while toasting marshmallows.

Gram also loved playing board games, baking cookies, and watching *Wheel of Fortune*. Honestly, sometimes I'd wished I could've lived here year-round because their house felt more like a home than my own after my mom was no longer there playing the piano, or giving me manicures, or putting fresh flowers around the house.

Looking back, I think my dad retreated into fixing things like the toaster or tinkering in his garage to avoid the quiet house, too, convinced he was doing his duty by keeping a roof over my head and food in my stomach. The fact that I look like my mom might've been a painful reminder, too, but I never asked.

Katy might feel smothered by my love and attention sometimes, but that has to beat her feeling overlooked.

"Anne Chase?" A stout nurse with flamboyant red hair has come to stand beside the sofa.

Hearing Richard's surname rattles me for a second. The world doesn't need two Mrs. Richard Chases. Changing my legal name back to Anne Sullivan should leapfrog to the top of my to-do list.

"Yes."

"I'm Clara. I'll take you to see your grandmother now." She beckons Katy, who tosses the magazine back on the coffee table and stands, as do I.

"Thank you, Clara." We follow her down the long hallway to the left.

Clara raps on the door before opening it.

"Miss Marie, you've got some visitors today," Clara says as we enter Gram's room—number 123, like her old street address—an end unit with corner windows and natural light. It's basically a large studio space with a full-size bed, a private handicap-accessible bathroom, and a breakfast bar area with a coffee maker, mini fridge, and small microwave.

The fading needlepoint carpet that used to be in Gram's bedroom plants a little ache in my heart. No matter how stoic a person, moving out of one's home at eighty-eight must be disconcerting.

Clara partly closes the door on her way out of the room.

Gram is seated in Grandpa's old lounge chair, which she brought here along with another moderately comfortable chair, both of which face a television placed in a small entertainment center. Above her bed is a watercolor of the bay I'd painted in 1997 that Gram had made me sign before she had it mounted and framed. I flatten my hand over my chest. Not terrible for a fourteen-year-old experimenting with wash techniques.

Gram looks up from the television as if we're nonthreatening strangers. Wispy short white hair curls away from her face. Her misty eyes squeeze my heart.

"What's wrong, Gram?" I cross the room to hug her, at which point the baby powder and hairspray scents steep me in nostalgia. Her bony frame might as well be a collection of toothpicks in my arms. I grasp her hands gently, fearful of hurting her tissue-thin skin. Thick shame about how long it's been since my last visit wedges itself in my throat.

I snatch a tissue from the box beside her and hand it to her.

She waves it off. "Those won't help."

"What will?" I take a seat, still holding the tissue. Katy is frozen behind me, waiting for instructions, so I gesture for her to hang tight.

"Nothing." Gram's voice is harsh, like she's mad at us because she's confused yet forced to cover her uncertainty.

Her cognitive deficiencies first surfaced around her eightieth birthday, although she masked them as long as she could. Once she hit stage 6 (or middle dementia), the doctor suggested that she move to a facility for constant care and supervision. He also told us to brace for paranoia, delusions, and more pronounced memory loss.

"How are you today?" I try.

"Same as always." She waves a hand. "Trapped here. Punished again."

"This isn't a punishment. You wanted to be someplace safe." At least she didn't fight her doctor or my dad.

"Don't get cute, Lonna." There's no mistaking that resentful tone. "You think you're better than me, but you were just lucky that you never wanted anything of your own."

Lonna is dead, so she can't illuminate this conversation. But I'm stunned, having had no idea there'd been animosity between them.

"I'm not your sister, Gram. It's me, Annie," I say, hoping to spark some recognition. "Bobby's daughter."

No one else calls my father by that name. Robert Sullivan, a civil engineer for the city of Baltimore. A taciturn man who probably would not answer to "Bobby" these days.

Dozens of angry wrinkles smooth as she fights to make sense of my words.

"Do you recognize Katy?" I nod toward my daughter. "She's growing up quickly."

When I wave Katy over, she approaches timidly, but leans in to kiss Gram's forehead. "Hi, Grammy."

Seventy-two years and three generations separate these two women, yet a bit of Gram lives on in Katy. You can see it in the shape of their mouths and the slightly snub nose.

"Annie . . ." A look of concern passes over Gram's face as recognition dawns. "Did something happen to Bobby?"

"No. I bought your house and moved to town. Remember?" I search her eyes for some recognition. "Maybe once the renovations are complete, you can come over for lunch and see all the changes. Would you like that?"

She's twining her fingers, rolling them over each other. "I don't know."

Katy moves to the shelf where Gram has set out two dozen framed photographs: Grandpa and my father, her parents and Lonna, me as a child. Others are landscape or object focused. She'd often had a camera handy, taking snapshots of strange things . . . like "For Rent" and "For Sale" signs, "Grand Opening" banners, new construction, and demolitions. It was almost as if she'd been intent on recording a history of changes in the town, no matter how seemingly insignificant.

When I'd first started drawing, she encouraged me to record the minute details. As I got older, she never much understood my interest in abstract impressionism. I'd tell her to enjoy the emotions at play, but she preferred realism, which is why she favored photography, I suppose.

"I like taking pictures, too," Katy says, setting a photograph of Grandpa and me back in its spot. She spins around to face Gram. "Let's take a selfie."

"A selfie?" Gram shoots me a questioning glance.

Katy sidles beside Gram, sets the camera app to portrait mode, shoots her left arm out and upward—iPhone in hand—and says, "Smile."

She snaps two quick photos, both of which portray Gram as stoic. Seeing my daughter smiling and making a connection with Gram increases my confidence that coming to Potomac Point will be good for us both. Gram reaches for the phone, shaking her head while turning it over. "That's sharp . . ."

"I'll print a copy and bring it next time for your shelf." Katy shrugs.

Gram's silver brows gather as she mutters, "You should try good old-fashioned film."

Katy laughs, then pauses in thought. "Darkrooms look cool in old pictures, with that red light and those tongs. Maybe I'll have access to one in my photography class."

"That would be cool," I say. "I'm sure this school will have some kind of art show to showcase students' work. You should start thinking up an idea."

"I actually have an idea of something I've been wanting to do anyway," Katy says.

"What's that?"

"A family tree collage."

It shouldn't surprise me that, like me at that age, she'd turn to artistic expression to work through her emotions. It also shouldn't surprise me that she's thinking about family at a time when hers is breaking apart. "How do you mean?"

"I'll collect new and old photos of Dad, you, myself, Grammy, and other extended family—with your and Dad's help. Then I'll tear them into bits and assemble them to look like the bark of a tree trunk and branches. At the ends of each branch will be a whole photograph of each family member."

"That's interesting," I say.

Katy nods. "I guess some of the old photos will be film based, but digital filters are pretty awesome, too, Grammy. Next time I come, I'll bring my laptop and show you how to edit digital photographs. We could photoshop your face onto Beyoncé's body if you want." She laughs.

Gram blinks, bewildered. "I won't be here."

My lips part. "Where will you be?"

"New York. And don't try to stop me this time." Defiance seeps from her pores. "I have to find Billy's parents and explain."

Katy mouths, "Who's Billy?"

I'm guessing he's a character from a television drama that she's confused with reality.

I play along with the hope of calming her, perhaps by transitioning to something mundane. "New York is exciting. Maybe I'll go with you."

She narrows her eyes, but I keep talking. "You did a nice job decorating your room, Gram. I always loved this carpet." I then point at my old painting. "Thanks for bringing that with you, too. I might never have studied art if you hadn't bought me my first set of paints and canvases."

She'd done it to give me a quiet outlet for my grief. I quickly realized how art affects us all, much like how music—both in its creation and its effect—stirs something inside. Connects us through familiar emotions. Art is the single most important gift Gram ever gave me.

Yet although proud of my early successes in high school and college, she encouraged me to give it up when Katy showed signs of needing more attention. *"Sometimes you have to make sacrifices, Annie. No one gets to have it all. Richard makes a lot of money, so you can afford to stay home and take care of your child."*

She hadn't been wrong. I wanted to experience playing with Katy at the park and finger-painting together and taking her to soccer practice. My professional career hadn't taken off like Richard's had, so I immersed myself in two roles I was certain I could do well. Joke's on me. Clearly, I failed as a wife. And Katy's inability to cope with her frustrations suggests I'm failing as her mom, too.

Katy casts a glance at the framed painting. She's probably judging it and probably deciding she might do it better, or at least differently. Professor Agate would be disappointed in my lack of daring now.

Gram blinks, her gaze darting from it to me. I can't tell if she recognizes it, but she has not become more talkative in old age. This visit will require a lot of prompts.

Her room is a touch too warm, but I doubt she has any iced tea or soda in that tiny refrigerator. "How's the food here?"

She clucks and waves her hand dismissively.

"Make me a list and next time I'll bring some of your favorite things from town. I see you have a microwave, so perhaps you'd like soup."

"I'm not hungry." She shrugs.

"You need to eat." I search my memory for her favorites. "Maybe chocolate pudding will stoke your appetite."

She loved pudding back in the day, and I'd loved to scrape clumps of thickened leftovers from the edges of the pot and chew them one by one.

No one says much, but at least Gram isn't as agitated or teary as when we'd arrived. An improvement. During a pause in conversation, I debate whether to bring up the recipe box.

Gram asks Katy, "What are you doing now?"

"Talking to my friends." Katy flashes her phone screen our way.

"Am I going deaf, too?" Gram gestures toward Katy with two fingers. "You shouldn't sit with your legs open. It's unbecoming."

Aha, Gram! There you are.

She uses the word "should" more than any other person I know. *You should behave like a lady and not get so muddy. You shouldn't question the rules. You shouldn't slurp your soup. You should listen to your father, and don't make waves. You should marry Richard now that you're pregnant.*

Katy's jaw twitches, but she closes the gap between her knees. "Sorry."

"Why aren't you in school?" Gram asks her.

"It doesn't start until next week."

Gram turns toward me, head tilted. "What month is it?"

"Late August," I reply.

She assesses Katy again. "You look like your father. Where's he?"

I'm not surprised that Gram remembers Richard. He makes quite an impression, and he'd charmed Gram with his big dreams. She'd get a

45

twinkle in her eye and smile at me. *"Annie, this one will be an adventure. A good match."* She'd had it half-right.

"At work." Katy turns stone-faced at the mention of Richard.

"Richard and I are divorcing, remember?" I say, pulling Gram's attention back to me.

"Divorce? Well, that's a shame. When you lose the one you love, a piece of your soul dies if you're not careful. Then nothing is ever quite right . . ." Gram's eyes cloud with sorrow.

It's sweet how she clings to Grandpa's memory. And if losing a husband of seventeen years is hard on me, I can't imagine how it feels to outlive a husband of forty-five years.

Gram clucks before asking me, "Do you still love him?"

Katy studies me, unblinking. Does she hope I say yes, or no? When I recall how he used to look at me and make me laugh, my eyes sting. But the past few years have seen more arguments than affection. He went from being someone who built me up to being someone whose waning attention filled me with self-doubt. I love our child. I respect his intellect. But in truth, we'd grown apart once I gave up fighting for his time, so my heart is less battered than my ego. Figuring out who I am now that he's no longer at my side is the most daunting aspect of our breakup.

"A part of me will always love Richard, but I'll be okay without him." Honest, if not direct. "That's why I've moved here. A clean slate . . . and now we can keep you company."

Gram frowns, eyes narrowed. "Why would you move here when you can go anywhere?"

"Good question," Katy pipes up.

"It's always peaceful here, Gram."

Gram's hands fidget with the arms of her lounger. "Call a spade a spade. It's dull . . ."

She falls silent and stares off, clearly lost in a memory, leaving me flabbergasted yet again. I set the recipe box on my knee, curious to see her response. "Gram, do you recognize this?"

Gram cranes her neck for a closer look, so I lean forward and place it in her lap.

She turns the box over for a moment, her hands gripping it tightly before shakily setting it on the oval table beside her and staring elsewhere again. I retrieve it and open the lid, displaying its contents one by one, beginning with the rusty nail. "I can't imagine why anyone would save this, but there must be a story behind it."

Gram doesn't answer. Her gaze shifts toward the table but at the same time is unfocused. I try the handkerchief. "How about this? Does 'W. T.' mean anything to you?"

It's possible these items belonged to her mother. My great-grandfather's initials were not W. T., though. I've been assuming all the items were related, but it occurs to me now that they could be random memories, like a time capsule.

When I get to the photograph, I hold it up. "Do you recognize this man? Grandpa didn't have that dimpled chin, but maybe this was someone you knew before you met Grandpa."

Her nostrils flare briefly, but her otherwise inscrutable expression tells me nothing.

I set the items aside and rest my hand on her knee. "The contractor found this box when he broke through the master closet. I thought it'd be fun for you to go back in time and share your memories."

"Fun?" The word flies from her lips, landing with an angry thud. "Are you *trying* to be hurtful?"

More questions crowd my thoughts, but Katy shakes her head at me in a silent appeal to drop the whole thing. She needn't be worried. It isn't my nature to torment people.

"Sorry," I say, although I have many more questions than I did when we arrived. Gram might not remember everything, but something in that box triggered her.

I stuff the items back in the box and squeeze it in my hands. If these items are *painful* reminders, why keep them at all?

Her eyes are as misty as when we first arrived. "I'm tired."

Katy hops off the mattress, eager to flee.

"Okay." Guilt trickles through me for foisting memories on her without warning. I set the box on the table and stand to help her out of her chair. "How about if I come back next time with that pudding?"

"My head hurts." She presses her fingertips to her forehead as I seat her on her bed. "No more about Billy."

Billy again. Not Bobby. Is he the man in the photograph? Does the *W* on the handkerchief stand for William?

"We'll let you rest. I'll see you next week." I bend to kiss her forehead and then pull the pink-and-red-and-white afghan folded on the side of her bed up to her waist.

"See you later, Grammy." Katy pats her shin.

I nod toward the door, giving my daughter permission to bolt.

Gram rolls onto her side, facing the wall. On my way out, I gather the tin box and then turn off the light and close her door.

Katy is waiting in the hallway.

"You were sweet to relate to Gram with photography. Thank you."

She shrugs. "Mom, please tell me you don't ever want to live like this. I mean, it's really sad. Cooped up in a little room. Unable to remember stuff. Not even hungry."

I throw my arm around her shoulder. "It's very sad. Scary, even. But I want to live long enough to see the amazing woman you become, and to meet my someday grandkids, even if I'm stuck in a bed and can only visit you on FaceTime."

Katy snickers. "Who says I'll get married and have kids? You heard Gram. Love kills your soul." She makes her hands into claws and fake swipes at my face.

I bat them away, chuckling yet preoccupied with Gram's paradoxes. "Not always."

We exit the building to walk beneath a sunny summer sky dotted with cotton ball clouds. The hint of saltwater tang floating on the breeze loosens the tightness in my shoulders, as always.

"I guess not if you're a guy." Katy ties her hair into a ponytail high on her head.

I slow to a halt. "Why do you say that?"

"Because most men are cheaters, and even when they're not, women get stuck doing everything. Why should I slave all day at work and then cook, do laundry, help with homework, and pick up after my husband, too?"

"Not all men cheat." Her cynicism is worrisome. "And some couples split household work evenly. I did everything because I didn't have a day job."

"All my friends' dads breeze in and out and play golf. And look at Pop-Pop. You always tell me about how, when you were my age, you were doing your own laundry and cooking for you and him."

Mistrusting men had not been the goal of those "responsibility" talks. Do all teens misinterpret their parents' life lessons, or just mine?

"Your dad and I married too young. But marriage can work if you know yourself well before you choose a partner. Either way, falling in love—being in love—is magical. I want that magic in your life."

"So I can end up hurt like you?" she asks.

Oof. Sometimes Katy's observations land like a sledgehammer.

"Without your dad, I wouldn't have you. You're worth ten times the pain of this divorce." I wink before sliding into the front seat and setting the tin box in the console between us. Of all the decisions to second-guess, I don't regret my marriage. Richard's rising star changed us, but it also allowed me to dote on Katy—moments to treasure that melt away too quickly.

Katy sinks onto her seat and opens the box's lid, peering at the items again. "Grammy doesn't want to talk about this stuff—if she even remembers it."

"She knows something. She mentioned someone named Billy twice . . ."

Katy grimaces. "She also called you Lonna, so don't get your hopes up."

"You don't think I should pry?"

My daughter stares ahead, sighing. "What's the point? We have bigger things to worry about, like having a kitchen."

True. There is plenty on my plate right now. Yet this little mystery piques my curiosity in a big way.

"Gram raised me. She was my rock." I followed her advice blindly—about college, about what to do when I got pregnant, and about how to manage Katy—even though she mistrusted therapists like Richard did. "I admit I'm a little shaken by the idea that she might not be who I thought. To think that she might not have loved her hometown, that she resented her sister, that she keeps painful secrets . . . It's not like there's much time to learn the truth, either. I don't know. It feels like fate dropped this box into my lap because I'm at a crossroads."

She wrinkles her nose. "Mom, if there's a reason Grammy hid that box, you might not like what you learn."

"True." I nod, staring at the road as we drive along the bay.

Katy's skepticism aside, I want to know about the elusive Billy T. and New York and what Gram wants to explain to his parents. At the very least, it's a distraction from the aftershocks of my divorce.

Then again, it's not often that buried secrets yield happy endings.

CHAPTER FIVE

MARIE

October 14, 1949

The pink wool swing coat I got for my eighteenth birthday is marvelous. The way it swirls when I spin and how its outsize pointed collar frames my face make me feel like a movie star, which is a welcome change from being plain Marie Robson. That sounds trivial compared with all the important things happening in the world. This coat won't bring about the end of the Cold War, but I delight in its power to transform *me*.

"Stop spinning. You look silly," Lonna says from my bedroom floor, where she's playing with her doll.

I meet her gaze in the cheval mirror and shrug.

She's only ten. What does she understand about fashion? *"You still play with dolls,"* I want to say but don't.

Lonna wearily shakes her head and then gives her doll a fake bottle. "Drink all this milk, Annabelle. And when you're finished, I'll burp you and change your diaper so you're comfortable."

Her gentle voice racks me with envy because she's exactly like our mother. Sweet and nurturing. Obedient. All the things I fake in order to please my parents and have invitations to school dances. If I pretend long enough, maybe I'll learn to feel the things "Dr. Robson's girls" are supposed to feel. I've no particular talent or gift—nor am I a great beauty—but I yearn to do *something* more exciting than spending the rest of my life in this town. Sometimes I regret reading about more interesting lives when I might be required to settle for one that fits me less well than this coat.

I lean over to pat Lonna's head on my way downstairs. "Have fun with Annabelle."

When I reach the living room, my father is encircled by lamplight and a hazy blue curl, reading and smoking his pipe. Like my mother and sister, I admire and want to please him. A conundrum, because to do so I must pretend to be someone else.

I hear my mother busying herself in the kitchen. Cook, clean, iron, repeat. The thought makes me shudder. My father came from Scottish immigrant parents who worked menial jobs to give their children a shot at the American dream. He met my mother while at medical school, where she worked as a secretary. Both of them strive to be their very best at all times. It's exhausting.

"Good night, Daddy!" I wave.

"Where are you off to?"

"The movies."

My father frowns, like he does whenever he deems something frivolous—which is not uncommon. "Come home directly afterward, please."

Swallowing a sigh, I agree. Outside, a horn blasts. "I have to go."

"Would you like money for your ticket?"

"Yes, thank you!" I rise onto my toes. His stern shell hides a soft underbelly. It gives me hope that one day I can talk him into letting me explore options other than college.

He removes his wallet from his pocket and hands me twenty-five cents, which will pay for the movie and two ice cream sundaes.

"Thank you." I wrap my arms around his neck. "I promise I won't stay out late."

My mother—a short, blonde beauty with a curvy figure hidden by an apron—peeks out from the kitchen. "Have fun, dear."

I blow her a kiss and then trot out the door to catch up with my friends. Susie's father bought a new Ford this Christmas—pea green with whitewall tires.

I slide into the back seat. "Nice car."

"Isn't it?" Susie smiles, proud of her father, our school principal.

Janice is studying me from the passenger seat. "I *love* that coat."

"Thank you." Unlike my sister, my friends appreciate glamour. "Let's hurry. I don't want to miss the beginning."

The car lurches away from the curb—Susie's not the best driver. It's chilly out tonight, so we'll have to keep the windows rolled up for the whole ride to the next town over, where the movie is playing.

"Joe Johnson is planning to propose to SaraJane when he gets back from Georgetown for the holidays," Janice says as we drive through Potomac Point.

I cringe at the thought of being married to Joe Johnson. He's arrogant and will probably be a bossy husband. "Will she say yes?"

Susie laughs. "Who wouldn't? He's got a bright future. In a couple of years she'll be a mom and set for life!"

I must've made a face, because Janice says, "You look like you've swallowed whiskey."

My friends are conventional, so I temper my opinion. "Is that all we get—a husband and some babies? Nothing of our own . . . no adventure?" My gaze darts from one to the other, while they stare at me like my skin has turned purple.

"Who says a handsome, nice man can't be an adventure?" Janice titters, unaware that she ranked handsome above nice, which highlights another difference in our priorities. "We can travel and do other things later, but we need to find husbands before we're too old."

I keep mum, but none of the mothers I know ever see the world. Maybe they're living their own dream, which is fine for them but leaves women like me out of luck.

Susie swats my shoulder. "You'll feel differently when you meet the right man."

She and Janice laugh, so I join in. So far every boy I've met is either too immature—like Ronnie Eggers, our high school's star pitcher—or too serious, like Fred Harrison, the school paper's editor, who only ever wants to talk about student government. The only men with the right combination of charm and daring live in Hollywood, which might as well be the moon.

"If Montgomery Clift asked for your number, would you give it to him?" Janice asks as we pull onto the north route out of town.

I giggle. "Of course, but he *would* be an adventure!"

We all burst into a fit of laughter, but then the car starts to shake and rumble. "Oh gosh!" Susie's eyes are wide. "What's happening?"

"Pull off the road," I say.

After she shifts into park, we all file out of the car and walk around, inspecting it.

"You've got a flat tire." Janice points to the rear driver's side tire.

"My dad's going to kill me," Susie whines.

"It's not your fault." I pat her shoulder. "Do either of you know how to use the spare?"

They shake their heads. I don't, either, and I don't want to dirty my coat.

"What do we do?" Janice asks.

"Wait for help," Susie says.

Waiting could take forever and we'll never make the movie. "I'll walk back toward town to get help."

"It's at least a mile or farther . . . That's not safe, especially in the dark." Janice shakes her head.

I'm not worried. It'll be practice for city life. Besides, there's rarely any crime in Potomac Point, and most of it is petty theft. This is the closest I'll come to an adventure this year. "I'm fine. I'll stop at the first house I see."

Before they can argue, I take off down the shadowy road. Humming helps distract me from how creepy it is. A few minutes into the walk, a motorcycle shifts gears in the distance. I tense, then shake my arms loose. Within seconds a headlight appears on the horizon, coming toward me pretty fast. My heart beats hard, but I wave my hands overhead to catch the driver's attention.

He slows, passing me before pulling over. Once he gets off his bike, he starts toward me. "What are you doing on the road? You could get hurt!"

I freeze in the face of the boy—no, the man—I've never seen before. There's a bit of rascal about his unruly dark hair, bushy brows arched high around rich brown eyes, and deep dimple in his chin. He's not classically handsome, but he's rugged and interesting looking. Perhaps an Italian or Greek. I'm not sure, but he's definitely not Scottish.

"Miss?" His Yankee accent—possibly New York or farther north—intrigues me more. He snaps his fingers. "Are you okay?"

My cheeks are probably turning the color of my new coat, but all I can do is blink and catch my breath.

"Sorry." I'm dizzy. "My friends are up the road. We got a flat tire, so I came looking for help."

"You should've waited together until someone passed by. What if I were a dangerous guy?" He's shaking his head. "Let's go fix the tire."

The whole time he's been talking, I've not blinked once. He's at least three years older than me, but he's no college boy. "What's your name?"

The words erupt without thought, but at the same time, I don't honestly care if I'm forward. He doesn't seem to, either.

"Billy." He wipes his hand on his pants before extending it, which is when I notice his gas attendant uniform. "Billy Tyler."

"That's not Italian." I slap my hand over my mouth, but he laughs. Still smiling, he says, "My mother is Italian."

My mouth is dry, but I answer, "Nice to meet you, Billy. I'm Marie Robson."

When he squeezes my hand, something shifts into place, unlocking an unfamiliar, exciting array of emotions.

"Come on, Marie. Your friends are probably nervous."

I've wanted to ride a motorcycle ever since I saw Loomis Dean's photographs in *Life* magazine of those women joyriding around Griffith Park in Los Angeles. One—Cecilia Adams—won an amateur all-girls trail race, too. But no one we know owns a motorcycle, and my parents consider it unladylike. My heart clutches so hard I'm breathless again. "You're right."

When I get to his bike, it isn't as big as it first appeared. A turquoise Indian Chief, with metal caps covering the tops of both wheels. Billy lifts one leg over the front tip of the seat to make space for me. He pats the seat behind him. "Sit here and wrap your arms around my waist, then hold tight. You can rest your cheek against my back if you don't like the wind."

With clammy hands and a tremulous smile, I climb onto the seat. My coat is too long. I can't hold it up and wrap my arms around his waist, so I do my best to tuck it under my butt. My body responds in confusing ways to Billy's firm, warm stomach—like I need to squeeze my thighs together.

"Hang on!" he says as he uses his body weight and foot to start the engine. It roars to life so loud it scares me.

My very being vibrates with the bike. My heart stutters—a moment of doubt—and yet I can't stop laughing as we start down the road. The wind blows my hair everywhere and freezes my hands, but I don't care. I feel free and brave and completely alive.

Too soon we come upon my friends. When I get off the bike, their wild-eyed gazes dart back and forth between Billy and me.

"This is Billy. He's going to help us."

He waves. "Hi, ladies. I'll get your spare switched out so you can be on your way."

"Thank you." Susie takes him to the trunk, while Janice sidles up to me.

"I can't believe you got on that motorcycle with a stranger." Her face is pinched and splotchy.

Ignoring her, I turn away and watch Billy heft the spare tire and roll it around before he stoops to loosen the bolts on the flat tire.

"What's got into you, Marie?" Janice elbows me as Susie joins us.

Is she blind? I whisper, "Billy Tyler is swoony!"

Susie tsk-tsks. "Your dad will never approve."

Maybe not, but that won't stop me from trying. "I'm eighteen now. I don't need permission."

"You don't even know this guy," Janice whispers. "He might be a creep."

"He's not." Don't ask how I know that, but I'm certain.

Susie is tapping her foot. "We'll never make the movie."

I hardly care, because my interest in make-believe has evaporated in the face of the real-life Billy Tyler.

It seems like thirty days instead of thirty minutes before he is finished changing the tire. He holds up the culprit—a big nail—and then puts it in his jacket pocket. "All set, but don't drive too far on the spare."

"It's fine. We'll go right back home," Susie promises. "Thank you. Can I pay you for helping?"

He waves her off. "No, thank you. Happy to help." Then he turns to me. "No more walking down dark roads on your own, Marie."

If walking down dark roads alone leads me to guys like Billy and rides on motorcycles, I'll be doing it every night. "But then I wouldn't have gotten to ride on your bike."

He tilts his head to the left, eyes crinkling. "You liked that?"

"Very much."

Billy hesitates, then says, "You want to drive it?"

Susie tugs at my arm. "We should go."

My gaze is locked with Billy's. "You'd let me? I don't know how . . ."

"It's not hard." He shrugs. "If you can ride a bicycle, you can do this."

Janice's mouth gapes. "You could get hurt, Marie. Let's just go."

"Hold on, Janice. Give me five minutes."

She and Susie exchange a look and offer tight-lipped nods.

"I promise she'll be safe," Billy says before he pats the seat. "Come on, Marie. Throw your leg over and hold the handlebars here. This is the front brake." He puts my hand over it to squeeze.

I'm grateful to be wearing pants. Once I'm straddling the big seat, I wiggle the bike side to side to test its weight. My heart races, but I repress my fear.

"Okay. So turn on the ignition"—he points to it—"then use your foot here on the kick-starter. Sort of jump on it with your weight and then rev the throttle and release the brake."

Every hair on my head prickles and heavy breaths sting my lungs. I glance back at my friends, who look constipated. My heart drums in my chest. I test the kick-starter, but nothing happens.

"Try again." Billy nods. "Really jump on it."

I hold my breath and throw all my weight down. When it revs to life, I screech, standing there holding on as it sputters between my legs. "Oh my God!"

"Relax," Billy shouts. "Now over here you can just click it into first gear and release the brake and just go a little way up nice and slow. If you get scared, hit the brakes. Stop as soon as you want."

I nod and do as he says. The bike heaves beneath me. I screech again, but don't feel too wobbly, actually, so I twist the throttle and drive forward about ten yards. Panic strikes, so I holler and hit the brakes, then turn off the ignition. I'm trembling yet laughing.

Billy catches up to me, his eyes lit with amusement. "You did great!"

I'm glad it's dark out because now my face is probably redder than my hair. I am not as brave as I thought, but I did it.

"Next time you'll go farther." He looks back at my friends. "We could try to ride together with me behind you, so I'd work the gears but you could watch and get a feel for it. If you want."

"Is that safe?"

He shrugs. "We'll go slow."

"Marie!" Janice calls.

I walk toward her, shucking out of my new coat. "I'm going to ride back with Billy. Can you take this in the car so it doesn't get dirty, then follow us and give it back to me at home?"

"Fine," Janice says, although the set of her shoulders tells me she'll scold me later.

Billy removes his bomber jacket. "Wear this."

"Won't you freeze?" I ask.

"It's not that far, or that cold. Besides, I'll be warm enough with you on the bike." He winks, and I nearly faint. No boy has ever talked to me this way, but I like how he treats me like a woman instead of a girl.

Susie says, "We'll be *right* behind you."

I nod and get back on his motorcycle. Just like last time, my heart pounds while he shows me how to start the engine. It feels different with him behind me, all squished forward so he can reach the handlebars. We turn around on the road and head back to town. I never even thought to ask where he'd been headed before I sidetracked him.

We drive past Main Street and head toward the water. "Go right at the stop sign and then take the second left onto Autumn. Number 123!" I shout.

He nods.

My friends will talk about this for weeks, but they can't tell others, or my parents will be furious.

When we stop in front of my house, Billy shuts off the bike, his mood less enthusiastic. "Nice house."

"Thanks." Our home befits my father's stature as one of the town's two doctors.

"Well," he says, "it was nice to meet you, Marie Robson. Hope you enjoyed your ride."

Janice gets out of Susie's car with my coat in her hand.

That reminds me that I'm still wearing Billy's bomber jacket. Reluctantly, I peel it off and hand it to him, but only after I palm the nail from its pocket. "When's my next lesson?"

He glances at my house again with a slight frown. "I dunno."

"Why not?"

He shrugs, kicking his toe against the pavement.

"Is something wrong . . . ?"

He squints at me. "You're not like other girls, are you?" He chuckles, drawing my attention to the dimple in his chin. "Give me your phone number."

Phew. "Blackburn-65809."

Billy repeats it and then kisses my cheek. "Sweet dreams, Marie."

When Janice catches up to us, he kick-starts his bike and drives off. The night sky swallows him long before the sound of his engine fades.

"Wow." I exhale a happy sigh.

Janice hands me my coat. "Marie, that was too much. What if you got hurt? And you shouldn't lead him on. When you get bored, he'll get hurt."

My front door opens, and my father's silhouette takes up the entire frame.

"Uh-oh." Janice's eyes widen. "Good luck." On her way to Susie's car, she waves at my father. "Hi, Dr. Robson."

"Good night, Janice." His voice is hard and flat.

My friends drive away, probably peeing their pants. I walk up the pavers, acting braver than I am. I try to offer a quick kiss on the cheek and breeze past. "Good night, Daddy."

"Hold on, Marie Jean."

Drat. My middle name signals a lecture.

"What happened with the movie, and who was that boy on the motorcycle?" His brow is furrowed.

"We got a flat tire on our way to the movie. Billy Tyler helped us with the spare. I think he works at the gas station."

My dad quirks a single brow. "Why did he follow you home?"

I gulp but can't think up a cover story on the spot. "Because I wanted to ride on his motorcycle."

Daddy's eyes grow four times their normal size. "You rode on a motorcycle with a stranger? That's not just foolish, it's dangerous."

"It was fun." If he knew I drove it, he'd ground me. "He went slow so Janice and Susie could follow the whole way. I was perfectly safe."

He rubs his face with one hand, shaking his head. "Motorcycles are *not* safe, or ladylike. Promise me you won't do that, or see him, again."

"You can't dislike him before you even meet him."

My father crosses his arms, chin tucked. "I don't need to meet him to know he's not the right kind of boy for you."

I love my dad—I do. He's a wonderful father and an excellent doctor. But his ideal—a quiet life in the suburbs—will not make me happy. Billy might not make me happy, either, but having a choice about my own life will. "I'm practically an adult. It should be my choice who I see."

His jaw muscles bulge as his expression hardens. "Unless you want to be grounded until you go to college, you will do as I say."

The threat makes me bristle. "What if I apprentice with that photographer we met at Polly's wedding last summer instead of going to college? When I get good at it, I can work for a magazine and travel."

He slaps his forehead. "Not this nonsense again."

"It's not nonsense, Daddy."

"You'll give your mother fits if you keep this up." He stops himself, holding his hands out. In a condescending tone, he says, "At university you'll meet a lot of interesting people. If you want to work for a while, you can become a teacher."

"I don't like kids." I fold my arms beneath my chest, aware that I'm pouting like one, but that's how this subject makes me feel.

"You will someday soon."

Most women do, but I'm not convinced. "What if I *don't*?"

I so need for him to hug me and tell me that he'll love me no matter what. That he believes in me and wants me to be happy, however that looks to me.

"Enough, Marie. It's late." He points toward the stairs. "Go to bed. We can talk about this more in the morning, but not in front of your mother."

"Yes, Daddy." I hang my coat in the closet and lug myself upstairs to my room as if my body weighs twice as much as normal.

The whole time I'm washing my face and brushing my teeth, I think about those few minutes on the back of Billy's motorcycle. The heat of his body still makes me warm, then I shiver at the recollection of his arms around me as he helped me steer, and the thrill of the wind on my face.

I hide the nail in my jewelry box. If Billy Tyler calls me, I *will* find a way to see him again, no matter what my father says.

CHAPTER SIX

KATY

"Where are you going, Katy?" Libby asks me when I turn in the opposite direction of the cafeteria on our way out of AP Physics.

She's a senior and the captain of the girls' varsity soccer team. I should make fast friends with her to get my mom off my back, but it makes me uncomfortable to be treated like a BFF by someone I hardly know. It's barely the second week of school. The most *anyone* can feel about me at this point is curiosity.

Not even about *me*, actually. More like my car, Apple Watch, and Hermès Clic Clac H bracelet. Then they seem surprised by my neighborhood because the old side of town is not where "rich" families live.

"Bathroom," I say.

"Cool. Find us in the cafeteria." She trots ahead to catch up to someone I don't know.

I duck into the girls' room, passing by all the students fixing their hair and putting on lip gloss, and shut myself in a stall.

After I drop my backpack on the ground, I sit on the toilet and breathe through the tightness in my chest. With my eyes closed I picture the table by the window in my old cafeteria, where I always ate with

Jen, Kelly, and Jo. I miss them, but Maisy White is constantly in their Instafeed now. They replaced me as fast as my dad has.

Maybe "replaceable" should be my middle name.

It hurts so much. Confirmation that people can't be counted on. That everything is bullshit.

I miss my old house and pool. I miss hugging my dad good night. Brody and Zoe get that from him now.

I drop freshly plucked hairs into the toilet bowl. Lately I can't focus half the time and don't want to the other half. Whenever I think about how my mom let Dad go without a fight, I want to hit something or cry. It's like both my parents have gone crazy.

Screwing up my grades would teach them, but it'd also be a huge waste of all the work I've put in the past two years. It sucks so bad to be pissed off and powerless.

My dab pen would take the edge off now, but the girls at the sinks might report me. There's still lunch, two more periods, and practice to endure before I can lock myself in my bedroom with the window open.

I pat my damp forehead with some toilet paper.

It'd be easier to navigate this place if I knew the pecking order: which cliques to avoid, what teachers to look out for, what kids to trust. The only certain thing is that I can't stay in this stall all period, so I flush the toilet, grab my backpack, and open the door.

As I stroll through the hall toward the cafeteria, kids are joking and running all around me, but I keep my eyes forward and slightly downcast. Once I breach the cafeteria doors, it's utter chaos. Groups of friends have claimed their regular tables. Kids are yelling to be heard over the din. The lines for the decent food stations are as bad as the ladies' room line at a Post Malone concert.

My appetite is nil because my stomach is in a vise. While alone in line trying not to look at anyone in particular, I'm so hot I could throw up.

I swallow, swipe my lunch card, and take my premade salad and ice cream sandwich to look for Libby, but it's like a game of Where's Waldo? in the massive dining hall. The one thing I'd thought might be cool about public school was ditching a uniform, but apparently Potomac Point doesn't do fashion. All the girls look the same. Long hair, gray hoodies, gym shorts.

As I make my way past some tables, I see Tomás London sitting alone. He's in my photography class.

A loner—but not goth or emo. He doesn't dress like the other boys—no sweats or khakis or gym shorts. His basic uniform is more hipster—fitted faded black jeans with a striped or printed shirt—although one day he wore red pants and a red-and-white-checked shirt. I didn't laugh out loud, but the rest of that day the Elmo song played in my head, so I've mentally nicknamed him after that Muppet.

He's not handsome, per se, but he's got an interesting, sad look, sort of like a darker-skinned version of that actor Timothée Chalamet. Rich brown hair with auburn highlights and greenish-hazel eyes that tip downward at the outside edges.

He glances up and catches me staring at him. We haven't said much to each other all week, but he nods toward an empty seat at his table. I almost glance around to see if he means me, but don't. After a second, I join him rather than spend the next fifteen minutes searching for Libby.

When I sit across from him, he turns his phone upside down and sports a friendly expression. The silver cross hanging around his neck glints. "Hey, new girl."

"Hey, Elmo." I cock a brow.

He tips his head. "Why 'Elmo'?"

"The red duds." I squeeze low-fat balsamic dressing from the little pouch. "Never seen an outfit that loud in real life."

He rests his chin on his fist, smirking. "Probably because whatever prep school you blew in from made you all wear uniforms."

Points to Elmo.

"Fair enough." I can't help smiling a little, despite my promise to hate every bit of this school so that my mom lets me go back to Prep next semester.

"Where are you from?" He drags a french fry through a mountain of ketchup and shoves it in his mouth. He's got a cool voice . . . sleepy. He seems so relaxed and wise, like he's been through this all before and nothing will surprise him. I decide he must have older siblings, and then I'm jealous.

"Arlington, Virginia."

"I hear it's nice up there." He repeats the same methodical drag with another fry. "You miss it?"

I'm way too raw to talk about this with a stranger, so I shrug and frown before taking a bite of my salad.

"So why's a genius taking photography?" He slurps soda through his straw.

"Genius?"

He pulls a face. "You're one of the mega-AP kids. And before you get all cringey, I'm not a psycho. Everyone here talks about the new kids."

I sink a little lower in my chair, tugging at the ends of my hair. "Don't you have something better to do?"

"Nope. That's the point." He smiles—more to himself than at me—and begins to draw circles in the remaining ketchup with his last fry.

"Great." Now I *know* I was right about not wanting to move here. For once, I've zero joy about proving my mom wrong.

He chomps that last fry. "You never answered my question."

"Why is it so weird that I can be a good student and like photography?"

"'Cause most kids in your shoes are eyeing the Ivies, not blowing credits on arts electives."

"Yeah, well . . . I'm not most kids." I stab my salad extra hard. Most kids don't have a furnace for a stomach and a hammer in their head.

"Just a rebel, then?" He raises a brow, half mocking, half teasing in a friendly way.

I smile again, despite myself. "Rebel" sounds better than "psychoneurotic" and the other terms in those books my mom keeps in her nightstand. "Something like that."

Maybe I should do a gap year—take art classes in Italy or something. My dad would hate that.

"Well, Jane Dean, you'll probably like the pit."

I frown. "Jane Dean?"

"*Rebel Without a Cause* . . . imaginary girl version." He raises his brows like I should've gotten that ancient reference.

I narrow my gaze. "You'll never top Elmo."

"We'll see." Tomás pushes his tray away and leans back, arms crossed.

His confidence makes me self-conscious. I unwrap my ice cream sandwich, break it in half, and offer him some. "What's 'the pit'?"

He takes the ice cream as he points through the large picture windows to a wooded area on the other side of the bus lot. "Some kids go there during lunch and frees to vape or drink or whatever."

My brows rise. Good to know.

Tomás is studying me while enjoying the ice cream.

"Can you show me?" I'm not sure I want to hang there, but I'm not sure I don't.

"Sure, Jane." He puts his phone in his pocket. "It's not really my thing, but if you're curious."

"It's Katy, by the way." I follow him, tossing my trash in the large green can on my way out the door. Tomás is wearing a thin oat-colored cotton shirt with a large outline of a skull on it, dark skinny jeans, and blue Converse sneakers.

I glance over my shoulder to see if anyone is watching us but see only our reflection in the windows. It would suck if people think Tomás and I are hooking up. Then three kids emerge from the woods on their way back to the school and I figure no one will think much at all about us heading there. We walk along a trampled path created by foot traffic for about twenty or thirty feet to a circle of fallen logs that resemble benches laid around a nonexistent campfire.

Tomás drops his backpack on the dirt and sits on a log, arms wide. "Here it is, in all its glory."

I sit and unzip a pocket of my backpack to get my dab pen, press the button, and inhale, then offer it to Tomás.

He shakes his head. "Like I said, not my thing."

I exhale a cloud of smoke. "Why not?"

"Don't need it." Tomás flicks his wrists. "I'm high on life."

He chuckles at his intentional cheesiness, but I can tell he means it, too.

"Never met a unicorn before," I mumble.

"We hide our horns most of the time." He looks up at the canopy of leaves rustling in the wind, pinpoints of light breaking through to stipple the ground. "Why do you use that stuff when you're smart and possibly talented?"

I scowl. "A unicorn *and* a mom?"

He shrugs. "I just don't get it, is all. Like, do what you want. I don't really care. It just seems like a waste when you've got money and other options."

"How do *you* know I've got money and options?" Jeez, talk about snap judgments.

"You've got your own car, don't you? You're smart . . ."

I scowl. "People are obsessed with my car."

"I told you, gossip spreads faster than that vape smoke." He crosses his ankles.

"Well, if you must know, this takes the edge off." I raise the pen.

He nods. "Pressure from the 'rents?"

That, and other things, like how sometimes I want to disappear. To escape being the freaky smart girl that everyone secretly hopes to see fail. To not have to worry about whether I can live up to my potential. To become someone else for a while. When I'm buzzed, I don't think about how often I don't like myself and am scared that people will figure out that I don't know what I'm doing. But I don't want to tell Elmo all that, so I press the button and take another hit.

"Well, we should get back before next period starts." He's reaching for his backpack and I'm exhaling another puff of smoke when a middle-aged man with a receding hairline comes upon us suddenly.

A school faculty badge hangs from the end of his lanyard. "Okay, you two, let's go see Principal Davies."

I cough, covering my shock, and throw a look at Tomás. He just sighs. I'm waiting for him to blame me, but he doesn't.

"Sure thing, Mr. Frey." He hefts his backpack over one shoulder.

"I thought we were allowed off campus during lunch and frees," I say, shoving my pen into my backpack, hoping Mr. Frey didn't see it.

"You are, but this here is technically school property, and we have rules against vaping and drug use." Mr. Frey gestures for us to follow him as he strides ahead by a few yards.

Damn. My mom might use this bust as an excuse to keep me from visiting my dad this weekend. I murmur to Tomás, "I thought you said this spot was cool."

"And I told you I don't come here. I didn't know it's monitored," he mumbles back. "Someone probably saw the 'new girl' heading over and decided to have some fun."

My face is hot. Someone in that cafeteria is laughing at me, but I refuse to cry. I raise my chin as we enter the building and head to the main office. Badass girls don't stay targets for long.

My stomach hurts, though, because this could get me kicked off the soccer team. And my dad will be furious and embarrassed.

"We'll have to administer drug tests." Mr. Frey turns toward the principal's office, but I stop him.

"Tomás didn't vape. It was only me. He shouldn't be in trouble or have to take a test." I'm a lot of mixed-up things, but I'm not a jerk.

Tomás quirks one brow.

"Is that true?" Mr. Frey asks us both.

"Why would I lie?" I frown.

Tomás says, "I'll take the drug test."

Mr. Frey pauses, but Tomás's willingness to take the test combined with my plea spares Tomás the humiliation and trouble with his parents.

"Go to class, Tomás." Mr. Frey waves him off and then points to a chair in the reception area where I'm to wait. Mr. Frey and Principal Davies will now forever look at me as a loser. Maybe I am a loser hidden behind a pretty face and good grades. Most days it feels that way, anyhow.

It sucks to be stuck in this chair, surrounded by glass walls that every student passing by can see through. I stop wiggling my foot and slump deep into the seat, close my eyes, and let my head fall back. The pot isn't helping to soothe the inferno raging inside. I dig a thumbnail into my arm so hard it'll leave a bruise.

That pain oddly calms me, and I begin to relax.

I need to figure out how to deal with my mom. I could drive up to Jen's. Her mom is cool and might help dial mine down a few notches. But if I embarrass my mom even more, she might not help keep me from getting kicked off the team. And I definitely need her to be the one to tell Dad about this. He's going to explode.

Maybe we don't need to tell him.

Or *maybe*, if he thinks I'm falling apart, he'll come home to save me from myself.

CHAPTER SEVEN

ANNE

"I knew your move was a mistake, Anne, but even *I* didn't think things would run off the rails this quickly." Richard's sigh fills my car as Katy and I drive home from our meeting with Principal Davies. Already glum, I don't need his "told you sos." I'm nauseated by her drug use. If our move is the precipitating factor, it makes this my fault—at least indirectly. "A fucking drug test?"

"Swearing doesn't help. Let's discuss solutions." I glance at our daughter, who is squeezed into the corner of the passenger seat with her temple pressed to the window, eyes unblinking, gaze focused elsewhere. My lungs hurt from holding in my alarm. "She's been suspended three days. School policy."

"It's barely the second week of school," he intones. I imagine him swiping a hand over his face. "This is not the kind of record I expect you to set, Katy."

My stomach tightens when he employs shame. Co-parenting has always been a challenge, with me constantly compensating for his demands with acceptance and praise. Our divorce makes it even harder. "Sarcasm isn't helpful, either."

"What's the deal with soccer?" His sharp voice cuts through the car like a knife blindly jabbing into space.

"According to the handbook, it can range from a suspension to being kicked off the team. Coach's discretion. The surrounding circumstances and the kid's attitude will be factors. When I Uber back to get Katy's car, I'll go to the field. He should be there at the practice."

"Maybe *I* should talk to him." Richard has wielded his chest-pounding effectively throughout his career.

I go cold at the thought. "I'd rather you let me appeal to the coach's empathy."

We endure a block-long silence. My guess is that he's at his desk, squeezing the hell out of a stress ball while mouthing additional curse words at me. I've got choice words for him, too, but I gulp them down.

"Katy," he finally says, "who's this Tomás person you've gotten hooked up with?"

"Don't blame him, Dad. He's just a kid in my photography class." Katy stares at the dashboard, her face a pale, stiff mask.

"Photography . . . another mistake." Richard huffs.

Katy clenches her jaw.

"Sorry you hate everything I do," she snaps before turning her face away from me. Not only doesn't her bravado fool me, but it also makes my heart sore and unsteady.

"Don't be dramatic. I'm your father. I'm allowed to have opinions about your education and hate the fact that you're on drugs. How long have you been smoking pot?" Richard's incredulous tone would be funny if this weren't so serious.

He's never attended a single parent meeting or public health discussion about teen life—mostly because his work hours conflicted with the lectures, but also because he thought Katy was somehow immune to it all. He's pooh-poohed most of my concerns over the years, too—*you're making mountains out of molehills*—so he knows little about the high rates of experimentation with alcohol and pot, especially among affluent, overstressed kids.

The strain of this conversation tautens my muscles.

"Since this summer, but only when I'm stressed." At the moment, the pot she smoked is keeping her pretty mellow in the face of her father's outrage. She's not arguing or crying, which is markedly different from how she deals with me. I can't tell if she respects him more than she does me, or simply fears losing him if she crosses a line. My breath catches when I recognize having felt that way about him in recent years.

"Jesus, how did we get here?" Richard asks of no one in particular.

The timing of her foray into drugs says a lot, but I clamp my jaw shut. Now he's probably turned toward the gigantic plate glass window behind his desk, staring out over the city, one hand grabbing his temple. Lauren's name dances on the tip of my tongue, but I won't put Katy in the middle of that fight if I can help it.

"Instead of looking backward, let's figure out a consequence and talk about how to stop this from happening again." I shoot a meaningful look at Katy, who then glances heavenward.

"Maybe you shouldn't ask the coach to go easy," Richard says. "Getting kicked off the team will teach her how fast drugs destroy lives."

He's right, but of all the fallout from this event, she's most upset about the possibility of losing her place on the team. If Richard and I had worked harder on our marriage, this might not have happened. Dammit, my skin is itchy all over, and guilt about the move makes me want to fix this for her. "*If* we were all under one roof and she was still at Prep, I'd agree. But in this case, I think the team is critical to her making friends and keeping active."

Taking that dig at Richard might not be productive, but better I unleash my tension on him than on Katy.

I half expect Katy to suggest a consequence she finds palatable—a technique she often uses to control the fallout. She's uncharacteristically quiet.

Richard clears his throat. "Then maybe the consequence is that she doesn't come up here this weekend. Frankly, I'm too angry to have a pleasant visit, anyway."

If I weren't driving, I would've closed my eyes in utter disappointment. Katy's mask of indifference slips long enough to reveal her flash of pain. I roll down the window, desperate for fresh air.

"Richard, you two need to stay connected now that you're living apart." Distancing himself will only make things worse for Katy, not better.

He sighs. "Let me talk to Lauren. She'll be concerned about Katy's influence on Zoe and Brody."

I almost slam the brakes.

"You did *not* just say that." I swallow a string of curse words. Since when do Zoe's and Brody's welfares rank above Katy's? "Lauren had better not take that position unless you want me to start harping about *her* influence on Katy."

"What's that supposed to mean?" Richard grinds out. If he were here, I might've thrown something at his head.

"That home-wrecker isn't in a position to judge *anyone*." My pulse is throbbing and my fingers ache as they tighten around the steering wheel. "Katy's a confused teen who made a mistake. Nothing more."

In my peripheral vision, I note Katy's brows rise in a show of surprise. For most of her life, we've shielded her from our arguments. I'm not sorry about that, but I'm also not sorry for this. When someone threatens my kid, I come a little unglued.

"Anne," Richard warns.

"Don't 'Anne' me. I've been as civil as can be expected about everything, but if Lauren tries to come between you and your daughter, she'll be very sorry." I need a lozenge to soothe my raw throat.

"Settle down. Things are bad enough without empty threats."

Empty? He really doesn't know me at all if he thinks I'd let anyone displace my child. "Don't tell me to settle down. We're all in this situation because of *you*, so be a man and take some effing responsibility."

Richard falls unexpectedly silent, and Katy is staring at me like my curly hair suddenly straightened. I roll my head to loosen my neck, but it feels damn good to get that off my chest. Unexpected momentum rises beneath me, as if I'm riding a cresting wave.

"I'm pulling into the garage. My thinking is that we institute random drug testing, and if we get positive results, Katy loses her phone and car indefinitely."

Katy's face currently resembles that of someone witnessing a murder. "Mom!"

I hold up a single finger. "You're getting off pretty easy, so you should zip it." Katy holds my gaze for two seconds before looking at her lap. I turn to the dashboard screen in my car, which still shows Richard's name and number. "Richard, any thoughts?"

"If she tests positive, I'm *selling* the car."

Katy makes a bitter face but wisely says nothing. His threat—while actually a punishment for me, too, as I'd be stuck playing chauffeur—is even better than mine, so I don't argue.

"Fine. In the meantime, Katy will see you on Saturday as planned. What time will you be at home?"

"I have to check my calendar. Zoe has a soccer game . . ."

Richard has attended so few of Katy's games I want to shout a truckload of obscenities, but that would only call attention to something that would further upset our daughter. Of course, her scowl tells me she's sharing my thoughts anyway.

"Let us know soon. Goodbye." I hit "End" before he says more. "You and I aren't done with this conversation."

Katy opens the car door and groans. "Why not? I heard the rules."

I follow her into the house through the door to the kitchen, where we come across Dan and Joe, one of his crewmen.

75

Dan looks at us with surprise. "Is Katy sick?"

"You could say that." I don't like to lie, but also don't want to humiliate my daughter in front of strangers. "Let me get her settled in her room. Excuse us."

"Feel better," he says to Katy.

"Thanks," she mumbles as I steer her out of the kitchen.

Dan already thinks I'm difficult. When word of this gets out, he'll also think I'm a lousy mother. This is not at all how I foresaw our entry into this new community—the picky single mom and her pothead daughter. I wish he and Joe would leave so I could have some privacy while I try to solve this problem.

When we get to Katy's room, she flings her backpack onto her desk and then face-plants onto her bed.

I sit on the edge of the mattress, staring at the back of her head as guilt erodes the lining of my stomach. "I'll ask your coach to go easy—which isn't the best parenting move—but only because the team will help you make new friends and stay healthy, not because of your transcript."

She cranes her neck to look at me, her expression riddled with mockery. "Duh. If you cared about my future, you wouldn't have pulled me out of Prep."

"Katy." I blow out a long breath. Yes, that school's admissions placements are stellar, but a student like her should be able to get into fine schools from anywhere. "Tell me why you've turned to drugs when there're one thousand better ways to deal with unhappiness or boredom."

She rolls onto her back and scoots to sit up against the headboard, grabbing her childhood lovey—a stuffed mouse she named Timmy. "Pot isn't a big deal. Everyone gets high—even some parents. The Hendricks and Capristos do all the time. It's legal in a bunch of states and probably will be here, too, someday, so it's no worse than beer."

I hide my shock about her friends' parents. If she thinks I'm that out of touch, she won't trust my advice. It occurs to me that during pregnancy, parents should be required to take crash courses as teachers, doctors, and shrinks. Chef and chauffeur classes would also help.

"Is that how you really feel?" Because I'm pretty sure pot is just an easy way to avoid dealing with what's really bothering her.

She stares at her feet without answering.

She's only just started this habit. Still, the other things that can happen when teens drink and do drugs—accidents, sexual assaults, arrests—thread through my thoughts. The list of possibilities is as frightening as it is endless.

"This started after your dad moved out." I close my eyes against the memory of her tears on that day. "Did you think getting high would change the facts?"

Again she says nothing.

"Oh, Katy." I sigh, helplessly. "Pot is legal in a few states, but it isn't legal for recreational use here in Maryland. Neither is alcohol for people under twenty-one. You're only sixteen. Your brain is still forming and doesn't have all the myelin coating to fend off some of the damage and addictive qualities. Plus they're finding links between teen pot use and later psychosis. The chances of you having a drinking or drug problem is much higher when you start so young than if you put it off until even nineteen or twenty." This is what years of volunteering for everything related to children teaches you. My eyes sting, aware that my plea falls on deaf ears. "Please, Katy. Don't waste all your potential."

She throws her head back on that word, then pulls her knees to her chest and rests her chin on them. "Do you think Lauren will try to keep me away from Dad?"

"I hope not." Having made a vow not to lie to my daughter, I can't, in good conscience, say no. "But if she does, I'll fight her."

"How? She's with him every day and we're not. He's going to Zoe's soccer game even though he rarely came to mine." Her eyes tear up.

I rub her knee, resentment toward Richard flaming like a blowtorch. Fanning that anger won't help Katy, so I swallow it. Some days I can't believe my stomach hasn't exploded from all the shit I've shoved in there. "I know that hurts. But he was younger and building his practice when you were little."

She scowls as if I've criticized her. "There you go again defending him."

"I'm not defending him. I'm reassuring *you* that he isn't more interested in Zoe's game than he was in yours. It's not his nature to bend for long. In another year he'll be no different than he was with us. But he loves you more than he'll ever like Lauren's children. It'll take time for us all to figure out a new dynamic, but we will. I promise."

"You never make promises you can't keep, so don't start now." She's still pouting, but I'm heartened that at least she trusts me to be good for my word. That's something, and I need a win—no matter how small—on a day like today. Her stomach growls. "I'm starving."

I bet she is.

"We'll get a pizza on our way back from getting your car. But listen, just because I'm not screaming doesn't mean I'm not upset."

"I know." She slides down a bit in the bed and starts twisting and tugging at her hair.

I touch a bruise on the inside of her forearm. "What happened here?"

"Nothing." She yanks her arm away, which makes me suspicious, especially when she changes the subject. "Take my phone. What's the difference anyway? It's not like I've got friends texting to hang out."

I reach for her arm again, worried about what other signs I might've missed. "Katy, let me see your arm."

When she relents, I pull it close to inspect for needle marks. Thankfully there aren't any, so I release her.

She tucks her arm at her side without further explanation, so I let it go.

If only I could close my eyes and wake up tomorrow to have everything be okay. Instead, I dangle like a spider in the breeze, evaluating the costs of my lousy options. Is it too much to ask for a fairy godmother, crystal ball, or magic wand for newly single mothers? I need a break so I can begin to work out my own problems—like what to do with the next fifty years of my life.

"Can we order the pizza?" Katy asks.

"Sure. Hand me your phone and your car keys."

She pulls the phone from her pocket and puts it in my hand. "Keys are in the outside zipper of my backpack."

After getting them, I have a change of heart. "Let's go. I'll order an Uber."

"Why do I have to come?" She looks so young with Timmy at her side—a reminder that she's immature and inexperienced, despite her grown-up face.

"You can talk to your coach when we pick up your car."

"No, Mom. Please!" She's vigorously shaking her head. "That's humiliating."

"You have to apologize and show remorse." I cross my arms to steel myself against her will. "Come on, I'll go with you."

Katy kicks the bed like a child. "Mom!"

"I'll meet you downstairs." I flee to avoid being worn down, trotting down the stairs while ordering an Uber.

"Anne?" Dan calls from the kitchen.

"Yes." I close my eyes, bracing for more bad news.

"Can you pop in here and triple-check this open shelving . . . the height, I mean?"

The shelves will be on a short wall and hold some cookbooks and bric-a-brac. I paste a smile on my face and round the bend. "Perfect."

Dan's brows show his surprise, then he gives me a double take. "Everything okay?"

Part of me wants to unload all of it so I feel less alone in this turmoil. But Dan isn't my friend, although I could use one. Another necessary change—making friends who aren't merely Katy's friends' mothers or Richard's partners' wives.

"Just a lot on my mind." To change the subject, I shift my gaze to the two base cabinets he's installed. "Those look gorgeous, don't they?"

For a second or two, I envy that Dan gets to create something every day. He's taken a risk and lives on his own terms. I haven't felt that freedom—or courage—since becoming a young mom. I thought coming back to Potomac Point would shake me loose, but it seems like I'm as overwhelmed and underconfident as my daughter.

"For what they cost, they'd better." He glances at them, nodding. He's often suggested substitute items throughout this project, but I know my budget and I know what I like. Dan says, "You must be eager to have a working kitchen."

"Let's just say it'll be a challenge to lose the weight I'm gaining from eating out so often." I tug at my belt loops.

"You look fine." He then coughs into his hand.

I release my jeans, self-conscious. "Thanks."

After living with Richard's nonstop opinions on everything from politics to my shoes, I can't decide if I like Dan's quietude or find it disconcerting.

"How's your grandmother doing?" Dan's left cheek dimples.

I blink at the abrupt change of subject. "Physically, she's comfortable and safe. Mentally, it's hard to know what's what."

"That must be tough," Dan says.

"It is." Especially now that she's a bit of a stranger to me for reasons that have nothing to do with dementia.

Yesterday I stopped by the school library after the PTA welcome coffee to page through 1940s yearbooks. None had any William T. who looked like the man in the photograph, though. A dead end. Given Katy's latest stunt, perhaps Gram's past shouldn't be my focus.

My phone pings. Richard's text informs me that they'll be home from Zoe's game by noon. My daughter will soon have stepsiblings. She resents them now, but she won't forever. Katy's family will grow while mine shrinks. A bitter pill I've no choice but to swallow. Zoe and Brody are as innocent as Katy in all this, but I begrudge them nonetheless and have no interest in accommodating them or Lauren.

Not for the first time, I face an ugly truth about myself: I have actively wished Lauren ill these past months. That bad karma has come around to kick my butt by making me watch my daughter suffer. Apparently karma knows how to best torment a mother.

"Trouble?" Dan asks, eyeing me closely.

Shoot. Anyone in need of easy winnings should play me in a high-stakes game of poker. "Just my ex trying to coordinate schedules with Katy. It's complicated because of his fiancée and her kids."

"Fiancée?" Dan's eyes are wide, and only then do I remember that he doesn't know about Lauren.

"Yep." At this point, I've got no pride left, so I don't even flush with the heat of humiliation.

"He moved on fast."

Before the divorce, in fact, but that's hardly flattering. I shrug because nothing will make this conversation any better or less awkward. Thankfully, Katy appears, if somewhat reluctantly. Hopefully, Dan thinks I'm taking her to the pediatrician. "Well, we've got to run."

I wave goodbye and usher Katy outside to catch the Uber before Dan asks more questions. Most men don't make me so nervous, possibly because I've been more or less invisible to them since I became a mom at twenty. Dan, however, pays close attention to everything.

Within moments of sitting in silence in the back seat of an overly perfumed Toyota Corolla, the events of the day wash over me. Katy is doing drugs. I can hardly wrap my mind around that. Plenty of my old classmates experimented, but it hadn't interested me. And despite everything I've read about the rise of pot use among teens, I honestly never believed Katy would try it.

Are Richard's and my threats and consequences enough to stop her from vaping again, and are they the best way to handle this problem?

I'm in so deep over my head I need an oxygen tank to breathe. My strength dissolves as my adrenaline ebbs, making me leery of meeting with Coach Diller. Not to make excuses, but my daughter needs help more than she needs punishment.

We get out of the Uber and walk past Katy's car, through the long shadow cast by the enormous brick-and-glass school building, to the fields. Katy's a yard or two in front of me, her shoulders rounded, her eyes fixed on the ground a few feet ahead of each step. The campus—a school that serves three townships—dwarfs her prep school. I don't know any of the other kids, parents, or teachers yet. The unfamiliarity breeds intimidation, and the reminder of what Katy feels coming here each day breaks me a little more.

One of the girls is tying her laces on the sideline. I wave when she looks up at us, but she looks down without a word.

I exhale and turn to my daughter. "Point out Coach Diller."

"The beard," she mumbles, chin tucked, hands shoved in her pockets.

Of the three adults on the field, only one has a beard. "Thank you."

By all rights, he should not bend any rules for my child. I was married to a lawyer and understand the concepts and importance of precedent and justice. Still . . .

With a deep inhalation, I step forward.

Katy grabs my arm. "Wait! Don't barge out there and interrupt practice. Jeez."

Her gaze is glued to the turf, and I can practically see her skin crawling. Hurting and lost and having had no prior experience with handling her own mistakes, she's ill-prepared for something so big and beyond her control.

"Good point." We stand back to wait for the coach to come off the field. Leaning against the chain-link fence takes me back to my high school experience. More geek than jock, I'd never played school sports, so the bond that teammates share eludes me. I'd been relieved when Katy inherited Richard's athleticism, knowing that gift would help her make friends more easily. Of course, Richard encouraged elite travel leagues and year-round training that I then had to manage.

Coach Diller makes his way to the sidelines, at which point he notices us. He sidles over wearing a disgruntled expression.

"Katy." He nods at her, then extends his hand to me. "You must be Mrs. Chase."

That name again. A hot brand to the heart each time. "Please call me Anne."

"I'm guessing you're here to plead Katy's case." He eyes us both.

"Katy's here to plead." I bow slightly before stepping back. My stomach drops when I see my daughter blanch. I'm not sure which is more taxing—watching her suffer or questioning my methods—but Katy needs to take responsibility for her actions. "I'm only here for support."

Katy disentangles her fingers from her hair. "Coach, I'm sorry I vaped. I know you don't owe me any favors, but I swear it won't happen again. Please don't kick me off the team. I really love soccer and promise I'll contribute a lot on the field. This team is the one thing I have to look forward to since the move and divorce and everything . . ." Her voice cracks and she trails off, but he caught enough.

She's gazing at her feet again. Her cheeks are red, her face damp with perspiration. Everyone experiences anxiety, which makes it very hard for me to judge whether, at any given moment, my daughter's involves typical or atypical levels of stress. She tenses when I touch her shoulder in support. I drop my hand, but seeing her squirm makes me ache with the need to offer comfort.

Coach Diller faces me, offering me the chance to add something.

"I'm sorry to meet under these circumstances," I begin. "All I can say is that this is a first, and hopefully a last, for Katy. It's been a tumultuous summer and transition, but now that I'm aware of this, I'll be keeping an eye out."

He crosses his arms with a sigh. "Katy, I'm no dummy. I know what kids are up to, so I won't pretend like you're the only girl on this team who's tried pot. But you got caught, so here's the deal. Come to practice starting tomorrow. You're suspended from playing in games for ten days, but then—assuming you commit—you're back on full tilt. However, if you smoke again, you'll be off the team. Are we clear?"

I could drop to my knees in thanks I'm so relieved. Katy pulls her thumbnail from her teeth and nods. "Yes, Coach. Thank you. I promise, I won't do it again."

"Good. Now I don't mean to be rude, but I need to get back to practice. See you tomorrow." He waves us off.

Katy and I head back to the parking lot together. When I put my arm around her shoulders, she shrugs me off while glancing backward to see if anyone saw us. I understand her impulse, but that doesn't make it hurt less. My role as her mother—the thing I most identify with—is being stripped away from me before I'm quite ready.

But I'm proud of her for facing the music, and of myself for letting her. Maybe this is the reminder I needed to begin letting go of managing her life so I can start to focus on reinventing mine.

"That wasn't so terrible, was it?" We get in her car, and I start the engine.

"For you, maybe."

"Katy, he was very reasonable." Finally, I can breathe. "You did that well, and I hope you meant what you said about the drugs."

Katy turns on the radio to drown out a lecture. "Can we get the pizza now? I'm about to faint."

Her nonanswer doesn't go unnoticed, but I let it go. It's been a rough day, but a good pizza will help. Hopefully, we'll get through the rest of the week without any more surprises.

CHAPTER EIGHT

ANNE

After a restless night of alternating between overanalyzing Katy and giving myself a pep talk about taking personal steps forward, I got dressed early and drove to Art Smarts to purchase a sketch pad and a set of Caran d'Ache Neocolor II crayons.

It sounded like a great idea at first. Something for myself. Excluding simplistic graphic design work for booster clubs and the PTA, I hadn't attempted anything artistic in a decade. Yet art helped me adapt to my new life at eight, so it may also help me now.

Sketching on my back patio on this sunny Thursday morning could be lovely if it weren't for a couple of things. One is that the french doors at my back merely muffle the hammers and saws and drills. Every so often a loud bang or shrill whir makes me jump in my seat. Another problem is that by now Dan's probably gotten wind of Katy's suspension. I don't love the idea of giving him more data to add to his poor opinion of me, but at least he hasn't nosed into our business.

She's lounging on the hammock in a sun hat, reading a short-fiction assignment from her AP Lit class. A passerby might think she's on vacation instead of under suspension. But seeing her finally start to relax a little makes it harder for me to treat this like a punishment. She's staying on top of her school assignments, and I've tasked her with weeding, laundry, and running errands. Hopefully, those extras will make her eager to return to the classroom on Monday.

The last snag is a case of nerves. No one but me need ever see these early efforts, yet my fingers fumble with the crayons. Unlike years ago, I don't get struck with inspiration in the face of the blank page—no sound, or color, or mood propels me. The crayon doesn't take over, and my body doesn't resonate with a developing idea. Rather than give up, I choose to practice by copying the nature around me.

A childishly mundane choice. My first strokes are halting and hesitant. Drawing does not return as naturally as riding a bike, that's for sure.

It takes effort to block out the distractions and focus on fleshing out the images of the sycamore, maple, and fir trees rimming our yard, which seem twice as large as they did two decades ago. I dip an old paintbrush in water and lift some color from a crayon to blend on the page. Voilà, watercolor. The work *is* amateurish, but the brush starts to feel good in my hand, like getting reacquainted with a long-lost friend.

Katy's sigh drifts down the terraced yard to remind me why she's here instead of at school—drugs. Doubts flare. Perhaps now *isn't* the time to indulge my own passions. In the grand scheme of things, what's another two-year delay—just until she goes to college? Of course, even then I'll be hard-pressed to stop worrying.

I press a hand to my chest at the thought of her leaving. She needs to spread her wings, but that requires me to let go of the most precious thing in my life.

Sometimes it seems as if my whole life is a test on enduring loss.

I glance at the weak work in front of me and tear the sheet from the book, crushing it in a flushed pique of embarrassment. While I'm wading in the shallow end of self-pity, my phone buzzes. Richard's name on my screen forces a scowl. He'd better not be canceling Katy's visit on

Saturday. She's currently engrossed in her book, so I close my eyes and brace for an unpleasant conversation. "Hello, Richard."

"Anne, it's Lauren."

I blink my eyes open. Her voice—sharp yet feminine, like a young Sharon Stone—is familiar despite my having heard it only twice before. Once by accident when she answered Richard's cell, and once the week before I moved, when I ran into her and Richard at Bagel Barn on a Sunday morning. That had been particularly awful—me in sweats and a T-shirt running out in the middle of packing moving boxes, them freshly showered and dressed, laughing together. Lauren can't see me now, but my palms are sweating. "Did something happen to Richard?"

The pang wrought by that concern makes me glower because I do *not* want to care about him any longer.

"Richard's fine. At least physically fine." Lauren sighs like some 1940s stage actress, as if whatever emotional crisis he's having is somehow everybody's problem. "Honestly, he's struggling with being stuck in the middle, so I think you and I need to talk, mother to mother."

My veins become lit fuses.

I slowly rise from my chair to make my way inside so Katy cannot hear any part of what is certain to be an explosive conversation. Inside the house, the hammers and drills will drown out every other word, but that's okay because Lauren and Richard's relationship strife isn't my problem. This woman's got gall to expect me to help ease things between her and Richard. "Does Richard know you've called me?"

Without answering my question, she says, "He told me about Katy's trouble at school."

I'm silent because her judgmental, pitying tone has me in a choke hold.

"Anne?"

I clear my throat. "Yes?"

"Oh, I thought you hung up."

"No, but I might." The painting over the mantel reminds me of the joy I felt painting it—of the sense of mastery of oils and my own style, so unlike the woman on the patio who just crumpled her work. Where did *that* woman go? "What do you want, Lauren?"

"Something neither you nor Richard can give me, I'm afraid. I know Katy wants to see her dad, but how can I be certain that she won't bring drugs into our house?"

Kaboom!

Throwing my phone against the wall will cost me money, so I refrain. "Interesting dilemma, because I'm pretty sure Katy wants something you can't give her, either."

"What's that?"

"Her father back under the same roof."

Lauren lets loose another dramatic sigh. I can hardly believe she's the kind of woman Richard prefers. "Okay, Anne. I thought we could be adults about this, but clearly I was wrong."

Her tendency for condescension must be how she and Richard first bonded. "Understand me, Lauren. My daughter is not a drug addict. She's a National Honor Society member, an athlete, an artist, and an all-around wonderful girl whose world has been thrown into chaos thanks, in large part, to *you*. She will not be bringing drugs to your house, so don't start with that nonsense. Richard is *her* father, not Brody's and Zoe's. If you don't trust Katy, then take your kids and go visit your parents or whomever you like while Katy is with Richard. Frankly, I'd prefer that because then she wouldn't have to spend time with *you*. But don't call me under some pretext just to make judgments about my child."

"If you plan on laying the blame for Katy's choices on me, it's no wonder she can't accept reality."

My entire body strings as tight as a cocked bow. "Back way up. Katy is taking full responsibility for her choice. But if you can't acknowledge how your stealing my husband has shaken her sense of security, then

I feel sorry for *your* kids and what they're learning from someone as entitled as *you*."

"Don't you think it's time we all move on from the whys of your divorce? Richard wasn't happy. That's not *my* fault."

Her words are like scissors to my heart. I vividly imagine her head on a spit. The violent urge actually scares me. "My divorce isn't even final, yet you're already meddling in Katy's relationship with her father. So, no, I won't simply 'move on' to appease you." Mentally, I add the C-word to the end of that sentence. "I'm pretty sure Richard wouldn't be *torn* if you weren't putting those thoughts in his head. At least he's not rolling over on this for you. Get used to that, Lauren. You may have stolen him from me, but you will never replace Katy. And if you try, you'll eventually lose Richard."

"Mom?" Katy must've slipped inside while I was on my tirade. My throat is sore, which tells me I've been screaming, too.

Great. Dan and Joe are probably ducking for cover. Maybe now that they've heard my temper, they'll work faster to be done with me. That'd be one upside of all this, anyhow.

"Are we done?" I ask Lauren.

"It seems so."

"Thank God. Lose my number." I hang up and chuck the phone onto the sofa. "Dammit."

"Was that Lauren?"

I hang my head. Another outburst to pick over when I'm alone. "Ignore her."

"She doesn't want me to come, does she?" Katy's eyes are misty.

"It doesn't matter what she wants, honey." I embrace my daughter, and to my shock, she lets me. It would be wonderful if her acquiescence wasn't the result of how upset she is. "Sweetie, I'm sorry you overheard that, but don't follow my example. Treat Lauren with respect so she doesn't have any leverage to use against you. Do you understand?"

Katy nods and sniffles into my shoulder. "I really messed up. Dad probably hates me now."

"I promise he doesn't hate you, honey." The memory of Richard teaching Katy to ride a bike—of the thrill in his young face—is another reminder of all we've lost. I ease away and move some of the hair off her forehead. "Be honest with him. Open up about your feelings."

She grunts. "Dad doesn't do feelings. He only cares about results."

"Then share the wins. You've gotten two As on your first real assignments, and you made the varsity team in a competitive district." I hug her again. "But also remember we all make mistakes. Don't let anyone make you see yourself as the sum of your worst behavior instead of your best."

When we break apart, she tugs on her hair again. The last time I suggested therapy, she got angry and Richard made me feel like a failure for needing outside help. Is it time to push back, or will that only make everything worse?

Her chin is at her chest when she mumbles, "I'm going to lie down for a while."

"How about we grab lunch?"

"I'm not hungry." She takes her book and clomps up the stairs.

Once she's out of sight, my shoulders droop, sinking me onto the sofa. I used to cry easily. It'd been cathartic. Restorative, even. But lately my emotions simply churn like they're stuck in a dryer that can't finish the job.

I could use a hug right now. Maybe I'll visit Gram. She might not remember me, but it could help just to see her. After a quick text to let Katy know that I'm leaving, I grab my keys and take off.

CHAPTER NINE

MARIE

"Hey, Gram. I brought pudding!" a pretty young woman says when she enters my room. "I would've made the stove-top kind if my kitchen remodel were finished, but this will have to do for now."

She cracks a cup off the pack and hands it to me with a plastic spoon from her coat pocket. The way she's smiling at me tells me I know her, but I don't know why she's calling me Graham. "Thank you."

"Let me help." She takes the cup back and peels off the lid before giving it back to me. Then she sits down in the empty chair and opens herself a pudding cup, too. "Almost like the old days."

I nod, although I'm confused. Do I like pudding? I test out a creamy spoonful. Chocolate. Pretty good.

The woman has already gobbled hers up. She heaves a sigh when she sets down the empty cup. "It's not nearly as good as when we'd eat right from the pot. I miss those days." Then she laughs to herself. "Maybe I've been kidding myself this whole time, thinking that returning here would be a magic fix for Katy and me. When Richard first asked for the divorce, I couldn't believe it. You remember how sweet he was in the beginning? All the plans we made? I still miss how he used to love to cook—his second-favorite study break activity during law school."

She winks at me in case I missed the innuendo, but I'm still trying to place her and this Richard. It's vaguely familiar but just out of reach, so I nod and continue to listen.

"I remember thinking that he reminded me of Grandpa back then—full of happy energy and affection. When he started working, he'd share everything about his day—what he was learning, the people he worked with. He'd thank me for being supportive and giving him a nice place to come home to. Always telling me how much he liked me and my kind heart. He hasn't said that in a few years, though."

Her expression loses all animation when she pauses. "When I first started to complain—about the fact that he no longer could sit through an entire movie without jumping up to take a call, or that he'd stopped holding my hand or putting his arm around me on the sofa, or how he left me to raise Katy except to second-guess me after the fact—I felt guilty because you and my mom were always such satisfied housewives. I mean, honestly, I never heard you complain to Grandpa. Not once."

She looks at me as if seeking confirmation. Is she talking about my husband, Martin? I got lucky with that one—loyal and patient. Compassionate. Easy to please. "Martin is very kind."

"The kindest." Her eyes light up for the first time, then her forehead crinkles. "I miss him, but I'm almost glad he isn't here to see all my failures."

Where is Martin? I need to tell him that even on melancholy days when regrets overwhelm me, I never regret marrying him.

The woman sighs again. "I really thought moving here would make it easier for me to move on, but it's only made things worse for Katy, and I'm still picking through my marriage, trying to figure out where I went wrong. The truth is, despite Richard's and my problems, I thought our foundation was solid. That our love lay beneath the frozen surface, waiting to bud again. Even when Richard was in New York for that deal after he announced his decision, I thought he'd realize what he'd be giving up—his *family*—and come home to work on our marriage. I mean, we were each other's first real loves . . . How do you really lose that?"

First love.

My sweet, dear Billy.

"Gram?" The young woman touches my knee, and Billy is gone all over again. "Did you hear me?"

"I'm sorry." My head is fuzzy. I can't help this woman, although I wish I could.

"It's okay. I didn't mean to dump all my problems on your lap. I just needed to talk to someone, and you're always a good listener."

I nod and force a smile.

"I have an idea." She stands, shaking off the past five minutes like a dog does water. "It's a gorgeous early-autumn day. Let's go outside and watch the boats on the bay."

"That sounds nice." With a slight hesitation, I take her hand. It's been a while since I've even been outside.

She links arms and pats my hand, calling my attention to my translucent, spotty skin. When did that happen? She steers me down the hall to the back door, which leads directly to a concrete patio with benches and tables. I shuffle along. When she opens the door, I raise my face to drink in the burst of sunlight and inhale the briny air.

We sit at a picnic table partially shaded by a giant sycamore tree canopy. The gulls soaring low across the sky draw my eye, as does the sunlight dancing atop the undulating water, sparkling clear to the horizon.

I close my eyes and shiver, thinking of the old wooden pier that stretches into the bay from the end of my street. People fish off it and launch small boats there in the summer, but during the winter it's eerily quiet except for the creak of the boards and the gentle lapping of water against its pylons. It's where Billy and I used to steal time together, early in.

I remember one morning I'd sneaked away to meet him at dawn, just a couple of months after we met . . . It's so clear I can relive our first kiss. That day the water vapor scattered the December light, making it look like steam was rising from the water. If you ignored the science and admired the effect, the bay had looked mystical.

With each step, breath clouds blurred my vision. The Polaroid Land camera my father had bought felt heavier than its few pounds, possibly because I'd taken it without asking. If he caught me, he would be angry, but not as furious as he would be if he found me with Billy.

I walked the length of the pier, its boards sagging beneath my weight. When I finally reached the end, rising mist surrounded me.

The big water views roused me. While staring at the horizon, I could pretend to be far away from Potomac Point—maybe even at the edge of the Pacific Ocean. Mother Nature was waking up. The foggy daybreak resembled an Ansel Adams photograph. How would he have captured the bay, or the geese gliding along its surface? Setting the camera aside, I crouched all the way down to lie on my stomach. I extended my hands and fingers forward as if framing a shot.

Water lapped below me. A bird broke the silence with its song. I synced my breath with the rise and fall of the small waves splashing onto the shore behind me. In my daydream I was a renowned photographer, hiking into unfamiliar territories to capture images to share with people who clamored for more.

A creak nearby snapped me from my musings.

"You didn't fall, did you?" Billy teased as he approached.

"No." I rose, brushing off bits of dirt and splinters from my coat.

When he reached me, he kissed my cheek and clasped my hands. "It's chilly."

An invitation if I'd ever heard one. I wrapped my arms around him, burying my face and cold nose against his chest. "I like it brisk, and we have at least thirty minutes before I have to sneak back." My parents slept until seven thirty on Saturdays.

"I don't like slinking around, Marie." He eased away. "We should talk to your dad again."

"We need to wait for the right time." This conversation made my stomach hurt. Putting him off insulted Billy, but I was stuck. Until I graduated from high school, I didn't have many options. "My dad can't see past your job. He doesn't care that you're a good person."

A great person, truthfully. The kind who'd moved here to help his sister, Angie, care for her toddler, Ben, after a car accident killed her husband. Their Catholic parents had disowned her when she converted to Judaism for her husband. She'd been foundering, trying to figure out how to raise a child on her own, until Billy came to her rescue. He was a true prince, but my father didn't care about any of that.

Billy shoved his hands in the pockets of his unzipped bomber jacket, which hung over his loose-fitting filling station attendant uniform. His manliness sent a little flutter to my chest. "I don't know, Marie. Angie still cries about how my parents won't forgive her even though they're missing out on knowing their grandson. If you keep up this way, you could end up like her, and I don't want that."

I shrugged in silence, worried about that exact thing. I liked Billy a lot—more than I'd ever liked any boy ever—but I wasn't ready to lose my family over him. "We don't have much time. Let's not waste it talking about my parents."

He dropped his chin with a sigh. "Okay. Tell me why you brought me here."

I bent to lift the camera. While I unfastened the leather case and exposed the camera lens, I asked, "Have you ever seen one of these?"

"Only in advertisements." He inspected it closely, raising it above his head, turning it about. "Does it really develop a picture inside this box?"

"Yes." I nodded. "Want to see?"

"Sure." He handed it back to me.

The light was still flat, so it probably wouldn't produce a crisp image. "Stand there at the end of the dock."

He held up a hand. "Won't my picture be a dead giveaway?"

"I'll hide it, but I'll take a picture of the scenery that I can show my dad if he catches me sneaking back into the house." Cunning was not a virtue my friends aspired to, but I couldn't deny my nature or make myself ashamed of it.

Billy's brows rose as he chuckled. "You're too clever for your own good, but it's one of my favorite things about you."

"Oh?" I did like compliments. "What are your other favorite things?"

Billy stepped closer and touched the ends of my hair, making me shiver. "These strawberry curls. Your boldness. The fact that you don't want to be like everyone else. I know, whatever happens, you'll make something special of your life. That's good, Marie. I hope I get to see it."

He was so close I wished he would just kiss me. This was the eighth time we'd secretly met up, and he'd been too much of a gentleman. "Maybe you will—we could travel around, you fixing cars, me taking pictures."

"We'd need money first, and your dad's approval." He dropped his hands and stepped back.

I suppressed a pout. "Let's not worry about that today. Let me take your picture. Stand right there. Be still, or it will be blurry."

"Like this?" His hands dangled at his sides, relaxed, and he tipped his head just left of center. A gentle smile softened his swarthy looks.

"Perfect." I widened my stance to steady myself and snapped the image.

"Now what?" He came closer.

"When we turn this knob, it pushes the paper through tiny rollers that use chemicals to transfer the image from the negative to the paper. We peel apart the two pages, and voilà, there you are!" I gave it a wave to dry it before I showed him. His wide-eyed amazement gave me a little thrill, but mostly I was ecstatic to finally have a picture of him that I could look at whenever I wanted.

"Wow! That's unbelievable." His broad smile set my heart ablaze.

Billy would never be able to afford that camera. That made me sad, because he worked as hard as my dad. Some might say harder, because he worked two jobs. "Would you like to try?"

"Sure thing." He nodded.

"Don't photograph me. Pick something else . . . like that copse of trees over there, or maybe the geese on the bay."

He lay on his stomach exactly the way he'd found me. "How's this?"

I was smiling so hard it hurt to talk. "Good!"

He aimed at the gaggle of geese and snapped the image, then carefully handed me the camera, almost as if he'd been afraid he'd accidentally break it. The camera probably did cost more than he made in a month, but I pushed that reality aside.

We were shoulder to shoulder when I turned the knob and peeled apart the paper.

His expression was nothing short of awe. "You know I'll never be able to give you nice things like this. That's why your dad thinks you can do better, and maybe he's right."

I wasn't naive. Money was important, but I could help take care of myself. "I've been given a lot of nice gifts in my life, but you give me something no one—not even my own father—does."

"What's that?" We were almost nose to nose.

"Hope. You make me believe in my dreams without making me feel peculiar for not wanting what everyone else thinks I *should* want."

"I like your spunk." He held my hand again. "I like you."

"I like you, too. A lot."

My breath was heavy, whooshing in and out of my lungs. *This is it. We're going to kiss.* I could feel it as we stared into each other's eyes, my heart racking my ribs. Everything was buzzing, in my head and all around me. When I closed my eyes and craned my neck, his lips softly brushed mine. I made a little noise just before his hands cupped my face.

Billy ran his tongue along the seam of my lips. I gasped but let it inside. The warm, wet stroke of his tongue against mine was so overwhelmingly sweet that my knees went soft. He held me up, but then set me apart, stopping everything before it got more heated.

I was somewhat bereft at the suddenness of his withdrawal.

"I need to get to work." His eyes were soft and glowing like amber. "When can I see you again?"

"Soon. I'll call you, and we'll figure something out. Another 'baby-sitting' job for Angie?"

"Or I could come over and give it my best shot with your parents. There has to be some way to earn their trust." Billy's face radiated confidence that I didn't have the heart to dash.

"I'll think about it."

"Thank you." His earnestness made my heart ache because I'd never seen my father change his mind once he'd made a decision. "I've got to go now."

"Did you walk all the way over here?" It had to be two miles from Angie's or farther.

He shook his head. "I dropped it off at the garage before walking over. Didn't want it to wake up your neighbors."

"Good thought." My father's ears were probably on constant alert for that sound.

Billy gave me a quick buss on the lips before dashing down the pier. I waved and then sauntered home slowly, elated by my first real kiss, yet worried. I might fall in love with him, and then what would I do?

Someone pats my hand, startling me from my thoughts. "It's really nice back here, Gram. Quiet."

When did Annie arrive?

Such a good girl. Sweet and easy, like Lonna.

She puts her arm around my shoulders and gives me a little squeeze. "Town's a lot different from when I first stayed with you and Grandpa. Redevelopment—sort of like what I need for my life! But it must be strange to you—all the changes."

I nod. Town is different. The world is different. I was born two generations too soon.

"What did you love most about life here?" Annie grins at me like she used to when she colored at the table while I cooked.

"The water." My hand trembles so I clasp it with the other.

"Yeah, that's one of the best parts." She slides a pleasant look my way.

"But I never loved it here as much as you did."

Annie folds her hands on the table, her head cocked. "Then why did you stay?"

I look at the water. "Once you lose your soul mate, there's no place to escape that grief, so I stayed where I knew."

She frowns. "But what about before Grandpa died, when you were young?"

"That's what I'm talking about." I snap my mouth shut, not having meant to say that.

Annie's mouth forms a little O. She pauses, then is careful with her words. "So there was a man before Grandpa?"

She loved Martin, so I look away. It's not loving Billy before Martin that shames me but everything that followed. Billy's and my reckless decisions. My own weakness. My father's rigidity and all its consequences.

Still, Annie presses. "Was that the Billy you mentioned the other week?"

My stomach rolls over. How does she know about him? "I don't want to talk about it."

"All right." She looks down before gazing up at the sky. Then it's as if she's talking to someone else, or maybe to herself. "Teen love is so grand and tragic. At nineteen I'd believed destiny had thrown Richard and me together. If he'd left me back then, I might've lived out my life worshipping the man I'd thought he could've been because I would never have come to know the man he actually is."

I knew the man Billy was—the best kind. If he'd had a selfish bone in his body, everything might've worked out differently. Painlessly. Not with me here in an institution.

My chest hurts, so I bend forward and grip my head. My muscles clench in anticipation of pain, but I keep my eyes closed.

"Are you okay?" the woman beside me asks. "Maybe we should go back inside."

No, please!

"Don't let them hurt me again." I clutch her forearm. "I promise I'll cooperate. If you let me go home, I'll do what my daddy says. I don't belong at Allcot."

"Allcot?" she repeats, playing dumb. "Who's hurting you?"

If she tells on me, that could make it worse. "No one."

"Are you sure?" She's staring at me so intently.

I know her . . . but I can't remember how. Lonna's hair is lighter. Who is she? "Is my father coming to visit soon?"

She blinks, her mouth forming a sad smile. "I hope so."

"Good." I'll be demure and beg him to take me home.

Her shoulders slump as a sailboat comes into view. Seconds later, her voice cracks. "You can't help me anymore, can you, Gram? I'm on my own now."

She dabs a tear from her eye and sniffles.

It isn't easy to watch someone lose her innocence, but sooner or later we all must face the harsh truth. "We're all on our own."

CHAPTER TEN

ANNE

By the time I surreptitiously inspect Gram for any bruises or injuries—which were absent, thankfully—get her settled in her room, and reach my car, my arms and legs are leaden. It's not as if I haven't noticed losing Gram bit by bit before today, yet that conversation made it more acute—made me lonelier. What was I thinking, dumping my problems on her lap when she's burdened with her own worries? Two weeks ago I'd thought she had only the frightening truth of her dementia to wrestle. Now, with her past and present overlapping, she's coping with old pain, too.

Who *was* Billy T., and what in the hell is Allcot? Her voice was laced with fear and need when she spoke of her father. Was he hurting her?

When I arrive at home, Katy's left for soccer practice. Hard to believe my conversation with Lauren happened mere hours ago. But I've handled that for now, so I take my laptop and a ginger ale outside to try to dig into Gram's latest revelation. A red-tailed hawk circles overhead while I type "Allcot" and "Maryland" into the search bar. A number of hits pop up, so I click on the first one.

Established in the late 1800s by Dr. Albert Allcot on his family's farm southwest of Baltimore, the facility served as a sanatorium for the "care and treatment of nervous and selected cases of mental diseases in women."

I push the laptop away. Holy hell!

That mission statement raises the hairs on my neck; 1950s mental health care isn't exactly known for being compassionate. I can't believe Gram spent time there, having never seen any inkling of a significant mental health disorder. She's always been solid. A little quiet at times, but we're all hit with bouts of melancholy.

Her memory is more sieve than anything else these days. She could be confusing something she once saw or read with her own experience. But the look in her eyes today—the panic—seemed real. My stomach gurgles.

After cracking open the soda tab, I pull the laptop back to read more. The facility closed down in 1978. I can't find more, and none of what's online will answer my specific questions. Gram made it sound like someone *put* her there. Who? Her father? Billy? And why? Is Allcot what Grandpa had been referring to that summer I overheard him? But then how would this information have helped my dad grieve my mom?

Don't let them hurt me again. I promise I'll cooperate. If you let me go home, I'll do what my daddy says.

Tears form, stinging my eyes. I'm wiping them with my sleeve when Dan steps outside.

Our gazes lock. The man misses nothing, but he doesn't press me. "Uh, we're packing it up for the day. Just wanted to let you know that we've got the sink, fridge, and dishwasher hooked up." He hitches his thumb over his shoulder. "The range and hood will be installed on Monday. I've put down plywood counters while we wait for the quartz. The kitchen's not yet fully functional, but you can keep a few more things on hand now that you aren't restricted to that mini fridge in the dining room."

I close the laptop, pushing my questions aside for the moment. "Thanks, Dan."

He turns to go, then stops. "I don't mean to pry, but I hate to leave a lady in distress. I overheard some of your call earlier. Can I . . . Is there anything I can do?"

I snort because, even from a distance, Lauren is messing with my life. When I can't take the quiet any longer, I ask, "How much of my call *did* you hear?"

He raises a shoulder. "Enough."

"So you know why Katy's been at home this week."

He nods, but his expression remains inscrutable. What must he think of my daughter and me? I'm working up the nerve to ask when he says, "I got caught drinking in the pit back in the nineties. Football coach made me do a lot of extra sprints during practice. Lost track of how many times I threw up during the two weeks following that bust." His smirk tells me he enjoyed his high school high jinks. "She'll be fine. Better she tests the boundaries now than when she's off at college."

My muscles slacken once I'm freed of the need to defend her or myself. It's refreshing to talk to someone who doesn't view every single event as a make-or-break moment. "Thank you for sharing that. Helps me feel less of a failure."

He waves me off and takes a seat. "You're a good mom."

"Am I? It was selfish moving her here when there was already enough upheaval."

Dan grunts. "It's not the worst thing when kids learn they aren't the center of the universe. Makes adulthood less of a shock."

The matter-of-fact statement brings me up short. I'd always resented the way my dad never made me the center of things, but his attitude did teach me to do things for myself.

Still, my daughter's anxiety and drug use complicate things—and now that I've learned Gram might've once had some kind of nervous breakdown, I'm more concerned. "It still seems sad to learn it so young, doesn't it?"

"Couldn't say. I've never been the center of anything." He averts his eyes.

I suspect he's shocked his admission slipped out. Teenage Dan always seemed to have had it all. He must've been the world's best faker. Been there, done that: My Arlington neighbors thought I'd been perfectly happy. What'd it get me? Nothing but more isolation.

"Thanks for checking on me, Dan. It's nice to reset after getting off on the wrong foot."

His brows gather. "Why do you think we got off on a bad foot?"

"Well"—I shrug—"you seemed impatient with my changes."

He shakes his head. "I just didn't want arguments when my original estimates were blown."

"I wouldn't expect changes for free."

"Then you'd be rare. Most folks don't 'see the big deal' when they ask for this alteration or that." He crosses his arms in front of his chest. "Then they bitch and moan on Yelp about the upcharges—which I won't publicly rebut—and that totally sucks."

"That does suck."

He tips his head, wearing a lopsided smile. "To be honest, I also didn't think you'd be able to live through this renovation so well."

"It's not as easy as I thought. But it's interesting to watch the daily progress." I sip the soda I brought out earlier. "Knowing how to build a house must be empowering. I mean, it's quite remarkable."

"Less remarkable than being an artist. Anyone can learn to do what I do."

"You're too humble, and too generous with your praise. I told you before, I'm no artist—not anymore." I fold and refold my napkin until it's a small triangle, recalling the sophomoric sketch I attempted earlier. I suspect he'd like me to talk more about art, but I've always found it difficult to put my feelings into words. Painting is a form of expression that goes beyond words, after all. "What drew you to construction work?"

"I couldn't see myself at a desk job. This is physical, mental, and creative." He shifts in his seat, leaning forward slightly. "My friend's dad had a small crew and hired me during college summers to help out. Got me hooked."

"I figured you love it from all the whistling I hear." I grin, my long-lost passion for work momentarily rippling the surface of my consciousness.

"Do I whistle that often?"

I nod.

"I don't even notice." He scratches his head. Somewhere in the yard a woodpecker drums a tree, breaking the silence. "Do you mind if I ask why you moved here, of all places?"

Before meeting his gaze, I set my chin on my fist. "My summers here were happy and slow-paced. Seemed like it'd be a great change for both my daughter and me. Of course, the town has changed a lot since then."

The west side of town, in particular, has flourished in the past decade, with new shops and restaurants spreading across the land like pachysandra.

"Yeah. Lots of change." He screws up his face.

"You don't like it?"

"It's good for my business. Good for property values. But I miss the leisurely vibe and time when I knew most everyone."

"I can still picture you on that lifeguard stand. You *did* know everyone back then."

He chuckles, shaking his head. "A lifetime ago."

"Hey now. Let's not talk like old people." I pat the table with my palm. "Not when I'm starting my life all over again."

Humor fades from his eyes. "Divorce is tough, but it gets easier. Give it time."

I envy the fact that he's passed through the grief and anger phases of this particular kind of loss. "Any tips?"

His expression screws up, likes he's conflicted about something. "Don't waste time being angry."

"Easier said than done, especially given the affair," I scoff, then regret the indiscretion.

"Trust me, I know."

"Your wife cheated, too?" I blurt, then cover my mouth with both hands.

"Real punch to the gut." He looks down, tugging at his earlobe. What an unfortunate set of circumstances we share. "I wasted a year being miserable instead of realizing I was free of the wrong woman. Now I know it was for the best."

I rest my chin on my fist. "God, you sound healthy."

"Like I said, time helps. That and throwing yourself into doing things you enjoy." One half of his mouth turns upward. "In a backward way maybe I owe Ellen for improving my bank account, thanks to the extra hours I put in to avoid thinking about or bumping into her."

"I can't ever cut ties with Richard and Lauren because of Katy." Even now, on my patio, the fact that Lauren will probably be part of our lives for years to come is a slam to my breastbone. "Somehow I have to accept that and get Katy to make the best of her blended family."

At least that's what a good mother would do. Does my secret longing for my daughter to hate Lauren make me a bad mother?

"That's a tall order." He wrinkles his nose in a show of sympathy. "I bump into Ellen only occasionally. Guess that's another upside of town's population boom."

Based on nothing at all, I imagine Ellen as a buxom redhead with bright eyes and a pouty mouth. "Is Ellen remarried?"

He nods, showing no outward sign of envy that his deceitful ex got a happy ending while he remains alone.

"Wow. You're really strong. Living far away hasn't helped me handle my jealousy yet."

His head tilts. "Why are you jealous?"

I raise my hands sideways like a set of scales and wiggle the right one. "Lauren's got a good career, classic looks—petite, blonde, patrician—my husband, a brand-new house, and two young kids who probably adore her." Then I wave the left hand. "I'm a divorced middle-aged mom who is failing at that job, and I've no idea what comes next."

"A—Lauren sounds cookie-cutter. B—you're not failing. Teens test boundaries. You'd be failing if Katy *didn't* try to pull some stunts."

I smooth my palm on the table. "You have no idea how much I want to believe that."

Dan leans forward, dropping his voice like he's about to share a secret. "Name one normal adult who didn't break a few rules in their teens."

I shake my head with a frown, unable to come up with one.

"Exactly." He sits back again. "I've never seen Lauren, so I can't comment on her looks, but you've got an intelligent, animated face, which is infinitely more attractive than a Barbie doll's. Plus, you're talented."

"Oh, stop. Please!" I self-consciously touch my curly ponytail and try not to think about the sun damage accrued over the years. "I'm not fishing for compliments."

"Still, I bet your husband regrets his decision soon enough."

I sigh. "Wouldn't that be nice."

"Is that what you want?" A loaded question if ever one existed.

"I don't know. I hate having failed . . . and I've never been on my own." I set my chin on my hand and look toward the trees, my mind sifting through memories, like how Richard, Katy, and I would snuggle in bed on Sunday mornings in those first years, or how he'd sneak up behind me at the stove and drop a kiss on the back of my neck while peeking at whatever I was stirring. "I liked being married. Or at least I liked parts of it. The companionship—when he was home, anyway.

Being a family unit. The sense of safety and belonging. But it's important for Katy to see me be independent and capable."

"Happiness is the best revenge, too." He clucks. "You've got a second chance to make your life whatever you want. Go for something big."

"Something big?" I tease. "I haven't been on my own since nineteen. It's probably best if I start small and build from there."

Dan nods. "I meant more in terms of dreams . . . Dream big."

I could dream big. If I'm prudent, my assets and alimony will last long enough to let me take my time finding a rewarding new purpose or career. But it had never been a lack of money that held me back from my original dream—more like a lack of faith. Or daring, perhaps. It's my nature to play things safe, but safety doesn't ever translate to truly great art. People don't get as excited about the familiar as they do the unexpected. Yet I stopped pushing myself before I ever took a truly bold step.

"I've been thinking about painting again, but I'm not the same girl who had all that creative optimism half a lifetime ago."

"And here I thought tortured artists were the *thing*." He chuckles. "You know, you might enjoy stopping by Trudy Miller's gallery, Finch Street Studio. She's terrific. Changes exhibits every month, and she's up on the local artist scene. You two might hit it off."

"I'll do that." I smile. I don't have to create art to enjoy it. And I would like a new friend. "Well, thanks again for the chat. I appreciate it but don't want to keep you any longer."

He's about to reply when Katy comes through the doors, sweaty from practice. "What's for dinner?"

Dan stands up.

I'd be more disappointed about the end of our conversation if I weren't happy that Katy's appetite has returned since we last spoke.

"Congrats on making varsity, Katy," Dan says. "The Tigers are a great team."

She nods. "Anne Arundel County champs last year."

"Coach Diller was friends with my older brother back in the day. He had a Division I scholarship to UVA. He's a good guy. Tough but fair."

"He's pretty cool." Katy starts to loosen her laces.

"Good luck this season."

She looks up at him as she toes off her cleats. "Thanks."

"See you tomorrow, Anne." Dan waves before ducking inside.

Once he's gone, Katy makes a strange face at me.

"What?"

"You tell me." She stares at me the way Richard always did when trying to make a point.

Suddenly it's like I'm standing naked in the yard. "Tell you what?"

"What's the deal with you and the contractor? I mean, he's not bad-looking for an old guy, but it is sorta cliché." There goes another eye roll.

I rap my knuckles on the table, slightly rattled. "Nothing's going on between Dan and me."

She mutters, "Probably how all these things start, though, right?"

"These things?"

She waves her hand around, scowling. "Forget it. I'd rather not picture you getting it on while I'm at school."

"Getting it on?" I sputter. "Oh, for Pete's sake. The divorce isn't even final, so I'm hardly in the mood for sex. But if I were, I'm not old enough for the idea to be so disgusting. Women my age are still having babies."

"Gross!" She fakes vomiting, which sets me back.

"You've never wanted a little brother or sister?" Not that I necessarily crave an infant at this point, but that dream hadn't died willingly. I don't know why I reacted like I did after the miscarriage, refusing to try again. Maybe on some level I suspected, even then, that things with Richard wouldn't last forever.

"I've got one of each now, remember?" Revulsion laces her voice.

Suddenly we're right back to steeping in her resentment about sharing a parent with a new stepfamily. "Honey, Brody and Zoe never did anything to hurt you. In fact, they're probably excited to have a 'big sister.' Try not to punish them because you're mad at their mother."

That took every ounce of my inner strength and dignity, because I'm actually a bit nauseated at the thought of Katy's life fusing with theirs.

She picks at her fingernail. "Can I be honest?"

"Always." My stomach tenses because no one precedes anything positive with that opener.

"Lauren's not the only one I'm mad at. I mean, yeah, bitch move to start an affair with a married man, but Dad was more wrong." She takes a breath, and I think I've escaped until she adds, "But *you* let him go without a fight. Why didn't you *try* to stop him?"

A flock of birds fly overhead while I'm transported back in time to when I'd been sitting on our bed, still in my pj's, watching Richard pack for his business trip while he told me about Lauren and his plans to file for a divorce. In retrospect, it was a fait accompli before he'd even zipped his luggage.

I lean forward, stretching my hand toward hers. "I thought about it at first, but tell me the point of fighting to hold on to a man who loves someone else." When she looks away, I add, "I don't want to be an obligation. Worse, to be wondering how unhappy my husband is every day. I'd rather be alone."

"Obviously *neither* of you cares how *I* feel."

Dan's earlier comment about teens learning their place in the world stops me from overpromising. "That's not true. We care a lot. But, honey, in two years you'll be in college and then on your own. Your father and I made seventeen years' worth of choices based on what we thought was best for you, but I couldn't stay with him after knowing who he wanted. And, frankly, I don't think I could've stopped him from leaving, even if I had tried harder. We did the best we could for as long as we could. We're not perfect people or parents, but that doesn't mean we love *you* less."

As I say those words, I feel one step closer to finding some peace.

Katy pouts. "I hate living apart and having to share holidays and vacations. It sucks."

"It does suck. I'm sorry."

We both fall silent. I resist the urge to find the right words to soothe her. Nothing I say will change our reality. It's like Gram said earlier—we're all on our own. Bleak as hell, but sort of true. So maybe Katy and I need to sit with the discomfort for a while in order for it to fade.

"I'm nervous to go to Dad's on Saturday knowing Lauren doesn't want me there." Her comment proves she's obsessing about this morning's phone call. She's got roughly forty-odd hours to prepare for the visit.

"Maybe you could plan to do something with your dad elsewhere. Go golfing or play tennis."

"That's so structured and weird."

I reach across the table to pat her hand. "The weekend forecast is great. Take your bathing suit and lie by their pool with a good book."

"That's part of the problem. It's all 'theirs,' not mine. I'm a visitor—a guest—at my own dad's house." Her eyes grow dewy, opening that pit in my stomach that spews acid.

"Didn't he make up a room just for you?" I recall him telling her that, although I've no assurance that it happened.

"A small one that I didn't decorate," she grumbles.

"To be honest, he took over decorating our old house, too." I shouldn't say things like that, but that was to console her, not to rag on Richard.

"Whatever. I'll deal." She blinks back her tears. "I'll go shower so we can get dinner."

"Okay." I put my face in my hands once she's gone.

She struggles so hard with her emotions. If Gram actually spent time in a sanatorium, I might've passed along a hereditary illness. For years Richard's certainty about Katy's behavior—calling it rebellion and teen hormones—made me question my concerns. I should've trusted my gut a long time ago.

CHAPTER ELEVEN

ANNE

Since Thursday evening, Katy's apprehension about today's big sleepover at her dad's new house has choked us like a cloud of smoke. Yesterday I tried distracting her with lunch by the water and a little shopping, but last night she pushed food around her plate and barely paid attention to the season six episodes of *The 100* we'd finally gotten around to watching.

Presently, my second cup of coffee is getting me through this fraught Saturday morning. "Honey, you won't have a thumb left if you don't stop chewing it."

Katy drops her hand from her mouth. "Maybe I should wait another week to visit Dad."

"I thought you wanted to see him?" I put the empty cup down.

"I do, but the whole pot thing this week just . . ." Her face is pinched and she's plucking her hair. "I wish Lauren wasn't going to be there."

So do I, honestly. I worry that she won't treat Katy like family—yet if she does, might Katy, who takes after Richard, also come to prefer the other woman? This divorce could well cost me my sanity.

I gently touch her hand to keep her from pulling out more hair. "Your dad loves you. Go break the ice. You can call me if you get upset. Retreat to your room when you need a break. If it's a disaster, just come home. But it's only for twenty-four hours—you can handle that."

Meanwhile, my stomach is in knots, for her and for me. Her first night with Richard and his new family is momentous, as is our first weekend apart. *My* first weekend on my own. That rattles my nerves, but I hide it from my daughter.

Hopefully, Richard stocked the refrigerator with her favorite snacks—string cheese and grapes. He used to be thoughtful that way and knew his way around the kitchen. He'd made a point of getting up early to make waffles with blueberries whenever she'd had a test. Early on he'd even paid attention to my favorites. And I'll never forget the sight of him cooking homemade chicken noodle soup—red-rimmed eyes, with Katy at his feet—the day after my miscarriage.

How did we go from that family to this one?

Some kinds of pain hit sharp but leave quickly, but this loss is more like a bone bruise—deep and slow to fade. "Text me when you arrive."

"You already track me on Find My Friends." She grabs her keys from the entry-table dish we painted together at one of those pottery-painting places when she was about six or seven.

Her quip nicks but isn't fatal. "Did you make plans to see Jen and the gang tonight?"

"Yeah." She hefts her duffel bag over her shoulder.

"That'll be nice. Tell them hi from me." I grab her in a hug. "I love you. See you tomorrow for dinner. Any special takeout requests?"

"Pasta?" She eases away.

"You got it." I can't resist dropping one final kiss on her forehead. "Love you!"

As she makes her way to her car, I wave and then stand there watching her drive away. To me, it feels as if my kindergartener is behind the wheel. She used to clutch my hand everywhere we went, and now she runs off.

Time moves too fast, refusing to pause on precious moments. She's growing up and will make her own life soon. But wherever she goes, she takes a piece of me with her. I pray I've taught her what she needs to know to face the struggles and savor the wins. That she knows, deep down, that she is my miracle and that she is loved without measure or reason.

I wrap my arms around myself—the only hugs I get these days.

When I close the door, my house is utterly silent. No hammers or buzz saws. No child or workmen skulking around. No one who needs me to run an errand, make a decision, cook a meal, or help in any way. It's so foreign I stand in the stillness, frowning, with only my shadow for company.

I rub my chest, then glance at the seagrass basket in the corner where my new art supplies are stored. After taking a few steps in that direction, I stop to stretch and wiggle my fingers, then place my hands over my roiling stomach. I'm in no frame of mind to create anything interesting, and even if I were, Thursday's effort proved I couldn't execute it.

With a sigh, I straighten the remotes, fluff the sofa pillows, and run Katy's slippers up to her room. When I come back downstairs, I'm jittery. Maybe it's the coffee . . . maybe not. I go to the kitchen to clean out that pot, then open the refrigerator and scan my options although I'm not hungry. Its shelves are full thanks to yesterday's grocery shopping. While in that checkout line, I'd noticed a poster advertising the town's street fair today. Now *there's* something pleasant to do. A little shopping will eat up a chunk of time.

Then I'll swing by Gram's to check on her before that three o'clock yoga class at Give Me Strength that I want to try. Hopefully, she's less distressed than when I left her on Thursday. Of course, lately our visits haven't been easy for either of us. I upset her, which then upsets me.

I open the old tin box and finger the red scarf and rusty nail. Nothing in here suggests time spent in an institution.

I snap the lid shut. Today is about taking a positive step forward. Time to do something for myself—to do anything that keeps me from looking back at Richard, Lauren, Katy, and Gram.

Yet no matter how I busy myself today, the toughest part will be the evening. I certainly didn't expect to cultivate a group of friends after only two weeks, but the renovation and Katy's escapades have sidetracked my socializing.

My only childhood friend here was Leslie Cummings. Her family moved to Charleston years ago, though, and she and I lost touch before we'd both graduated from college. My carefree sorority-party days ended immediately upon seeing two pink lines on a pee stick. Leslie would be shocked to learn that I'm living here. Maybe I'll look her up on Facebook later.

In any case, all my neighbors are married except for Mr. Conti, the elderly widower three doors down, so they'll be busy with couples plans. I should hit up that gallery Dan mentioned and introduce myself to its owner today, and once the volunteer committee for the school art show gets into gear, I'll make a friend or two there as well. But until all that falls into place, my Saturday night dates will be with Ben & Jerry's and Netflix.

Opting not to shower before exercise, I dress in yoga pants and a T-shirt and grab my mat. On my way out the door, I peek at myself in the mirror—a mess of curls and stress. Not at all the "pert" girl Richard used to exclaim I was in the mornings. But this isn't Arlington. I'm a stranger here, so it doesn't matter if I'm looking "sporty." And my over-size Dior sunglasses should provide ample cover.

When I get to town, the sleek-looking fitness center—white painted cement block, plate glass, silver accents—stands out against the otherwise quaint beach-town character of the surrounding shopping district. Beneath a bluebird September sky, shop owners are carrying products in and out of their stores. Small crowds are roaming the tents, tearing through boxes and racks, bargain hunting. My stomach growls, reminding me that two cups of coffee are not enough sustenance. I park on Main Street and jog toward Sugar Momma's, the vivid pastry shop whose striped awning flaps in the breeze, then order a pistachio muffin the size of a softball and an Earl Grey tea to go.

The woman working the counter is humming along with some Khalid song I recognize only because of Katy. Her little shop is bustling with chatty customers, and I make a mental note to remember to bring my daughter here next week.

Rather than sit alone at a table, I nosh on the muffin while strolling through town. It's a little dicey balancing it and the tea while thumbing through racks, but soon enough I devour the muffin, freeing up one hand.

As I peer down the middle of the road, the chaotic street fair rambles on for blocks. At the far end, the rainbow colors of a bouncy house wobble amid a mob of children, sweeping me back to the lavish birthday parties we'd thrown for Katy. Foolish wastes of money that she surely doesn't remember well, but we'd taken great joy in spoiling her. Some of my favorite memories are of me surrounded by gaggles of young children screeching and running wild, messy with ice cream stains.

I shake my head, dragging myself from nostalgia. Yearning for yesteryear won't help me figure out what to do with myself now, so I focus on the next tent.

L'Armoire is quite stylish, selling dresses and jumpsuits from Vince, Burberry, and Nanette Lepore. But my life isn't about client dinners and "ladies who lunch" anymore, so it would be wasteful to buy fancy new clothes. I do love the bold floral prints of Samantha Sung dresses, though.

Ultimately nothing speaks to me, so I move on. Playin' the Blues showcases piles of distressed denim and faded T-shirts that run more to Katy's tastes than mine, but I won't shop without her. She'll hate anything I choose for no reason other than my liking it automatically makes it uncool "mom" clothing. I toss the jean skirt back on the pile and try the next tent.

Mirror Mirror, a cosmetics store, catches my attention. Katy doesn't wear a lot of makeup, but she loves skin care products. Never one to primp much, I'm unfamiliar with them but select some "miracle masks," a cellular three-minute peel, and a "facial in a box" to plan a fun surprise for tomorrow night when Katy returns. Maybe I'll order takeout sushi and try to convince her to watch *A Star Is Born* again, too.

My bag of goodies jostles against my hip as I continue my exploration amid the commotion.

I stumble upon Little Lamb, where the most gorgeous baby clothes make me sigh. We were broke students when Katy was born. Richard's parents funded his law school tuition, and the rest of our money went toward renting a tiny apartment and food, so Katy never had such beautiful outfits. Still, she looked and was precious.

Massaging the base of my neck, I bite down on my lip while ogling the frilly soft things. So tiny. A bittersweet reminder of the time of life when every discovery brought more wonder and joy. The infancy days, long before worries set in and surpassing milestones became Richard's obsession.

My God, the exhaustion and sore nipples and mommy brain fog had turned me into a monster some days. Thankfully, Richard had been at home—studying, but there—during those earliest years. Katy had completely fascinated him at the start. He'd been so young and exuberantly certain of our future. Determined to create a dream life for us all. He'd swept me up in his fantasy, and by the time I realized that career was overtaking family on his list of priorities, it was too late to reel him back. Now the memory of our once-tight little family hollows out a chamber in my heart.

Those days of being satisfied with my place in life and confident about my mothering skills and my marriage feel more like an old movie than my own past. Turns out the truth of my life is a series of missteps and reactions more than careful planning and choices. An artist turned wife and mother turned divorcée. Now I'm little more than a stranger to myself.

I'm dabbing my eyes like some loon when a familiar voice calls my name.

"Anne?" Dan's standing just outside the tent.

Thank goodness for my sunglasses.

"Oh, hi!" My cheeks are probably as pink as the baby clothes that made me weepy.

His gaze falls on the little dresses, then he tips his head. "Will I be turning your spare bedroom into a nursery next?"

"God, no!"

That came out harsher than necessary, making me grimace.

Dan's hands rise in surrender as he snickers. "I didn't think so, but one never knows."

"If I were pregnant, it'd be the Second Coming." My hand covers my mouth, but thankfully we both laugh.

If I had another shot at motherhood, would the wisdom I've earned through experience make me better at it? Doubtful, since I haven't mastered being Katy's parent, and I'm running out of time with that, too. That inescapable future—my daughter's burgeoning independence—can knock me over like a strong wave.

"I got sidetracked by the beautiful things." I leave the precious clothes behind and walk into the sunlight, only to be mortified anew. Yoga pants in public—what was I thinking? They leave nothing to the imagination and reveal every imperfection. "I didn't expect to run into anyone I knew."

Then again, it's a big event for a small town, so it shouldn't be a surprise that he's here. In fact, subconsciously I might've even hoped to bump into him.

"Good place for early Christmas shopping." He holds up a bag, thankfully oblivious to my musings. "My sister, my niece, and my mother—all done."

For years I purchased all the gifts for Richard's family. Lauren can't possibly know them well enough to select the perfect items. Richard might not care, but come Christmas, the Chases will miss me a little, I bet. "That's a lot of ladies."

He shrugs, looking pleased, which I find very sweet. "They spoil me. I'm not good at mushy, but I pick good gifts."

I don't know why something so simple nearly brings me to tears. "That's nice, Dan."

"Yeah. I'm lucky." He scans the area around me. "Where's Katy?"

"Visiting her father up in our old neighborhood. Her first time in his new house with the girlfriend and her kids. I'm flying solo!" Blah, blah, blah . . . my gosh, as if Dan cares. I sound like a ninny.

He crosses his arms, bag dangling along his side. "Ah, so you have some time to yourself."

I'm trying really hard to have it feel as wonderful as his tone suggests it should be. It *is* easier to feel alive—feel hope—in this crowd than sitting alone at home with nothing to do and no one to care for. If I keep moving, then someday—maybe not too long from now—twenty-four hours will pass without a thought about Richard and Lauren. Without me second-guessing everything from marrying Richard to my motives for moving here.

"I was thinking of going to that gallery you mentioned," I reply. "What was the name again?"

"Finch Street Studio. It's right around the corner, on Finch Street." He gestures with his head.

"Who would've guessed?" I tease.

His brows rise. "Why don't I join you? I can introduce you to Trudy. She and I go way back."

"Oh really? Sounds like there's a story there." My face is hot again. I adjust my sunglasses, self-conscious and worried that he'll think I'm flirting when I don't mean to.

"High school sweethearts." He winks, furthering my concern. "She broke my heart, but we stayed friends."

I can't recall anyone named Trudy back in the nineties. Then again, I was at home and in bed by nine in those days.

"Ah. You have an ulterior motive for escorting me, then." I shoot him a knowing look.

"Nah. She's been happily married for twelve years." He swings his shopping bag toward Finch Street. "Shall we go?"

There are worse ways to spend a Saturday afternoon than visiting an art gallery with a handsome man. "Why not."

It's literally one block off Main and sits on a corner lot. While the storefront is mostly plate glass, the shop's brick sidewall is entirely painted in spectacular graffiti—a Warholesque image of a woman in sunglasses, done in teals, plums, shades of pink, and yellow. "Very cool."

"Have you ever done anything like that?" Dan asks.

"Graffiti?" While I appreciate pop art, my stylistic preferences lean toward the isms: impressionism, postimpressionism, and abstract expressionism. Not exactly suited for sidewalks and commercial exteriors.

"No. I mean on that scale . . ." He widens his arms, bag still dangling. "Huge."

I shake my head. "Fun project, though. Something for the entire community to enjoy."

"If someone gave you a wall, what would you paint?" he asks as we approach the gallery door.

"It would depend on my mood at the time." I laugh, trying to picture myself standing in front of drywall in a home or an office lobby.

It's absurd to consider, but a cartoonish image of Lauren beneath my bootheel flickers to life. Not exactly Monet.

"If it were right now . . . ," he prods, stopping on the sidewalk.

I flush, suspecting he hopes to be wowed while knowing he won't be. But, dammit, I can at least give it a try. With my eyes closed, the sounds of the street fair and nearby gulls filter into my thoughts. Drawing a breath, I let my thoughts wander before opening my eyes. "Maybe an abstract image of the sky over the bay just after a late-day storm, with rosy-orange sunlight behind the clouds, and the faintest hint of a rainbow in the distance."

Another juvenile attempt at symbolism. My skin is on fire, but I don't cover my face or look away. One could argue that childishness suits my current stage of rebirth. Would Professor Agate accept that as me taking responsibility for my creation? Ha!

A slow grin appears as Dan studies me. His amber eyes glow like the backlit clouds in my imaginary painting. "I'd like to see that."

"Please don't hold your breath. I'm not up for a funeral." I chuckle while he pulls the door open. Only after we step inside do I acknowledge that maybe I could paint the bay—not to impress others or to sell, but for myself. For fun. When was the last time I did anything just for fun?

The gallery design is fairly typical—polished wood floors, stark white walls, high ceilings, and bright lights. The theme of the exhibit must be wildlife naturalism. I'm drawn to a gorgeous image of a mother lion on her side, nursing two cubs. My being lifts in the face of the universal imagery. I'm so awed I almost touch it.

"You like that?" Dan asks.

I nod. "It's wonderful. Powerful."

"In what way?" He studies the image. "Seems more peaceful than powerful."

"I think the artist chose a lioness to counter the way society—and children—often make mothers feel vulnerable. But our bodies are amazingly life-giving and nurturing. Mothers give without taking, and that requires strength and courage."

A flush spreads across my chest following my little speech, although that is exactly what my professors would demand. Dan doesn't dismiss my comment or make a joke, as Richard might have. He's considering it, so I let myself enjoy the moment of thinking critically about art. It's been years since I've taken time to visit a museum or gallery.

A rather elegant, slender blonde looks up from her desk in the back corner and grins. "Dan!"

She brushes her clothes as she stands and strolls toward us. Her flowing black slacks and halter-style top flatter her figure. A jaw-length bob and fuchsia lipstick lend a sharp, smart look, too. I'm not surprised he dated someone this pretty, but her chicness makes me rethink what his ex-wife might've been like.

She kisses Dan on the cheek, then thumbs away the lipstick smudge before turning and extending her hand to me. "Hello. I'm Trudy."

"Hi. I'm Anne Chase." God, I need to change my name. "Actually, Anne Sullivan . . . or soon to return to that name anyway."

Bumbling again. Katy's right: I've got no game.

"It's nice to meet you, Anne." Trudy's eyes twinkle in the light. She's something of a sprite—full of energy and perhaps a bit of mischief. "Are you new to town or just visiting Dan?"

"Oh, I'm not with Dan." I wave my hands—my shopping bag crinkling as I do—failing miserably at sparing us both the embarrassment of being considered a couple thanks to my overreaction. "I mean, I know Dan, of course. He's doing work at my house. I moved to town with my daughter a few weeks ago and am renovating my grandparents' old Cape." More verbal diarrhea. Glaring proof of my lack of practice socializing with adults about topics that have nothing to do with children. I make a private vow that if Trudy and I hit it off, I will not bore her with my divorce or parenting woes.

"Ah. Welcome to Potomac Point. Are you in the market for artwork as part of your renovation?" She crosses her arms, pleasantly awaiting an answer.

I shake my head. "Not at the moment, sorry. Dan suggested I meet you and see your gallery."

She pats his shoulder in a sisterly fashion. "Isn't that lovely?"

"Anne's an artist," Dan adds.

"Was." I wave my arms, but rein them in quickly. "It's been a long while since I've painted."

Dan says, "The stuff in her living and dining rooms is as good as anything in here." He points at artwork around the room.

Trudy's gaze sharpens. "Have you a website or portfolio I might view?"

"Does PTA-related graphic design count?" I chuckle. "But seriously, I gave up my career a decade ago to raise my daughter."

That sounds lame, but I can't embarrass Katy by exposing the nitty-gritty of why she requires so much of my time. Even now, when I *should* have more free time, I've got to be on the lookout for drugs and other types of rebellion.

"Maybe you can start up again," Trudy says. "I love to support local artists. In fact, in December I showcase them, complete with a festive opening-night party on the town's Holiday Stroll celebration. Does that deadline motivate you?"

"Oh, no, thank you. Even if I could produce something worthy, that timing is too soon. I'm in the thick of moving in and getting my daughter transitioned. But I'll definitely drop in to support the others."

"Well, I'd love to schmooze, but I've got a ton of work today. Maybe we could grab coffee and talk art. There aren't many of us who like to dig into that, you know."

"I'd love that, thanks." I beam. Then a vision of Katy at Richard's—stressed and awkward—taints my joy.

"Call me here and we can put something on the calendar." Trudy squeezes Dan's hand. "Always great to see you, Dan. Thanks for stopping in. If you have questions about anything you see, give a shout. Otherwise, I'll leave you to browse."

"See ya, Trudy." Dan waves and I nod, releasing her from our conversation. He leans toward me. "Told ya you'd like her."

"Yes, you did." We head outside together, and I pause on the sidewalk. "Listen, I appreciate your encouragement about my art, but I've got too much on my plate with Katy, Gram, and the renovation. Maybe I'll paint again someday, but if I'm forced before I feel it, the work will suffer and that won't help my confidence."

"Sorry. I don't mean to push. Ellen used to get on me about that a lot. My sister's poor kids probably hate when I visit or yell from the sidelines." He chuckles at himself, but all I can think about is how nice it is that he makes time for his sister's kids' events.

"I have to ask: Why do you care so much whether or not I make friends and paint or whatever?" The question surprises us both.

He stares into my eyes, making me a little breathless. "When Ellen took off, it threw me way off my game. I felt like hell. Wallowed for a year, unable to cope with the kick in the teeth. The failure as a man. The doubts. That all makes you do things you regret . . . big mistakes." He almost shivers while glancing at his feet. "I guess I thought you could bypass those mistakes and regrets if you got back into doing something you're great at."

His chivalry melts my heart like it's been warmed by the sun.

"Wow. That's . . . that's very kind, Dan." And revealing. I start walking because standing together on the sidewalk locked in a personal conversation feels too intimate. "Honestly, I can't imagine you wallowing or making big mistakes."

"Trust me. I did." He snorts.

"With women?" If I could cover my face without looking immature, I would. What made me blurt that?

"No. Women were the last thing on my mind." He scrunches his nose. "Trust issues, thanks to Ellen. Sadly, I dove headlong into a months-long combo of alcohol and belligerence that resulted in a bad fall from the top of an extension ladder." He points to the scars on his forehead and arm. "It's lucky I've got such a hard head. Only suffered a moderate concussion and a bunch of stitches. But these battle wounds keep me in check on lonely days when I'm tempted to wallow."

"Oh dear." I know that heartache so well my chest hurts when picturing him stumbling around, drunk and suffering. "I understand. Lately I've come to better appreciate the benefits of a good pinot noir."

"Who doesn't?" He rubs the back of his neck like he might regret sharing such personal details.

We stroll a few steps in silence before I add, "I'm doing okay, though. Katy keeps me focused and moving forward."

His mouth presses into a tight line as we hit Main Street. "What about when Katy's not around, like today? I know she's your priority right now, but you're more than Katy's mother."

Am I? It's been my primary role for almost seventeen years. I can't recall the last time I defined myself as something other than a mother, daughter, or wife (*ex*-wife). A sudden thought slams into my consciousness, causing me to stop in my tracks. Before the pregnancy, I had goals of my own. A plan—the Columbia fine arts master's and all that would follow. That's the Anne whom Richard fell in love with, as I fell for the ambitious dreamer he'd been. He didn't waver from his course, but I strayed far from mine. Did the Anne I've become make me a stranger to *him*, too? Is that why he doesn't love me anymore?

Dan grabs my arm when I stagger. "Hey, ignore me. Who the hell am I to project my stuff onto you? As long as you're satisfied, that's all that matters."

He smiles in a feeble attempt to pretend he doesn't still believe he hit the nail on the head—an apt idiom for a contractor.

"Thanks." I blow out a quick breath to reset myself. "I'm sorry Ellen hurt you that much. How long ago did you divorce, if you don't mind my asking?"

"Five years."

"Wow." He's been single a long time. "No one special since then?"

He shakes his head. "Nah. I don't think it's in the cards for me. The thing that came between Ellen and me wasn't the other guy—not really. And I can't fix my . . ." He waves his hand. "Never mind."

Hm. There's more to his story, but I won't press. "So you keep it casual."

"Casual is good. No one gets hurt."

"Makes sense." I smile, but it's far too sad for me to actually be happy. Will that be me—a future of casual affairs with no one to love or to love me?

Dan steers the conversation elsewhere, pulling me back from an abyss. "How's your grandmother doing?"

"Same. It kills me to see her slipping further and further away. Half the time she doesn't recognize me. It must be terrifying to live in a worldful of strangers like she does now."

"I'm sorry that's happening on top of everything else you're going through."

I nod. He's really very kind—like the young man I remember. So different from my first impressions this summer. "To be honest, she mentioned something during my last visit that was upsetting—a place called Allcot—and acted afraid of being hurt. I did some digging and found out there used to be a mental hospital by that name years ago not far from here. I've no idea if she actually spent time there—or if she was afraid of it as a child and now is confused and thinking that that's where she's been stuck."

Dan's brows pull together. "I'm sure you would've heard something if she'd ever been hospitalized."

I'd agree if Grandpa's whispered words weren't in the back of my mind. "Her 'secret box' proves that she isn't big on sharing."

"Your father can't help?"

"Doubtful." First I'd have to reach him instead of his voice mail.

"Cousins? Aunts or uncles?"

"I hesitate to disclose Gram's secrets to them without her permission."

"But you're telling me things." He crosses his arms.

"That's different. You don't really know her, and you won't judge her. I worry they would. We were never all that close to begin with. It's complicated, and I'm running out of time because Gram is out of it more often than not."

"Are you just curious about the past, or is there a deeper reason to push?" Dan asks.

"Both. There could be a hereditary mental health issue I should know about. But the bigger part of me needs to know more about what shaped the woman I most looked up to, the woman who shaped me. She's struggling with these memories. With regret, maybe. If I figure out what happened, maybe I can help lessen her regrets before she dies."

"That's a tall order for someone with advanced dementia. Does she remember the past long enough to be haunted by it?"

"It seems like she spends more time in the past now than the present, actually."

He clucks, shaking his head. "Wish I had better advice."

"I'm just grateful to have someone to bounce ideas off of."

"Want to grab a bite?" Dan asks, gesturing to Oak & Almond across the street. "I don't know about you, but I think we deserve a nice lunch after all this heavy talk."

"Oh, that's nice, but I planned to swing by my gram's before yoga class." I'm not dressed for a nice restaurant, and this feels a wee bit too much like a lunch date. I'm not ready to date, although if I were, Dan might be a nice jumping-off point. "Can I take a rain check?"

He nods. I can't tell if he's disappointed, but *my* chest is a little heavy. "Of course. Have a nice visit."

"Thanks. I'll see you Monday."

"Bright and early."

I've enjoyed hearing him whistling through my house. It'll be quiet when he finishes his work. We part ways with a smile, and I walk back to my car.

It's only after I'm driving to Gram's that I realize I've thought only once in the past hour about how Katy is handling Richard and Lauren. I check my phone. No texts. Everything must be fine.

It's been ages since I've been utterly free to do as I please.

Look at me. My first day without Katy isn't so bad after all.

CHAPTER TWELVE

MARIE

"Gram, you should've prepared me better for dealing with teens." Annie sips the tea she made us in the microwave.

"No parent has the secret to getting through those years without bumps." Bobby thought he had all the answers back then. Just like I had at that age. Fools, all of us.

"Probably not, although it seems like it gets harder with each generation. Technology has heightened a lot of anxiety and depression. Kids are bombarded with information. It's overwhelming. Even here in this little town we can't get away from it all." She sighs and sets her cup on the table. "Did my dad give you trouble?"

"We didn't argue a lot over little things—teen rebellions." Oh, the long hair, the loud music! "I worried about the big things—like if he would get drafted to Vietnam." That still makes me shiver.

The military—war—it all makes me nauseous. This country can't stop waging its wars.

"Oh gosh, that must've been nerve-racking," Annie says, eyes wide. "I guess we're both lucky that didn't happen."

Lucky, yes. And grateful that he didn't enlist like Billy did long ago. For me, Billy had said, but I never wanted that. I can still picture the look on his face when we argued about it—the day when everything had started to go wrong.

"I hate that idea," I'd told him, pacing Angie's living room in front of the unattractive cream-and-brown floral-patterned sofa while the upstairs neighbor's TV blared through the ceiling. How Angie lived with that night after night was a mystery. It must've kept Ben awake. At two, he could be a real handful. Billy adored his nephew, though. They were darling together. He said he didn't need kids, but seeing them together made me realize I might like having some after I'd had a few years to travel.

Angie was in Ben's room, reading him a book before putting him down for the evening. I tried to keep my voice calm but wanted to shout and storm off. Yet I couldn't walk away from the man I loved to share everything with, and who understood me.

"Marie, please settle so we can talk," Billy said.

I spun on him. "Why would you join the army?"

"To be respectable. To be a hero."

I didn't care if he didn't have what my family considered a respectable job. "I'm afraid, Billy. The military is dangerous."

He shook his head. "The war's been over for years."

"But there are other options. You could go back to your parents in New York and train for a different career. After I graduate, I could look for an apprenticeship up there, too."

"Moving and training cost money I don't have. The army will train me and give me a steady paycheck. Later it'll even give me money for college. And after meeting you and seeing your family, I want more for myself now, too."

I couldn't exactly argue against a chance for a free college education. "But if you go, how will we see each other?"

"We won't for a while, but we can write. You'll be busy finding an apprenticeship with a photographer somewhere, right? Maybe once you learn what you need to learn, I'll be stationed somewhere interesting, like Europe or Asia. We could get married so you could come live with me. Imagine the things we might see—the cultures we'd experience. You could work freelance for newspapers or magazines everywhere."

I was stunned into silence. The kitchen clock ticked on, and in the distance, Ben fussed.

Billy cleared his throat. "We don't have to. I mean—"

"You want to marry me?" My thoughts kept skipping, like they were stuck in some kind of strange loop.

"Well, yeah, Marie. I mean, we love each other, right? I'll ask you proper . . . but—" He couldn't finish because I lunged at him and squeezed him hard. I didn't even know I wanted to get married until he said that, and then I just knew. I loved Billy. I really loved him.

He kissed my head and kept talking. "I know you worry about not having your dad's support if you don't go to college, but maybe you could move in with Angie to live cheaply as an apprentice around here. Then, once we're married, you can find work from wherever I'm stationed. We'd probably get moved a few times, so it'll be a real adventure like you want. No more being stuck in Potomac Point."

His plan held some appeal, yet all I could think about was how many people had died in combat not *that* long ago. I looked into his eyes. "The Communists aren't giving up. There could be another war."

"Don't think of the worst-case scenario. Think of the best—we could be in Belgium keeping the peace and preventing the Soviets from taking over. Imagine the images you could capture." His eyes shone with a determination that my fears would not deter. He tugged at his greasy work overalls. "I'd trade in this ugly thing for a service coat. Picture me, defending our country. Wouldn't you be proud?"

My heart ached. I admired his courage and patriotism but hated him risking his life.

He cupped my face. "Your father's right about one thing. I can't ask you to throw all your chips in with me and expect you to live like this—with *no* chance at the life you want." He nodded around his sister's cramped place. "I don't want to hold you back, but if you want me to be part of your future, this is the best way. And if you hate military life, I can quit in eight years and get a different job or go to college. No more greasy hands and oil-soaked clothes."

Frightened tears clogged my throat and nose. I wanted to leave this town. And I wanted Billy. But a military life—even for a few years—seemed alien and rigid. "I don't know. This is so sudden for such big plans."

"No matter what future you choose, you won't be happy with a rift in your family. Look at how much that eats at Angie. I don't want that for you." He kissed me. "If we run off to New York half-cocked with no real plan, your father will never accept me. But he'd *have* to respect me if I'm defending our country."

My heart hardened against my father. If he would only have helped us instead of fighting me, we would've had more options.

Billy stared out the window as if watching the movie of his future life playing on the clouds, so he didn't notice my scowl. "I can do this. I *want* to do this, actually. I think I'd be good at it."

A toy basket with bright painted blocks was at my feet. "Does your sister agree with this?"

"She starts her new job next week, so she won't need as much support from me." Hagman's Insurance firm had hired her as a secretary. "I'll still send her a little money each month. Plus my leaving her 'alone' could be the push my parents need to finally reach out to her and Ben." He pulled me into a tight embrace.

"Won't *you* miss Ben?"

When Billy dropped his arms, I instantly grew cold. "I thought you'd be proud. Excited even. I support all of your dreams. Can't you support mine?"

"My dreams don't put me in danger." I could hardly believe I was arguing against a plan that would enable us to leave Potomac Point together.

"You don't know that."

"*Sciocco testardo!*" I stomped my foot and pouted.

Billy laughed and kissed me. "I should never have taught you that."

"Your sister's right. You're as stubborn as they come."

"Must be why we get along so well." He wrapped me in another hug and planted a kiss on my head. "I have to leave for work. Just think about what I've said."

I squeezed him tight. He loved me enough to change his whole life to be with me. How could I be upset about that? "I'll think about it, but don't you dare enlist before I agree."

If I could change my father's mind about Billy and college, maybe he could help us come up with another plan. Maybe he'd even give me the money he would've paid for tuition to put toward studying photography, and then Billy and I could get married later and move to New York.

Billy kissed me. Lush and warm as always. Everything smelled better, tasted better, and felt better with him.

When we broke apart, he took my hand and led me out of the apartment and down the stairs to the lobby. "Will I see you later?"

"Tomorrow evening my parents have bridge club at the Parkers'. I'll meet you here."

He nodded. "It'll be nice when we don't have to hide."

I couldn't argue with that, so I didn't. Playfully, I pushed him out the apartment door, then waited two minutes before exiting and going the opposite direction, but not until I stole one last look at him as he rounded the corner.

My heart was simultaneously aflutter and heavy. Along the walk home, I kicked pebbles. Billy was right. I'd never made real plans, just bellyached about feeling constrained by expectations and imagined a more interesting life. The thought of Billy in combat gear made me want to throw up.

I didn't expect a proposal today, but Billy's version of life together wasn't as dull as the marriages around here looked. I'd love to travel, but army life sounded as strict as life with my dad.

By the time I got home, my blood was pumping through me in hot spurts.

My family was in the living room. The stupid song "Buttons and Bows" was playing, making me angrier. How could I let Billy put his life at risk if I wasn't even willing to fight here on the home front?

"What's the matter?" My mother set her book on her lap.

Lonna glanced up from her dolls, and my father folded his newspaper in half.

I wiped the frown from my face and kept my voice even. "I need to talk about something serious."

My father leaned forward. "What's going on?"

"I'm worried terrible things might happen if you don't try to see things my way."

"Is this about your friend?" My father's gaze narrowed.

I stood erect, as if defying a firing squad. "Yes, it's about Billy."

"Not this again." He sighed. My parents exchanged a look, although my mother didn't appear as adamant as my father.

"Yes. This *again*." I was shaking because once I admitted that I'd continued seeing Billy these past months, I had no idea what kind of hell would break loose. "We've been spending time together, and now he's got it in his head that if he joins the army and we get married, he can help me see the world and you'll respect him. But I don't want him to end up in a war in some backwards attempt to please *you*. Please, Daddy. Trust me. He's a good person. Can't you please give him a chance and also help me pursue something other than college?"

My mother sank her teeth into her lip. Lonna shook her head at me.

"If he were a good man, he wouldn't have let you lie to your parents. And what kind of example are you setting with this behavior?" His cheeks were crimson; his eyes, hard. "Consider yourself grounded until further notice."

I remained there, chest puffed out, but shaky inside. "You can't ground me. I'm an adult."

"Oh boy," Lonna mumbled.

"I most certainly can." Daddy rose from his chair, but my mother reached for his hand, stopping him from advancing on me.

I trembled, but kept picturing Billy lying on some field somewhere. "Not if I don't live here."

I didn't know where that came from, but I wasn't sorry. Billy's plans frightened me more than my father tonight.

Daddy shrugged free of Mom's grip. "And where, exactly, would you go?"

Good question. My heart raced.

"To live with Billy's sister." Heat filled my entire body. Lonna pulled her knees to her chest, her eyes wide and afraid.

My father's eyes clouded. His face pinched so tight he spat when he spoke. "Lonna, go upstairs to your room."

I gulped. This wasn't a good sign. Once she left, he stepped closer, his voice low and hot. "Marie Jean, what has this boy done to you? Are you pregnant?"

"No!" We hadn't done anything like *that*.

He looked at me as though I was a stranger. "I don't believe you."

"I swear, Daddy. He respects me. Why do you keep thinking the worst of him and me?"

"Because you've been lying to us," he shouted.

"I only lied because you won't be fair."

"Lewis . . ." My mother's gentle voice instantly disarmed the room.

My father scrubbed his face with both hands. "This boy is having a bad influence on you, whether you see it or not."

"That's not true. He's been begging to talk to you again. It's me that's been lying, looking for a way to convince you."

"Why, Marie?" my mother asked.

"Because I love him, Mom." I was crying, which made me mad. I didn't want to be a baby, but I was scared. For Billy, and for myself. I couldn't honestly imagine life without my family, but I couldn't imagine it without Billy, either.

"You can't love him. You hardly know him. This is infatuation, and it will pass when you go to college." My father crossed his arms.

"It's not infatuation." How insulting. "We want to get married."

He waved his arm in a brusque manner. "Get that out of your head. You're going to college, and that's that."

"You never listen to me, but Billy does. He's willing to change everything to help me create a life that excites me. You only want me to live life your way. If you force me to choose, I'll choose him. But if you give us a chance, maybe there's a way to make everyone happy without him having to join the army." I turned to my mother. "Don't you want me to be happy?"

"Of course I do, but why won't you listen to our advice?" she asked, her voice pained.

"Because it's my life—"

"Your life, that *we've* sacrificed things for to make better," my father interrupted. "I'm not going to let you wreck your future over this man."

My arms slapped against my sides. "I don't want to wreck my life, either! But I need to keep Billy from enlisting just to please *you*."

My parents exchanged a look, and then Dad crossed his arms. "Marie, someday you'll understand why we cannot support this relationship. I'm telling you that this Billy can't make you happy. Not in the long run. You have to trust me."

"Why can't you trust *me*? Listen to what I want instead of what you think I want. I don't need all these things that you think are important."

My mother's eyes watered, so she looked at her lap. Daddy inhaled slowly.

"This discussion is over." He returned to his chair. "You start university in September. For now, you will come home after school until we can trust you. I mean it, Marie Jean. If we catch you lying again, there will be grave consequences."

I chafed at his control, ready to burst into flame. There would be grave consequences either way, it seemed, but I'd be damned if I let him decide my future when he wouldn't even consider my opinions. Without another word, I raced past them and ran upstairs to my room, closed my door, and fell on my bed in tears.

He'd called my bluff, so I'd have to make good on my threat. When everyone was asleep, I'd pack my bags and then go to Billy tomorrow. I couldn't live in sin, so we'd have to elope right away. I'd find some way to convince him not to enlist. After graduation, I'd get a job and we would work together to make a new plan.

Move to a bigger city to find better jobs and make our own rules.

Someday, when my parents saw how happy we were, they'd forgive me. What choice would they have?

"Gram, why are you crying?" A pretty woman with curly hair hands me a tissue.

I look around but don't recognize this room. It's not my bedroom. I don't know where I am. Where did everyone go?

She touches my arm, looking at me with a pitying smile. "Gram? It's me, Annie."

"Annie." I nod. Annie . . . Little Annie? "You're so big now."

"I am." She chuckles. "Do you remember what you were thinking about a minute ago?"

I shake my head. It's probably good that I forget, because my body feels heavy, like it was something sad.

"Well, my yoga class starts soon, so I need to go. I'm trying to be Zen, with Katy up at Richard's. Being single at this age wasn't part of my plan." She sighs, zipping up her little jacket.

I grab her hand. I didn't end up with the life I first meant to create, but Annie has been like a summer breeze all these years. "Even the wrong road leads to some wonderful surprises. You have been a gift."

Annie's eyes water. "Thank you, Gram. So have you."

CHAPTER THIRTEEN

KATY

The glass-and-wood house looks like a bunch of corrugated boxes stacked on top of each other. As cold-looking as Lauren. And it's nothing like the house my dad had chosen for *us*. *Our* house had classic features like pillars and mahogany paneling and crown molding. He loves that stuff so much his office has them, too. Why did he let Lauren talk him into this ice cube when he never liked modern design before?

I slam my car door closed after grabbing my overnight bag from the passenger seat. Visiting my dad shouldn't make my throat tight and my eyes sting. My mom's advice about playing nice and not giving Lauren ammunition rattles around my brain, but my stomach blazes as I head into enemy territory. Blinking and breathing deep, I trot up the walkway and knock on the door. That's weird, too.

My dad jogs toward me—I can see him through the glass. He's wearing his game-face smile. The one he uses with friends and colleagues, not the one he gives me when I beat him in a tennis match or hand over my report card. He's probably nervous that I'll do something to upset Lauren. That he cares more about her feelings than mine smarts.

"Hey, honey. Come in." He takes my bag from me as we ease out of a brief hug.

He's probably still pissed about the suspension. I'd talk to him about that if Lauren and her kids weren't here. "Hi, Dad."

"Are you hungry?" He motions for me to follow him into the bowels of this museum. The floors look like hardwood but are tile. Fake and cold, like Lauren. "I've got hamburgers and hot dogs on the grill. Chopped onion like you like. Fresh tomatoes."

I nod, although the flames in my gut leave little room for an appetite.

Everything in this house is done in shades of white and gray. Like, everything. Even the art. Oversize black-and-white photographs in clear glass frames. Charcoal drawings and monochromatic paintings abound.

My mother would hate it. I do, too, although it is all fine art. I'll have to inspect it more closely later. For a second, an image of Tomás breaks through my mood. His photography is good, so I can see him producing something like the cool black-and-white close-up of the Guggenheim's exterior hanging on the wall.

When we reach the kitchen—which is crowded with lacquered white cabinets capped by concrete counters—Lauren and her kids are seated at the round kitchen table with four seats.

Crap, I've been so busy dreading seeing Lauren I forgot I'd be meeting her spawn for the first time.

"Kids, this is Katy!" Her voice might sound bubbly, but I know the truth. I wonder if she told Dad that she called my mom. "Katy, this is Zoe and Brody."

Zoe is almost six; Brody is four. Both are blissfully clueless about the layers of subtext taking place. I can't blame them for being here or loving their mother. She's probably really nice to them, and if I saw her on the street, I'd think she was pretty in a classy Princess Kate way. My mom isn't sleek and stylish, but she's got an interesting face and charm, like Emilia Clarke in *Me Before You*. She's smart and passionate and ten times a better person than Lauren.

I wipe my scowl away before one of the kids notices, although I'm pretty sure Lauren already caught my vibe, because she's watching me without blinking.

Again my mom's voice is in my head, encouraging me to act like a big sister, but I don't feel anything for these kids other than envy that they have my dad now. Come to think of it, I wonder where their real dad is and if he's pissed off like I am. "Hi, guys."

"Hi!" Zoe exclaims brightly before shoving a Cheeto in her mouth. She must look like her dad, because she's a brunette with hazel eyes, unlike Lauren's blonde hair and blue eyes.

Brody's intently glued to an iPad, so he barely registers my arrival. He's got sandy-colored, pin-straight hair, a wide mouth, and the skinniest arms I've ever seen.

My dad drops my bag on an island that might be bigger than Mom's and my new kitchen, and pulls a stool over to the table. "I'll take this one. You sit there between Zoe and Brody."

I force a grin even though it's clear that my presence was not factored into anything about this house. Four chairs? Six would've been smarter, even if only so they had room for Zoe's and Brody's friends.

Lauren tries again. "We're glad you came, Katy. Welcome to our home."

"Our home," as if I need a reminder that I'm more guest than member of *this* family. And just because she doesn't know I overheard her call to my mom doesn't mean I can pretend to be happy to see her. I raise my brows and nod—it's the best I can do. Meanwhile, did she actually wear that fancy jumpsuit to a kids' soccer game?

"Do you want some Cheetos?" Zoe thrusts one at me. She's still in her emerald-green team shirt, although she must've kicked off her cleats somewhere.

"No thanks." I can tell she's disappointed. Her offer was sweet, unlike many kids I babysit who don't share. Maybe I'd like her if I were just the babysitter. But I'm not. All I can think about is how my dad made her youth soccer game a priority when he rarely had with mine. Still, I try. "Did you win your game?"

"Nope." She swings her feet beneath her seat, unapologetic and unfazed.

"Bummer." I pour myself some lemonade from the pitcher on the table. "Maybe next time."

She shrugs.

My dad is carrying the tray of grilled meat inside when Lauren brushes some of Zoe's curls from her face, saying, "It's not important who wins. It's about having fun and trying your best."

I snort. "That's not what I was told."

Zoe frowns, her lower lip sticking out like she's confused. Lauren exchanges a look with my dad.

He sets the platter on the table and ignores my remark, making me as confused as Zoe, because winning is pretty much his life mantra. When he settles on his stool, he's towering over us all. Meanwhile, Brody's chin wouldn't clear the table without his booster seat, and he's not interested in eating.

"So, the drive up here wasn't too bad?" Dad piles tomato and lettuce on his burger, then overloads it with mustard while rolling his neck around. My stomach twists from the discomfort of being here.

"Not bad, so it'll be easy for you to come to me, too. There's a trail along the bay where we could run." I miss our Sunday-morning routine—the one time each week I could count on private time with him. Dad would wake me at six to run the Custis Trail together, and then we'd pick up bagels and coffee to bring home. Mom would always have some egg concoction warming in the oven.

"Sounds great." Dad briefly makes eye contact with Lauren. "Maybe soon."

In the back of my mind, I know it would be kind to compliment the new house, be friendly toward my soon-to-be stepsiblings. Yes, that would make me more likable and please my father, but it would also make me a phony. I don't care what else happens, but this divorce won't turn me into a phony.

I load my hot dog with onion, mustard, and ketchup, and eat it without saying much. It's awkward as anything, but it's all I can do not to break out in a flop sweat. I wish I weren't so worked up, but all the friction is firing through me like electricity.

"Is there any plan for the day?" I ask once I've swallowed my food. "I mean, there doesn't need to be, but I don't know. This is like . . . strange. Right?"

My dad reaches out for my hand. "It won't always be strange."

I withdraw. He's not sorry about any of it. Is sex with Lauren really worth blowing up our family? For a wild second, I almost blurt my question. Luckily, I don't. But I see him—too well. He wants me to make this easy for him, but all I want is to go back to the time when it was Mom and Dad and me.

Brody giggles at something on the screen. My mom never allows devices at the table.

Before Dad takes another bite of his burger, he asks, "Did you bring a bathing suit? Maybe we can relax by the pool for a while. You can tell me about the new school and your classes."

Zoe dances in her seat. "Mommy, can Megan come over to swim?"

"Not today, honey. We're having a family day." Lauren smiles at my dad and then me.

I can't believe I don't combust on the spot. It's bad enough when my mom pretends that everything is fine, but Lauren is a phony bitch and I seriously want to smoosh her face.

"Mommy, please," Zoe whines. "You promised I could have a sleepover this week but you keep saying no."

"Zoe, stop. We talked about this already." Lauren makes a "serious mom" face.

Zoe persists, and, I admit, I like her moxie. She points at me. "She won't care if I have a friend here."

"That's true. I don't care." I really don't. In fact, it might take some of the pressure off me.

"See!" Zoe's face brightens as she claps vigorously. "Please, Mommy."

I keep waiting for my dad to jump in like the hammer he always is, but he shrugs, leaving the decision to Lauren. Wait till my mom hears this. Actually, I won't tell. It'd only upset her.

"Let's clean up lunch and swim for a while, and we can talk about it later," Lauren concedes.

Zoe looks self-satisfied, so I bet she knows her mom will give in. I stand to help clear the table and put things away, which doesn't take more than five minutes. When we finish, I grab my bag. "So where am I sleeping?"

"I'll show you your room." Dad steers me around the island and back to the stairwell in the front of the house. "You have your own bathroom, so you don't have to share with the kids."

"Thanks." That's a bonus.

We get to "my" room, which is pretty bland. One narrow floor-to-ceiling window gives me a partial view of the backyard and pool. The walls are—wait for it—gray, but the bedding is a mix of creams, grays, and lavender. Tasteful, but no personality. Neither Lauren nor Dad ever asked me what I might like. A clear signal that this is "the guest room," not *my* bedroom.

"Meet you at the pool?" Dad asks.

I nod. "I'll be down once I change."

He gives me another hug and musses my hair. "I'm glad you're here, Katy."

He waves as he closes the door behind him.

I can't escape the gigantic mirror as I unzip my bag. Staring at it, I think about something my dad told me in one of his zillion lectures about success and getting what you want. *"Katy, when it comes to people, the key to every successful negotiation is knowing what the other person needs, and what they fear. Don't assume that if you give someone what they need, they'll go along. To clinch it, you show them that if they don't do as you suggest, then they will end up with what they fear."*

I want my dad to leave Lauren and come home. But does my dad fear anything, and can I use that? It's manipulative, but he's the one who taught me to think that way, so he can't exactly get mad if I turn it on him. For now, I'll spend the day looking for ways to remind Dad what he's missing by choosing this family over ours. I'll even play in the pool with Zoe and Brody so I can't be accused of sabotaging anything. Eventually I'll find a crack to exploit.

Energized by my plan, I pull gym shorts over my bikini bottoms and leave my bag on the bed to unpack later.

My dad is the only one at the pool. He's finishing a lap, and when he stands in the shallow end, water sluices down his shoulders.

"Where's everybody?"

Dad climbs out of the pool and dries himself with a towel before sitting on one of the patio chairs. "Lauren's getting the kids' suits on."

"Oh." I sit at the edge of the pool and dangle my legs in the cool water. It's a great big pool—almost black-looking water, with an infinity edge that overlooks the sloping backyard.

"Now talk to me. Aside from the nonsense with the pot smoking, how are you?" Dad pulls a foot up over his knee and crosses his arms. Down to business.

"Fine." I kick the water.

"Katy . . ." He waits for me to look up. "I'm serious. How are you handling the move, the new team, the new school?"

The fire ignites in my gut. "Can we talk about something else?"

"Why? Are you keeping something from me?" His foot hits the ground, and he leans forward in his chair.

"No, but I know you want to hear that everything is awesome so you don't have to feel bad about being happy here." I snap my mouth shut, having said too much already. I look away, blinking back stupid tears.

"Do you honestly think I'm moving on with no regrets?" His voice is deceptively calm.

"Looks like it to me," I mumble, still averting my eyes. And to Mom, I bet, but I don't say it.

"Is that what your mother is feeding you?" His tone sharpens.

"No!" That sucks, so I scowl at him. "Except for the time in the car, Mom never talks about you or Lauren with me. She tells me only that I have to be nice to and get along with Lauren. She said that even *after* Lauren called her to complain about me."

"Lauren called your mother?" His brows go up.

Ooh. There's a crack! "Yes. She was worried I'd bring 'drugs' to the house."

"And your mother told you this because . . . ?"

"I walked in on it. Mom was yelling, so I heard the tail end of the conversation."

Dad glances toward the house but says nothing. "When you're older, you'll understand all this better. For now, just know that I'm very sorry that you're paying for the mistakes your mom and I made in our marriage."

"Just not sorry enough to change your mind." I pout. I shouldn't but I can't help it. I don't know what mistakes my mom made—other than getting pregnant and choosing to keep me. They've always said that was a mutual decision and that they wanted to get married, but I'm not an idiot. Anyway, Mom didn't cheat. He did.

He looks at the ground. "It's not that simple, Katy. I love Lauren. And if you give her a chance, I think you'll come to like her."

I slip into the pool and under the water. The quiet helps. I don't want to talk about this anymore, so I focus on how the water glides over my skin, and on the little bubbles tickling me as I slither into a somersault before bursting through the surface for air.

Dad's still there, and Lauren and her kids haven't come back yet. "Tell me about your classes. How do they stack up against Prep?"

"I thought it'd be a lot easier, but it's not. It's about the same. There are just more kids in my classes."

"So your grades are good?"

"It's only been two weeks, but I got a one hundred on my AP Gov PowerPoint. Wanna see it?" At least in this he'll be proud.

His eyes gleam as his expression relaxes. "Sure."

"It's on my laptop." I push myself out of the water and towel off. "Be right back."

After wrapping the towel around me like a dress, I head back inside and up to the guest room. The door is partway closed, but when I push it open, Lauren is by my bed, going through my bag.

"What are you doing?" I snatch it from her hands.

Her cheeks turn red. "I'm sorry, Katy, but I was checking for drugs."

I. Can't. Even.

"You have no right to go through my things," I shriek.

"Please lower your voice." Lauren walks over to close the door. "I shouldn't have sneaked behind your back. That was wrong, but this is my house and I will not allow drugs where my kids could stumble upon them."

"My mom already told you there wouldn't be any drugs."

"I couldn't take her word for it." Her arms are straight at her sides. She's unnaturally calm, unlike my parents.

"You think she'd lie and put your kids at risk?" I fight the urge to push her. "*She's* not the liar. *You're* the one who can't be trusted."

Lauren holds up one hand, speaking quietly. "I'm not going to argue with you about things you don't understand."

"Oh, I understand just fine. You want to pretend you didn't get with my dad while he was married, but what you did was selfish and low. At least admit that much." I'm screaming so loud, spittle flies from my mouth.

My dad barrels through the door. "What the hell is going on? Zoe is downstairs crying."

"I caught Lauren snooping through my bags." I throw my bag back at her chest. "Here. Finish the job. Sorry to disappoint you, but you won't find any drugs."

As if I'd risk that after her call to Mom and my coach's warning.

"Katy, calm down." My dad grabs my shoulders, but I shrug away.

"Why should I calm down? She's the one who violated my privacy. Is that supposed to make me feel welcome?" I stare at him, my jaw clamped tight.

"Of course you're welcome here, Katy." My dad turns his back to Lauren after giving her a hard look. His pinched brow reveals his conflict, and his voice is dangerously even. "Lauren's being overprotective. She's worried for her kids' safety. It's not personal."

Lauren looks upset that my dad isn't happy. She drops my bag back on the bed without completing her search. "I've already apologized. I should've spoken with you directly, not gone through your things. That was disrespectful. And this is your dad's house, so you're always welcome here, Katy."

I glance from her to my dad and back, then shake my head. "You know what, that's bull. This room doesn't reflect anything about me— there's not even a photograph of me in here or anywhere. I've never even been given a key, so don't pretend this is my house or room. I'm a guest here, like anyone else. Coming was a huge mistake." I start throwing my things back in my bag. "I'm going home."

"Katy, stop. Please. We have to work through rough patches," my dad says.

"Like you did with Mom?" I spit out.

Calmness lights Lauren's face—proof that I just threw away my upper hand with that insult—but I don't even care. My chest hurts as if a thousand elephants are stampeding across it. I jerk the zipper shut. "If you want to spend time with me, come to *me*."

I storm across the room, hoping to brush past my dad, but he catches me. "Katy, slow down. Don't go . . . . You can't drive like this."

For a few seconds I'm dazed. He's not hugging me and apologizing. He's not insisting I stay. And he sure isn't yelling at Lauren. He's letting me go, just like I've feared all along. Razors of pain shred my lungs as hot tears tumble down my cheeks. I don't look at him, don't say a word, just jerk free and pound down the stupid floating staircase without looking back.

I throw my bag in the passenger seat and with shaky hands fire up the ignition, screeching backward out of the driveway. I don't remember the drive home because all I do is think about how I've ruined everything.

I'm so stupid. I didn't listen to my mom, and now my dad is probably relieved I took off. He calls twice, but I don't answer. What would I even say? "Sorry I'm the big mistake you're stuck with for the rest of your life"? Meanwhile, Lauren probably spent the last hour or whatever convincing him that I'm the problem. I'm too much trouble. But she caused this. She's pushing me right out of the picture with everything she does, and he doesn't even care.

I run into the house, grateful that my mom's car isn't there. Once I'm in my room, I thrash around, pounding on my furniture and then my thigh, trying to make the pain go away. On my desk lies the pocketknife my parents gave me last summer for my Outward Bound trip in Colorado.

Collapsing onto the chair, I then flick the little blades and scissors open and shut, remembering how good it felt when I dug my nails into my arm earlier this week. Sunlight glints off the blade, like it had off the water in my dad's pool where he and his new family are enjoying the afternoon. My phone vibrates, but I ignore it. Probably him again.

A fat tear slides down my cheek. My heart is beating so hard it might crack a rib. I could do it. It wouldn't hurt that much. But if I do, I can't undo it. I'll have a scar. A reminder. Someone else might see it and judge me.

Maybe just once is okay. It will help . . . I'll feel better.

I slide my fingertip along the knife blade, determined despite strained, rapid breaths. Maybe the scissor blade is less risky. I don't know. I don't want to die; I just want relief.

My hands tremble as I extend my left arm and hold the blade against the inside of my forearm.

No. Too hard to hide there. I don't want to wear long-sleeved shirts all year long.

Getting high usually numbed the pain, but I'll be kicked off the team if I'm caught smoking again. This is safer and quicker.

I move the blade higher on the inside of my biceps, just below my armpit. My breath is heavy, chest heaving rapidly. Oh God. Am I really going to do this?

Before I overthink it, I clench my left fist and slash my upper arm with the blade.

Ah!

It stings at first, angry blood oozing down my biceps. Then a bloom of relief—euphoria-like—takes over. I'm floating outside my body, filled with peace as my brain quiets down. It's so good. I can breathe without pain. I'm in control and calm . . . It's better.

I drop the blade on the desk and stare at the cut. When that immediate sense of ecstasy recedes, my mouth is agape with shame. New tears blur my vision. I grab some tissues to press against the wound, then throw them in the trash and run to the bathroom to wash away the disgrace.

The water is so hot it hurts my skin, but I want the punishment. Moments later, I think I hear my mom calling my name and stomping around, but it's more like a dream than reality. Especially with steam billowing all around.

I'm standing beneath the showerhead, crying quietly when my mom blows into the bathroom, shouting my name. She rips open the shower curtain, crying, the bloody pocketknife in her hand.

Our gazes lock, and I almost throw up as I choke out, "I'm sorry, Mom!"

"Oh, Katy!" She whimpers, shivering.

The knife clatters on the tile floor as she grabs me into a bear hug, both of us sobbing as water douses her and the bathroom floor.

CHAPTER FOURTEEN

ANNE

I can't stop shaking. Katy's bawling reverberates off all the tile, each sob a puncture to my heart. I don't want to let go of her, but the bathroom is flooding with water from the shower spout. "I love you, sweetie. I'm sorry you're hurting. I'm so sorry."

Tears gush down my cheeks. My breaths come in gulps as my thoughts alternate between fear and relief. When Richard called to tell me about the disastrous visit and Katy's refusal to answer his calls, I raced home expecting trouble . . . but not this. Never this.

I break away long enough to shut off the water, then yank a towel from the rack and wrap it around her, smoothing my hands over her head and her face while sending up silent prayers that she hadn't done worse to herself.

Her piercing blue eyes cloud and her features all crumple at once. "Don't tell Dad. Please, Mom. Please don't tell Dad."

She's bawling. I kick the knife at my feet aside before helping her safely step out of the tub. While she clings to my chest, I whisper, "Sh. Sh, sh, sh."

I kiss her wet head, wishing for the power to absorb all her pain so she would be free of its burden. My baby hurt herself on purpose.

That is so much bigger than anything I can understand and handle. And it's not something I can keep from Richard, no matter how much she pleads.

For years he's talked me out of hiring a therapist to help with Katy's anxiety. *"She's a teen,"* he'd say. *"All teens act like this."* I'd caved instead of trusting my gut. We're soaked in blood and water now because I didn't stand up to my husband.

When Katy's crying dissolves into hiccups, I guide her to the toilet and make her sit. Without saying a word, I raise her arm and inspect the cut. It's pretty superficial, thank God. No need for stitches, although it is about two inches long. After retrieving first-aid supplies from the vanity, I drop to my knees, dry the area surrounding the slash, apply antibiotic ointment, then cover it with a large, square Band-Aid.

Katy's body goes limp while she looks at everything but me. I reach for her face, cupping her cheek and then turning her chin until she can't avoid my gaze. "Can you stand?"

She nods, so I rise and lend her my arm, although I'm still wobbly.

"How about you put on some comfy clothes and then come downstairs. I'll make tea and we can order pasta for dinner." My heart continues to thump unevenly.

New tears spill from her eyes. "You're going to tell Dad, aren't you?" She hunches, shoulders quivering.

I clasp her biceps and briefly touch my forehead to hers. "We have to tell him, honey. He's your father. He's worried about you—that's why he called me."

Katy puckers her face before hanging her head, so I hug her again. I'm entirely out of my depth. The only parenting tool I can access is to hold on tight and pray we both make it through this storm. "It'll be okay. We'll figure this out together, I promise. Tonight, try to relax. Can you do that?"

"Are you ashamed of me?" Her voice cracks.

"No!" I shake my head. "Never. I'm scared and I ache for you, but I'm not ashamed. You are my *everything*, Katy. My star and angel. My light and heart. If anything, I'm upset with myself for underestimating your pain."

Katy's eyes reveal doubt, but she tugs the towel more tightly around her body and makes for the door. Once she disappears, I stoop to pick up the pocketknife. My daughter's blood turns the sink bowl pink as I rinse its blade. Fresh tears—hot and stinging—coat my eyes.

My gorgeous, talented girl was distraught and then harming herself while I was half flirting with Dan and enjoying my afternoon. Heavy loads of guilt climb all over my back, buckling my knees. I should've listened when she suggested putting off her visit. At the very least, I should've texted her to see how it was going.

What if she'd accidentally cut too deeply? I smooth my finger along the knife's edge, sick at the thought of her slicing her skin open. This is what happens when I take my eyes off her and do something for myself.

Once the blade is dry, I fold it together, then slip it into my pocket. Icy water cools my face but does nothing to reduce its splotchiness. I dry my eyes, then go to check on my daughter. Tapping at her door, I ask, "Are you okay?"

She opens it, wearing pajamas, and nods.

"Good." I touch her wet hair. "Would you still like pasta for dinner?"

She pulls back slightly, then twirls her hair in her fingers. "I'm not hungry."

I stroke her cheek to satisfy the instinct to touch her, as if reassuring myself that she is still here with me. "I know, but it's important to eat something. How about sushi?"

"Maybe just instant oatmeal," she says.

"Done. Dry your hair and grab your slippers, then join me downstairs. Maybe we can watch something on Netflix." I don't want to leave her alone for long.

"Okay." She doesn't ask for the knife back, which I take as a good sign.

I pad downstairs, dread rising because Richard's awaiting a call. After filling a bowl with water and oatmeal and popping it in the microwave, I dial my ex.

"She's home?" he asks without pleasantries.

"Yes. She was home when I arrived."

"Good. Now I can be angry."

"Not so fast, Richard." My voice wobbles, but I collect myself. "Katy cut herself."

"On what?" he asks, clearly not understanding what I'm telling him.

"She took the pocketknife we bought her and slashed the underside of her upper arm. I found her sobbing in the shower."

"Jesus Christ!" he booms. He always shouts when he's scared. It's not something I've seen often, as he doesn't scare easily, but for all his discipline and strength, he falls apart in a crisis. It sounds like he's pacing when he repeats himself. "Jesus Christ."

Well, if that's his idea of praying, we're out of luck.

"It's pretty superficial and she's calmed down, but I think it's time to take her to a therapist. She needs someone to talk to—a neutral professional whom she trusts." I hold my breath, bracing for blowback.

"You shouldn't have moved, Anne. It was too much too soon." His gruff judgment sets my teeth on edge, but I close my eyes and count to three.

How can I argue when I've wondered the same thing? But even before the move, Katy struggled with her emotions. Whatever transpired earlier today brought everything to a head. "It's more complicated than that, Richard. I've warned you for years that this is a deep-seated issue." My thoughts shift to the possibility that Gram spent time in a psychiatric facility because of something that happened with *her* father. "Tell me exactly what happened at your house."

While I take the oatmeal out of the microwave and grab a spoon, he pauses long enough to suggest he's not blameless.

"Dammit . . ." It sounds like he's scrubbing his neck or face with one hand. "It was going okay, but then Katy caught Lauren searching her suitcase for drugs."

"What?" My body flashes hot, then cold, while a roar gathers in my chest. How dare she!

"She was worried that Zoe or Brody could stumble upon them. But she knows she handled the situation badly and apologized."

Handled it badly—is that all she thinks? My exploding thoughts override most of whatever else he's blabbering. "I told Lauren there wouldn't be any drugs."

"Katy mentioned that Lauren had called you. I'm sorry for that. I assure you, Lauren and I have discussed all of this, and neither of these things will happen again. You have my word."

Ever since he broke our vows, his word means nothing to me. "I want more than that, Richard. I don't want her around Katy. Not until Katy wants to see her."

"That could take months." He sounds panicked.

I don't care if it takes years. Our daughter shouldn't be subjected to someone she can't trust. "That's not Katy's fault. Lauren set off this spiral. Doesn't that matter to you?"

"Anne, I'm devastated, but it's not fair to lay all the blame on Lauren."

My entire body vibrates to the point where I nearly kick a chair and throw my phone. "Tell yourself whatever lets you sleep at night, but for the foreseeable future, find ways to see your daughter that don't involve your girlfriend. Take Katy away for a weekend. Have her visit when Lauren isn't around. I don't care. Work it out, but don't expect your child to open her arms to Lauren just because you want it to be easy." I draw a breath. "We're in crisis mode, Richard. We need to tread carefully and support Katy. Speaking of that, her school has an art show later this fall. Katy's idea for a family tree project will require both our help. It'd be nice if you'd get involved and make a point to come to her show. And I don't want any more arguments about getting her into therapy. In fact, we need family therapy, too."

I grab my head to stanch the throbbing. If only I'd forced these things years ago. All this time I'd convinced myself the only person hurt by my biting my tongue had been me.

He blows out a long breath. "Fine, but can we look for a therapist somewhere in between our towns? You know my schedule. If I have to come all the way down there, that'll take nearly three hours in round-trip drive time."

My spine softens with his unexpected acquiescence. I dab the tears in my eyes. "I'll do my best."

"Can I talk to Katy?"

"She's getting dressed." I sprinkle a touch of brown sugar and a handful of raisins on the oatmeal. "I'll have her call you later, but listen. She begged me not to tell you, Richard. She loves you yet is terrified of you, and she's convinced she's being replaced by Zoe and Brody. Whatever you do or say, please don't use shame or guilt. Just love her. Accept her, flaws and all."

"I do!"

My chin dips involuntarily. "Well, she doesn't always feel that way, and her perception is what matters." I hear Katy starting down the steps. "Keep your phone nearby."

"Okay."

"I'll get in touch once I find a therapist. Bye." I hang up and tuck my phone in my back pocket as Katy hits the bottom tread.

"Was that Dad?" She's as pale as her white terry cloth robe.

"Yes."

Her face scrunches up. "Is he furious?"

"He's concerned. He also told me what Lauren did today. I *totally* get your anger."

Her eyebrows rise above wide eyes. "You're not mad?"

"No." I hand her the bowl of oatmeal. "Let's sit on the couch."

She shuffles across the floor and plops cross-legged into one corner of the sofa, then reaches for the bowl. I sit beside her, letting her take two spoonfuls.

"Honey." I grip her knee. "I think we need to find a counselor."

"No!" Her shoulders droop along with her mouth. "I swear I won't do it again, Mom. Please don't make me a freak."

"Sweetheart, you're not a freak. But you obviously have big worries that neither Dad nor I are equipped to manage. I actually think we should *all* get advice learning how to be this new kind of family. Plus it'd be a huge help to have someone you trust teach you to manage your stress so this doesn't happen again." Tears form the instant I recall finding that bloody knife on her desk. "Katy, I don't know what I'd do if anything terrible ever happened to you. It terrifies me to think about what might've happened if that cut had been deeper. Please, honey."

She pushes the oatmeal around with the spoon, her eyes misty, her cheeks red. In a weepy voice, she asks, "What's wrong with me?"

I gently take the bowl from her and set it down before snuggling closer and pulling her head to my shoulder. "Nothing's *wrong* with you. But maybe you've always worked so hard to be perfect you've worn yourself thin, making the stress of this divorce and move harder to handle—and these things are never easy in the first place."

Katy mumbles, "Gee, wonder where I learned that?"

Oof. I'm pinned to the sofa by that dagger, mostly because it's laden with the weight of truth. There's some caustic irony: compensating to ensure Katy didn't end up with my issues has inadvertently pressured her into pursuing perfection. I close my eyes, defeated by that possibility. "Fair point. But all I've ever wanted was to give you what I didn't have—a parent who's fully invested in you. Not because I wanted you to be perfect, but because I hoped it'd help you to grow up secure and confident."

I ease back a bit to see her face.

"Sorry it didn't turn out like you expected. Just another way I've let you down." Her eyes are dewy as she presses at the Band-Aid on her arm.

I hold her tight again. "I *never* said you let me down."

"You don't have to, Mom." She pulls away. "You and Dad both think I'm some kind of superstar. I'll never live up to that."

"Honey, we never meant to make you feel like that. We only get excited about your potential. It's supposed to be a compliment. The sky is the limit for you."

"Stop," she warns.

"I'm sorry. I don't know what to say. I'm scared. But attacking me doesn't change what's happening inside you."

We sit in silence while she sniffles. I'm fending off self-loathing, but it's difficult. I should've fought harder to better address her anxieties sooner.

Suddenly a bitter laugh threatens to explode. I beat myself up for mistakes exactly like she does. Is that learned behavior or a genetic tendency? Either way, I can't stop my daughter from doing it when I can't even stop myself.

If she's subliminally mirroring me, then my interactions with Richard these past months might be tearing her in two.

"I have a question, and please be honest. Do you feel pressured to dislike Lauren for my sake?" I hate Lauren and, in my heart of hearts, do not want her to be close to my daughter. But *my* petty jealousy shouldn't be foisted upon my child. When Katy doesn't answer, I add, "No matter how I feel, you should form your opinions based on how she treats you. Don't start off hating her out of loyalty to me, or because she hurt me."

"But she didn't just hurt you. She screwed up my life, too," Katy moans.

"She crossed some lines, which makes her an easy target." A target I love to hit again and again because that's easier than admitting to the more complicated nuances in my marriage, as if refusing to examine them closely will keep them from hurting me. "The truth is, somewhere along the way, your dad and I stopped making each other a priority. I wish we both would've worked on that before it was too late, but we didn't. I might not have been the one to walk away, but I have to take some blame for our breakup, too." There. I said it aloud, and it didn't kill me.

She picks at fuzz on her robe, absorbed in her own thoughts. The way her eyelids twitch and narrow tells me she's forming a plan. Richard taught her how to strategize, and I'm not sure I like it much.

"If Dad realizes that he made a mistake, would you take him back?" Hopefulness floods her eyes.

For a fleeting moment I consider lying because I'm terrified that she might hurt herself if there's no chance.

"I'd be tempted to for *your* sake, honey." I kiss her head again in a lame effort to dry her tears. "But while there are things about your father that I'll always admire, we weren't making each other happy, and that's not good for us or for you."

She slumps. "Now holidays and vacations and birthdays will always be a little sad."

I nod, my nose and eyes clogging with tears. "I'm sorry. But I promise I'll be flexible. It won't upset me when you want to spend some of them with your dad."

In truth, that will kill me, but she shouldn't have to take on my pain.

"Why should you spend a holiday alone when he's the one who did this? Let him spend the holidays with his new family." She scowls.

I shake my head. "You're here with me every day for the next two years. It's important that you stay connected to your dad. Even when you're mad at him." I abhor the parallels between her and Richard and my father and me. At least I had my grandparents' affection. What man can Katy count on to embrace her just as she is? "Speaking of your dad, he's waiting to hear from you."

She throws her head back and flings her arms over her eyes. "This sucks so bad."

"You know what I always say . . . Do the sucky thing first so you can relax the rest of the evening. Call now. I'll give you some privacy."

She stares at her phone while I take her half-eaten bowl and rinse it in the sink, giving her some privacy.

Instead of cleaning up, I exit the house through the french doors and squint in the face of an orange sun hanging low in the sky. A cool breeze feathers across my skin, teasing the hairs on my arms. After gathering some dried leaves and brush, I grab a few fatwoods from the bin and select three nice logs to tent above it all.

Before I go inside to get a lighter and the marshmallow sticks, I give myself a moment to cry. Warm tears flow, carrying the fear that seized me when I found that knife, the acidic burn Katy's spilled blood imprinted on my heart, the exhaustion of trying and failing to be a good mother.

The forested back edge of the property shrouds me in privacy with an added magical quality, as if woodland fairies are lurking, whispering secrets I'll never understand. Gram's secrets. Secrets about life and love and parenting. Secrets about happiness. I wipe my cheeks dry. Behind me, the babbling fountain helps me to relax.

Landscape lighting will turn on soon, highlighting an abundance of ornamental grasses, goldenrods, irises, peonies, gladiolas, and hydrangeas that furnish a riot of colors and scents that rivals any resort. It may not be the grand three-acre lot and massive gunite pool we left behind, but this space gives me peace.

Feeling stronger, I duck inside to grab the s'mores supplies, shaking them in the air to entice Katy outside after she's finished her conversation.

Thank God for fatwoods. Within a few minutes, a healthy fire blazes in the firepit. Later the fireflies will glow like festive golden Christmas lights floating around the yard. With each chirp from the cicadas, my muscles relax enough for me to stretch my legs out in front of the fire. The smoky aroma lulls me.

Memories from youth arise—time spent sketching back here. The pounds of burgers Grandpa, Gram, and I ate. The times I'd argued the genius of Alanis Morissette or taught them the Macarena.

They were always good dancers, and I could tell Alanis's lyrics intrigued Gram, although she wouldn't admit it. Another secret facet of Gram I never took the time to understand.

Earlier today she'd remembered me. I'd almost asked her about Allcot, but then she'd looked at me with such affection I couldn't bear to ruin the beautiful moment between us. It might be one of our last.

I blink back the tears brimming and stretch again.

So much history in this yard. If the trees could talk, what story would they tell? What did they witness as they stood sentry, watching over generations of Robsons and Sullivans? Could that history teach me anything about how to navigate this frightening time in my life, or am I doomed to end up like my father and Gram, alone and not all that happy?

CHAPTER FIFTEEN

ANNE

My eyes burn from too little sleep.

I dribble syrup over the stack of toaster waffles and set them in front of Katy, suppressing the urge to tear her robe off and check her arms and legs for more damage. The knife is hidden, but after spending hours scouring the internet last night to research cutting, I learned that she can use dozens of household items—thumbtacks, pen caps, razors, carpet staples—to do the job. At some point today I need to collect as many of these items as possible to remove the temptation.

Whenever I close my eyes, I'm bombarded by the images uncovered during my research. So many children. So many scars. So many chat boards stuffed with messages from frantic parents seeking help.

I count myself lucky to have caught this at the beginning, and to not have a demanding career splitting my attention now. Preventing my daughter's further self-harm is my absolute priority. Yet I long to return to those pleasant hours yesterday when I'd shopped and met new friends and daydreamed about painting. That glimpse of what my life could be—the mirage—has all but vanished.

Katy needs me more than I need those things right now.

"What would you like to do today?" I sit beside her with my coffee and gently sweep one hand over her head. Research taught me that distracting cutters with pleasant activities is a useful tactic. "We could go shopping—I found some cute stores in town. Or we could go to a hip little coffee shop I tried yesterday. If you'd rather stay home, maybe you'd like to start working on your project for the art show? We could dig around the attic looking for old photo albums."

"I don't want to do anything." She doesn't look at me, choosing to focus on the stack of waffles. A million questions about what she said to Richard yesterday crowd my thoughts, but I won't pry.

My muscles and brain ache from the weight of worry that has been building since finding that bloody blade on her desk. "Sweetie, it's a gorgeous fall day. Let's find one activity that gets us out of the house for a bit."

She closes her eyes with a sigh. "I just want to be alone for a while."

It's humbling to want to spend time with someone who'd be happier if you'd disappear. I am sixteen again, sitting at the dinner table, trying to hold my father's attention. Or, more recently, thirty-six and seeking to recapture Richard's.

Yesterday Katy begged me to let her feel however she felt. I could test that out—leave her alone to wallow or think or zone out. God, that feels wrong, but maybe *I'm* what's wrong.

I sit back, staring at my plate, debating with myself. It's like running a gauntlet. Does she really want me to go, or is she pushing me away to test my love? I can't tell. In fact, I don't know anything right now except that my head aches. "You could . . . or maybe we could do some yoga first?"

Katy sips the milk I poured. She slants me a look. "Being stared at and pretending to be in a good mood doesn't sound relaxing."

"That's not what I'm suggesting. But can't we find *something* to smile about?"

She sets down her silverware and frowns. "Why is smiling better than feeling what I feel? Yesterday sucked. Lauren sucks, too. I never want to see her again, so tell me how lattes, shoe shopping, or old photos will change that, or how faking happiness will make Dad dump Lauren."

Her anger paralyzes me. The more I encourage her to let it go and forgive, the worse her mood becomes. It's fricking disheartening, that's what it is. She wants to be treated like a grown-up? Fine. "Okay. Pout and grumble and scream every ugly thing you can think of to say about them. You're entitled to your feelings and to act on them however you want. But just know that nothing you do or don't do will make your father leave Lauren. For what it's worth, I don't think plotting some kind of sabotage is healthy."

"But it's fair. After what she did—to you *and* by invading my privacy—she deserves it. I thought about it all night, and it still makes me so mad." Katy wraps a white-knuckled fist around her fork, so I lay my hand on hers to get her to relax.

"Who ever said life was fair?" Certainly not my parents or grandparents. Frankly, they preached the opposite.

Katy's eyes practically pop out of her skull. "You're *always* telling me to be fair."

I shake my head, thinking about how to parse my words. "Having integrity and learning to compromise isn't a promise that the world will be fair, but at least you'll always respect who you see in the mirror. *That's* priceless."

An eye roll so dramatic it might've stripped paint from the ceiling quickly dashes any motherly pride I got from sharing that nugget of wisdom.

We're both irked at this point, so I might as well go for broke. "I did some digging last night and found a good therapist in Morningside. I'll speak with your father today to get his schedule so I can make a family appointment."

Katy's shoulders fall and her brows bunch together with a scowl. "Why do we have to make a whole thing out of this? I swear I won't do it again. Please, Mom. Dad will hate wasting his time on therapy."

"Your well-being isn't a waste of our time. It's our primary goal, for God's sake." If Richard could only hear the dread his disapproval inspires.

"Maybe I wouldn't be a basket case if you didn't hover all the time. Did you think of *that*?" she barks.

"Stop it, Katy." My voice remains steady even though I'm shaken. Jesus, she's like Richard with her sharp, shrewd mind. "You might be right, but that doesn't mean you should be disrespectful or use it to manipulate me into blowing off what happened yesterday. If anything, you should be glad we're *all* going for help. Maybe the therapist will help me parent you better."

Katy shoves back from the table, glaring at me while she snatches her plate and proceeds to stomp upstairs to her room. A slammed door punctuates her unspoken sentiment.

I sink my forehead to the table with a thud. Can I acquire a whole new set of parenting tools this late in the game?

Many years ago, my dad warned that parenting is a thankless job. It insulted me at the time, but now I get it. You do the best you can in any given moment, having no idea if any of it is working or will turn out all right in the end. End? There's no finish line, and no one is handing out gold medals.

Katy's resentment hurts. Her perceptions might not be 100 percent correct, but her feelings matter. They're her experience, and I don't want to do anything that makes her life harder. Which leaves me up in the air. I am crushed to discover that, in addition to needing to figure out how to be a single, middle-aged woman, I'm not nearly the parent I'd hoped to be.

Despite the mess on the table, I refill my teacup and take my phone outside to the patio, where the sunshine and birdsong might lift my spirits. With great effort, I consciously relax the muscles in my face to erase my scowl.

I need advice but can't count on Gram to be lucid. If my mom had lived, she would probably know what to do. She was wonderful . . .

With more hope than expectation, I dial my father.

"Hello?" Now that he's sixty-five, his deep voice is accented by a slight warble.

"Hey, Dad, it's me." I prop my feet up on the table, crossing them at the ankles.

"Oh, hi, Anne. How are you?"

If only he *wanted* to hear the truth. This is a mistake. Suddenly aware that I might start to hate him if I tell him about Katy's pain and he remains as disinterested in consolation as he was with me at her age, I don't give him the chance to let me down. "Fine. You?"

"Fine."

A pause.

Conversations like this make me curious about what made my mom fall in love. Sure, he's attractive and smart. He's enjoyed a steady career, and my mom never suffered the indignity of a husband's wandering eye and restlessness. But Dad doesn't do sparkling conversation or warmth—at least not that I remember.

When he doesn't ask a single question, I say, "I've visited Gram a couple of times."

"That's nice of you. The cleanliness of that facility impressed me when I checked her in."

"It's antiseptic." I twist my teacup in a circle on the table, frowning. "She's confused me with Lonna at times."

"Well, that's not a surprise. Dementia is tricky."

"Hmm." He sounds like we're discussing a distant cousin's welfare, not his mother's. "You know, you should come see what I've done to the old house. You could catch one of Katy's tournaments, we could visit Gram . . ."

"Maybe. I'll look at my calendar."

"Oh, Dad." I pull a Katy and roll *my* eyes. "Do I have to beg you to find some time? There's been a lot of upheaval in my life, in Katy's, and in Gram's." My stomach clenches in the face of his indifference, then drops when it occurs to me that pleading for paternal support might be part of what Katy hoped to kill by cutting herself. I curl forward, sickened that my daughter is following in my footsteps. What's becoming clearer is that I need to make many changes before I can think of helping my daughter.

"Sorry, Anne. You handled a bigger loss than Richard at a much younger age, so I've assumed you were pushing through this divorce just fine."

Pushing through is not the same as thriving. I don't know that I'm fine at all, or if I've ever been fine since they covered my mom's casket with earth. I'm shaking with frustration. "What about Gram? She's losing touch with reality every day. Don't you want to see her before she has no idea who you are?"

He sighs sharply. "I don't think my mother ever knew who I was, nor I her. She was better with you than she ever was with me. I'd rather keep my few good memories than end our relationship on a sadder note."

That comment flattens my heart.

"Maybe Gram wasn't the ideal mom for you, but she showed up every day and raised you. She did her best. Doesn't that count for anything?" I stop short of throwing his old warning about the thanklessness of parenting in his face.

It makes me wonder, though, if it isn't so much about the things you do as a mother, but the way they are received. Gram seemed like a great parent to me, but maybe she and I were a lot alike, so I understood her motives. Likewise, my parenting might work for some kids, but sadly not my own.

So where does that leave me? Do I need to change everything about myself to be a good mother for Katy, or is there nothing I can do that will make her like and appreciate me and my intentions? I'm so damn confused at this point I can hardly breathe.

There is an interminable pause before my father speaks. "I'll check my calendar. Promise. But I do have other commitments—out-of-town seminars and such."

"I'll text you Katy's art show date. At least promise to come for that." I shake my head, doubting I'll get a call unless I follow up. "Before you hang up, I have a question. Did Gram ever mention the name Billy? Or Allcot?"

"Not that I recall. Why?"

Damn. I fudge a little, preferring not to hit him with theories about first loves and hospitalization without facts. "These names have come up when I've visited. I know it could be nothing, but they sound important to her. I googled Allcot. There was a sanatorium by that name that closed down in the late seventies."

"Not ringing a bell."

"So you never heard anything about Gram going there, or saw her take medication?"

He's quiet for a moment. "When I was young, she'd lapse into moodiness and forgetfulness. My dad would tell me to be patient because she'd been through a lot. But he never gave me details, so I stopped asking."

If Gram was moody, she'd hidden that from me. Or, rather, maybe by the time I came around, she'd gotten over whatever it was that had troubled her when she'd been younger. I wish I had a diagnosis to share with Katy's therapist.

"So you've never learned more?" I prod.

"You can only knock at a closed door so many times . . ." He sighs. "Maybe Emily knows more."

Emily is one of my father's cousins—Lonna's eldest daughter, with whom Lonna was particularly close. I haven't seen or been in touch with

Emily or the other relatives since the family celebrated Gram's eightieth birthday. "Does she still live in Florida?"

"Far as I know."

I swallow my frustration, but only because I, too, could've kept in touch if it'd been important to me. The truth is that Emily can be a ferocious braggart, especially about her kids and grandkids. Still, it's discomforting to realize I'm a little bit like my dad when it comes to keeping in touch with family.

"Well . . ." I fish for something neutral to talk about. "What's going on with you? Thinking of retirement yet?"

"No." He chuckles. "What would I do with myself?"

He enjoys his work. It defines him in every way. Much like Richard. If I'd chosen to be like them instead of emulating my mother and Gram, would Katy be better off now? Would I?

"Golf? Travel? Maybe date around?" He's had two girlfriends since my mother died. Lynn had coaxed a ring from him, but then she backed out in the eleventh hour. Years later, he met Didi, who became a nice companion for another decade, but then she moved to California to be close to her grandkids. My father has been alone since then.

"Eh, I like to be productive."

That's the truth, although he's also pretty frugal.

"Well, I'll text you that art show date. It's important to me, Dad. I'd like us to rally around Katy. She's having a hard time with the divorce." There. I've laid myself bare. I want my dad to show up for us this one time.

"Okay, Anne. I'll be sure to come for that."

I release my breath. "Thank you."

"Sure. Take care."

Take care. Not *love you, miss you, can't wait to see you*.

I stopped expecting hugs and teasing from my dad by the age of ten, yet sometimes I still yearn for a show of affection. Richard isn't stoic like my father, but his way of loving can feel conditional. I've worked hard to offset that for Katy, but it doesn't seem to have made a difference. It didn't help my relationship with Richard, either. And the fact that I'm stewing in regret on my patio by myself proves it didn't do me any favors.

I stand and stretch, but nothing releases the weight in my chest. For all I know, Katy is inside right now finding some other instrument to carve up her skin. Happiness seems so out of reach in the face of all the changes we must make.

Effective therapy will require our full participation. Richard can't cooperate begrudgingly. Biting the bullet, I dial his number.

"Good morning, Anne. How's Katy?"

"Bitter. Unhappy. Challenging . . ." But snark doesn't make it less real.

A silent beat allows us both to take a breath before he speaks. "At the risk of starting an argument, have you considered keeping that little house as a summer place and renting a condo up here for two years so she can return to her old school? I think that would help."

My teeth hurt from clenching my jaw so tight. "Or you could slow down your race to the altar."

"That's not the same thing."

"It *is*. My moving here hasn't been any harder on Katy than your becoming a father to new children so fast. She feels like she's losing you. And don't get me started on Lauren." I tell myself that Katy's living with me in this small town is healthier than staying in the pressure cooker up there with Richard and his new family. But what if I'm wrong?

"Fine, Anne. I don't want to fight with you. For fuck's sake, I'd thought this bickering would end when we got divorced."

His framing our marriage that way makes me want to cry. We did bicker more often in recent years. Our marriage might've been happier if I hadn't set aside all my own ambitions in the service of my family. If I'd had gallery events and interesting friends, the balance of power between Richard and me would've been more equal and Katy would've had more than one example of success to consider. Hindsight is seriously kicking my ass lately. "I don't want to fight, either. Therapy should help us all communicate better. I found a reputable doctor in Morningside."

Another interminable pause has me chewing the inside of my cheek.

"I spent all night staring at the ceiling considering this," he begins. "Don't you think therapists create as many problems as they solve—handing kids pills like they're passing out Smarties? We're smart. We can read up on this and figure it out."

If it weren't maddening, his hubris would amuse me.

"Between your career and your new family, exactly when do you plan to become an expert in child psychology, too? I've read every parenting book on the planet, and that hasn't helped one bit. And now I'm here on my own, so I can count on even less help from you on a daily basis. This has reached dangerous levels that neither of us is equipped to handle. Especially not now that I suspect my gram might've had some kind of mental breakdown before my father was born."

"Where's this coming from?"

I rub my face. "We found some memorabilia during the renovation, and when I questioned Gram, she mentioned some weird stuff . . ."

"She's got dementia," he scoffs. "It's probably all nonsense."

"It's possible that she's blending her memories with those of people close to her. But it fits with the melancholy my dad always spoke about. I'm still investigating, but I'll feel better after a doctor diagnoses Katy and explains why she's turned to self-harm. Katy doesn't want my advice, but she might engage with a professional. Someone who keeps her confidences. A dispassionate adviser who won't judge her. Please, Richard. We can't afford to take any chances."

Did I hear a sniffle? "You're right."

"Thank you. If you send me a handful of dates and times when you're available in the next two weeks, I'll set up a family appointment."

"Okay. I'll check with Lauren, too. She has a closing coming up—"

Horror pries my jaw open. "What's Lauren's schedule got to do with anything?"

"She's part of this family now, too."

My heart turns to ice. "She's also part of the problem, and Katy's not ready to see her yet."

"We're the adults. If Lauren is part of the problem, then she needs to be part of the solution."

"Down the road, yes. But our first appointment should be private. Katy's raw and she doesn't trust or like Lauren. I assume you told her about the cutting . . ."

"She won't share it with anyone, but she had to be informed." The edge in his voice suggests they had their first real fight over all this. Will this fine crack in their relationship splinter or seal?

Seems I still hate my husband's mistress-soon-to-be-wife, but for once that doesn't make me feel like the bad guy. "Katy will be mortified."

He huffs. "I'm doing the best I can juggling Lauren, her kids, my firm, and now all Katy's trouble."

"No one said parenting was easy, but we all have to deal with the commitment we took on. You're a senior partner now, so you should be able to move your schedule around."

"You've never appreciated how hard I work or the personal sacrifices I made for our family." The truth is that, at first, his work ethic made me proud. But as time went on, I began to resent his career as if *it* were the other woman in our lives. Then he'd accuse me of nagging, when all I'd ever wanted was more family time. "You and Katy have both benefited from my success."

"Until it cost us everything that mattered." I pat my hot, damp face, embarrassed by the confession. "I know you don't see it that way, but that's how I feel. We were happier when we had less."

Surprisingly, he doesn't argue. There's some commotion behind his end of the line. "I'll send you dates later and check in with Katy this afternoon."

"I'm sure she'll appreciate that. Bye." I set the phone on the table, heavy from the high cost of all our mistakes.

My tea is ice-cold, and scudding clouds have rolled in off the bay. With my eyes closed, I indulge the dangerous, wistful what-if: What if I hadn't gotten pregnant at twenty and married Richard? I might be an artist, living in Northern California with an interesting, eclectic group of friends. Might've experienced myriad lovers, too. The fantasy shimmers like pixie dust for a few seconds, but then the idea of life without Katy blows through to scatter that glitter. No career or fame or lust would eclipse being her mother. Not even with all the hurt and anger and anxiety flooding my system.

There must be some way to turn this around. My thoughts drift to my grandpa and the advice he would've offered, like the time he came out of his shed and found me crying under the maple tree because Tori Decker had taunted me at the town pool by stealing my sketch pad and showing it to the other girls while laughing at me.

Being an outsider and somewhat of an introverted preteen had made it difficult to form friendships. But that wasn't what hurt most—I didn't even want to be Tori's friend because she never struck me as kind. Her poking at my drawings, though—the place where I'd poured all my pain and joy—planted doubts when there'd been none. Rejection is a part of art, but my first critic being so wicked to my face in public was a breathtaking moment I've never forgotten. She'd planted seeds that sprouted with my early career's failure to thrive.

My gaze settles on that neglected shed, which remains in the corner of the yard because I couldn't bring myself to tear down that last reminder of Grandpa. He and I had cleared cobwebs and stored patio furniture in there at the end of each summer. The mundane memory swathes my heart in warmth, then inspiration strikes.

It was here that my grandparents handed me paper and paints as an outlet for my complicated emotions. Art saved me then, and it might help me now.

It might even help my daughter, too.

CHAPTER SIXTEEN

ANNE

Richard is working on his tablet beside me when Katy returns to the waiting room after her introductory session with Dr. Grant. I tap his arm while smiling at our daughter. Hope as fragile as soap bubbles fills my lungs. "Hi, honey. How'd it go?"

"Did you like Dr. Grant?" Richard slips his tablet into its case.

Katy shrugs. "She wants to talk to you guys."

Richard sighs.

As subtly as possible, I elbow his side. "Oh good. I'm eager for her help."

Katy's mouth pinches. "Yippee!"

"That's not helpful." Richard stands. "We're here for you—at almost three hundred dollars an hour—so I'd like you to take this seriously."

I would stomp on his foot if Katy weren't here. Meanwhile, she plunks onto a seat and whips out her phone. Not a good sign.

"Aren't you coming with us?" I ask.

She shakes her head. "She wants to talk to you alone."

Richard and I exchange a glance. "Okay. We'll be back soon."

When we enter Dr. Grant's office, she stands and comes around her desk, hand extended. "I'm glad you're both here today."

"Of course," we say in unison, then fall silent. I don't know what I expected, but Dr. Grant is young—maybe my age at most—and looks more hippie than MD in her flared jeans and velvet tunic.

"Why don't you each take a seat." Dr. Grant gestures toward the sofa and chairs. Her office is arranged like a cozy living room. Creams and pinks, soft lights. Very calming. My muscles involuntarily relax, but my brain is on high alert.

I take a seat on the sofa. Richard chooses a bucket chair and sits, feet spread apart, elbows to knees. "So how do we fix our daughter?"

"Your daughter is very astute, I see," Dr. Grant replies, wearing a professional smile. "She suspected that would be your attitude."

Richard shrugs. "Is wanting to solve this a bad thing? I love Katy and don't want her to hurt herself again."

"Of course you don't. No one is suggesting otherwise. But words like 'fix' and 'solve' aren't necessarily the terms we should be thinking about when it comes to complex emotions and anxiety."

With a heavy sigh, Richard slides deeper into the seat and crosses a foot over one knee. "Fine. How do we *help* our daughter stop hurting herself?"

"Before you can help, it's important to understand the things that can cause this kind of behavior—"

I interrupt. "I've done some research and learned that cutting is a way to control her emotions. The physical pain releases endorphins and gives her something other than the emotional pain to focus on."

Dr. Grant nods. "Yes, that's all true, but again it doesn't get to the source—the *why* of Katy's inability to cope with emotional pain without those measures."

True. I'll shut up now.

"Let me guess, it's all my fault for being too hard on her, and for asking for the divorce," Richard grumbles.

"Let the doctor talk, Richard," I say, embarrassed that we've both interrupted her already.

Dr. Grant returns Richard's gaze. "High expectations *can* increase anxiety in some children, and divorce causes additional turmoil. Adolescents are learning to manage things like love and sex and adulthood, so when a family splits apart, it can shake their sense of what those relationships are supposed to look like, and what they can rely on." If Katy hadn't exhibited troubling behavior long before the divorce, I might take comfort in Dr. Grant's blaming Richard. But, in fairness, both he and I have, in our own way, imposed a lot of expectations on Katy. I see that now. "However, it's likely that Katy was born with a propensity toward anxiety—"

"Her extreme reactions to frustration began around four," I interrupt. Again. But the history is important. "Before that, she was an easy baby. Content and able to occupy herself. She listened well. She wasn't impulsive or rebellious."

Dr. Grant's friendly expression is contradicted by eyes that warn me of unpleasant oncoming news. "Recent studies suggest that parenting styles, particularly the mother's, can impact a child's anxiety levels. So, for example, if a child is naturally good at self-control, but then a mother usurps that child's autonomy, it actually increases anxiety in that child."

Hot tears spring to my eyes. Since hearing Katy's accusations, I've combed through all the minutes of our life together to see what I did or could do or should do differently, only to now have my worst fears confirmed. *I'm* the reason my daughter is hurting herself. My actions have hurt the person I most love in the world. I'm a worse parent than my father.

I gulp a breath, needing oxygen.

Richard sets his hand on my forearm. "Anne is an excellent mother. She dotes on Katy. Supports her. Keeps her organized and gives her everything she needs."

I clutch Richard's hand, blinking back tears. If my throat weren't swollen, I would say thank you. It's unbearable to think that *nothing* I did was right.

Dr. Grant pulls a tissue from a box and hands it to me. "Yes, that's what Katy says. She describes you as very loving and supportive. But in this case, the way in which you go about it may inadvertently be contributing to Katy's anxiety."

I blow my nose while an endless loop of *"You're a bad mother"* plays in my head. My thoughts harden against the criticism. What does she know about our family after a mere forty-five minutes of listening to a confused sixteen-year-old's perspective? Dr. Grant's not wearing a wedding ring. She probably doesn't even have children, so she knows nothing about how parent-child dynamics rarely emulate the examples set out in theory or in parenting books. Every single decision is an audible and some days are a win simply for lack of a catastrophe.

I inhale slowly and blow out a breath. My family needs help, so I must keep an open mind. "I'm sorry. I don't quite understand."

She hands me the entire box. "Sometimes when we swoop in and take control of our kids' lives with all the best intentions—to protect them, to push them, to help them reach goals—we simultaneously rob them of a sense of autonomy and control over their own destinies. That loss of control is often at the root of anxiety."

Is that what I've done—robbed her of something so critical instead of filling her with love and confidence? I swallow the bile that rises up my throat.

Dr. Grant turns to Richard. "Likewise, when a parent imposes his own goals and values on a child, it can also create problems if those conflict with the child's."

Richard scowls with a dismissive shake of his head. "Sorry, but what decent parent doesn't want their child to do well in school, learn to compete, and become their best self? That's all Anne and I have ever asked of Katy."

He's not wrong. We do want those things for her, and they seem like normal things to wish for. I'm so confused. Are parents not to ask for or expect anything? Do we just let kids raise themselves?

"Again, it's the methods—not the motivations—I'm asking you to rethink. In the coming weeks, try stepping back and giving Katy a little more autonomy. Let her make mistakes, learn from them, and grow, so she realizes she can manage her life on her own. When she figures that out, her anxiety will decrease. And as anxiety decreases, she won't need to hurt herself to exert control."

My body and brain are numb from the thought of dismantling all my habits and building a whole new model of parenting. Thank God I've asked Dan to price out the shed conversion. Taking Dr. Grant's advice will require me to put up a cot in there and paint daily from dawn till dusk.

"Autonomy?" Richard stands and paces, his voice laced with incredulity. "Like when she decided to smoke pot at school and almost got kicked off the soccer team?"

"Actually, yes. That lesson was a big one for her, and I'm certain she learned from it. But let's talk about the vaping for a second. It's not uncommon for kids with anxiety to turn to alcohol and weed to take the edge off. It doesn't mean she'll become a habitual user or turn to heavier drugs." Dr. Grant doesn't seem the least bit fazed by Richard's incredulous expression. "So again, while I'll use dialectic therapy to help Katy develop better coping tactics, I'd like you two to work on your relationships with her, and with each other. This is, in many ways, a family problem, and everyone needs to work together with patience, trust, and love—not shame. I like to tell parents to strive for alliance, not compliance."

Richard shoots me a look that so resembles Katy's pre–eye roll face I might laugh if I weren't so upset.

"May I ask a question?" I pull my hand to my lap after having raised it like a schoolgirl.

"Of course." Dr. Grant leans forward, elbows on her thighs, hands clasped.

It hurts to swallow and I'm damp with perspiration. "Are we too late to undo the damage? She's almost seventeen. I read that, in many important ways, kids are formed by early grade school."

"I don't believe it's ever too late, especially if Katy wants to do the work. I sense, deep down, she does and is willing to work with me in earnest."

"So what are the rules or specific 'don'ts' I should keep in mind?" I ask.

Dr. Grant chuckles, although I see no humor in any of this. "It would be nice if it were that clear-cut, but there isn't one right and wrong way. You can have discussions with and make suggestions to her, but it will be best to let her make the final decisions. Think of this as giving each of you back some freedom, too. By taking the pressure off yourself to be Katy's everything, you can use this time to fulfill some of your own goals. That will also relieve Katy of the burden of being the center of your world."

My throat is so tight it hurts to breathe. The irony that I gave up everything to help her only to now learn that doing so is what actually hurt her levels me. When new tears flood my eyes, I don't even try to hide them.

Richard stops pacing to stand beside me and set a hand on my shoulder. "Okay. Enough hindsight quarterbacking Anne's and my parenting. We were young parents who did the best we could. We're still doing our best, and laying the blame at our feet after the damage is done isn't helpful."

He's in full lawyer mode now. Sober. Resolute. Confident. I envy that and appreciate his desire to ease my pain, but the truth is that we probably wouldn't be here if we had been terrific parents.

"I don't think you're bad parents. Hopefully, when you've had time to digest everything, you'll see that. I'm only suggesting a few changes to help Katy." Dr. Grant falls silent.

"So what comes next?" I can't believe I'm reaching for Richard's hand a second time, but there it is. As tense and distant as we are most days, I'm glad he's at my side right now.

"Let's start with weekly sessions with Katy. At home, try to keep the obvious things she could cut herself with out of sight or put away. Continue to suggest healthy outlets, encourage friendships with new kids, help her get in touch with her core identity—the things she loved as a child are instructive—all of that will help her build up her esteem and give her other ways to channel her frustration and emotional pain. But don't force any of it. Drop a suggestion and then let it lie. Also, substitute behaviors—things like rubbing ice on her skin or snapping a rubber band on her wrist—might help prevent more cutting while therapy gets underway."

"And what about my fiancée? How do I get Katy to accept her if I'm not allowed to expect it?" Richard grips his hips.

I drop my chin, but there's no hiding from the pain of listening to him fight for Lauren.

Dr. Grant's pleasant demeanor shifts to something equally cool as Richard's. "Mr. Chase, I'm sure your priority is on building a more open and accepting relationship with your daughter. Despite what she might say to you, she has a very high need for your approval. Obviously, she'll have to accept your new life in time, but that will happen more quickly if you two rebuild your connection before you force the rest."

Richard's frustration is no surprise. His parents divorced when he was thirteen, yet he powered through it like he does everything else. He's never had confidence problems or trouble focusing on his own goals, so he honestly does not understand Katy or me. It's why he wasn't exactly empathetic about my dissatisfaction with my father, or my insecurities about my art, or even my desire for his undivided attention. That core difference between us is one reason we drifted apart.

"Before you leave, please don't think that I'm judging you—or that you have failed. You have raised a very bright young lady who loves you both. Sadly, these days almost twenty percent of teens engage in some form of self-harm. Social media and other societal pressures are ever present. In our case, Katy's tendency toward brutal honesty will actually work in our favor, because she's willing to engage in difficult discussions. And if anything comes up, or you have questions as we go on, please call me."

My legs are so weak I'm not sure they can hold me upright. "Thank you. I'll work on doing better."

"Not better—different." Dr. Grant touches my arm.

Richard shakes her hand but remains silent as we leave the room. As soon as we close the door, he mutters, "We need a second opinion."

I stop. I might harbor some doubt, too, but this isn't about my preferences or his. This is about Katy. "We have to be on the same page, Richard. Please. If Katy likes Dr. Grant, we should stick with this for a while and internalize what we just learned."

"Strip away all the flowery words and you get to the bottom line. She *is* blaming us—*you*—for this, and that's bullshit. You're a good mother, Anne." Without warning, he hugs me. It's nothing more than some echo of affection from our past mixed with his own fear and lack of control that's pushing him to squeeze me so tight, but I surrender anyway because I need this hug for the strength to change myself.

"Mom?" Katy stands by the chair where we left her, with tears in her eyes. "What's the matter?"

Richard and I break apart. "Nothing. Your father and I just have a lot to digest after talking with Dr. Grant. We're committed to reducing the stress in our family. Are you?"

When she nods, we all hug. For this moment, I allow myself to hope that everything will be okay.

"This is probably more costly than you were anticipating, but I assumed you wanted temperature control, plus electric and plumbing . . ." Dan licks his lips before pressing them in a tight line. Golden morning light pours through the kitchen window, but nothing has warmed me since my meeting with Dr. Grant this week. Biting my tongue yesterday when Katy opted out of a team dinner "to study" and not forcing a healthy breakfast on her this morning has me exhausted, irritable, and veering toward depressed. But an art studio, once completed, will move me in the direction the doctor suggested. One of peace and satisfaction that I'd come back to Potomac Point to find, too.

Dan and I haven't spent any time alone since I declined his spontaneous lunch invitation last weekend. I've consciously avoided him, mostly because he's perceptive and I don't want him to pick up on everything going on with Katy. Even as we speak, I'm busying myself cleaning the coffee maker to avoid eye contact. I'd felt a little stir of something at the street fair, but at present my withdrawal is for the best.

I focus on the estimate. Although it's more costly than I hoped, there's no price tag too high for Katy's and my mental health. "It's fine. My bigger concern is getting it done as quickly as possible."

He scratches his head. "Well, your master bath will be done soon, so I can get started on this in another week. Joe and I can probably bang it out in two weeks."

That feels too far off. "Start on this first, then finish my bathroom. I'm fine sharing the upstairs bathroom with Katy a little longer."

He frowns. "What's the rush?"

I can't divulge Katy's cutting, so I cover. "I might attempt something for that local artists show at Trudy's gallery. Plus Katy has to work on her school project for the show, which takes place in late November. It'd be great to have this space for us to work in together."

A genuine smile tugs at the corners of my mouth. Art is one interest that Katy and I always shared when she was younger. I picture us quietly working side by side. You don't need to talk to feel a connection.

"All righty. Guess I'll get started today." Dan folds the estimate and stuffs it in his back pocket. "I'm happy you made this decision, and not just because it means more money for me."

"So am I, thanks." I'm turning to take my coffee outside when he touches my shoulder.

"Anne." He drops his hand. "You've been jumpy since the street fair. Is everything okay?"

I guess he's missed the bad jokes cracked in passing and commiseration over local traffic. "Yes. I'm fine."

Dan scratches his jaw, his gaze narrowing. "So I didn't do or say anything on Saturday that upset you?"

"No." I reach for his arm without thinking. "I'm just tired. When I thought moving here would bring me peace, I forgot to consider that I'd be looking after Gram in addition to dealing with a divorce and a disgruntled teen. And with the ongoing renovation, I've got no quiet place to decompress."

He crosses his ankles and leans his butt against the edge of the counter, graciously not saying "told you so" in the process. "Well, we'll be working outside at the shed for the next two weeks, so you'll have some privacy in here. The bathroom will only take another week after that, then you'll be free of me."

I nod as if that makes me happy, but in truth I've mostly enjoyed seeing Dan every day.

"Did your grandmother enjoy your drop-in on Saturday?" A dimple forms.

"Actually, we had a really lovely moment before I left her." I've thought back on it several times this week. *Even the wrong road leads to some wonderful surprises.* The implication, though, is that Grandpa had been the wrong road. Sometimes it's better not to know *everything* about a person.

Still, I can't stop wondering what happened between Gram and Billy T., and whether that had something to do with Allcot. I called

Cousin Emily yesterday, but she'd only ever heard the same vague references about Gram's troubled past as my father had. Lonna must've figured it was her sister's secret to share or not. One dead end after another.

"That's real nice," Dan interrupts my musing. "Guess the mysteries of the box will remain a mystery, though?"

"Seems so." I shrug. "But that leaves me free to focus on the future."

"Good point."

"In fact, I'm meeting Trudy for coffee in thirty minutes and then going to a yoga class, so I'd better go clean up a bit."

His grin lengthens my spine. "Tell Trudy I said hi. I'd better get your studio ready so you can wow her with something special down the road. I'll make a supply run for the shed conversion."

"Thanks." I pat his arm again in an effort to keep the door of friendship open for the future. "I'll hop online today and order paints and an easel and the rest of it."

"Sounds good." Dan waves as he wanders out of the kitchen.

I need to run a brush through my hair, but first I breeze through the french doors to the patio, where I can breathe. With my back to the house and my eyes closed, I listen to the fountain, drawing the morning air into my lungs and sending my fears out on a long breath.

As long as I take one step at a time, I can become a mother—a woman—Katy can rely on and look up to. She will stop hurting herself and gain confidence. Our lives will move forward without veering too far off track.

Maybe, if I'm really lucky, I'll eventually find my own happiness, too.

CHAPTER SEVENTEEN

ANNE

I'd volunteered at Whitman Prep from Katy's entry in kindergarten through her early years of high school, so I knew most of the moms. Or, more accurately, I knew the stay-at-home moms who had the free time to help improve the quality of extracurriculars and equipment. Today I walk through the massive public high school doors a virtual stranger.

My stomach is gurgling like that of a middle schooler hoping not to humiliate herself in a quest to meet one person who might become a friend—and I have typical levels of anxiety. This is what Katy experiences every day, which overtaxes her fragile grip on her anxieties. I should talk to her and make sure she's—no . . . wait. My new job is to stop fixing things for her. If she's not asking for help, I won't butt in. Feels wrong, but I'm putting my faith in Dr. Grant.

Kids bustle around the hallways, changing classes, as I make my way to the security desk to check in. Katy would be mortified if she thought I was trying to check up on her, so I keep my eyes forward and don't scan the horde. Can't risk messing up the two weeks of slight progress we've made since first meeting with Dr. Grant. Every time I've wanted to jump in and make something easier for her—from little things like teaching her how not to burn garlic to big things like responding to her father's invitation to come for another overnight visit already—I've politely excused myself, gone to my room, closed the door, and paced around talking to myself for two minutes.

I feel uncomfortably disconnected from Katy, but she's less irritable with me and—as far as I can tell—hasn't hurt herself again, so my bedroom floors will need rebuffing sooner than later.

"Good morning." A cheerful, balding man sipping from a large mug of coffee holds his palm out, awaiting my ID.

"Good morning." I hand him my license. "I'm here for the art show parent volunteer meeting."

He taps the sign-in book. "Go ahead and sign in. That's in the Edgemont Room, which is down the stairs behind me and to the left."

"Super. Thanks." I sign in and place the visitor sticker he hands me on my shirt. "Have a nice day."

"Stop back to sign out before you leave." He goes back to his coffee and whatever he was watching on his phone.

Before turning the corner at the bottom of the stairs, I hear the murmur of the crowd within. I press a hand to my pounding heart and then square my shoulders and enter the windowless room five minutes ahead of schedule.

A few small clusters of women are chatting over coffee and doughnuts. As expected, most look to be in their late forties or older. Many have probably lived in this county for most of their lives. As my gaze flits around the room in search of a welcoming smile, I catch the eye of one redheaded woman, who smiles noncommittally before returning her attention to her posse. With nothing to do and no one to talk to, I sign in and pour myself a coffee that I don't need.

It's only when I search out a seat that I see Tori. Tori effing Decker. I would've liked not to have hesitated, but my lips part and my muscles tighten. At least she isn't close enough to hear the rush of sound in my ears.

Two decades have passed since that summer she made life at the public pool a living hell. There've been times since then when mean-girl revenge fantasies had me picture her balding, with sun-ravaged skin, and alone on Saturday nights. The truth is that she's still quite attractive—even if she pays for that particular shade of golden hair and regular Botox—and she also still wears her beauty like a crown.

I don't recall hearing anything about her getting pregnant young, but, then again, I'd stopped summering in Potomac Point at seventeen. Despite queasy insides, I follow the advice I'd offer Katy and confront the beast. My heart thumps wildly, but at least I don't trip.

"Hi, Tori. This is a surprise." Did that sound friendly? The expressions of the two women she's speaking to don't reveal anything that leads me to believe otherwise.

"It certainly is." She's dripping in diamonds—tasteful ones, but overdone for a parent meeting.

I exchange introductions with the other women, Kwana Johnson and Ginny Ackerman.

Tori cuts in: "I had no idea you moved to town. Weren't you from Baltimore?"

"Yes, I was, but I've lived in Arlington since college. Just moved here in August. My grandmother's ill . . ." Babbling shows her that she makes me nervous, so I stop.

"You're so young to have a teenager." Her friendly sort of laugh doesn't fool me, but I *am* confused. She's only a year older than me.

Rather than respond directly to her remark, I say, "My daughter, Katy Chase, is a junior."

"Katy Chase . . . ," Tori muses, brows pinched, finger tapping her glossy lips. "Does she play soccer?"

Kwana and Ginny stare at me pleasantly, but my stomach turns to lead and then sinks to my feet. "Yes. For the varsity team."

"So does my stepdaughter, Mia. Mia Collins." She puffs up like a peacock. I have no idea who Mia Collins is, but apparently Tori is someone's second wife—like Lauren. I wonder if her someone likes to dress her in those extremely snug clothes and expensive accessories.

"Then I'll probably see you in the bleachers." Just like that, all my anticipatory joy is replaced by trepidation.

She opens her mouth, then closes it. I suspect she might've been ready to make a snarky remark about Katy's temporary game suspension—assuming Mia talks to her parents about those kinds of things—then thought better of showing her ass here at a school meeting. That's progress, I suppose. Or simply proof that, like me at present, she's a bit out of her natural element.

A woman in distressed gray jeans, ankle boots, and a funky pink tunic speaks up from the front of the room. "Okay, ladies, let's get started."

Everyone takes a seat. If I could've moved away from Tori without appearing rude, I would've. Instead, I'm wedged between her and Kwana. My skin prickles like it's covered in fire ants.

"Welcome back to another year and another show. For those who are new, I'm Samantha Savage. My son Greg is a senior sculptor. This will be my fourth and final art show here at the high school. As you know, the faculty will be talking to the kids about themes. Last year, we intermingled different artwork throughout the hallways and other spaces to force students and families to view *all* of the amazing pieces, but parents complained that it made it harder to find their kids' work, so it looks like we may be doing segregated displays for the various disciplines like photography, drawing, painting, and sculpture. It's our job to follow instructions, set up installations, organize snacks and beverages, publicity, etcetera."

Fudge. We're just the workhorses. Creative input not welcome.

I raise my hand anyway.

"Yes, Miss . . ." Samantha points at me.

"Hi, I'm Anne. I'm new to the area, but not to art shows. I just wonder if the setup is a done deal, or if there's still time to consider intermingling the work? We could create a map and index for those parents who aren't interested in viewing other kids' work." I flash a hopeful smile, remembering the excited anticipation of others seeing my work at high school and college art shows. The school should encourage admiration for the kids' works from more than just their own parents. It takes guts to put yourself on display that way.

When I notice other moms' heads bob in support, my chest expands.

"I can take it up with the teachers, but admin hates fielding angry-parent letters." She then continues with her speech while I fan myself because of the heat coming from Tori's side-eye. "When you signed in, you should've included your email, which we'll use to create a group directory. Next, I'm going to pass around a sheet where you can choose where you most want to help. Setup, cleanup, food and beverage, and so on."

I raise my hand again, emboldened.

"Yes, Anne?"

My mouth is a bit dry. "Another way to get parents invested in viewing *all* of the art might be to turn the show into an auction and donate the proceeds to the PTC."

More heads bob excitedly at that idea, but Tori clears her throat. In a sweet-as-pie voice, she says, "That's the kind of thing that sounds great at first, but if you stop to actually *think* about it, you see the problems it creates. Can't you just hear little so-and-so crying because no one bid on her piece, while another kid boasts about his work having the highest bid?"

Not to be bested by her, I reply, "That could be handled with technology. I'm sure there are silent auction apps out there that let bidders make private bids. None of the kids ever has to know whose art was more or less popular, or the exact dollar amount spent on any piece."

"It's an interesting idea," Samantha says. "As a member of the PTC board, we're always looking to supplement our fundraising. Let me talk to the teachers and look into options that address Tori's concern, but I like the outside-the-box thinking, Anne."

"Thank you." I sit back, vindicated and enthusiastic. Although Katy originally took this class to spite Richard, it's turning into a wonderful diversion for us both. Helping with this show is bringing back memories of Mrs. Tivoli, my high school art teacher. Passionate yet shrewd, she'd pushed us outside our comfort zones in the best way.

Dr. Grant said that healthy outlets were a good idea. Once the studio is finished, Katy and I can retreat to that sanctuary to work through our emotions in different mediums. Katy's been snooping around the shed and asking about when Dan will finish, which is a hopeful sign.

When the meeting ends, we all stand. As I'm saying goodbye to Kwana and Ginny, Tori says, "Hey, Anne. Hang back a sec, could you? I want to hash out this idea of yours a bit more."

My entire body freezes. "Sure."

When we are segregated from the stragglers, Tori says, "A word of advice?"

I cock my head and shrug.

"Don't make me look stupid in front of others, or your daughter's drug problem might slip out."

My body goes as cold as the bay in December. "First of all, Katy doesn't have a drug *problem*. Secondly, I wasn't trying to make you look stupid. You raised a good point, and I offered a solution. Isn't it better for all the kids if we raise money?"

She narrows her eyes like she doubts my motives. "What ever became of your artistic aspirations?"

My cheeks are hot. "I sold some paintings early on, but my focus turned to raising Katy this past decade." I would mention getting back into it if she were kind and this was a friendly conversation.

"Let me guess . . . single mom?" She raises her perfectly tweezed eyebrows along with her chin.

No use lying. She'll dig around for the truth anyway. "Recently divorced."

"What a shame, Anne. Must be tough." She shakes her head, wearing the slightest sneer so that no one but me can accurately read her body language.

Tori wouldn't have any compunction about hurting me through my daughter. Katy can't defend herself against a grown-up bully, so I play dumb. Resisting the urge to recoil, I touch her shoulder. "I appreciate your sympathy."

When she flinches, I take advantage of her hesitation to make a break for it.

"You have a great day." I stop to thank Samantha for considering my idea before fleeing the scene. Each time Tori's phony smile and threat replay, my chest tightens. During the drive home, my thoughts darken. That witch could undo all the work Katy, Richard, and I have been doing these past weeks.

When I finally arrive, it's as if I've dragged a hurricane through the door with me. I chuck my purse on the couch and let out a growly noise while punching a pillow just as Dan exits the powder room.

His brows rise. "Whoa. Maybe you're better off telling me what happened than killing your sofa."

"Tori Decker—*Collins*—is a Bitter Betty." I stomp, fists at my sides like a bad cartoon. Only then does it occur to me that Dan might be friendly with her. They grew up here, after all. I slap both hands across my mouth.

Dan's eyes twinkle above a slow grin. "That's about right, although I'd use a different B-word."

I drop my hands and shake them out, uneasiness souring my gut. I'm so tired I could literally collapse on the sofa and sleep until Christmas. Tears begin to brim.

Dan tips his head, staring at me. "Where'd you run into her?"

I clear my throat so my voice won't crack. "I went to a parent meeting hoping to make a friend, and there she was—my preteen nemesis. I hoped maturity might've mellowed her and even made her embarrassed by her young self. But *no*, same old Tori."

Dan takes a cautious step toward me. "What'd she do?"

"I made a suggestion, which she countered with a potential problem. When I offered a solution, she quietly threatened to out Katy's 'drug use' if I didn't watch it." My breaths come up short as my chest tightens again. "She thought I was trying to embarrass her, but I was only looking for ways to help the kids."

Exhaustion borne from watching Katy from a distance for signs of cutting, holding myself back when I've wanted to rush in to comfort her, and worrying about Gram's continued decline has me unsteady on my feet. I'm trembling. In the safety of my living room, the tears finally come.

"Anne." Dan sets his hands on my shoulders and gently pushes me to sit on the sofa. "I'm not defending Tori, but what's the worst that would happen if she makes good on her threat? It's not like Katy would have to wear a red 'A' every day. Plus, you're not the only mom in that room whose kid has made mistakes."

"You don't understand. Katy can't take any more stress." I grab a tissue off the sofa table and wipe my nose.

"Katy seems tough to me."

I look into his warm hazel eyes. "No, she's the opposite of tough." The need for comfort and consolation overwhelms me, so it all comes tumbling out. "She's hurting herself. She ran out on Richard that Saturday of the street fair. I got home and found her in the shower, bleeding. We've hired a therapist who's making us question everything we've done—mostly *me*—as parents. It's frightening enough without Tori or her stepdaughter making life harder for Katy. That could get dangerous fast." I wipe my wet face and sniffle.

Dan hesitates, his body tense, as he slowly reaches out to pat my shoulder. "I'm sorry."

I bury my face in my hands while crying. Before I know it, Dan has me cradled against his chest while he silently waits for me to cry it out.

Between sniffles, I recite the short version of Dr. Grant's opinions and unload all the guilt and conflict I'm battling in my own head about my role in everything from my divorce to Katy's problems.

A few minutes pass where he says nothing, letting my tale of woe settle around us without judgment. It's both a luxury and a discomfort.

Dan withdraws his arm from my shoulder, so I sit upright. "You're too hard on yourself, always trying to be a perfect parent. That's impossible, you know. I've never met one, have you?"

"No." That doesn't help, though. I've never measured myself against others, only against my own goals. Being the best damn mother had been my number one goal. I'd followed the examples set by my mom and Gram—women who stayed at home and paid attention to me, took care of and anticipated my needs, taught me right from wrong.

Was that all a lie, or a mask? Gram and her "wrong road" . . . So I, too, took that wrong road by giving up my own passion and funneling all that energy into Katy, only to now learn that, in doing so, I robbed her of her own identity, and robbed myself of one, too.

"I doubt Dr. Grant wants you to beat yourself up. Sounds like she just wants you to make a shift for both your sakes. You're lucky, actually. You get the chance to make changes before it's too late. This could be the best thing for both of you, right?"

I snort and shake my head. It's like he's a mind reader. "I swear, I have no idea why your wife left you. You're a good guy. You'd be a great parent, frankly."

"Thank you." He crosses his arms and stares at the coffee table, like he's about to shut down. "I would've liked kids, but it wasn't in the cards."

"You're still young enough." Men have kids in their forties.

He looks at his lap, lips twisted. With a shrug and red cheeks, he blurts, "I'm infertile."

"Oh!" I lay a hand on his leg, then remove it as if his thigh were a hot pan. "I'm sorry. I didn't mean to pry."

"It's fine. I mean, it was brutal, but I accepted it. Ellen couldn't, though. She didn't want to adopt or find a donor. It got between us, and then she moved on. I can't blame her—I mean, she could've waited until after the marriage ended—but I get her wanting a husband who could father children."

Just because a man can father them doesn't mean he should. My thoughts run to my own father, of course. I wonder if Ellen's new husband is as good a father as Dan would've been.

"I'm sorry." Like me, he's been humiliated by betrayal. But worse, his ex-wife's attitude about his infertility might've emasculated him. No wonder he keeps things casual with women. "Thank you for trusting me with that personal story."

"Seemed like turnabout was called for today." His downcast eyes compel me to take his hands and squeeze them.

"I really appreciate your friendship. Honestly, I'd be completely lost without it."

"Don't mention it." He waves me off. "Now, if you're feeling better, I should probably get back to work and finish that shed for you and your daughter."

I nod. When he stands, I do, too. "Katy's growing impatient to work on her collage project up there."

"So you *did* make a good decision." He winks and wanders toward the french doors. "See you later."

"Bye." After he closes the door, I sink back onto the cushion. Male infertility isn't something I've ever thought about. My friend Wendy was infertile, but she had several support groups. In my experience, men tend to handle everything on their own.

Katy's a little bit right about me. I *do* like Dan. It'll be lonely when he's no longer working here, and that scares me.

But right now I have a bigger concern. How will Katy react when I tell her that my volunteering might have inadvertently put a target on her back?

CHAPTER EIGHTEEN

KATY

"I'm sorry. I volunteered to support the arts in the school and to make some new friends, but my involvement could further antagonize your teammate's mother. Does that concern you?" Mom asks.

I snap the rubber band on my wrist, which draws her attention. We exchange a look, but she doesn't freak out. At least not on the outside. It's been like this since my first meeting with Dr. Grant. Mom watching me but holding back, waiting for me to take the lead. But I'm sure she doesn't quite trust me not to cut myself again.

She shouldn't, because I don't trust myself.

"Mia is nice," I say. "Everyone on the team already knows about the pot. I don't care what a few moms think, so that Tori lady can't really make it worse for me." I don't want people to think I'm a bad kid, but from what I can tell, most moms are pretty forgiving. "And, hey, now I know Mia and I have something in common."

"What's that?" Mom's eyebrows pinch in question.

"Evil stepmoms." I brace for a lecture about my attitude. Part of me is relieved when it doesn't come, but the other part is a little sad. It used to be too much; now it is almost too little—or just unnatural. We've got to find a middle ground.

"Well, you're right—your teammates know everything, so the only one Tori can torture is me." She makes a wry face and taps her fingers on the counter. "I'd like to stay on the committee to establish my own roots in town, and the school is an easy place to meet other women around my age."

"It's fine, Mom."

"Great." She smiles. "On to a fun topic. Would you like to check out our art shed? It's nearly finished."

She asked me not to peek during the construction because she wanted to do a big reveal, but I did try. Dan had the doors wrapped in plastic, so I couldn't see anything. "Sure."

Mom loops her arm through mine, and we go out the back door and up the terraced yard to the shed. Dan repainted it the same shade of peacock blue as our front door and shutters.

Mom opens the new glass doors and waves her arm like a game-show model. "Ta-da!"

"Wow." I gaze up through the skylight Dan inserted on one side of the roof. We are awash in sunlight, surrounded by white walls and pale gray laminate floors. "This is seriously cool. When you said art shed, I expected something more rustic. This is like a real studio."

"A private haven." She crosses to the small shelf where she's got paint supplies and cleaning solutions. Mom's easel is in the corner beside a built-in collapsible tabletop, a three-legged stool on wheels, and a dorm-size refrigerator.

On the opposite wall, there's a long worktable for my photography and collage work, and a tripod, flash, and reflector. We have one big white cabinet for storage. A shallow black sink gives the room a sleek look. "No one can bother us once we close those doors."

She nods. "I'm glad you love it, too."

Her face is glowing. It's the first time she's looked excited in months. Memories of her humming in front of an easel rise like a slap to my face.

"Is something wrong?" she asks.

Dr. Grant says I should be honest, even when it's hard. Like now. I snap the band. "Do you . . . do you ever regret having me?"

"What on earth makes you think that?" Her expression is one of horrified shock.

"I know I wasn't planned. You and Dad probably wouldn't have gotten married if it weren't for me. Then you gave up your art to raise me, and now Dad's left. You got the worst end of the whole deal."

She takes a step in my direction, reaching for me, then stops herself. I'm sorry that she feels like she has to weigh each interaction so heavily now. "Katy, never ever have I regretted having you. I would've kept you even if your father and I hadn't married. And I *chose* you over my art—no one forced that on me, least of all you. Honey, please don't ever doubt that. I've never loved anything or anyone as much as I love you." She's got tears in her eyes.

A wave of something crashes over me. Happiness, maybe. It's been a tough few months, but my mom really loves me. I'm sorry that the drugs and cutting have made her worry so much.

"Thanks, Mom. Sorry I upset you." I surprise her with a hug. "Remember that messy stained sweatshirt you painted in when I was little?"

"I still have it somewhere. Maybe I'll break it out for old time's sake." She squeezes me really tight, as usual. But it feels good now, in the heat from the sun streaming through the skylight.

We break apart when the doors unexpectedly open behind us.

"Oh, sorry." Dan is standing there with two small gift bags in his hands. He smiles at my mom. It's so obvious that he likes her. I'm not sure how I feel about that. "I didn't know you were doing the big reveal today."

"I couldn't wait any longer," Mom says, then points to the bags. "Whatcha got there?"

"A little surprise for you both. I was planning to leave them for you to find, but . . . well, here you go." He hands us each a bag, then crosses his arms.

"You didn't have to do that," Mom says. But she's already removing the tissue paper. She pulls out two tubes of oil paint.

"I asked Trudy for ideas. She thought you might like these. Apparently they're 'rare' colors—something about antiquity Naples yellow having a 'soft glowing light' and that Mesa Verde green having a 'granular quality.' I don't know. It's just a little something to wish you luck." He shrugs. It's funny to see a big man like him blush, but I keep my snark to myself.

"Thank you so much. They're lovely." She and he exchange a look that makes me feel like an outsider. Not as bad as I do around Dad and Lauren. I don't hate Dan like I do Lauren, because he didn't mess with my family. "Katy, open yours now."

I almost forgot I was holding the bag. I toss the tissue on the work desk and pull out a set of colored photo gels. "Wow. This is awesome, Dan. Thanks."

Normally I hug someone who gives me a present, but that would be weird with Dan. I don't know what to do, so there's a brief pause during which I can't help but think about the fact that my dad hasn't been overly interested in my photography class.

"You're welcome." Dan nods. "I hope you can use them."

"Totally." This is a little awkward. I hoped that maybe, now that Mom and Dad have been talking more since meeting with Dr. Grant, there was a chance Dad would leave Lauren and come home. But if Mom starts to date, that won't happen. I better leave before they read my face. "Mom, I'm going to go see Grammy and ask if I can borrow her old photo albums to make copies of pictures for my project."

"Oh, I was about to start dinner . . . ," Mom says.

"That's okay. I'll be back in time."

She opens her mouth but then closes it. I bet she wants to come with me. "Okay. Try to return in about an hour."

"Fine. I have homework to do tonight, too." I set the gels on my new work table. "Thanks again, Dan. This was really nice."

"Good luck digging up some interesting pictures." He waves.

Hopefully, Grammy can remember the faces in the photos. Otherwise I'll be making stuff up on my family tree.

I swing through the house to grab my car keys and the digital camera I use for my class, then hit the road for the care center. My first solo visit. Grammy might not recognize me without my mom, which could go badly. My stomach is tight, but I do what Dr. Grant suggests: picture the worst-case scenario—Grammy getting upset and flustered—and think about how I'd handle it. The staff is there to help if that happens, which helps me relax.

Clara's at the registration desk when I walk inside.

"How's my grammy today?"

"Quiet, dear."

Quiet is good. Or at least it's better than agitated. I don't like picturing Grammy being bewildered all the time. It's the saddest thing to see.

"Okay. I won't be long." I smile and head toward her room. All around me, only depressing sounds—coughing, beeping, the shuffle of someone on a walker, the TV set too loud—break up the silence. This is a place where loneliness kills you minute by minute.

Before entering her room, I knock on the doorframe, though I doubt she hears me over the TV. "Hey, Grammy. It's me, Katy."

She looks up from *NOVA* and gathers the thin throw blanket on her lap. "Katy . . ." It seems like she's working on placing me. "Where's Annie?"

Relief loosens my shoulders. "At home."

"Oh." She starts tugging at her clothes. Without my mom around, she's as unsure about how to talk to me as I am with her.

Might as well dive right in. "I actually came to ask you a big favor."

"I can hardly do favors from here," she grunts.

"You can do this one. I'm starting my photography project for the school's art show." I reexplain my collage idea. "I'd like to take your picture today, and then look through your old photo albums with you so you could tell me who everyone is."

Grammy shrugs. "Okay."

"Thanks!" I remove the lens from my camera. "Ready?"

She finger-combs her silver curls, then sets her hands in her lap. She stares at me but doesn't smile. That makes me happy because a smile would've been phony. These pictures should reflect who she is . . . or who she's become, anyway. That sober face is honest, and more than anything else in my life, I need truth.

When I zoom in, I notice our similar noses. How else might we be alike, and would we have been close if I'd grown up in this town? There's something about Grammy—something repressed but strong—that makes me curious. When I finish, I cover the lens.

"Are your albums in this cabinet?" I set the camera aside, crouching down to hunt for them before she answers, but looking over my shoulder.

"I guess." Grammy's face pinches.

I hesitate. Old pictures could bring up a lot of memories. Is that good or bad? Not sure, but it might help me solve "the big mystery" my mom is curious about.

Three fat albums sit at the bottom of Grammy's entertainment center. They're old-school—leather bound, worn, pages stuck together from lack of use. The top book is recent enough that I recognize my mom as a child. She was cute in her own weird way—all curly haired and wide-eyed. Pop-Pop looks nerdy. His hair was fuller back then, but he had the same faraway look on his face that he still wears most of the time.

"What was my mom like as a kid?" I ask.

A little smile pulls at Grammy's thin lips. "Sad for a while, of course. Losing your mom that young . . . That hit her hard. But she was sweet, like Lonna. Considerate. Sensitive."

"So basically the same as she is now?" I'm not sure what to think about that. If we don't change much as we age, that means that I'm always going to be a mess.

"Not exactly. She had big goals back then . . ." Grammy trails off, shaking her head. "I thought she'd be different from me, but she turned out the same that way."

"How do you mean?" I stare at Grammy.

She turns her head. "It's not important. You two are happy, and that's what matters."

Hmph. If she only knew. But I won't upset her when she has almost nothing to be happy about these days.

There's a wedding photo from my mom and dad's small affair. All I know about that day was that they got married by a justice of the peace in Virginia, with two college friends as witnesses. Dad's parents didn't support a big party because they weren't eager to "trumpet" the unwed pregnancy. But after the wedding, Pop-Pop met my other grandparents at a private celebratory dinner at their country club, and Gram gave my parents the first and last months' rent on a cheap apartment as a wedding present.

A little shiver runs through me as I trace the image. I was there that day, too. Hidden beneath Mom's loose-fitted peach dress and a bouquet of white roses. Dad is looking at her like she's everything. I scowl and almost rip the page from turning it too fast.

There are only two pictures of my mom's mother in the album, but we have more of those at home. Some of these people must be Lonna's kids and their families. In any case, Mom can definitely identify most of these people for me. What I need to find is the *really* old stuff that only Grammy will know.

I drag the most beat-up album to the top of the pile.

"Can you tell me a little about these people?" I point to a vintage black and white of a family with a Christmas tree in the background. Grammy looks to be about ten, and Lonna might be two. I point to the stern-looking man in a suit. "Is this your dad?"

"Yes." Grammy is stone-faced. "Dr. Lewis Robson. And that's my mother, Marjorie, and my sister, Lonna."

"Must've been nice to have a doctor for a dad," I say.

"He was a proud man," she concedes. "That's not always good, you know."

She's looking at me accusatorily, like I'm proud or something. Or maybe she's mad at *my* dad, who is also proud. The iciness of her voice tells me something bad went down between her and hers. "Your mom is pretty."

She stiffens. "Pretty, but weak. She never stood up to anyone."

My mom likes to smooth things over, too. I used to think that was weak, but now I don't think that's always true. She didn't abort me. She doesn't use me to get back at Dad like Ashley McAfee's mother does. She stood up to Lauren and Dad for me, and she's handling everything else I've thrown at her without totally losing her shit.

Absently, I touch my scar. Luckily my short sleeves hide it from Grammy.

Dr. Grant says honesty matters, but she also says that looking for something positive in a bad situation can keep you from feeling hopeless. The only real mistake is to *pretend* not to feel what you really feel before you try to see it from a different perspective.

"Do you have any pictures of *your* grandparents in here?"

I'm thumbing through the pages, and she stops me. "That's Granny Alma and Pop-Pop Karl Busch. They came over from Germany after the Great War, when my mother was twelve."

"Cool." I stare at the unsmiling blond couple.

Grammy shrugs. "Life was harder then. People too."

Must be why no one in pictures from that era is ever smiling.

"They're all dead." Grammy's expression is distant, like she's off in thought. The more she tells me, the more her sad, isolated life breaks my heart. If Dr. Grant can't help me, I could end up like her in seventy years.

"I wish I had a sister." I don't know where that came from, but sometimes I'm jealous of bigger families. Maybe this divorce wouldn't be so bad if there were more than just the three of us. But I can't imagine ever feeling close to Zoe and Brody. Not when I hate their mom so much, anyway.

"Lonna was okay, but we were nothing alike."

"My friend Jen fights with her little sister, Bridget, all the time." I nod.

"Lonna blamed me for a lot of the tension in our house." Grammy sighs. "I caused some of it, but my father—he never listened to my opinions. He always thought he was right, right up to the day he died. He never apologized, not even after what he did."

"What did he do?"

Her gaze is so far away—hollow-like. "He killed Billy Tyler."

CHAPTER NINETEEN

MARIE

"What do you mean?" Katy asks, eyes wide, snapping me out of my hot haze. "Like malpractice or something?"

This is a pickle.

"Figure of speech." I turn away and stare out the window, hoping she'll drop it. At least I didn't blurt that my father nearly killed me, too. Strictly speaking, he isn't directly responsible. But Billy Tyler wouldn't be dead if it weren't for my father's rigidity. And I might not have all these memory problems if his response to my grief had been the least bit compassionate.

That grief is pulling at me now. My chest aches, but I let the memory come.

From my bedroom in Angie's apartment, I heard Ben vrooming his toy truck in the living room. The clock read 11:20 a.m. Angie's footsteps lumbered across the apartment—presumably to answer the doorbell—as she mumbled something to her son. Rolling over to cover my head with the blanket, I then stayed in bed with the blinds pulled—as they'd been for two weeks—and sniffed the sheets for any trace of Billy.

My eyes watered spontaneously while I clutched the cotton. That was all I'd left. Those sheets, the few shirts in the closet, the ring on my finger. I squeezed my eyes shut against the memory of our snowy January wedding day—me in my simple green silk dress and roses, and Billy's butterfly kisses, Angie and Ben and the somber justice of the peace.

Billy had wanted us to wait for my parents' approval, which he assumed he'd get after basic training. But after the argument with my father, I'd made good on my threat to move out, determined not to let him control my life. My mother had cried; my friends had distanced themselves from their "fallen" friend. I wouldn't live in sin with Billy, though, so we'd married right away. I'd thought he'd change his mind about the army after that, but becoming a husband had only made him more determined to prove himself worthy and provide for me. By early February, he'd left me with Angie and gone to Fort Knox, Kentucky. At that time, I was still finishing high school and missed Billy something awful. I couldn't wait to be reunited—if briefly—on his graduation day. But right after that, he'd been sent to *Japan*. I'd still had another month until graduation, and my parents and I had remained in a standoff despite my suspicion that my mother would've come to me if my dad hadn't forbidden it.

Nothing about life with Billy had turned out as I'd envisioned. All I knew of Japan was kamikaze pilots, and images of the reconstruction of Hiroshima and Nagasaki, and of repatriated soldiers being welcomed home by people who looked and dressed so different from anything I knew. Worse, I was not at all as brave as I'd thought. Still, I'd promised Billy that after my high school graduation, I would join him. He'd said we would find a photographer there to train me and I could take pictures of the country's recovery.

Billy had written letters telling me about rice paper walls and "honey buckets" and the "Red purge." He'd sent me a beautiful red silk scarf with Mount Fuji and cherry blossoms and promised that there was so much to see that I'd never run out of material. He'd sounded both dazzled and proud of himself, which gave me faith. The adventure I'd always wanted was on the horizon.

In June, I'd discovered that I'd gotten pregnant the night of his basic training graduation. I'd been shocked, and sad to be alone that day—except for Angie, of course. It had seemed as if I'd been swept into a swift current—everything kept moving whether I was ready or not. The baby had complicated everything, and yet it was a miracle. A little part of Billy had been growing inside me. I'd written to him, wondering about traveling safely by ship. We faced many issues but had thought we had time to figure them out.

Neither of us had foreseen the start of the Korean War.

Then Billy was gone—his smile erased forever.

The cavern in my heart expanded.

I started at the knock on my door.

"Marie?" Angie's gentle voice called.

"Go away, please." I couldn't face her. She'd lost her brother because of me and my family, but she was too kind to turn me out when I'd nowhere to go.

Ignoring my command, she opened my door. "There's someone here to see you."

I whipped the blanket off my head and sat up, about to bark that I didn't want visitors, when my father stepped into view. My body quaked as my heart pounded. Each beat splintered my stone-cold chest like the surface of a frozen pond. All that pain was his fault.

Daddy clasped his hands in front of his hips. "Marie."

I stared at him, unblinking.

There wasn't a spark of warmth between us. No fondness or happy memories could rise above my pain. Only anger. Only blame. "I have nothing to say to you."

He muttered something to Angie, who shot me an apologetic glance before leaving us alone.

I flopped back onto the bed and yanked the covers over my head, curling onto my side and around a pillow.

My father's footfall approached before the mattress depressed. From the edge of my bed, he sighed. "Marie, you need to get out of bed."

Like a child playing hide-and-seek, I kept silent and stiff, wishing he would disappear.

"Your sister-in-law called us out of concern. She says you won't eat and haven't showered in days." When his hand gripped my calf, I flinched and stuffed a corner of the pillow into my mouth to keep from screaming.

"You can't hide in this room forever," he said. "I'm sure this isn't what he would want for you."

That did it. I shot up and shoved my father's arm. "Don't talk about Billy like you knew him. Not when you refused all his attempts to get to know you. If you would've just tried, he wouldn't be dead. This is your fault. It's all your fault!" Hot tears streaked my cheeks. My throat ached. I hugged myself, dropping my head to my knees before rolling back onto my side. "Just go away, please."

"I can't, Marie. Your mother and I are concerned." A long pause ensued. I couldn't imagine what he was thinking, but the urge to kick him off my bed throbbed in my legs. "Your mother wants you to come home. You can't burden Angie anymore. She has enough on her plate."

I snorted. "Why would I come home after the way you cut me off?"

He stared at the floor. Cheeks red, voice roughened by emotion. "Perhaps we've all made mistakes, but it's time for our family to come together."

"Don't you get it? You're not my family anymore. Billy was my family. Angie and Ben, they're my family now." My voice scraped my throat raw.

To his credit, he didn't argue. "Angie's worried about your mental state and knows she can't give you the proper care." There was another pause and attempt to avert his gaze. "She told us about the miscarriage."

A knife to my gut. I could almost feel blood spurt from my mouth. My baby—the one I'd never known I wanted—gone within a week of losing Billy. The doctor couldn't tell me why. *"Sometimes it's God's way."* I gulped for air.

Daddy stood and began opening my dresser drawers. "Come on. You can't go on this way. Go shower, and I'll organize your things. We'll check you into Allcot for a few weeks of rest and therapy, and reevaluate everything after that."

"You can't tell me what to do." I folded my arms, scowling.

"If you refuse to cooperate, you'll only make it harder on everyone. Hasn't there been enough pain? Whatever has happened, you are my daughter. If I must, I'll force you."

"You'd have me committed after everything else you've done?" My ribs constricted around my lungs.

"Regardless of your take on these past few months, your mother and I love you and want you to get well."

"Get well?" I heard Ben crying in the background, probably upset by our raised voices. "You can't force me into a hospital just because you don't like the way I'm grieving."

He continued to empty my drawers and neatly fold my clothes, unfazed by my shouting. I jumped out of bed and pounded on his back. "Stop it. Stop! I'm not going with you. You can't make me. Just leave. Leave!"

He grabbed my fists and tried to hug me, but I wrested myself free and backed into the corner like a mouse facing a hungry cat. We stared at each other—him calm and certain, me quaking.

"It's clear to me that you are having a breakdown and need help, Marie. But how you get that help is up to you. I won't drag you out by your hair, but if you don't come home within the next day, I'll return with your mother." He nodded and turned around, leaving me alone in the room.

The walls—covered in faded green floral wallpaper—closed in inch by inch. I sank to the floor, nauseous, and cried while his footsteps receded and the apartment door closed.

A moment later, Angie poked her head into my room. "I'm sorry, Marie. I had to call your family. I'm very worried about you."

Traitor. She knew how they had treated her brother. How they'd treated me.

"I'll leave, don't worry. You won't have to deal with me." I pushed myself up and continued the packing my father had started, numb and clueless about where I'd go next. Maybe Susie's family would let me stay there for a week.

She crossed the room and clutched my arm. "Marie."

We stared at each other, both of us with watery eyes. She tugged me into a sisterly hug, patting my head. "I know it's hard, but I would've given anything for my parents to come to me in my grief. To offer support and a safe place. Don't follow in my footsteps. Go home. Heal. Move forward. That's what Billy would want for you. You know I'm right. He never wanted to come between you and your family."

I eased away, embarrassed. Worse, ashamed. She was grieving, too, and my behavior wasn't making that easier for her. After everything I'd cost her, I couldn't add to her worry. "I'm sorry I've caused you so much trouble, Angie."

She squeezed my hand. "I know the pain of a loss so big you think you can't go on. My brother helped me when I needed him, and I'm helping you by making you go home as he would want. Trust me, Marie. When you're doing better, come visit me and Ben. We'll miss you, of course."

I nodded and watched her leave my room. It was so quiet. Nothingness. I closed my eyes and wished I could fall into that empty void and sleep forever.

Within thirty minutes my bags were packed. I stared at Billy's clothes, the flag from his funeral, the medal. A tangle of angry tears and self-loathing knit in my gut. Symbols of a life cut far too short. Of a brave, bold man who, for a brief time, had loved me completely. But I couldn't take them with me when my impetuousness was why they existed. They belonged with Angie and Ben.

I stripped the bed and remade it with fresh sheets—not as well as Billy, who'd been neater than I. And kinder and more forgiving. Who'd valued family above all else.

I squeezed the ball of sheets and took one last deep breath, filling my lungs with that faint hint of my love. Maybe the only thing I could do was accept the punishment for my pride and my mistakes. Reunite with my family, like Billy had always wanted. Do as I was told without fighting it.

I didn't deserve to be happy anyway.

"Grandpop looks psyched in this picture, Grammy." A dark-haired girl is pointing at the black-and-white wedding photo of Martin and me taken in his family's living room in front of those ugly floral drapes. I married Billy in a simple day dress, but my parents bought me a lace gown with sheer nylon sleeves and a matching veil for my wedding with Martin. Anyone paying attention to my smile would've noticed my eyes weren't ecstatic. Martin was, though. Look at him—dashing in a suit with a white carnation boutonniere.

"No boy has ever looked at me like I'm *all that*," the girl says. She's family . . . I think. I should know her name. What is her name?

"Martin was a good man." I fold my hands in prayer for a second before interlacing my gnarly fingers. "He and Bobby deserved better from me. I tried to do the right thing . . . every day." I pick at my scalp. "But some days I just couldn't *feel* anything." I cluck.

"Mom says that you should judge yourself by what you do right, not by your mistakes. She also says that Grandpa was always happy and that she loved being with you guys in the summer. So whatever you think you did wrong, you must've done a lot of things right." She takes my hand and squeezes it. Katy! That's her name. Annie's child.

She closes the photo albums. "Thanks for letting me borrow these. I have to go home for dinner now, but Mom or I will bring them back soon, okay?"

I nod and pull my blanket higher as she kisses me goodbye.

Katy has a look in her eyes that reminds me of myself at that age—questioning and restless. "Katy, wait."

She stops. "Do you need something?"

I nod. "If I were your age, I think we'd be friends."

"Thanks, Grammy." She cocks her hip, shifting the weight of the albums in her arms. "But we can be friends now, right?"

"Yes, dear. But make me one promise."

"Bring more pudding?" Her blue eyes twinkle.

"Oh, that too," I say. "But you're at that age when a lot of people will tell you who you should be. Promise me you'll listen to your own heart first."

Katy sets the books on the kitchenette counter and comes back to give me another hug. "I'm trying really hard."

I'm glad she didn't make an easy promise. She's a serious child, and she's going to get it right. I pat her hand as she pulls away. "Good girl."

CHAPTER TWENTY

ANNE

Katy returns and dumps the photo albums on the dining table. "Well, that was interesting."

"Was Gram able to be helpful?"

"Oh, yeah. She was very informative. Turns out Billy's last name is Tyler and he's dead." My lips part before Katy finishes. "*And* her dad might've had something to do with that. She said he killed Billy, then she backpedaled. It's hard to tell what's real with the way she weaves in and out."

"She accused her father of murder?" I'm gobsmacked.

"I was thinking it was more accidental—like maybe he treated him for something and it didn't work. But then she acted like she'd been exaggerating. But if he is dead, there should be an obituary, right?"

"You're right! And now we have a last name." I pop off my chair to get my laptop from my bedroom. When I return, I say, "I'm nervous. Are you?"

Katy nods.

She hangs over my shoulder while I type "William Tyler obituary Maryland" into the browser's search bar. After scrolling past the first two, which are more recent, I see one dated July 7, 1950, and bite my lip. "Here goes nothing."

"Whoa!" Katy hovers over my shoulder, reading my computer screen. "Grammy was *married* to Billy?"

I'm blinking, rereading William Anthony Tyler's obituary for a third time.

> **Tyler.—William Anthony**, son of Matthew David and Josephina (**Sciotto**) **Tyler**, was born Nov. 28, 1927, in Brooklyn, New York. He was killed in action on Jul. 5, 1950, in South Korea at the Battle of Osan; aged 23. He held the rank of Private First Class, whose specialty was Light Weapons Infantryman with 21st Infantry Regiment, 24th Infantry Division. He was awarded the Purple Heart and is survived by his parents, and his wife, Marie Jean **Robson**, of Potomac Point, Maryland, and his sister, Angela Tyler Berg, and her son, Benjamin William Berg. In his life he made many friends, who remember him as an honest man. He was a kind and loving husband. Funeral services will be held July 10 at St. Mary's Church.

I never met Billy—never knew of his existence until this month—yet my heart is leaden. A tragic ending to his life and, judging by the date of his death, his abbreviated marriage. Gram married even younger than I did—she could only have just graduated high school that spring. And now her lack of enthusiasm each Fourth of July makes more sense to me. But why would she blame her father when Billy clearly died in combat?

Her secretiveness points to an elopement. Many women married young in that era, so her father's objections must've been something specific. But what was not to like and respect about a soldier?

Unless she'd been pregnant like me . . .

"You should marry Richard now that you're pregnant," she'd told me. I'd worry about my father's paternity, but he wasn't born until 1955.

"Does Pop-Pop know about this?" Katy asks.

I shake my head, certain at first, then slowly questioning myself. He'd claimed not to have heard Billy's name before, but there's no guarantee that my father would tell me the truth. We've never shared the kind of relationship I've tried to build with my daughter. "I don't think so."

Had Gram's young widowhood been what Grandpa had been referring to when he spoke of all she'd been through? A war-hero husband shouldn't have needed to be a secret, so there must be more to this story. That makes me shiver.

"Don't ask her about this, Mom." Katy plunks onto a chair beside me, arms flung across the table. I quickly scan them for evidence of more trouble. Nothing so far, although she still pulls at her hair and snaps that dang rubber band often. "She didn't talk about it for a reason."

Gram was married to someone else. Was grief what kept her from doting too much on my dad—the fear of loving and losing him, too? Was grief what sent her to Allcot, if she even went there? My thoughts scatter, so I'm hardly listening while weighing whether or not to share this revelation with my father.

"You know, she told me today that if she were my age, she'd want to be my friend." Katy smiles to herself.

The answers I seek can wait another day.

"Did she? That's a lovely compliment." It would've been nice to witness that beautiful moment, but it might not have happened if I'd been there.

"It makes me a little sad that we didn't visit more often when she was healthier—not that I'm trying to make you feel bad. I mean, my schedule is always crazy, and I probably wouldn't have wanted to come if you'd asked. But now I see what we missed, you know?"

I don't want to cry, but my heart is so full of happy tears I can't help it. "I do know. Maybe it's a lesson that we need to slow down and be in the moment more often."

"Yeah. Like now." Katy shoves a fat photo album in front of me. "Can you help me with my project? I need to know about all these relatives."

"Did Gram fill in some blanks?"

"Some. She got a little spacey for a while, but then she came back. She told me about her grandparents from Germany. I'm so used to it just being you, Dad, and me it was kind of cool to see all these other people that are part of my family—technically, anyway."

I stroke her hair. "You know, maybe when things settle down, I can try to organize a little reunion. See if I can get together some of my dad's cousins and their kids for one last hurrah with Gram."

Katy nods and opens the oldest album. We sift through the pages, selecting images best suited to her vision for the photo-collage family tree. It's surprising how many faces I recognize thanks to the rainy day when Grandpa and I had picked through these albums and talked about the people in them.

When we've finished, Katy says, "I invited Tomás to work on his photography project in our studio next week if that's okay."

I blink. "Is he the boy who was with you when you were caught smoking pot?"

She screws up her face. "I told you and Dad he had nothing to do with that. He just happened to be there."

"Sorry. It's just—that's the last I'd heard his name. I didn't realize you'd become friends."

My daughter spears me with a look. "He's in my photography class and he's really good at it. We're just friends, though. Like total 'friend zone' friend."

"Isn't that what I said?" Always with the eggshells beneath my feet. It's exhausting.

"You sound like you don't believe me."

Now she's a mind reader, too.

"I do," I say. "But when you act touchy, it makes me suspicious."

"I'm not touchy. I just don't want you to act all weird if you meet him, that's all." She slaps the open album closed.

I cross my heart. "I won't act weird."

"Like you can control that . . ." She smirks.

"Katy!" I slap her arm in jest.

She chuckles. "It's okay. You can't help making a big deal of everything."

Noted. Sort of.

Motherhood is a tricky road with no map. I've taken many wrong turns, but I'm learning, slowly, some new ways to communicate with my daughter. She's been a little easier around me as a result. "Let's make a deal. I won't make a fuss about Tomás if you stop making one about Dan."

Katy's mouth twitches. "That's different."

"How so?"

She looks me dead in the eye. "Because Dan likes you."

I flush. "He's a kind person, and we're friends."

"Okay, ostrich." She neatly stacks the old pictures we've pulled out to copy. "Will you return these albums after I make copies of stuff at Walgreens?"

I'm glad to drop the topic of Dan. "Sure."

"Great!" Katy pops out of her chair, toting the heavy albums. "Smells like dinner should be ready."

"Go use the meat thermometer to see if the roast is done while I close up all this." I point to my laptop.

After Katy goes into the kitchen, I turn back to the obituary. Billy Tyler's sister is likely dead, and I couldn't call his nephew out of the blue even if I could find him. I keep googling Billy's name in search of more information, but he is essentially a ghost, like millions before him.

If I die, there won't be much of a footprint left behind, either. No legacy other than Katy.

That's always been fine with me, but the closer she gets to flying the coop, the less being her mother feels like it should be the entirety of my entire life's accomplishments.

———

On Friday morning, Dan arrives with the goal of wrapping up my master bathroom work no later than Wednesday. As happy as I'll be when my house is cleaned up, I'll miss his company. We've fallen into a pattern of sharing lunch on the patio lately. He's told me about his black Lab, Arya, and the first house he remodeled—a bungalow on Orchard—and his dad's losing battle with lung cancer, and his favorite blog, *Wait But Why*. Lots of little details that paint a bigger picture of a simple, loyal man who commits to the people and things in his life.

"Good morning." I pour him a cup of coffee.

"Hi." The kitchen brightens when he steps inside. Dan hasn't brought up the other week's little breakdown or Katy's cutting since we spoke of it, so I try not to assume it's the first thing he thinks of whenever he sees me. He sips some coffee while its steam still curls above the cup. "What's on your agenda today?"

"Well, I'm having lunch with Jackie—a tech-savvy mom on the art show committee—to see which of the auction apps might work. Then I thought I might finally sit down in my new studio, brush the rust off these hands, and paint something." I shake off the nervous tingles that idea sets off. Since my first attempt at sketching again in a decade, I'm feeling more confident and inspired. More deserving of something of my own despite everything else that needs my attention.

He brightens, setting his coffee on the counter. "That's terrific. I can't wait to see what you do."

"Oh gosh. Today will be more about practicing technique than creating art." In fact, there will be lots of practicing in the coming weeks.

He nods. "Understood. Still, that's great. I hope you find some peace in that studio."

"It's so beautiful. You did an amazing job. The skylight and glass doors let nature in. It's perfect."

"It's my favorite reno of this job." He smiles.

"Mine too." My face feels like banked embers. "You've been so kind to us, buying those gifts. I wish I had some way to repay you for everything."

The room temperature rises in the beats between my comment and his reply. He clears his throat as he runs a hand through his hair. "Well, if you're offering, there is one thing I'd like."

He's very still, as am I—as long as you don't count the artery throbbing in my neck.

"What's that?" My shirt is sticking to my back.

"The next time Katy spends the night with her father, join me for dinner." His brows are arched high in question, his grin hopeful.

I immediately tug at a long curl of hair. "Oh. Well, you know my divorce isn't even final . . . I'm not sure I'm ready to date."

He waves the notion away. "No labels. An adult night out, that's all."

"A casual night with a friend." I nod, knowing it is more than that, but comfortable with the boundary for now. "Okay, then. It's a *not*-date," I tease. "Katy is working up to seeing Lauren again, so I'll let you know when they put something on the calendar."

"Terrific." He's beaming, amber eyes lit from within. "Guess I'd better get to work so you can finally soak in that tub you bought."

I snap my fingers and point toward the bedroom, laughing. "Yes, get on that, please!"

When Dan leaves, it occurs to me that I should probably talk to Katy about this so she doesn't feel like her feelings don't matter. I have a life to live, but I want to move forward in a way that minimizes the risk of either of us ending up hurt.

———

"This is the one. It's free and we can set parameters, like minimum incremental bids—maybe one dollar? And we can rig it to ping auction participants when they've been outbid, so they can simply increase their bid by another two dollars. The only person who will know what a piece sells for is the one who buys it and the two volunteers in charge of the auction," Jackie says, her eyes still scanning the software app's site.

"Of course, we can't stop parents from talking or sharing that news. Some info will leak." I twist my lips, weighing the benefits of the auction against the potential downside.

"I don't see a problem. Every parent will bid on their own kid's work, so everything will sell. I doubt we'll see massive bidding wars over anything, either. This is just a fun way to get parents and kids involved in the show. It's better than charging five or ten bucks' entry fee, which could dampen the size of the crowd."

"Good point." I nod. "I'll text Samantha this info and see what she says."

Jackie closes her laptop and sips from her wine. She's pleasant and probably five to seven years my senior. But like me, she tends toward hanging at the fringes of large groups, which is why we hit it off. In any case, it's refreshing to be establishing new friendships with people who have no connection to Richard, his clients, our old country club, or even Katy's friends.

"So have you lived here long?" I ask.

"Ten years, give or take." She slides her laptop into her gorgeous black leather satchel. "My husband quit the corporate world to come home and run his father's insurance business. Decent money and he works fewer hours."

I stir my iced tea. "Sounds like a good trade-off."

She snickers. "I still miss Chicago. The restaurants. The shows. The shopping!"

"Town has a lot more shops and restaurants than when I was young." I sip my drink. "I think you're lucky. My ex wouldn't consider stepping back from his career to spend more time with my daughter and me."

Jackie wrinkles her nose, laughing. "You're right. I should be glad Scott still enjoys my company after almost twenty-five years together."

The waiter brings our bill, so we each throw down twenty bucks.

"I'm going to ask Scott if he knows of any nice single men in town." Jackie stuffs her wallet in the satchel.

"Please don't. I'm not in the market for that yet." I think of Dan, though, and smile.

Jackie narrows her gaze. "That smile makes me think maybe you already have someone in your sights."

"I don't know. Not really . . . I mean, there's a guy and he's nice and there might be something there. But Richard damaged my ability to trust."

"Makes sense . . . but don't wait too long or someone else might snap up your Mr. Nice Guy." Jackie slides out of her side of the booth. "So I guess I'll see you at the next meeting."

"Yes. But if you change your mind about trying yoga, you should meet me at a class some morning. It's really a great way to relieve stress."

"Stress?" She mockingly chugs the remains of her wine. "Who's stressed?"

I grin. "Certainly not us."

When I get home, I bypass the house and head straight to the shed.

With the exception of the slight mess Katy's left on her desk from the other night, it's pristine—the perfect canvas for my fresh start. Before I begin, I open my Spotify app and connect to the little Bluetooth speaker. A George Winston playlist will set a nice mood. I grab some paper towels, solvent, and tubes of oils, and then—for the first time in a decade—pull up to an easel and sit in front of a canvas.

It should be easy. That's what my mind repeats, yet my damp hands and thready pulse tell a different story. Professor Agate is in my head again. *"Be fierce and barefaced. Hide nothing."* I stretch my fingers, which suddenly feel arthritic although they aren't. Beyond the skylight, cumulus clouds populate a blue sky. To relieve the pressure of producing something stunning, I begin with an old exercise in blending techniques—painting clouds.

I first paint the canvas with a base white to start. Next I mix a dab of marine blue and titanium white on the palette, then use the fan brush in a back-and-forth sweeping motion to create the sky. Occasionally I add a heavier sweep of blue or white to avoid flatness and let the light bounce around the background.

Next I choose a titch of manganese violet to add to a new white blob, and use a number 6 filbert brush to make little circles of clouds. Years away from the canvas show in my overblending. Sighing, I squiggle a number 10 palette knife to create different clouds and add back dimension by leaving some thicker paint on the canvas.

I sit back, chest heavy. This used to feel natural—like an extension of my soul—but now it's as if I'm a novice again, exploring the canvas for the first time. Like any skill, painting well requires constancy. Momentum builds from there. If I hadn't quit, I might have become as good as George MacDonald, a contemporary in Richmond who makes his living on his work. Instead I'm in a shed—granted, a lovely one—painting clouds badly.

Closing my eyes, I push aside recriminations. I knew I'd be rusty. Get over it, Anne. Eventually it will all come back.

I attack the canvas with a fan brush.

Time flows without notice, so I gasp when Katy enters the shed.

"What are you doing home?" I ask.

Her gaze is fixed on my painting. I fight the urge to cover it. "The bus for my game doesn't leave until four, so I came to grab a snack."

"Oh, that's right! Your game." I need to clean up so I can go cheer.

"What's this?" She leans forward, inspecting the work.

I wave her off. "Nothing. Just playing around."

"Why clouds?" Her gaze is narrow. "Seems simplistic compared with your old work."

"It is, but I'm really rusty. I need to get the feel of it again." I set my brush down. "Since you left *your* project out, I figured you wouldn't mind if I took a peek. The base of the trunk looks really cool."

She casts a glance across the room. "Thanks. I've done some hand tearing and some cutting with the craft knife."

Hopefully I didn't wince, although the thought of her in here alone with a knife really pushes me to the edge. "Have you picked out the photos you will use as the 'fruit' on the branches?"

"Not yet."

While she's thinking, I decide to tell her about my decision to accept Dan's invitation. "Listen, I want to tell you something. Dan asked me out to dinner. Not a '*date* date' exactly, but it could lead there in time. I don't need your permission, but I'd like to know if it bothers you."

She twists her mouth and nose. "A little."

Whatever her flaws, she's honest to a fault. "Can I ask why? Has he done or said anything that makes you dislike him?"

"No. It's not him." She picks at her eyebrow as her face pales. "It's just . . . once you start dating someone, then there's no hope that you and Dad will call off the divorce."

Her eyes shimmer, making my whole chest ache. I had no idea she was clinging to that fantasy, but it's probably normal. Throughout the summer, a little part of me wanted that for all of us, too.

I hug her, which she doesn't fight. "I'm sorry this is all so hard."

She eases away, wiping her eyes. "I'm being selfish, I know. I just miss seeing Dad every night, but I don't expect you to take him back for my sake. You deserve someone you can trust."

"Thank you." I kiss her head before fully releasing her. Her concession is a marathon win and shows the progress we've made these past few weeks. "Now, how about I make us a quick quinoa salad with leftover chicken and tomato before your game?"

She nods and follows me out of the shed. "Mom?"

"Hm?"

"It's good that you're painting again, even if it's only clouds."

I smirk, teasing. "Let me guess. You're happy because painting will leave me less time to keep track of you?"

"Well, duh." She makes a silly face—something I haven't seen in too long. "But really, it's nice to see you doing something that makes you happy. Something you're good at, too."

I stop, touched and teary, which seems like too much emotion for her small statement. Yet the otherwise simple aside marks a turning point for us. For the first time in months, Potomac Point feels like less of a mistake.

CHAPTER
TWENTY-ONE

ANNE

A sharp note of grapefruit lingers in the air and clings to my skin. As expected, my new tub is divine, although soaking in bath oil for twenty minutes has made my fingertips prune. They also fumble with the clasp on my necklace. It's as if I'm sixteen again. When I've wished for my youth back, this isn't what I had in mind.

I wriggle into the saffron ruched cotton dress, which is extra snug thanks to weeks' worth of comfort eating. Twirling from left to right in front of the mirror, I see that, in my excitement about having a reason to dress up, I've overshot. On my way to the closet to look for something much more casual—jeans and a flowy top—the doorbell rings.

After grabbing a tissue to blot my clammy forehead and neck, I shake out my hands while trotting across the living room. Standing at my front door, I blow out the breath I'd been holding. With my heart flitting around my chest like a moth in a jar, I open the door to greet Dan.

"Wow." His appreciative gaze raises all the hairs on the back of my neck. "You look beautiful."

"Thank you." I nip at my lower lip. Dark jeans hug his long legs, and he's rolled the sleeves of his fitted, untucked striped shirt. Unlike Richard's manicured hands, Dan's are rough and manly. That's more noticeable when he isn't in his work boots and scrub clothes. "You clean up pretty good yourself."

"Thanks." His gaze is fixed on me. His shoulders are relaxed. He's not fidgeting. Clearly he's been on a few dates since his divorce. Pointing at my shoes, he asks, "Are those comfortable?"

I kick one of the spiky heels up and joke, "Comfortable enough to sit through dinner."

Dan wrinkles his nose. "Well, actually, I got us tickets to the Taste of Potomac tonight."

"What's that?"

"Twice a year a bunch of local restaurants offer small-plate meals to ticket holders for a fixed price. Basically, you stroll around from place to place, sampling light meals paired with glasses of wine. A ton of folks participate, so it's social. I thought you might enjoy the chance to get to know town better, and it's more interesting than sitting in one place all night." Dan is a man full of surprises—thoughtful ones, to boot. "But it's a walking tour. I should've run it by you first."

I touch his arm. "Not at all. That sounds fun. I'll change into more comfortable shoes, though. Give me thirty seconds."

Dan steps inside while I dash to my room, kick off the heels— gratefully—and find footwear that complements my dress without cramping my toes and arches. When I return to the living room, he's studying a photo of Katy and me, which he sets down when I approach. "Has she used the studio yet?"

"Yes. Her worktable is a mess of ripped photos right now." The X-Acto knife still gives me pause, but she hasn't used anything other than a rubber band to inflict pain on herself since that one cut. Hopefully, she won't need that crutch too much longer. "Thanks again for the lightning-speed conversion effort."

"No big deal. Glad it's keeping her occupied." He drops his chin, as if regretting the implication of the offhand remark.

"So am I." I grab my purse to signal a preference not to discuss Katy tonight. She's been less surly with me lately. What other things might've been different for our family if we'd seen a therapist years ago? Life seems to be improving, but my stomach is still hard as a rock most days, waiting for another shoe to drop. Her spending time this weekend with Richard and Lauren will be a huge test. Katy said she was ready to try another sleepover, so I suppressed my protective instincts and let her make that call. Lauren will never be my favorite person, but she understands the stakes. "Shall we go?"

"Of course." He holds the door for me—a gentlemanly gesture I appreciate.

I stop beside the immaculate silver Audi A4 in my driveway. "No truck?"

"I'm off duty." As if that explains his preppy choice in cars. Dan opens the passenger door for me.

Once I'm sealed inside his car, my nerves jingle. No matter what we said, this nondate date *is* a date. Dan consumes most of the front seat. It's delicious and terrifying, so I roll down my window. Casual, casual, casual.

He swivels toward me. "Here's the deal with this event—you can go to any and all of the stops in any order until ten. There are two Italian places, one gastropub, a Thai teahouse, and a French restaurant."

"Sounds fun."

"Where would you like to start?"

I consider the options. "Let's start with your least favorite and end with your most."

"Save the best for last?" He shifts the car into reverse and pulls out of my driveway, a dimple creasing his cheek.

"Always." I twine my fingers together to keep from fiddling with my purse strap. It's been eighteen years since my last first date. Or any date with someone other than Richard. As suspected, it isn't easier at thirty-seven than it was at nineteen. In fact, it's harder. Will there be a first kiss? I squeeze my knees together and knot the purse strap around my hand.

Dan's tapping his right hand against the steering wheel to the beat of some country song, but neither of us says a word. My stomach might as well be a tumbleweed rolling down the road, and I forgot tissues, so I can't blot the perspiration on my forehead.

"I have a confession to make," Dan finally says.

Uh-oh. "What's that?"

"Well, even though this is a not-a-date kind of date"—he slants me a sideways glance above a crooked smile—"I'm still kinda nervous."

"Oh, thank God. Me too." I press my palm to my chest and chuckle. "This is all new to me, but why are *you* nervous?"

"You're a little intimidating." He keeps his eyes on the road, but I can see the flush rising above his collar.

Now he's pulling my leg. "What could possibly be intimidating about a middle-aged, divorced, stay-at-home mom?"

He takes his eyes off the road only long enough to give me a glimpse of his frown. "You're smart and went to a great college. You're independently wealthy. You've lived somewhere other than Potomac Point. And you're talented."

"You're talented, too, Dan. Look at how you've remade my home and that shed." I replay his list of my attributes in my head, having not seen myself in that light in forever. "Thank you, though, for the compliments."

"Just trying to explain the knots in my tongue."

Only a confident man could make himself that vulnerable. The car no longer feels as small or hot. "That's surprising, though. You can't have a shortage of dates."

We roll into a parking spot in front of Mama Bella's.

"I've known most of the women here too long—or at least long enough to remember where all the bodies are buried, so to speak. And anyway, I was a mess for some time after my divorce, as I told you. It's not easy to trust again." He turns off the car.

"That's the worst part. Before I left Arlington, my neighbor, Evie Connors, told me to get on Tinder and Bumble as soon as she heard about Richard and Lauren." I shudder. "Can you imagine? Even if I was ready to actually date, I wouldn't put myself on those shelves, so to speak."

"Friends made me sign up for that stuff, too, but most of the women were too young for me."

Most men *want* younger girlfriends, like those women are some testament to their virility. Then again, maybe that was part of Dan's problem. Young women who want kids might be reminders about why his first marriage ended. That thought plants a little ache in my chest.

He exits his car, so I do, too. The town looks festive. Store lights are aglow, and tiki torches are located outside the participating restaurants. Couples mill around, hand in hand.

"I'm looking forward to this," I say.

"Me too."

His hand grazes my lower back as we scale the few stairs to the restaurant, and I almost cry. It's been so long since I've been touched that way, I'd forgotten how lovely it is.

When we get inside, Dan retrieves our tickets from his wallet to show the maître d', who marks them and hands them back to Dan before leading us to a two-top near a window. The stereotypical dining room looks like something from a soundstage, with classic checkered tablecloths and Chianti bottle candleholders. Trellises smothered by plastic ivy are pressed against the wall.

The maître d' snaps his fingers to grab a waiter's attention and says something in Italian before he bows and returns to his station.

Before I sip from my water glass, the waiter swings by our table. "Tonight our Taste of Potomac menu consists of Eggplant Rollatini with a little Romano and fresh basil, paired with a Chianti. I can't substitute the small plate, but if you'd like to upgrade to a different wine, that's an option for a small fee."

Dan looks at me.

"I'm fine with the Chianti." I probably should pass altogether because my alcohol tolerance is low and wine can make me drowsy. Then again, I can't imagine being drowsy when my nerves are crackling.

Once the waiter leaves, Dan leans forward comfortably. I resist the urge to back up, although his energy rubs against my skin. My heart is beating so fast I won't need to work out for a week.

"It's a bit cheesy in here, but even though this is my 'worst' of the bunch, the food's not too bad."

"I don't mind cheesy. It's kind of cute. Besides, the real test of any restaurant is its smell. I'll take garlic and onion over nouveau decor."

He relaxes into his chair. "How's your grandmother doing?"

"The same. Good moments and bad." I'd already filled Dan in on the obituary, though I didn't mention her animosity toward my great-grandfather. "The good ones don't last long, though, so I hesitate to squander precious time together by pressing her with questions about the past."

"How heartbreaking." He sets his chin in his palm. "As for Billy, some people never get over their first love, I guess."

That's part of why Richard's rejection hurt so much. But lately I'm more confident I'll get over him. "The thing is, Gram did get a second chance at happiness. My grandfather was a wonderful man who gave a lot more affection than he probably ever got, honestly. The more I think on it, the sadder I get. He obviously knew of her past, so I wonder if he always felt like second best."

"Did he seem unhappy?"

"Not to me, but how could he be happy if she wasn't as invested?"

"Guess that depends on his expectations."

"You think he didn't expect his wife to love him deeply?" I unfold the napkin on my lap.

"How do you know she didn't?"

"She said Billy was her soul mate."

"So? She loved Billy one way, and she loved your grandfather another. They raised a son and a granddaughter. Lived in this community together for decades and socialized. He could've been plenty happy as long as the way she loved him met his expectations."

"What's that even mean—met his expectations? Love is love."

He frowns, shaking his head. "Everyone loves a little differently—some show it more than others, some need more reassurance than others. Just like some people are happy with very little, and others can have the whole world and still be unhappy. My mom spent most of her life cleaning toilets, raising a bunch of hellions, and losing my dad at forty. Still, she woke up every day and chose gratitude. She always says, 'Laugh hard when you can. Cry hard when you must, but do it quick. Ain't no reason to waste time being sad about what you can't change.'"

"In other words, low expectations make for happier lives." I imagine my own mother must've subscribed to that same philosophy. My few real memories of her are all warm ones—filled with her smiles and laughter—despite being married to my aloof dad. "She sounds like a great mom."

"She is a great mom. Like you."

I shake my head. "I'm hardly great."

The waiter arrives with our wine and rollatini. I take a huge gulp of wine, grateful for the interruption.

After the waiter leaves us, Dan asks, "Why do you say that?"

I wave the question away, not wanting to talk about motherhood on my first unofficial date. "Let's talk about something else."

The rollatini is tender and cuts with the side of my fork.

"Okay." He nods and chews his first bite with a pleased expression. "How do you like this?"

I taste it. "If this is your least favorite place, then we're in for some great food this evening."

We each sip some wine, and my muscles are finally relaxing when I hear a voice that makes my entire body tense.

"Lookee here." Tori sidles up to the table with her husband, who's a decade or more her senior. He's got kind eyes and radiates warmth, so she got better than she deserves. "Dan Foley out on a *date* when, for years, you've been telling everyone you aren't interested in dating. Guess you just needed to meet the right person."

There's a brittle quality to her voice, almost as if he rejected her at some point. If so, my association with him will only make her more hateful toward me. It's a selfish thought, but I don't want her to take it out on Katy.

"Tori," Dan replies, neither confirming nor denying our status as he stands to shake her husband's hand. "Andrew. This is Anne Sullivan. She's new to town."

I could kiss him for using my maiden name.

"Hello, it's nice to meet you, Andrew." I shake his hand. "Hi, Tori."

"So how'd you two meet?" Tori might be smiling, but her eyes are calculating.

"Dan did some work at my house." I take another swig of wine.

She nods, facing Dan. "Imagine my surprise at seeing her again after so many years. Who would've guessed we'd end up volunteering together at the high school?" Tori casually anchors her hand on her hip. "I see Samantha is following up on your idea. I hope it doesn't blow up in our faces."

The implication being that I will be responsible for what happens and how everyone reacts to that. If it weren't for Dr. Grant, I might take on that responsibility. But I'm learning. We are all responsible for the way we respond to hardships.

"My son, Tony, thinks he's the next Picasso," Andrew teases with a pleasant roll of his eyes.

"Anne knows all about those dreams, don't you?" She hasn't changed much at all since those days when she tormented me at the pool.

Ignoring her, I focus on Andrew. "Maybe he is. You never know."

"*That's* the problem." Andrew thrusts one hand upward. "It's so subjective. There's no security in it."

"No," I concede. "But art feeds the soul, so at the very least it's a great hobby."

Looking back, I can't believe I got so swept up in Richard's and Katy's needs that I set it completely aside.

Andrew taps the side of his nose twice before pointing his finger at me. "Good point. I'll remember that the next time he leaves a mess in the basement."

Tori looks like she's swallowed a lemon, and I can't pretend I'm sorry.

"Honey, let's grab a table before I pass out from hunger." Andrew lays his hand on Tori's back. "Nice to meet you, Anne. Dan."

He nudges Tori to go to the table where the maître d' has been patiently waiting.

My face sags the instant they leave, aching from holding a phony smile in place. "I've lost my appetite."

Dan, of course, ate his rollatini while we'd all been chatting. "Don't give her that kind of power."

So blunt, like my daughter. "If it were only me, I'd be fine, but Katy is still in a fragile state."

Dan rests his chin on his palm. "Bubble Wrap protects things, but it never makes them less fragile."

"I know." I push my empty wineglass away and toy with the silverware, back to talking about motherhood, despite my intentions. "I want to teach Katy to stand up to bullies, but that doesn't mean it's easy.

I'm sure I sound completely overprotective, but when you have kids, nothing hurts more than when they're in pain."

"None of us gets through without cuts of one kind or another."

His casual reference to her cutting causes my sharp inhale. "And not everyone gets stronger from the struggle. Some crumble."

He shakes his head, waving that concern away. "Katy won't crumble completely."

"How can you be sure?" I narrow my gaze.

He turns over a hand in a matter-of-fact gesture. "Because she's had your love and support her whole life. You've already given her everything she needs to dig deep and move forward."

Tears form, but these are grateful ones. "I hope you're right." I chuckle as I dab at my tears. "You remind me of her—always saying exactly what you think."

"Don't you?"

"No. After my mom died, my dad withdrew a lot. My mom's parents lived in Florida, so I barely saw them, and Gram and Grandpa did their best in the summers, but I knew they were older and tired. I tried not to complain or argue much because everyone had a lot on their plates."

"That takes a lot of strength, especially as a kid."

I grimace. "Says the man who never keeps his opinions to himself."

"When you say it like that, I sound awful." He hesitates with a half shrug. "But I'd hate to have left things unsaid if I suddenly dropped dead, you know?"

"That's bleak." I would laugh if those words didn't strike a chord. "I honestly never thought of it that way."

Dan points at me. "From the look on your face, you've left some things unsaid."

To Richard. To Katy. To Gram. To my dad. Yep. Plenty of things, yet none I'll admit to here. I'm definitely still a work in progress. "I admire your approach to things."

"I'm a lucky guy."

I doubt most infertile, divorced men would use the word "lucky" to describe the hand life dealt them. "You certainly appreciate the little things."

"It's been a conscious effort since this." He points at his facial scar.

A reminder of a dark time, much like the scar on Katy's arm will be for her. Maybe she, like Dan, can turn it into something positive. "What are you most grateful for?"

"My freedom."

I chuckle. "Spoken like a true bachelor."

"No." He leans forward, fingers interlaced. "Freedom to choose. There's a worldful of people who don't get to choose anything. Not their spouse. Not their leaders. Nothing. But I can, so even when I'm dealing with something crappy, I try to choose the best reaction."

"So the secret to happiness is as easy as choosing it?" I tease, mentally testing being happy for Richard and Lauren. It'll take lots of practice, but it is easier when sitting across the table from Dan.

"Maybe." There's a little twinkle in his eye when he tosses a few dollars' tip on the table. "Let's head out of here. Maybe we can avoid dealing with Tori again if we keep moving."

Good plan, although, truthfully, I'd forgotten all about her. "What's next on the list?"

"Thai."

Two hours and many meals later, we leave the last restaurant—a French place called Bistro Henri. Dan stopped drinking four stops earlier, but I've enjoyed the wine at each venue. At first, to help settle my nerves and ease me into the kind of banter that makes for pleasant dates. But then Dan made it all so easy—effortless—to talk I was drinking without even realizing it. Now I'm a little tipsy—maybe a lot—but it's kind of nice to float down the sidewalk. Until I trip.

Dan catches me. "Whoa there."

His arms are solid and warm, so I lean against his side for the last twenty yards to the car. "I drank too much."

"It's fine." He keeps an arm around me while he opens my car door and gets me settled.

I let my head fall back against the headrest, my thoughts a jumble, my body pleasantly warm and tingly. When Dan gets behind the wheel, I reach out and touch his arm. "Thank you for the nondate date night. I agree with you—Bistro Henri was the best meal."

He laughs. "Not sure you can call crème brûlée a meal, but it's a nice spot."

"Very." A romantic one, with candlelight and French jazz and the aroma of browned butter filtering through the air.

I have a great view of Dan's profile from this angle. He'd look good bald, although he still has a shock of thick hair along with a strong nose and chin, a defined jawline, and thick brows. His few wrinkles are like a patina, improving the looks of his boyhood self.

My stomach is fizzy with anticipation. I haven't kissed anyone other than Richard in forever, and toward the end there were so few to speak of I might have forgotten how.

When we pull into the driveway, I panic because Katy's car is missing. Then I remember that she's with Richard. That must be going well, because no one has called me tonight. As soon as jealousy bites down, I choose to be happy for my daughter and her father. It's hard to do when Richard hurt me so much. But what's done is done, and now I'm sitting beside a handsome man who likes me.

"Let me walk you up, Anne."

"Thanks." He's at my door before I've gathered my purse. Good thing, because I'm unsteady on my feet.

He holds my arm as we stroll up the walkway. I fumble for my keys at the front door. Once it's open, I turn to face Dan. He's so close. He smells good. "Would you like some coffee . . . or decaf?"

He hesitates. "Not tonight. You should drink some water, take an aspirin, and get some rest."

Again with the chivalry. I'd argue, but he's right, and I'm not ready for anything more physical than a simple good-night kiss.

"Guess I'll say good night, then."

"Sweet dreams."

Before he turns to go, I catch his shoulder, lean in, and plant a kiss on his mouth. Just a brief brush of our lips, yet it sends a delicious shock through me.

Dan thumbs my jaw, his eyes searching mine. His jaw tenses before he cups my face and kisses me—one deep, hot kiss—then he drops his hands and steps back. "I'll check on you tomorrow."

Through my daze, I manage, "Okay. Thanks for a lovely evening."

"My pleasure." With a tip of his head, he turns and goes to his car.

When he revs his engine, I close the door, thinking the pleasure is all mine.

CHAPTER TWENTY-TWO

KATY

Lauren has been kissing up to me all day to impress my dad. Worse, he's totally buying it. Seriously. I always thought he was a genius, but lately I'm not so sure. As if she's actually my superfan just a month after she thought I was bringing drugs into "her" house. On the upside, I've snapped the rubber band only seven times today, which is better than I expected.

The one decent thing about this new family is Zoe. She's actually kind of funny, and not a ding-dong. Poor Brody will be brain-dead by ten if no one takes away his iPad. I don't get that at all. My dad didn't let me have a phone until seventh grade, yet this kid is constantly watching movies and playing video games. He had zero interest in the art project I tried to get him and Zoe to do with me earlier. Neither the scissors nor sparkle glue or anything else tempted him for more than two seconds.

Zoe made a decent collage for someone her age. She cut a ton of hearts in different-colored construction paper and layered them before smearing them with glitter. It was going well until she dumped glitter in her hair.

Lauren got a little annoyed at the mess, but she didn't say a word because my dad praised me for trying to be nice. Not that he was around much this afternoon. Something bad must be happening on a deal, because he stayed in his office behind closed doors for a good part of the day. Lauren didn't seem too happy about that. His work always consumes most of his time, so maybe she'll get bored and call off the wedding. #goals

Lauren and Dad are putting the kids to bed, so I've cleared the dining table and put all the crayons and glue and construction paper mess in a box so I can spread out my family tree collage and the rest of my supplies.

The trunk looks awesome, if I say so myself. My hobby knife lets me shred the pictures in interesting and intricate shapes, so I've got varied thicknesses and textures throughout, like a real tree—with deep and shallow ridges and cool peelings. The branches will be trickier, as I figured out with the lowest set, because their shapes vary greatly. All in all, it's looking pretty cool. Definitely different from what other kids in my photography class are working on for the art show. Mine's not a pure photography project, but I prefer mixed-media work.

I hear Dad jogging down the steps, so it's not a surprise when he comes up behind me and lays his hands on my shoulders. He kisses the back of my head. At first all my muscles relax, but then my chest hurts because we hardly ever get time alone.

"Sorry I had to duck into my office today, but it couldn't be helped."

"It's fine." Not like I'm not used to it.

"How's everything going—at school, at home?" His eyes flick to the X-Acto blade.

"Fine, Dad." My cheeks burn. "No cutting."

"I'm glad." His jaw relaxes. "Anything new?"

I think about Gram's past but decide not to share it. Not like that's part of his family anymore, anyway. "Mom and I got to use the studio this week."

"What studio?"

"She had Dan turn the old shed into this awesome art studio. He did a great job. Bought her some special paints and me some photo gels. They're on a date tonight, actually." I watch for his reaction to see if he's a little jealous, but he's unreadable. "Mom's painting again. There's a local artist show before Christmas, so she's hoping to submit something."

"She is?" His gaze grows fuzzy, then he gives a little shake of the head. "Good for her. So what's all this?"

Gotta hand it to him for pretending to care, because he's never been that into my art. Mom says he used to be proud of her back in college, but I've never heard him brag about her paintings. In our old house they were hung mostly upstairs in the bedrooms, except for the two displayed in the foyer, where everyone could see them.

"This is my family tree—for the school art show." I fan my fingers while explaining my vision for the end product. He listens as I sift through the stack of photos to find the one of him that will hang from my parents' branch. "This will be you."

He studies it like he can't remember when it was taken, which shocks me. June 5, two years ago. His and Mom's fifteenth anniversary. They'd both gotten dressed up to go on a big date to Plume in DC. There's no way he can look at his twinkling eyes now and not have some doubt or regret. "I look pretty good here."

I nod and say nothing, although a little part of me wants to remind him that he looked that nice because they were out celebrating their marriage. Instead, I hold up a beautiful picture of my mother from when we were all on their friend's sailboat—her hair is blowing and she's laughing at something. "I'm using this one of Mom."

Dad takes it for a second. He's staring at it almost like he's forgotten how fun she can be when she's not heartbroken and stressed out. When tears coat my eyes, I blink fast to clear them.

Lauren appears, ruining the moment. Dad hands the photo back to me. "Good choice."

"What's all this?" Lauren's voice is way too bright.

I'm twisting my hair around my finger pretty tight, but I release it and think about Dr. Grant. With as much politeness as possible, I explain my project. A little thrill whips through me when I catch her eyeing the photograph of my mother. Take that!

"Very original," she finally says, then pats my dad's arm. "Maybe Katy would like us to leave her alone while she works."

While I hadn't minded my dad's company, I definitely don't want to hang out with Lauren any longer than necessary. "Thanks."

Dad squeezes my shoulder. "I'll check back in on you in a bit. Do you need anything to eat?"

I shake my head. "All good."

Within a minute I hear the TV come on, so I get back to work. I hum a made-up melody while cutting all the little pieces and gluing them together, making each branch as realistic as possible by varying the thickness and size and shape of the cuts and torn pieces to mimic bark. Mom had helped me map out the base sketch of the family tree going back four generations so I'd have a plan to follow.

Around ten my dad and Lauren breeze past the dining room on their way upstairs. "You still at it?" he asks.

I nod. The deadline for submissions is not far off, and I want to make it perfect. I doubt they're giving out ribbons, but if they do, I want a shot at winning something. Some things have changed, but I'm still my father's daughter.

"Turn off the lights when you come up." Dad kisses me good night. "We'll see you in the morning."

"Good night." I wave him and Lauren off. It's weird to see him go to bed with someone other than Mom. Dad doesn't seem uncomfortable, which kind of makes me want to smear glue over that nice picture of him. I swig some water to rinse my pasty mouth.

Eventually my mom will be doing the same thing . . . probably with Dan. Soon I'll have no place to hide from my parents' midlife crises. Ugh. But at least Dan is a decent guy, unlike the phony liar my dad picked.

Not even ten minutes later, the roller-coaster ride of my feelings from the day catches up to me and makes me yawn. My back is stiff from sitting so long, so I leave everything spread out to continue working in the morning.

My dad's bedroom door is closed. This whole situation still sucks. I doubt I'll ever like being here. The awkward dinners and uncomfortable holidays of my future bear down, making my body ache so much that brushing my teeth feels like a weightlifting challenge. I snap the rubber band twice, and then am practically asleep before my head hits the pillow.

—

My eyes are so dry it hurts to open them, and I might have bruises from this ultrafirm mattress. Last night I woke up at least four times, maybe more. Sunlight slants through the drapes. I grab my phone. Eight o'clock.

A quick scroll through Insta shows Jen and Kelly at a party with Maisy—532 likes and two dozen comments. I haven't been to a single party this year, which is strange but not actually terrible. I pause on Tomás's post—a crazy close-up shot of dew on a petal—less than 100 likes. I like it and scroll on, then decide to go back to my own project since I'm up.

After braiding my hair and pulling on a sweatshirt, I tromp downstairs. It sounds like my dad and Lauren are moving around the kitchen, talking about something. I avoid them and turn into the dining room, then come to a dead stop.

My body breaks out into a cold sweat and my heart pounds.

"Zoe!" I stumble to the table, where she's added glitter and cutout hearts to my collage. "What did you do?"

"Collage like you showed me." She's got her hands on the table and is bouncing on her toes. "It's pretty now."

"This was *my* project," I bark, but then restrain myself when her little brows pucker and fear crosses her face.

She slides off the chair, teary, and runs into the kitchen, calling for her mom.

I'm shaking. My thoughts skip around with no ability to figure out how to salvage my work. Oh God. The hours and care destroyed in mere seconds.

I pull at my hair and squeeze my temples with my palms, trying not to let the scream explode from my chest. My throat hurts so bad.

My dad rushes in. "What's happened?" Then he sees the mess Zoe made of my work. Without a thought, he asks, "Why did you leave this out, Katy?"

I whip my head around. "What?"

Please take my side. Please take my side.

He gestures to the table. "Zoe's little. She didn't know this was important. You should've protected your work."

"How was I to know that? It's not like I'm around little kids a lot. I thought it was safe in here. You *never* let *me* play alone in our dining room when *I* was little." My voice cracks midaccusation.

"I'm sorry. We were making french toast and didn't notice that she'd slipped away." When he reaches for me, I flinch.

My breath is shallow and sharp. He doesn't care about this because he doesn't care about my art. French toast? I can't remember the last time he helped Mom make breakfast. I hate him right now. I hate this house. I hate Lauren. I hate everything about all of it and wish I could close my eyes and disappear. Why can't I just disappear?

My chest hurts like I swallowed a chunk of bread without chewing it enough.

Zoe and Lauren appear, and Lauren nudges Zoe forward. Her tiny face is splotchy. "Sorry, Katy."

Tears run down my face, but I swipe them away. Zoe didn't mean to do anything wrong, so I mutter, "It's fine."

But I turn my back to all of them and begin to clean up my things. Do I even have time to begin again and make another set of copies of all the photographs? At least the one of my mom is untouched by the glitter bomb, so I carefully tear it away from the tree.

"Katy," my dad says.

With my body half-turned away from them, I don't make eye contact. "Can you leave me alone for a minute, please. Let me deal . . ."

I start cleaning without waiting for an answer, but hear them shuffle away. Of course he didn't try to stay with me. Instead he went to console *them*. To help *them* get over this "little blip." He never fights to stay with me—to help me or see me. I place all the unused pictures back in the box I brought, but the canvas is ruined. Not even my mom could come up with a way to save this. My careful, intricate work destroyed. I snap the rubber band four times.

More tears streak down my cheeks. Blood is pulsing in my ears and little earthquakes rack my muscles. The craft knife is lying there—right within reach. My breaths come harder and faster, burning my lungs.

I squeeze my eyes shut and picture Dr. Grant, but my collage is ruined and my dad is consoling Zoe instead of me. He only pretended to care about this project. He probably pretends to want me to visit, too, but would be happier if he could move on to his new family—the one he didn't get by mistake.

It's so easy to flick the blade open. Slim and sharp . . . right here. Right now. I shouldn't. I *know* I shouldn't. But the rush tempts me. That relief. Just for an instant. Just one more time . . .

The rubber band isn't enough release for *this* . . .

In a flash I gash the middle of my forearm, but this time it is deep. Too deep. I cut with too much anger. The knife hits the table.

"Dad!" I scream, scared and gripping my arm to stanch the blood flow. "Dad!"

He runs in. His eyes bug out when he notes the blood dripping on the carpet.

"Oh, Jesus Christ." He whips off his T-shirt and ties it really tight above the cut to slow the blood flow. He's ashen, his voice shaky, not angry. "Jesus Christ, Katy. Why are you doing this?"

I'm crying too hard to answer. But the truth is I don't know why my head goes to all the dark places faster than a bullet train. Lauren appears and gasps.

"Should I call nine-one-one?" She looks at my dad.

"No. She needs stitches, though. I'll drive her." He's got his arms around my shoulders. "Let's wrap it in gauze and then go. Lauren, call Anne."

She shakes her head, taking a step back. "Richard, I don't think—"

He gestures toward me in a jerky motion. "I've got my hands full. Call Anne and tell her I'm taking Katy to Virginia Hospital Center to get stitches. She can call me in the car."

Lauren swallows, turns, and disappears, presumably to find my dad's phone.

My dad ushers me into the bathroom and turns on the faucet. The cold water stings. He pats it dry, not looking at me or speaking. Just focusing on cleaning the cut as he pours soapy water over it.

"Ow!"

"Sorry." He works quickly, wrapping my arm in gauze and taping it. "Keep your arm up, okay. Now let's go. I want to get it stitched up."

My chest hurts from crying. I hate the disappointment and fear on his face. He's never looked so confused. Just like me. My mom's going to freak, too.

I'm so stupid. Why am I so stupid?

CHAPTER TWENTY-THREE

ANNE

The sunlight might as well be a stake driving through my head. With one eye open I peer at the clock. Nine already? I throw the comforter aside and drag myself out of bed, with a quick, terrifying glance in the mirror. After tightening the sash of my robe, I try finger-combing my tangles. A splash of water and a washcloth take care of the mascara smudges but do nothing to stop the pounding in my head.

On this morning after my first date in forever—even if we didn't officially label it—I stare at myself expecting to look like a different woman. But nothing has changed—not on the outside, anyway. Inside I'm a slightly giddy divorcée thanks to a pleasant date with my teen crush.

The morning stretches out in front of me. Katy probably won't be home until the afternoon. Yoga? No. Not today. I'm too antsy. Restless. Maybe I'll take my coffee to the studio and paint something—something red and pink and orange. Something happy.

Thankfully there's enough french roast in the bag to take care of this hangover. I scoop some into the filter, turn on the coffee maker, and trudge to the charging station to check my phone.

It's a great surprise to find that, in my stupor last night, I remembered to plug it in. The benefit of good habits, I suppose. Please, God, don't let me have drunk-texted my daughter last night. When I open the screen, a text from Richard pops up: WHERE ARE YOU?

My system is still shaky from the hangover, and now my heart is off and running. There's a voice mail notification from Richard, too. I hit speakerphone and grip the counter, but as Lauren's voice fills the room, my knees give way.

"Oh God. Not again!" I grab the phone and hit redial, but it goes to voice mail. "Richard, it's Anne. I just got the messages. My phone has been charging all morning, but I'm coming up there. I'll meet you at the hospital."

As I turn in small circles in the kitchen, my vision is blurred by tears. Unable to drive in this condition, I call Dan.

"Hey, Anne. How are you feeling this morning?" He chuckles.

"Dan . . ." My voice cracks. "Katy's in the hospital. I need to get up to Arlington. I'm sorry to bother you, but I'm too shaken to drive."

"I'll be right over."

"Thank you." We hang up without more discussion.

In less than five minutes, I've brushed my teeth and thrown on jeans and a pullover. I'm waiting outside when Dan shows up.

He gets out of the car as I barrel toward the passenger door, and catches me by the shoulders. "Anne, take a breath."

I raise my head to look at him. "I thought she was doing better."

"I know." He strokes my head before releasing me, and we get into his car.

"Please, let's hurry. I overslept, so I didn't get the messages sooner." I fasten my seat belt and wipe my cheeks.

"It wouldn't have made any difference," Dan says as he starts the engine.

"Yes it would've. I could be there already."

We're rolling backward down the driveway. "I only mean that it wouldn't have changed the circumstances."

The circumstances. Such a sterile way to describe what's happening with my child. My daughter is falling apart while I'm lolling around hungover.

"I don't understand why this happened. We've been following Dr. Grant's advice." Mostly. I still hovered a bit, keeping an eye out for setbacks. Surreptitiously checking her body for marks. "How did I miss the signs again?"

Dan reaches across the console and grabs my hand. It's so different from last night, when I'd been like a moony teen, daydreaming about sex with someone new. Look at what happened the second I took my eye off my daughter.

He squeezes my hand. "Pull yourself together before she sees you."

I nod as we zoom toward the highway and up to the ER at Virginia Hospital Center. The repetitive "Be strong" mantra running through my head is occasionally punctuated by ridiculous questions and unfounded accusations toward Lauren and Richard and Dr. Grant. My phone rings.

"Richard?"

"Anne, we're leaving the hospital and heading home. She got a few stitches. No real harm."

A relieved sob escapes. "I don't have your new address. Text it to me and I'll meet you there. I'm still twenty minutes away."

"I'm not sure that's a good idea."

I go rigid. "I'm nearly there and I need to see our daughter. Please."

"Okay."

"Can I speak to her?"

"Sure."

"Hey, Mom." Katy's voice is coated in shame. "I'm sorry."

"It's okay. I'm sorry I wasn't there when you needed me." I hate that she feels so alone in the world. I'm always here for her. Always. "I'll see you soon, okay?"

"Okay."

I'm holding the phone so tight my fingers ache. When she doesn't say more, I end the conversation. "All right. Just relax. We'll work everything out."

"Bye." She hangs up.

I picture her huddled in the corner of her dad's car, depressed and staring at what will be another scar on her arm. I might scream and flail my arms and kick the dashboard if it wouldn't make Dan think I've lost my mind. He wouldn't be wrong.

"I'm sorry, but we have to go to Richard's." I rub my eyes. "They've left the hospital."

"That's fine. Just tell me where to go."

I update his navigation with the new address. "Thank you for doing this today. God, I'll have to face Lauren in their new home. My life is so far from what I thought it would be. I don't understand how everything got so bad."

He taps his fingers on the steering wheel while chewing on the inside of his cheek. "I'm sorry this is happening again and that nothing's bringing you any joy."

"I didn't mean that how it sounds—I didn't mean you. I just—I'm terrified."

"I know." Dan turns on the radio, recognizing my need to retreat into my own head for the duration of the drive.

When we finally pull into Richard's driveway, I scowl. "I can't believe this is where he's living."

Dan shrugs. "You don't like it?"

"There's no way *he* likes this." I shake my head. "It burns me that he lets Lauren rule the roost."

"Not sure comparison is healthy or relevant," Dan says.

I drink too much wine, eat sugar, and have slacked off on my yoga practice. It's pretty clear I think healthy is overrated. Still, he has a point.

Dan asks, "Would you like me to wait out here for you?"

"Thank you, but I have no idea what will happen once I'm inside. I could be hours." My emotions churn like a hurricane-ravaged sea, but I let go of this life raft. "And it might embarrass Katy to know you're sitting out here."

"I don't want that. Call me later and let me know you two are back home safe, okay?" he asks.

I squeeze his hand, new tears brimming. "I will. Thank you. Thank you so much, Dan. I'm sorry I'm such a hot mess."

"It's fine, really. Go take care of your daughter."

I practically jump out of the car and run to the front door.

Lauren answers, her face drained of color. "Anne. Katy and Richard are in his office."

I nod, waiting to be led to my child. The monochromatic house almost makes me worry for Richard. He's trying to please Lauren, but I know my husband. He prefers color and warmth and classic architecture. This cannot feel like home to him, no matter how much he lusts after his fiancée.

When I first glimpse Katy, she is curled on the love seat, chewing her thumbnail. Our gazes lock and I'm awash in all her pain and fear and shame. She springs from her seat, and we catch each other in a fierce embrace. I'm kissing her head and murmuring to her, forgetting all about Richard and Lauren.

In my mind is a warring set of dialogue. Half of it condemning Dr. Grant and her advice, for we are in no better position than before. The other half telling myself to calm down and recognize that real change takes more than a few weeks.

Vaguely, I hear Richard clear his throat.

I whisper in Katy's ear. "What do you want to do? Stay and talk? Go home?"

"Go home." She's holding me tight, and I'm glad to be needed. To make her feel safe.

"I'll drive your car." I ease away and look at Richard. "I'll take her home."

He shakes his head. "Hold on. We should talk first."

"I'm taking Zoe and Brody to my mother's for a while." Lauren's neither warm nor cold when she speaks. I'm grateful she isn't inserting herself into our discussion, and I am sorry that her kids were exposed to something this adult. They must be cowering upstairs.

"Thank you, Lauren," I manage. My face is hot. I don't like having to make apologies to my husband's lover, but right is right. "I'm sorry your kids were frightened."

"It's been a rough morning for everyone." Lauren tries to catch Katy's eye. "I'm sorry about your project, Katy. I hope you feel better soon."

Her project? I never thought to ask what caused this breakdown, but I wait until Lauren has left the office. "What happened?"

"Zoe ruined my project," Katy says.

I grab my chest. She'd been so proud of how it was coming along.

Richard holds up a hand. "If it's all the same, let's take a breath first. Maybe get some water."

"Actually, I need to use the restroom." That coffee I drank an hour ago has filled my bladder.

"Right around the corner from the base of the stairs." Richard points toward the entry.

I squeeze Katy's hand. "I'll be right back."

My footsteps echo throughout the space. When I finish using the powder room and open the door, I come face-to-face with Lauren's children. They are cute despite solemn, wary gazes and ashen faces. I envy Lauren that her children are still young and she hasn't screwed them up yet.

251

All this time I've let that envy eat me up, as if she stole all my happiness and will end up with some picture-perfect future. The truth is, she'll have to deal with Richard's shortcomings just as I did. And her kids will tax her in ways she can't yet imagine. There's nothing perfect about any of our lives, even if she looks more put together than I do on any given day. Lord knows what her kids think of me right now or how they feel about Katy.

"Hello." I offer my hand and smile. "I'm Katy's mom, Miss Anne. You must be Zoe and Brody."

They nod, while Lauren stands behind them, one hand on each child's shoulder.

"Hi," Zoe says. Tears fill her eyes. "I'm sorry I ruined Katy's picture."

None of us needs more pain this morning, so I crouch to her level. "I'm sure you are. Don't worry. It'll be okay, Zoe."

She tucks her chin and turns toward her mom, burying her head.

Lauren and I trade a silent glance—an acknowledgment of the struggle we both face to help our children get through the transition. This isn't only about me or Katy, and I need to remember that the next time I seethe with hatred toward this woman. Katy will never accept this new family if I keep resisting it, too. And I don't want to inadvertently cause these two children pain.

"Have fun at your grandma's house." I move away because nothing better comes to mind. My heart aches, though. Katy put so much effort into that collage.

I find her and Richard in his office. For a change, he's on the love seat with her instead of sitting behind his desk. My body is like a struck bell, reverberating with too many emotions. My daughter's distress, the strangeness of seeing Richard and his new family in their home, trying to find common ground with Lauren . . .

"Sorry," I say because nothing better comes to mind.

Richard clears his throat and looks at me like I'm a beloved old friend he forgot he missed. "Did you drive up here?"

"No. Dan brought me, so I can drive Katy's car home."

"That's good." Richard hesitates. "Is Dan someone I should make an effort to know?"

How civil we are. How utterly, depressingly off it all is.

"Dan was my contractor. He's a friend." I don't want to talk about him now, and certainly not with Richard.

Richard's gaze narrows, as if reading between the lines. I feel struck again by something palpable between us. A vestige of emotions from our many years together. He clears his throat. "As Katy mentioned, Zoe accidentally ruined her project."

"How?"

"Katy left it out last night, and Zoe added to it, thinking it was another collage like the ones they did earlier in the day." Richard runs a hand over his face.

Again, I'm assaulted with conflicting tugs at my heart. I adore that Katy tried to find a way to connect with Zoe, yet at the same time it hurts that her new family doesn't include me.

"I'm sorry, sweetheart. I know how much time you put in on that. But we can start again. I'll help if you want it . . ." I trail off when it occurs to me I might be overstepping. Right. Wait for her to ask for help. Waiting seems so unnatural, as if I don't care or can't be bothered.

"Katy," Richard says. He's uncharacteristically jittery. "You scared me today. For the first time in forever, I feel completely powerless. I thought things were getting better. Even this morning, you acted like you were able to handle Zoe's mess."

Katy's eyes don't leave her lap. She simply shrugs. Of course she doesn't have answers. We're the grown-ups. We're supposed to have the solutions, but we don't.

"Honey, would you like to talk to Dr. Grant? Maybe she can see you or us today . . . an emergency visit?" I ask. We all underestimated the depth of Katy's situation. We were kidding ourselves to think it could be resolved so quickly.

Before Katy gives us an answer, Richard interrupts. "First I need to understand what happened this morning. You seemed in control. You asked me to leave you alone. I figured you wanted a minute to gather yourself. I wouldn't have left if I'd had any inkling you planned this." His face is drawn with guilt.

"It wasn't a plan, Dad. I was trying not to freak out on Zoe. But then you took her side—"

"How did I take her side?" He raises his hands at his sides.

Katy scowls. "You blamed me for leaving my stuff out, like I should know Lauren's kids didn't have the same rules that I always had. You let Zoe and Brody do whatever they want. It's so weird how you let Lauren make all the rules, too, like you don't care. If the rules weren't important to you, why were you so hard on me all the time? It's like I don't even know you anymore." She's crying again.

I want to swoop in and scoop her up, run from here, and never look back. But I can't do that.

He looks to me for help and quickly realizes I'm not able to fix this for him, either.

Richard drops his head into his hands. "I'm sorry, Katy. I didn't mean to take a side. And I'm sorry if it looks like I have a double standard." He grabs her hand. "If I do, it's only because you are *mine*. I love you. When I'm demanding and difficult, it's because I want to see you reach your potential. Zoe and Brody aren't my kids, so I let Lauren choose the parenting style. It's that simple. It's got nothing to do with my feelings about them. Does that make sense?"

She nods, but I can't tell how much she understands versus how much she just wants this conversation to end. But I'm moved by his plea, and it makes me wonder if part of the reason he'd been less involved in raising Katy is because I jumped in and took care of everything before he had an opportunity.

Richard blinks back his own tears, and seeing that unlocks something new in my chest. We all sit in silence, although I bet their heads are buzzing like mine. I want so badly to make it all better, but the only way our family dynamic can change is if we don't try to sweep this under the rug.

Richard coughs into his fist and looks up at me, every one of his thirty-eight years dragging at his face. "I'm sorry, Anne. I'm sorry I didn't handle things between us better. I should've come to you to work on things before leaving. Maybe we could've found our way back to the way we were in the beginning. I don't know . . . and I'm sorry about that. At the very least, I should've left before starting up with Lauren. I'm ashamed and regret how that hurt you—hurt you both." He squeezes Katy's thigh, his voice raw. "I wish I could change it, but I can't. Katy, I was selfish, but it has nothing to do with how much I love you. Please believe me. And, Anne, even if my love for you has changed form, I'll *always* care. We grew up together, and you'll always matter to me."

It's not all the remorse I wish he felt, but it's the most he's shown since the day he walked out our door. I swipe my own tears but can't speak through my tight throat, so I just nod an acknowledgment.

He turns to Katy. "If I move out of this house for a while and rent a place so you and I can spend time alone until things settle or normalize, will that help?"

My lips part, but I clamp them together and hold my breath, hoping not to influence her decision either way. It's tragic that it took this to make him reconsider the speed of his plans, but at least he has finally put Katy first.

She rubs her eyes with the heels of her palms. "It's not just about that, Dad. I mean, yeah, I'm really sad that we're not still a family—"

"We are a family—" he says, but stops when her shoulders drop.

"Not like before. We don't live together, and you have this whole new family. But that's not everything. I just, I don't know. It's been building for a while. I'm like an empty shell—I don't belong anywhere and everything is pointless. I miss my old friends, but even they replaced me already. Who can I trust? And I hate when people tell me I'm smart or pretty or talented or whatever. It's so much to live up to all the time. I don't know what I want . . . I don't know why I get so upset so fast, like a tornado. I'm just broken."

I cross the room and squeeze myself beside her, opposite Richard. "Honey, you're not broken. You're becoming an adult, and that's a scary, confusing thing."

"Please don't try to pretend *this* is normal!" She points to her stitches and starts crying.

"I'm sorry." I look to Richard, but he's as helpless as I am. "I only wish you'd see what I see, which is someone wonderful."

"Wonderful?" She flinches; her lip curls. "Like when I vaped? Or cut myself? Or when I'm mean to you or Dad or Lauren? Yeah, I'm so wonderful."

"You can be wonderful *and* still be misguided. They aren't mutually exclusive," Richard says.

"Katy, you never answered my earlier question. Did you want me to call Dr. Grant?"

She looks up at me with those deep blue eyes and nods.

I excuse myself from the office and make the call in the entry hall. Voice mail. Not a surprise on a Sunday. I leave a message, but am distracted by the photographs of Lauren and her children.

They are gorgeous images. Laughing eyes and dimples and wind-blown hair. How sublime that period of motherhood had been—young children are sponges, soaking up love and information and making you see the world again with wonder and awe. I miss those days. The blissful ignorance of believing that simply loving my child would ensure that she matured without troubles or setbacks.

When I return to the office, Richard has Katy cradled against his chest. With one hand he gestures for me to join in a group hug, so I sink to my knees on the floor in front of the sofa and embrace my daughter and my ex.

CHAPTER TWENTY-FOUR

ANNE

I find myself running down rabbit holes every time I replay what happened Sunday morning. It's worse here, with all the mothers on this committee gushing about their kids' art projects. Katy hasn't said what she'll do now that hers is destroyed, nor has she asked for my help. It's killing me to stand aside, but I'm biting my tongue.

Forcing myself to stay present, I turn to Jackie. "There are so many spacious, light-filled common spaces where we can display the artwork."

We continue following Katy's photography teacher, Ms. Pope, through the hallways, taking notes on what should go where.

"They renovated the common spaces about four years ago. Tax dollars in action." She casts a glance around and shrugs one shoulder. "Not bad, although upgrading the science labs would've been smarter."

I wasn't around during those budget debates, so I don't respond directly. "Maybe the money raised by the art show can be earmarked for lab upgrades."

She chuckles. "Anne, you're such an optimist. Sadly, I bet most people only bid on their own kid's work, and I doubt they'll spend too much on what they could get for free."

A pent-up sigh tugs at the corners of my mouth. "Well, I'm looking forward to the show and will definitely bid on several items."

Jackie nods. "Same."

I smile, happy to have struck up this budding friendship, but it also makes me more aware of Katy's struggle to find her place in town. Friendships take time and effort, so I know she and I need to be patient. In nine weeks, the only person I've gotten to know *well* is Dan. And just as I'm getting to know Trudy and Jackie, Katy's backslide means she needs all my attention. Dr. Grant's advice clearly is not enough, so it will be a while before either woman becomes a true confidante. But what of Katy? Whom can she turn to outside of her parents?

I scan the hundred-item list of artwork in my notebook, marking the ones assigned to this atrium with the number 4. On the eve of the event, beverages and snacks will be served in the main lobby. Thankfully, Tori opted to volunteer on that team rather than this one. Our run-ins are restricted to the soccer stands. She's friendly in public, but who knows what she says behind my back.

"So that's it, folks. If you have any questions, email me. The students are getting excited. Some have even turned work in early." Ms. Pope's playful emphasis elicits gentle laughter among the mothers, all of whom have ridden herd on their kids about homework and other deadlines at one time or another.

I laugh along with the rest, although it's hard to fake it when my daughter's starting at square one this late in the game. The mental image of Katy's newly stitched-up forearm practically scratches my eyeballs. Even Zoe's genuine remorse can't make *that* disappear.

Since Sunday morning I've nursed a chronic headache. Sleep is more of a wish than a reality, too. Dr. Grant has scheduled three sessions with Katy within the coming ten days. I'm not supposed to hover, but how am I supposed to have faith in my daughter's ability to handle herself when all evidence points to the contrary?

Our group is breaking up when Ms. Pope calls to me. "Ms. Chase, can I speak to you for a minute?"

"Sure." Assuming she has questions about the auction pamphlet and map that I'm making for the event, I bid Jackie a good day and wander over to Katy's teacher. "What can I do for you?"

"I wanted to ask about Katy. She's been quiet in class these past two days, and this morning she withdrew from the art show."

My lips part. Nothing smarts like being caught on your back foot when it comes to your kid.

"She didn't tell me that." I cover my face with one hand, shaking my head involuntarily. "She'd been working on this amazing collage, but her young stepsister ruined it with glitter and other cutouts on Sunday morning. Katy was devastated, but I assumed she'd start again."

"That's a shame. Participation in the show isn't mandatory, but I hate to see Katy losing interest in class. She has natural talent and a good eye."

"Thank you. I'll pass that along and encourage her to reconsider. Maybe there's time to produce something less intricate." The urge to sink to the ground in a defeated heap of flesh and bones is strong. "Thank you for telling me what you're seeing. If things get worse, could you email me? There's a lot going on at home."

"I'm sorry to hear that. I'll be sure to keep an eye out." She checks her phone. "Now if you'll excuse me, I've got to run. Thanks for volunteering to help with the show."

"My pleasure." Empty words said out of habit. My mind is already elsewhere.

On my way to my car, I glance across the parking lot toward the stadium, where the soccer team will soon be practicing. Katy would be beyond mortified by my arrival on the sidelines, so this conversation will have to wait until later. Experience tells me that unpleasant conversations are best cushioned by serving a favorite meal, so I swing through the grocery store on my way home to pick up salmon and salad greens.

My thoughts are still spinning as my street comes into view. Seeing Dan's truck in my driveway causes me to slow down. With a heavy sigh, I pull past him and into the garage.

The rearview mirror gives me a chance to watch him as he gets out and closes his door. Tall and solid . . . patient. But I cannot start up a romantic or even semiromantic relationship with anyone right now. Katy's relapse has me more worried than ever, and after Sunday it's clear that I'm still making peace with the fact of my divorce. Opening myself up to a man now is a recipe for disaster. Still, it's hard to walk away from a good one when, by all accounts, they're impossible to find.

I hoist my grocery bag from the passenger seat before going out to greet him. An autumnal sun beats down, but that's not why I'm perspiring. "Hey."

He shoves his hands in his pockets, respecting the distance I've left between us. With a half shrug, he says, "I thought I'd hear from you by now."

"I'm sorry." My grocery bag gets heavier—or maybe that's my heart. "I've been preoccupied, and, honestly, a little embarrassed. Between getting drunk in front of you and then dragging you up to Richard's . . ." I shake my head. My face is flaming even as golden leaves drift to the ground in the breeze.

He takes a hesitant step forward, eyes soft yet focused on mine. "Anne, I told you, I've made all kinds of mistakes in my life, so I don't judge you or Katy."

The gravity of him pulls at me, but I resist the urge to run in for a hug. I won't use him for comfort when I can't give him anything in return. "If things were different, Dan . . . but my life's so complicated. Scary, even. Getting Katy through this is going to take all my energy, so I've got nothing to give anyone else."

"What about you?" He doesn't budge except for a sad quirk of his brow. "Who'll get you through this?"

Tears coat my eyes. I'm afraid to let him in. Afraid to trust him not to hurt me, especially when I haven't healed from Richard's betrayal. "I don't look it, but I'm strong. I'll be okay."

No matter how depleted I am, I'll keep digging until I strike another seam of resilience for my daughter's sake.

Dan drops his chin for a second, then shakes his head. "You shouldn't have to settle for 'okay.' Let me help."

My fortress walls crumble. When I let him hug me, the grocery bag hits the pavement. He smells like cocoa and a cozy fire—like safety. With my eyes closed, visions of lazy mornings with the Sunday paper, walks by the bay, and calloused hands on my skin open a pit of deep longing.

"I wish our timing were different, but jumping into something—even something casual—so soon after Richard . . . and with Katy's issues. Bottom line—I can't give you anything when I need everything I've got to save my child." Reluctantly, I ease away. "I just found out she's withdrawn from the art show and isn't participating in class. It breaks my heart when she tugs at her shirtsleeve to hide her stitches. Every time she snaps that rubber band, my blood turns to ice. Her shame and pain are so raw, and that'll all be harder for her if you're hanging around."

He nods. "I don't want to make anything harder. But promise you'll call if you need anything. Or when things get better."

"Sure . . ." There's no way of knowing how long it will be before Katy and I are ready to open our home and hearts to anyone.

His shoulders droop, and his voice drops. "Promise."

"Yes, but don't wait around." We stare at each other, stock still, as if movement will destroy the thin thread that binds us. Eventually, I gesture toward the garage, turning my body away. "Well, I need to start dinner."

He doesn't move at first, as if he's going to stand there and watch me while I go inside and close the garage door. Then he inhales so deep I feel a breeze brush against my skin. With a wave goodbye, he says, "I'll see you."

My heart squeezes so hard I almost bend at the waist. After he backs out of the driveway, I go inside and close the garage door. Sniffling helps stave off tears, but I need a tissue by the time I reach the kitchen.

Dan has been a fixture in this house since we moved in. His absence significantly lowers the temperature. But Katy will be home soon, so I push down my sorrow and clean the salmon before smearing it with teriyaki sauce and sesame seeds, and firing up a pot of jasmine rice.

While that's cooking, I set the dining table, as if pretty napkins will make the conversation easier. Gram's photo albums remain on the buffet. I keep forgetting to return them when I visit, but I'll remember tomorrow. If Gram's lucid, that'll give me the boost I need. Maybe she'll finally fill in the missing pieces about what happened after Billy's death, and if she did, in fact, spend time in Allcot.

I hear my daughter enter the house before I see her. "Dinner's almost ready."

"I need a quick shower." She's got her cleats kicked off and is jogging through the living room, ponytail bouncing behind her, looking nothing like a girl with demons tearing her apart.

Her impulse to give up on the art show is understandable, but also disappointing. Yet I don't want to heap guilt on her when she's vulnerable, which leaves me squished neatly between that rock and hard place people always talk about.

Suddenly Katy materializes behind me in the kitchen. "Did you make salmon?"

I turn in time to catch a glimpse of pleasure in her expression. A tiny win for us both. "I did. And sticky rice, and salad with carrot ginger dressing."

"Thanks, Mom." Her hair is wet but combed, and she's dressed in lightweight sweats, a T-shirt, and socks. Without makeup and earrings, she looks younger and defenseless. She opens the fridge to grab a seltzer. "Want one?"

"Sure." I set the broiler pan on the stove. "If you bring the plates in, we can serve right from here."

She disappears and reappears in seconds. Once we've filled our dishes, we return to the dining table. Katy doesn't remark on my restraint, but she must notice. Tension builds inside until I can't hold in my concern any longer.

"I saw Ms. Pope today at the volunteer meeting." I chew a bite of salmon, watching for her reaction.

She pauses, knife and fork in hand, but doesn't look up. "Please don't make a big thing or lecture me."

My stomach sours, so I set down my fork. "It's not a lecture, but can you at least tell me why you've pulled out of the show?"

She shoots me a "duh" look. "Because there isn't time to redo my collage and keep up with homework and tests and soccer. Photography won't help me get into college, so I'm focusing on what matters most."

I hear Richard's voice behind those words, but keep that to myself. "Schoolwork always comes first, honey. But hobbies are great outlets . . . and your teacher says you have natural talent."

Katy rolls her eyes. "She's being nice. Teachers always exaggerate when they talk to parents. Trust me, no one will miss my artwork."

"I will." I press my lips together after that rookie mistake.

Katy snorts, and mutters, "That's pretty funny considering how you blew off your talent for ten years."

My jaw hangs open. "I had a baby to raise."

"I haven't been a baby for a long time." She shovels rice into her mouth.

Instinctively, my eyes drop to her arm. "But I still need to look out for you."

My heart pounds. Totally wrong thing to say, proven by the hurt in her eyes. I reach for her hand, but she pulls back. "Katy."

"Stop," she warns.

"I'm sorry. I don't want to hurt you, but I'm terrified, and attacking me doesn't change what's happening with you."

She chugs seltzer without meeting my gaze. "Dr. Grant says I should have control over my life. If you aren't going to listen to her, why send me there?"

"I *have* been listening and letting you decide for weeks, but that doesn't mean we can't talk about your feelings first."

She sighs, whipping a hank of wet hair behind her shoulder. "Why do you care if I do the art show?"

"Because you were excited about it. And because I don't want this incident to set a precedent of handling setbacks by quitting."

"Why can't I quit? You and Dad did," she mumbles.

My eyes nearly pop out of their sockets at that deflection. "What?"

She tucks her chin, glancing up from beneath her lashes. "Dad left, and you did nothing. Worse, actually. You ran away and made me come with you."

She might as well have pulled my chair out from beneath me. These past few weeks her behavior toward Gram and me, time in the studio, and acceptance of my interest in Dan led me to believe we'd moved forward.

"Katy, I'm trying my best here, but you can't insult me over and over like I have no feelings. And you can't keep blaming your father and me for everything that isn't going well in your life. You want to make decisions, then learn to own responsibility for them. You have almost everything a person could want or need—brains, beauty, talent—to build a wonderful life. Nothing is in your way—"

"Stop, Mom. Just stop." She pounds on her chest. "Look at me!" She thrusts her forearm so close to my face the stitches almost tickle my nose. "Look! I'm not full of potential. I'm a fraud, and all the pep talks in the world can't make me special."

The sound of her heavy breath silences me, then my own lungs seem to collapse. I retreat to Dr. Grant's advice of letting her feel what she feels.

A tear rolls down Katy's cheek while she finishes her rice. I slump, my limbs too heavy to move, and stare at my uneaten salmon while listening to the sound of her fork scrape the plate. My impotence leaves me filled with hopelessness.

"Thanks for dinner." Katy risks a glance at me, likely sensing I've no fight left. "Can I go do homework?"

Though my heart is lodged in my throat and my brain is scrambling to think about what potential weapons she could find up there to hurt herself with, I manage, "Yes."

Katy takes her things to the kitchen while I remain motionless at the table. A moment later, she's slung her backpack over her shoulder and is heading toward her room.

I've no idea how long I sit in silence, gazing at the painting above the buffet, replaying the conversation that went sideways so fast it was like being swallowed by an avalanche. Rubbing my temples is not helping to quiet Dr. Grant's opinions about the damage my doting—or hovering, as Katy would claim—set in motion sixteen years ago. Changing my behavior is damn hard work.

What if I can't reverse our course before more devastating consequences destroy my child?

CHAPTER
TWENTY-FIVE

MARIE

This is what's left to me. Lying in bed, watching the shadows of branches and leaves dance on my walls like some hypnotic movie. Lonna should've let me die so I could be with Billy. Now I'm stuck here in this prison.

So many regrets, mistakes, loss.

Wish I could sleep forever.

A sudden knock on the door makes me flinch. It's too soon for another session with Dr. Morgan. If I never have another, it'll still be too many. There has to be a way out of this place.

I rise up on one elbow to see which jailer has come, then frown. Who is this woman? Her face seems familiar. I'll pretend until it comes to me. "Hello."

"Hi." She shifts the weight of books in her arms, studying me like she's looking for some kind of clue. "It's me, Annie."

I don't know anyone named Annie. She must be a new nurse, yet her clothes are all wrong. Unusual, actually. She's not in uniform, and

I've never seen ankle boots quite like those before. Still, I'll play along. "Of course, Annie. What's in your arms?"

She raises the stack. "I brought back the photo albums Katy borrowed."

Oh my. She must be a patient. The poor thing is delusional, talking to me like we're friends when I have no idea who Katy is and don't own those albums. "Those aren't mine."

"Sure they are. Actually, I had fun leafing through them and seeing the whole family. Made me miss Grandpa, though." She spins in place, looking around. Grandpa? She's not Lonna, and she doesn't look like any of my cousins . . . well, maybe a little, but that hair is too dark. "Shall I put them in that cabinet?"

Cabinet? I see a bookshelf unit against a wall. It must be new. What's happening? I should stop taking all the pills they force on me. "Sure."

When she stoops to put the thick books away, I sit up and hug my pillow to my chest while studying Annie. There's something sweet about her. Something easy and kind. Biddable, even. Maybe she'd be willing to help me escape.

Annie turns around and approaches me with such familiarity. I go stiff when she bends to drop a kiss on my head, then she sits on the mattress and strokes my shin. "How are you today?"

"Not good," I admit. I glance over her shoulder to see if a nurse is there, but Annie wandered in here all alone. There's nothing to lose by taking my chance. "Can you help me?"

"Of course, although I admit I came today hoping *you* could help *me*." She pats my leg. Her lips may be curved upward, but concern weighs down her eyes.

"Me help *you*?" I narrow my gaze. "Tell the truth, are you a patient?"

She chuckles. "No, silly. I'm here to visit."

A visitor who's clearly mistaken me for someone else. I'm sure of it. But she *is* kind. She might help anyway.

"I'll do anything you want if you get me out of here. I can't take another treatment. I ache all over." Tears clog my throat, but I won't cry. There's no time for that.

"Treatment?" Her jaw tenses, like she's a true friend. Like Billy. Without warning, she touches the back of her hand to my forehead as if I'm a child. "I think you're getting confused. Maybe you should rest."

"No. I have to leave. My father won't listen to me, because he trusts Dr. Morgan." I fist the blanket in my hands. "He doesn't know what it's like. Please. Help me get out of here."

"All right. Stay calm. But before we go, tell me more about these treatments." Her posture is relaxed, but her voice is shaky. "If I understand the problem, I can help convince your father."

Good idea. An ally. And if Daddy doesn't listen, then I'll run away, even if I have to sell my ring for bus fare. Billy would understand. He wouldn't want me to suffer here. "What do you want to know?"

"What is the treatment? Shots?"

I shake my head. "I wish that were all."

"What else, then?" She scooches closer, leaning in, lip caught beneath her teeth.

It's embarrassing, but I close my eyes, determined to do what I must to escape. "They hold me to the bed, then the doctor puts paddles with wet sponges around my head and charges them. Next thing, I'm mostly out of it, but there are lingering tremors, gauze is stuck in my mouth, and they hold me extra tight." I open my eyes to find Annie holding her breath. "My whole body hurts after, and I worry about what it's doing to my brain."

Annie covers her chin, mouth, and cheek with one hand. "Oh, Gram. I'm so sorry."

Graham?

She pities me. I don't like that, but if it helps me, I won't complain. "Don't be sorry. Just help me. Please!"

"I will. But *why* are they giving you shock therapy?" She waits for an answer. I don't know why that matters, but there's no other choice but to trust her.

"For 'depression.'"

She nods solemnly. "Depression . . . because of Billy."

I scramble back against the wall, my breath quick. "Who told you about Billy?"

"You did, and then I found his obituary. He was your husband, who died in the Korean War."

She refers to it funny, like the war's already over. I haven't seen a newspaper in weeks, but no war ends that fast.

"I don't remember telling you anything." I rub my temple to erase thoughts about Billy and the baby. My head is pounding as hard as my heart.

"It's all right. It helps me understand more about you. But shock therapy seems extreme for grief. Is there more to it? Another diagnosis, perhaps?"

I hang my head. She must be a nurse in disguise or something to be asking me these questions. Maybe if I tell the truth, she'll think I'm getting better and let me go sooner. "It's all in the file."

She sucks her lips inward, nodding. "I'd rather not waste time digging for the file when you're so eager to leave. Can you just remind me? Is it bipolar disorder? Schizophrenia?"

"No." I shake my head, scowling. "One night I took all the pills in Daddy's medicine bag. My sister found me, and now I'm here indefinitely."

Annie gathers me into a hug. "Oh, Gram. I'm sorry you were so devastated—that you suffered, but I'm glad you lived."

I have no idea why she keeps calling me Graham, nor do I care. I just want to leave. "You said you'd help me."

Her eyes are red. "I did, and I will." She stands, tapping her mouth with her fingers. "Put on some clothes and then we'll go."

Oh my goodness. Freedom is at my fingertips. I could cry. "Go where?"

"To my house. Change out of those jammies while I deal with the nurses." She nods.

I reach for her. "Wait! They won't let me walk out. We'll have to sneak out."

"Don't worry. They'll listen to me." She pats my hand. "Trust me. I promise everything will be fine."

Her certainty and honest face make me believe her. I get out of bed and change into a comfortable if dowdy dress. Nothing in this closet looks familiar. The styles are strange, too, but I'll make do.

Annie is taking a long time to come back. She was probably some crazy patient who's been taken back to her own room. I'll never get out of here.

I sink onto a chair, deflated. Then Annie reappears.

"All set?" she asks.

"Yes." I rise, oddly unsteady. "Can we leave?"

"I have special permission, so don't be nervous." She cradles my arm like I'm a geezer. I don't fight, though. If she can walk me past the guards, I'll do whatever she wants.

When we leave the room, nothing about these halls looks right. It's all new, and I don't remember this lobby at all. The front porch is gone, too. Now *I'm* confused, so I stop.

"What's wrong?" Annie asks, halting.

"It's all different." I rub my head again, convinced I can smell the bay. The sun is low in the sky, and my stomach rumbles.

"It's okay." She tugs at my arm. "You can close your eyes while I drive. Maybe things will clear up when you wake."

"All right." I let her lead me to her car, which is small and sleek and nothing like my father's and friends' cars. This must be a dream, and when I wake up, I'll still be stuck in my hospital bed.

She settles me in my seat. "Close your eyes and rest."

I'm a little afraid, but the sun beams through the window to warm my face. With my eyes closed, I strategize. The truth is that I'll do whatever my dad says I have to do to avoid going back to Allcot. I'll go to college. I'll marry the right sort of person and have the right sort of family. *Anything* he wants, as long as I never have to be shocked again.

Annie touches my shoulder after she parks the car. "We're here."

I open my eyes and can't breathe. That house might be glowing in the rosy sunset like some beacon of joy, but I'd know it anywhere. "This is my father's house."

"It's my house, I promise." She walks around the car to open my door and help me out. I look at the teal blue front door and white-washed brick of the Cape Cod–style house. That's new, but everything else looks familiar.

"This looks like my father's house," I say to no one.

She guides me up the steps and we go inside, where it's nothing like Daddy's house. The carpets and wallpaper are gone. The fireplace is in the same place, but it's completely different. I've never seen appliances like hers—never.

"Well?" she asks. "Do you like the changes?"

I shrug. I don't want to insult her, but this furniture and the light fixtures are odd. Maybe she's from Europe or California.

The door blows open behind us, and a sweat-soaked young girl comes in carrying plastic bags that smell like food—salty food.

I blink.

Katy! She's a spitfire, like I was at her age.

"Hi, Grammy." She sets the bags on a dining table, then looks at her mom. "I got dinner like you asked and used the change to top off my car."

I chuckle. "You're a sly one, Katy."

Annie's eyes widen. "You recognize her?"

"Of course I do." What's the matter with Annie, thinking I don't know my own great-granddaughter? The real question is how I got here, but I won't ask. It will only worry Annie if she thinks I can't keep track of my comings and goings. "She's a photographer, like me."

There's an odd pause—and a lot of tension. I recognize the atmosphere from my teen years, but then Annie claps her hands together like I'm a toddler taking first steps. "Actually, I turned Grandpa's shed into an art studio. Would you like to see it?"

I nod. "All right."

Annie waves for Katy to join us. "Come on, Katy. Let's show Gram the studio."

Katy doesn't look very excited, though, but I don't ask why. Nothing worse than being forced to talk about things.

Annie has added new steps to the terraced yard and an open firepit. It's all quite pretty. I miss sitting at my kitchen table and watching the birds here in the privacy of my own property. I wouldn't recognize Martin's old shed now that it's been painted that peacock blue and given fancy french doors.

We step inside the bright space, which feels airy thanks to pale walls and a skylight.

"Lucky for Martin I never imagined a shed could look like this or he would've had to find someplace else to store his mower and our patio furniture." I chuckle. It feels good to laugh.

"You would've been ahead of your time if you had," Annie says.

In some ways I had been ahead of my time, but not strong enough—or maybe not passionate enough—to overcome setbacks and pursue my youthful dreams.

A painting in progress sits on the easel. It looks like dark boxes, but I'm sure they're symbolic of something else. Annie never did like painting things exactly as they are. Still, my heart fills to see it. "You're back at it after all this time."

"Relearning the basics," she demurs.

I pat her hand, which is lightly clutching my arm, presumably to keep me from stumbling. "Be patient with yourself. Persevere and it will happen."

Annie nods, but she and Katy carefully avoid looking at each other.

"Katy, don't you have a school project?" My memory is vague, but she talked to me about that, didn't she?

"Not at the moment," she answers, then abruptly changes the subject. "I'm hungry, and the food is getting cold."

"Let's eat, then." Annie turns off the light, and we all return to the house.

Annie goes to the kitchen to get plates and silverware while Katy rips open the bags. One by one, she sets out all the little white takeout boxes.

While waiting for them to settle into their seats, I study the painting above the buffet. It's soothing. Another of Annie's, I suspect. When I encouraged her to dedicate herself to helping Katy years ago, I never thought she'd stop painting altogether. I should've known better, especially when I'd let one horrible summer color my entire outlook for decades. Martin blamed the ECT, yet sometimes I wonder if I used that excuse to cover apprehension that existed before a single paddle touched my head.

Annie returns and fixes me a plate with vegetable lo mein. She and Martin had loved lo mein when she was young. I never did crave Asian food like they had, but anything beats the soggy meals at the care center.

When Katy reaches for the rice container, I see stitches on her arm. I point. "What happened to you?"

She withdraws her arm like my question is a bear trap, and glances at her mom. "I cut myself."

"You should be more careful." I sever my lo mein into manageable lengths.

"Yeah." She falls quiet, and so does Annie.

The tension ramps up, again reminding me of many dinners in this room with my parents. Maybe no family gets through adolescence without drama and pain.

I keep eating, still unsure how I got here. The changes Annie made do make my home more stylish. She's always been stylish, I suppose. And everything changes with time.

Katy pushes her plate away. "I should shower."

"Wait," Annie says. "Gram is still here. How about you spare us a little more time?"

Katy stretches out, crossing her arms and ankles. Pretending to be relaxed—maybe believing she is. She reminds me of myself at that age, poor child. But I get it. Old people aren't interesting.

"Nothing changes," I say, resigned to the absurdity of life.

"What do you mean?" Annie asks before sipping from her glass.

"Families." I choke for a minute when my water goes down the wrong tube.

"Gram?" Annie juts forward, but I wave her off.

"Stop worrying," I say when I can talk. "When my time comes, it comes. Let God take care of the rest."

"Exactly." Katy nods.

Annie shoots her a look I can't read. "I just want to make sure the people I love are safe and happy."

"Good luck with that," I mutter, knowing that we are ultimately responsible only for our *own* happiness and have very little influence on someone else's.

Katy laughs, drawing a sharp look from her mom.

There I go causing trouble, like always. Throughout my life I've inadvertently hurt the people I care about and the people who care about me.

Distracted by Katy's giggling, Annie ignores me while speaking to her daughter. "Go ahead and laugh, but maybe if you'd consider some of the good advice you're given, you'd be happier."

"'Cause *you're* so happy," Katy mumbles.

"Don't be sassy," I cut in to undo the damage I started.

"Sorry," Katy says. "But it's true. You're not happy, Mom."

"I think I'm doing pretty well under the circumstances—and doing it *without* insulting others. You know, if you started helping other people out instead of always thinking about what's *not* going your way, you'd get a new perspective on your own problems." They exchange another look I can't read.

I'm too old for family feuds. It's exhausting. I'm getting fidgety. It's almost time for *Jeopardy!*, and I miss my easy chair. "I'm tired."

The girls stop bickering.

"Would you like me to take you back?" Annie asks.

I nod.

"Katy, please clear the table. I'll be back in thirty minutes." Annie tips her head.

Katy springs from her seat. "Sure."

"Are you ready?" Annie asks me.

"Yes. Thank you." I push up from the table.

"Bye, Grammy." Katy collects the plates. "See you later."

"Bye now." I wave and then let Annie help me down the walkway and back to her car. I can tell she has a lot on her mind. About Katy. About me. Maybe even about what comes next for her.

As we pull down the street, she asks, "Gram, do you remember what you told me earlier today?"

I shrug, having no memory of anything before dinner. I don't want her to know that. It's embarrassing to forget so much all the time.

"Well, I just want to say . . ." Annie's voice sounds strained. "I want to thank you for how you and Grandpa took me in all those summers."

I wave my hands to stop her. Thank me? Pish. "I did what anyone would do."

"That's not true. You made a big commitment at a time when you could've been free. It can't have been easy to entertain a sad, young girl for three months at a time year after year."

Could've been free. My throat hurts. Could be phlegm, but I doubt it. "You were always a good girl."

"I wish I'd known more about your life when I was younger. Understood your passions. Your past."

My past. I'd hoped to bury the last of it with Martin, but it never dies.

"And I'm sorry that I haven't visited you more often these past few years. You shouldn't have had to spend so much time alone." Annie reaches across to squeeze my hand.

"I'm not your responsibility." I pat her hand.

"That's not the point." She shakes her head. "You gave me love and stability when I needed it most. You kept me safe and busy, and filled me with shortbread cookies." She winks.

Oh, those cookies! They were good, but now I don't have a kitchen.

"What I'm trying to say is that I'm sorry I've been absent. I want to do better. I know life always didn't go where you'd wanted, but for what it's worth, I'm glad you met Grandpa, had my dad, and took care of me. I love you, Gram."

I don't understand why she started this conversation. "Okay, Annie. I love you, too."

She smiles before biting her lip. "Can I ask a question?"

I sigh. She's full of energy tonight, but I am not. "Yes."

"If you could go back in time—to my age or even younger—what's the one thing you would do different?" She holds her breath.

I have no idea why that matters, but it seems very important to her that I tell the truth. The whole truth, even if that isn't easy.

"When I was young, I thought my bold ideas—at least by that era's standards—made me special. But ideas without action are just . . ." I twirl my hand in the air. "Instead of making a plan, I reacted to the forces around me. That cost me a lot, so then I lived scared. Made safe choices." Like a strobe light, pictures from my past flash before me—Billy's funeral, Bobby's birth, my thirtieth wedding anniversary. "Martin was a good man. Kind. Loved me despite my flaws, which was a gift. I was grateful, and blessed with Bobby and you, but a homemaker's life wasn't easy for me. Although there were high points, I'd get restless because it wasn't what I'd envisioned for myself. What-ifs can be like poison. In the end, I never did the one thing I wanted—leave town and become a professional photographer." I stare out my window because I don't want to see her eyes.

"It's not easy to be bold when your whole world gets ripped away." Annie isn't talking to me, I don't think.

"You're upset."

She nods. "We're struggling—Katy and me. Nothing about coming back here is what I thought it would be."

"Most things aren't." I clear my throat, reflecting on my past advice. I don't want Annie to have my regrets or to believe motherhood makes it too late to chase a dream. "Life's going to drag you down a bumpy road. You'll stumble and get hurt. But once in a while it's flat and wide-open—exhilarating and drenched in sunlight. If you play it safe, you won't get hurt as much, but it won't be exciting, either.

"The happiest time in my life was when I saw that open road ahead. I let early mistakes hold me back. Then when I was older, I decided I'd missed my chance, but that was wrong. Until you're old and sick like me, it's never too late." I turn to Annie. "Let go of the life you made with Richard and build a new one on your terms. Let Katy learn to navigate the bumps. You're a better mom than I ever was, but don't lose yourself in *that* role, either. Decide what makes you happy and go after it, otherwise you'll have regrets. You hear?"

She glances at me, nose red as her eyes. "I do, Gram."

"Good girl." I nod, glad for the chance to set her on a better path. I stare at the road ahead, which is bathed in the glow of a harvest moon.

Like a heavenly light.

There was a time when I wanted to die to be with Billy. Then I scraped together enough happiness to keep going. Now I don't want to see Billy or Daddy or Martin in the afterlife. Please, God, let heaven be simply a place of freedom from regrets so I can rest in peace.

I never lived in a city—never made a name for myself—but I made a home, and a piece of me lives on in Bobby, Annie, and Katy. If my mistakes teach them to do better, then I've accomplished something worthwhile before I die.

CHAPTER TWENTY-SIX

ANNE

I'm at the dining table, mainlining coffee and making a grocery list, when Katy slings her backpack over her shoulder and calls out goodbye as she heads off to school.

"Have a good day," I say as she's closing the door.

Another swig empties my cup.

It'll take the entire pot to get me moving after spending the night processing my grandmother's attempted suicide, stint in a sanatorium, and ECT. Researching 1940s mental health care and electroshock had brought no comfort. In fact, one of the YouTube videos uploaded from that era reappeared in a nightmare that woke me at three o'clock.

I scrub my hands over my face.

Her current memory loss is likely related to the treatments. The one bright spot is that she didn't seem to recall telling me everything. The stigma she must've faced in the fifties is probably to blame for why she never wanted her son or me to learn about it.

Grandpa had known, though. My respect for him is only deepened from knowing that his love saved her from utter isolation.

It would be easy to blame my great-grandfather. To hate him, even, for being cruel. But what would I do if Katy attempted suicide? I would listen to medical professionals and try anything that I was told would save her. I wonder if he, like me, second-guessed everything he ever did as a parent.

That makes me shudder.

Now I can only hope my and Katy's presence these past months has brought Gram some comfort and that her parting advice last night gave her closure. Not only did Gram's thoughts align with Dr. Grant's theories, but they made me realize that my acting from a place of fear, and reacting to Richard's and Lauren's and Katy's behaviors and expectations, gives me less hand in my fate than that of a leaf floating down a stream.

The time to set a clear vision of the life I want is now. I tear the grocery list off the tablet and write "Life Goals" across the top of the clean sheet of paper. That's the easy part. Tapping the pencil against my lips, I consider what brings me joy.

- Art
- Family
- Love

That's the bottom line: a creative outlet, healthy relationships with the people I love, and romantic love are what I most crave.

Is it possible to create a plan to achieve those broad things? With respect to family, I suppose the plan is to continue working with Dr. Grant to learn better ways to communicate with Katy and Richard. Organizing a family reunion to reconnect with extended family and surround Gram with hers before she can't recognize anyone is another step to take. And maybe once I inform my dad about his mom's young life, it will soften him.

I underline "Art." It'll take time to work back to the skill level I once had, let alone improve upon it. But it's not too late for me to be a professional artist, especially when my expectations are more realistic than they were at eighteen. Am I brave enough to submit something to Trudy's local artist show without worrying about whether it is my "best" work? I scrunch my face, then dial my new friend.

"Hello?" Trudy answers.

"Hey, Trudy. It's Anne."

"Oh, Anne. What's up?"

"Well, Dan converted my old shed to a little studio, so I've dusted off the old tools and am painting again." I flush from head to toe but force myself to keep going. "I'm wondering about the submission deadline for your December show."

"That's excellent! November fifteenth is the deadline, but if you tell me the size of the canvas and style of the work you plan to submit, I can plan for it and give you a little extra time. I'll be doing the installation of everything on November twenty-ninth and thirtieth."

Mid-November gives me a few weeks. It's doable. "Let me think about it and get back to you."

"Terrific. So was the shed Dan's idea? What a great use of dead space."

"It was my idea, but he took it to a new level."

Trudy chuckles. "Dan has a tendency to go all-out when he gets excited about something."

I smile, then frown because I miss him around the house. "Must be why he's so successful."

"Mm-hmm. Hey, I am about to run some errands before the gallery opens. Are you free for a quick lunch later? We can chat more about the show."

"Sounds great. Text me where and when to meet you."

"Done. See you later!"

We hang up, and I sit back staring at the last item on my list. Love. Such a fragile, vulnerable thing. My heart is still weary from Richard's infidelity.

Pushing the pad aside, I then take my empty mug to the kitchen. This fabulous kitchen. The pop of turquoise makes me smile every single day. Dan did an outstanding job.

A slideshow of images flash—him with his brow furrowed, measuring a wall, him carrying boxes of tile to the master bath, him kissing me good night.

I pull out my phone and open my favorites list, then pause. I'm not ready. Not yet. Katy is far from out of the woods, and now I've committed to painting something for the art show. Those two things must take precedence, or I'll fail at everything.

After I have a little success of my own, I'll reach out to Dan. Hopefully he's as patient as he seems.

CHAPTER TWENTY-SEVEN

KATY

When I get home from soccer practice, my mom's not in the kitchen, but I smell a roast in the oven. She's probably in the studio, where she's been spending more time these past few days. I grab a bottled water on my way outside.

When I reach the shed, Mom's back is to the door. As I step inside, the scent of oil paint takes me back to the days when I'd color at my dad's feet while he was studying for the bar exam and she was working on her art. Dad laughed a lot more back then. Mom too. Maybe if she hadn't quit working and painting, they would've stayed in love. And if I'm the reason she gave up art, then I'm also the reason everything fell apart.

She glances over her shoulder with a smile as I sneak up behind her. I'm surprised she heard me because she's so intent when she paints.

The painting is haunting. Abstract impressionism—her favorite. To me it resembles a dark forest broken up by points of gold and orange shining through the "trees." No pathway to follow, though. Just the hope of something better on the other side of the woods. "How long have you been out here?"

She glances at the clock. "On and off all afternoon."

"What inspired this?" I point at the picture, assuming it's a message for me.

"Nothing. Everything. Something Gram said . . ." She swivels back to her painting.

Before we worked with Dr. Grant, she'd hit me with a thousand questions about my day, soccer, friends . . . anything and everything. She'd backed off a bit when we'd first gone to Dr. Grant, but then after I cut again, she hovered more. Since our fight earlier this week, though, she's given me a ton of space. "I told Tomás he could come use the studio tonight. His small house is chaotic with all his siblings."

I brace for her to say something more about my dropping out of the art show.

"That's fine." Nothing more. Is this a trick, or is her getting back to painting meant as a subtle nudge for me to pick up the camera?

My stomach growls. "When will dinner be ready?"

She glances over her shoulder again, eyes going round. "Actually, it might be overcooked!"

I frown. "Mom, what's going on?"

She puts down her paintbrush and turns in her chair. "What do you mean?"

"Since we argued, you haven't asked about the art show even once. If it's some kind of reverse psychology to get me to submit something, it won't work." I cross my arms and stare at her, but my chest is heavy.

She rubs her thighs with a little huff. "Is that supposed to be an apology for all the rude things you said to me in front of my grandmother?"

I flush from my head to my toes and fiddle with the rubber band. "Sorry."

Mom grabs my hand. "I know." She nods toward my desk chair. "Sit for a second so we can talk."

Dr. Grant encourages me to listen without feeling attacked or judged, so I sit.

"I've been thinking a lot these past few days—about Dr. Grant, Gram, you, and me." Mom blows out a breath. "I wasn't much older than you when I got pregnant, but I was determined to be the best mom—like I remember my mother. I had visions of me knowing you better than you knew yourself, and you adoring and respecting me."

Her resigned tone hurts my heart because she thinks that I don't feel those things, but that's not true. I just lash out when I'm upset.

She continues, "I was certain I could teach you to be wiser than your age and keep you from making mistakes. But Dr. Grant is right. You can't learn from *my* mistakes—you need to make your own so you learn how to pick yourself up and go on. And I can't be a perfect mother because there isn't any such thing. Every mother is different and human, and we make mistakes just like you. We have baggage, like you. We get it wrong and have to start again, like you."

"You're not a bad mom. You're a great mom most of the time." My face and arms grow tingly.

"Thank you." She stands and pulls me up into a hug. "I love you. I'll always love you. And if you need me, you have only to ask for help. But I finally understand that the longer I run your life, the longer it'll take you to be comfortable doing that for yourself. So if you don't want to be in the art show, that's your choice."

I nod, but it feels like the ground is moving beneath me.

She steps back and drops her chin. "There's more."

Oh boy, another tectonic plate shift makes me nauseated.

"Your father and I have been talking about what a hard time you're having down here. We want you to wake up happy and look forward to your day. To school. To your future, Katy. So, if you want to go back to your old school with your old friends, then you can move in with your dad and finish high school at Prep, and stay with me on the weekends and summers."

"You don't want me anymore?" My ribs pinch my lungs.

"Of course I want you with me, but this place is *my* dream, not yours. I forced you—selfishly—to come with me. Maybe a little part of me was afraid that if you stayed with your dad, you'd leave me behind, making all the years I'd given you seem like a waste of my life. But that's not true, or fair to you.

"I gave you everything I had because I love you and it made me happy to be with you—not so that you would owe me your life in return. In the end, everything I did was done so you would flourish. I have to let go now so you can do what you need to do to be happy." She blows some curls from her eyes. "If you do stay—which I would love—it'll be different around here because I've also realized some things about myself. I've been a wife and mom so long I hardly remember who Anne Sullivan is. So while you're figuring out your stuff, I'll be figuring out what *I* need to be happy, too. It's not fair for either of us when I tie all my joy to you."

Shit, this is scary. When I snap my rubber band a few times, her gaze drops to my wrist before meeting my eyes.

"Do you want to talk about how you feel, or would you rather sleep on it?" she asks, holding her breath.

She's scared about me cutting again. The urge is still there—I can't lie. The rubber band helps, and I don't want more scars. My goal is to make it to my next appointment with Dr. Grant without another scar. "I'll think about it. Right now, I need to shower before Tomás shows up."

"Let me get that roast out of the oven before it's totally ruined." She removes her smock and hangs it on the hook.

I'm not great at telling people how I feel, but there are a lot of feelings right now, so I catch her by the hand.

"I love you, Mom." I hug her really hard. She holds me so tight I'm surprised we don't both pass out.

We break apart without saying more. She kisses my forehead, and we head to the house so I can clean up. The hot shower doesn't fully soothe my uneasiness.

No matter what she says, she'll be sad if I go live with Dad. Dealing with Lauren more often sounds worse than sticking it out here. Graduating from this high school will also mean less competition within my class for the top schools. That ups my chances for UVA or Georgetown. Some of the girls on my soccer team are nice. I could try harder to insert myself into their groups. And then there's Tomás. He's nice. And cute, in a geeky kind of way. When that makes me smile, I frown.

Sometimes I wish I could see the future and know everything will be okay.

Downstairs, Mom's plated slices of roast beef with roasted potatoes. Comfort food, as she calls it. We don't say much while taking our seats. I guess we're the same—all mixed up and trying to figure out what to do next. Rather than talk about that more, I change the subject.

"Did you ever ask Grammy about Billy's obituary?"

"I did." She bites her lip. "To be honest, there's a lot more to the story." She launches into this whole thing about Grammy and suicide attempts and ECT. I can hardly believe any of it. "It puts a lot of things in a new perspective. My mom doted on me completely before she died, and then Gram did after that. My whole life I thought they were examples of 'perfect' motherhood.

"But knowing what Gram suffered—what she lost and why—has helped me start to look at our life differently. For the better, I think. It must've been frustrating for her, trying to be that square peg in a round hole. But I know she wants something different for us now. I think the first step is that we respect each other and honor our own needs. That said, I emailed Dr. Grant about Gram's suicide attempt because depression can be genetic."

If my stomach was queasy before, it's worse now. "Do you think I'm suicidal? 'Cause I'm not. I don't want to die."

"No, honey. I don't think you're suicidal, but depression can run in families, so we should treat it like heart disease and diabetes. We give our doctors all the facts so they know what to watch for."

"Does Pop-Pop know?"

She nods. "I told him yesterday."

"Why?" I drag a potato through some of the beef gravy. "I mean, it's not like it makes much difference to him now."

"I hope it explains why she wasn't warmer to him when he was young. It wasn't personal, but she was still close to her grief and wrestling her choices. Maybe that will help him make peace with it before it's too late." She shrugs, fork and knife in hand, with a huff. "Or maybe it won't make a damn bit of difference to anyone but me."

"What about Grammy? Does she remember telling you all her secrets?"

She leans forward, chin on her fists. "I'm not sure. But I hope, in the moment she unloaded it all, it gave her some closure."

The doorbell rings before I can ask more. "That's probably Tomás. Please don't be weird."

"I'll do my best," she says drolly. She was actually okay the last time he came to work in the studio, so I shouldn't worry.

I trot to the door, feeling a little lighter after Mom and I have cleared the air. Surprise, surprise—Elmo's in sweats and an old T-shirt instead of his typical hipster clothes. I must be staring, because he says, "I was helping my dad with the leaves."

I nod and wave him inside.

Mom waves. "Hey, Tomás. Are you hungry?"

She never said what she thinks of him, but she must notice how different he is from the guys I used to hang out with—and not only because he's half their size.

"I ate already, but thanks." He shoots me a look. "Are you finished with dinner?"

"Yeah."

"You two go on. I'll deal with the dishes," Mom offers.

"Great. Thanks," I say.

Tomás waves to my mom. "Nice to see you, Mrs. Chase."

I get why my mom flinches every time someone calls her that. It's a crappy reminder.

I lead Tomás outside.

"Are you bummed you aren't putting anything in the show?" he asks, slowing down.

"A little." I snap the rubber band.

His gaze drops to my wrist, and he twists his mouth. "When do those stitches come out?"

I stare at him, mortified. "Soon."

He's studying me. "I want to say something, but don't take it wrong. It's, like, not a judgment at all, but I think I know what the deal is with that rubber band. I had a cousin who cut herself for a while, but she's better now. It gets better."

Rather than hide, I hold my arm out. "I've only done it twice."

"That's really good." He surprises me when he takes my hand and squeezes it. My body fills with warmth. He's so not my type, but I like Tomás. Like, I might *like* him like him.

I pull my hand back but resist the urge to rub my thumb on my palm where his fingers had been. "Thanks."

"For what?"

"For being straight up. Not playing dumb. It's actually nice to be able to talk about it with someone besides my doctor or my parents."

"Trust me, there's no way you're the only one at school who cuts."

"You think?" I can't imagine other kids as screwed up as me.

"Think about it. No one sees this side of you at school because you project this tough act. Most kids envy you—the girl with everything—while they sit at home wishing they had your life."

"Joke's on them." I try to laugh it off, but it's hard in the face of my stitches. How ridiculous that anyone would envy *me*. Then I think about how I look on the outside, how my old friends look in their Insta feed, and I get a crazy idea. "What if we took pictures of my arm? Like a series of photos—a statement about high school and stress . . . sort of the anti-Finsta poster girl."

His brows rise so high they're covered by his bangs. "It's super brave to be that real. Like really real."

"My camera is in the studio."

"I'll shoot them for you. You just tell me how you want them—you know, angles, close-ups, whatever."

I glance around the patio, but it's too dark for good photos outside. "Okay. If they come out good, we can submit them as a joint project."

"Cool." He smiles. "Where do you want to start?"

"I guess in the studio. Go ahead up. My camera should be on the desk. I need to grab my X-Acto knife, otherwise it won't make sense." After the second cutting, Mom removed the knife from the studio and put it in the kitchen junk drawer. I can hardly blame her for taking a precaution.

He grimaces. "That's bold."

I shrug. "Be right back."

When I duck inside, my mom asks, "Is everything all right?"

"Yeah. I need my knife." I see a moment of terror cross her face before I go into the kitchen. "Don't worry. It's for the pictures."

"What pictures?" She blinks.

Tomás is already waiting for me, so I quickly relay my idea. My mom's heart is beating so violently I can see an artery in her neck pulsing.

She swallows hard. "If you think you're ready for that, I trust you. Take the pictures and see how they turn out. If you change your mind, that's fine, too."

That had to be super hard for her. I might change my mind, but right now I'm inspired, and not just because Tomás called me brave. "Thanks."

After I get up to the studio, I slide onto my seat with my forearm on my desk facing upward and the blade lying beside it. He takes one photo from a standing position, then he crouches to be even with my arm. When he's that close, I can smell his deodorant—it's spicy. And his hair is so thick and shiny I want to touch it. When I hear the click, I shift my arm back and tug at the rubber band with my other fingers. "Take this, too."

He does.

Then I look at him. "Might as well go for it." I hold my forearm up under my chin. "Somber or smiling?"

"How do you feel?" he asks. Such a simple question on the surface, but so complex.

I feel powerful, like I'm taking control over my scars. The courage makes me want to smile, so I do.

Tomás takes two more pictures and then hands me the camera. He stretches his arms behind his back. "I bet more pictures have been taken since we were born than in all of history before that. People are obsessed. Dinner plates and selfies—it's all kind of dumb. I only want to take pictures that mean something, like these."

"Does everything have to mean something? Sometimes it's fun to see a picture of a really cool cake."

He tips his head side to side like he's considering that. "Except all those meaningless pictures have replaced actual conversation."

I shove his shoulder. "You sound like my mom."

"I'm an old soul, I guess." He laughs. I like that, because his laugh sounds like freedom.

He *is* an old soul, which also explains why he doesn't run with a crowd. Elmo doesn't fit in, but he doesn't care. There's something liberating about that. He's got no trouble making decisions or deciding what he wants. He's not so screwed up that he's abusing himself. Why does he even want to hang around me?

Tomás kicks my foot playfully. "*Jane*, you seem . . . preoccupied."

I meet his gaze. "My mom just offered to let me go live with my dad so I could go back to Prep."

He pulls back, frowning. "Is that what you want?"

I glance at my feet and shrug.

His head tilts sideways, his eyes downcast. "I thought you didn't like Lauren."

"I don't."

He rubs his scalp. "Your mom is pretty cool to let you choose."

I'm not sure what to make of her, like all of a sudden she's made this big U-turn on me. She's basically giving me everything I said I wanted, but the truth is, what I actually want is to be like Tomás—centered and certain.

He is pretty quiet now, but I don't ask what's on his mind.

While I'm plugging the camera into the computer, Tomás flicks my arm. "Sorry if I'm being weird. You should go back if that makes you happy."

"What do you think I should do?"

"You should stay so I can have access to this place," he teases. Then he clears his throat. "And 'cause I'd miss you."

A satisfied sigh forms before I can stop it. "You're so honest . . . like you couldn't care less what other people think. How do you do that?"

"I care what *some* people think, like my family." He shrugs. "But high school is just four years of my life. Why worry about most of those people's opinions when I'll move on soon enough?"

Like my old friends have moved on without me.

He smooths his hand along the edge of the desk. "I figure stuff will work out like it's supposed to."

"But what if you're wrong? What if nothing works out right?"

He laughs. "I guess I'll deal with it then."

"So you really don't try to control anything, not even the stuff you wish would last?"

"If something is important, I'll work hard for it. But the best surprises come when stuff unfolds naturally, like getting to know you." One half of his mouth lifts, and the air in the shed charges. My heart skips a beat, too.

I hold up my injured arm. "You don't have high expectations, do you?"

"Don't put yourself down." He slides closer. "I like you, Katy. You're smart and sarcastic. Sometimes even funny." He makes a face at me. "Most important, you're not a phony . . . That's rare. Who cares if you've got some issues? Everyone does."

I'm not sure if I want him to kiss me or if I'm afraid that will ruin everything, so I bump shoulders instead. There's no rush. I'm not going to go back to Prep. "I like you, too, Elmo." I open Photoshop to prevent the conversation from going further. "Ready to see what we've got on here?"

"I came to work." He winks.

I think we both know that's not the only reason he's here, and I'm kind of happy about it, which says a lot, since I can't remember the last time I felt happy.

CHAPTER
TWENTY-EIGHT

ANNE

"Before we go in, I want to tell you again how proud I am. You're so much braver than me." I reach across the center console and grab Katy's hand, too aware of the six brightly colored rubber bands around her wrist—another statement, or badge of courage. "Are you worried about how other parents might react?"

"Not really." She shrugs. I wouldn't believe her except that she's been working with Dr. Grant a few times each week for the past month and been honest about the urge to cut. Bit by bit, she's finding new coping tactics. "The whole point is to make people uncomfortable so they see what's happening with kids. Since the photos went up this week, two students have DM'd me for advice about cutting."

"Have they?" Both hands hit my chest. "That's amazing. It must feel good to make a difference."

"I don't know if I feel *good*—I mean, it's sad to hear those stories. And it's not like I'm 'cured,' and have answers. But Dr. Grant helps me figure out how to talk about the daily struggle without making it sound hopeless."

The daily struggle. It'll be many months or longer until I can fully relax, but Katy is taking ownership and putting in the work.

We've found a nice rhythm in our house and with new friends. My hostility toward Richard has lessened since that teary apology in his home office, but I'm still working on accepting Lauren as part of our future. This morning I submitted a painting to Trudy for the Holiday Stroll opening event in a couple of weeks. It's not my best-ever work, but it represents my first real step forward, which is the most important thing.

Anytime I've thought to call Dan, I stop myself, uncertain of what to say. It's been a few weeks since we last saw each other in my driveway. Whatever might happen between us in the future, it would need to progress very slowly. That seems like a selfish thing to ask of someone whose kindness I've already rejected.

In any case, tonight is not for mooning over Dan or preening over my own progress. Tonight is about Katy and the rest of the teens who are putting their hearts on display at the school art show.

"Well, I guess we should go in. Pop-Pop and Gram might already be here." I open the car door. In recent weeks, I've visited Gram almost daily. Even Katy has come with me more often. After Ms. Pope told Katy and the other students about Jay Fleming, an area photographer, Katy shared his book *Working the Water*—environmental photographs taken in and around Chesapeake Bay—with Gram and convinced me to take us all on a field trip to his gallery in Annapolis last weekend. The trip was a bit ambitious, as Gram got confused and anxious throughout the morning, but it's still a memory I will cherish.

Katy follows my lead. "It's nice that Pop-Pop came all the way down tonight just for this."

"He's trying." That's as much as I can say. Despite my pleas and his knowing the truth about his mother, my dad will never make a sea change. He's a loner, and I'm finally learning not to take that personally. "I'm not sure how long they'll stay. The crowds and noise could be hard for Gram."

"It'll be nice if she recognizes us, even for a few minutes."

I cross my fingers. "Let's hope."

When we enter the lobby, I scan the crowd for my dad. He's six feet three, so it's always easy to spot his strawberry-blond hair. When I do, I wave and tug Katy through the crowd to reach them.

"Thanks for coming, Dad." I kiss him and Gram hello.

Katy hugs Gram first, then my dad. "Thanks for coming to my show."

"It's crowded." Gram sticks close to my father to keep from being jostled. She hasn't addressed Katy or me by name, so I'm not sure she's fully cognizant of who we are yet. She appears comfortable with her son, though.

I don't ask.

"Crowds are good—more buyers for the fundraiser," my dad says. "Shall we get started?"

"Have you seen my dad yet?" Katy asks, standing on her toes, searching for Richard. I take a deep breath and brush imaginary lint off my sweater. This will be the first time he and Lauren have socialized with my family for Katy's sake. My stomach isn't cooperating, but I manage a calm facade.

Sure enough, Katy spots Richard's black-and-silver hair and begins to wave her hands in the air.

My dad puts a hand on my shoulder. His uncharacteristic physical show of support nearly makes me cry.

I pat his hand and whisper, "It's okay. Richard and I have to come together for Katy's sake."

"Good for you," Dad says quietly.

When they reach us, Richard gives Katy a bear hug. I can tell he's whispering something in her ear. As always, seeing them together produces a bittersweet pang in my chest. When they break apart, he kisses my cheek and shakes my father's hand. "Robert."

"Richard," Dad says, stone-faced, with a single shake and quick release.

It's stiff and awkward, but we all survive. I can count on my father to say very little, which in this case is a good thing.

Richard blinks when he spots Gram. "Marie, this is a surprise. You look well."

"Thank you," she says, not offering her cheek. Her blank look suggests she can't quite place him. Or maybe she is being cold on my account. Hard to tell.

Lauren squirms. My gut tightens with enmity that might never subside, but my daughter's courage inspires me to rise above it. "Hello, Lauren. Thanks for coming to support Katy."

"It's a big thing she's done." Lauren nods, clutching Richard's arm.

"It is." I turn toward my family. "Dad, Gram, this is Lauren. Lauren, this is my father and grandmother, Robert and Marie."

Gram is quiet, Dad is polite, and I'm glad that part is over.

"So where's your project?" Richard asks.

"Downstairs, outside the cafeteria." Katy tugs at his arm. "Come on."

Gram can't navigate this crowd quickly, so I wave them on, having already seen Katy's work when I helped set up the exhibit last weekend. "You guys go ahead. We'll catch up."

Richard and Lauren exchange a look. "Are you sure?"

I nod, having no wish to extend a conversation with my not-yet ex and his lover.

As soon as they are out of earshot, my father grumbles, "He's an idiot."

I can't help it. I laugh aloud. It's great to shed the sorrow and self-pity. To not feel like as much of a pathetic reject. Somehow in the midst of all the chaos these past few months, I've turned a corner. "Thanks, Dad."

"I saw a new painting in Mom's room when I picked her up," he says as we begin our slow march through the halls, Gram in between us.

"I've been playing around a bit. The canvas is a great place to unload my feelings."

"That's great, Anne." He smiles. "Your mother would've loved your work. I wish she were around to see how you've grown, and to meet Katy."

My eyes get dewy. "So do I, Dad. But you're here, and Gram. I really appreciate the effort, and Katy does, too."

He nods. "Will you sell your work again?"

"I submitted something to the local art gallery for its December local artist exhibit." I smile, conjuring the abstract painting of my house, done in warm shades of gold and rose and plum. "I've been getting to know the owner, Trudy. She's savvy and witty. I really like her." Of course, that makes me think of Dan, who'd encouraged me to meet her.

"Mom!" Katy calls over the crowd inside the cafeteria. When I see her, she's holding a bouquet of vibrant gerbera daisies.

"Where did those come from?" I ask when we catch up to her. Then I see Tomás behind her. "They're gorgeous."

I give Tomás a quick hug, careful not to be too "weird" and embarrass Katy. He's been at the house several times this past month. The mutual attraction between them is obvious to me, but I suspect Katy is too afraid to risk ruining the friendship. I don't blame her. In fact, I understand exactly how she feels.

Truthfully, I half hope I'll bump into Dan here tonight, which would spare me the discomfort of making a surprise phone call. He knows so many people in the community—he could show up. It's why I've worn makeup.

"You guys did such a good job with this." She and Tomás turned their work into a collage, although it isn't as intricate as her original idea. This piece involves a simple line drawing of her profile. Outside the profile are images from her social media accounts—happy faces, friends, soccer games, vacations. The "good life" images we all post to trumpet our "success" to friends and frenemies alike. Inside the profile are the images of her stitches, the other scar, the rubber band, and an honest selfie of her scarred arm beneath her chin.

I don't know how many teens will see themselves in this work, but I certainly see elements of my own life represented. The brave face I wear in public. The private battles and losses. Maybe I did one thing right as a parent, because my daughter sure is more astute about human nature than I was at her age.

Tomás gestures to Katy. "I can hardly take credit. It was all her idea. I just took the pictures."

"Well, they came out great. Time to bid!" It's so hard to say that because seeing the close-ups of her stitches and scars is like a stab to the gut. But it's a heroic piece of art, and I will bid an outrageous sum because I want it for us. A symbol of our triumph over adversity. Of the rainbow after the storm. I whip out my phone and use the app to make a bid.

Gram points at the collage. "Katy, this is good work."

Finally, she's with us. It makes my heart lurch.

"Who's this young man?" she asks, looking at Tomás.

He extends his hand. "Hi. I'm Tomás London, Katy's friend. I helped with the collage."

"Very nice." Gram pats my dad on the wrist and makes a very motherly motion for him to scoot. She turns to me. "Annie, keep an eye on Katy. Young hearts break easy."

Knowing her history sheds new light on this statement and much of her past advice. "I will, Gram. Don't worry. What do you think of all the artwork tonight?"

My auction app pings, letting me know I've been outbid. I quickly ante up and resubmit the new bid.

Gram says, "We never had anything this grand at my high school."

How different her life might've turned out if she'd been born in this generation.

My dad is asking Katy something when a voice behind me makes me bristle.

"Anne, weren't you on the setup committee?" Tori asks.

I step away from my family to minimize the fallout of whatever might be coming. My best guess is that she'll dress me down because she doesn't like the placement of her stepson's work. "Yes. Why?"

She glances at Katy's collage with bug eyes and then back to me. "Why would you let her put that up?"

At first, my body goes hot and cold. But Katy's bold public move has robbed bullies like Tori of the ability to make her ashamed. When I realize that Katy has coated herself in Teflon, it's all I can do to unclench my fist and stop myself from clocking Tori. "Katy wanted to make a social statement, and I support her."

Tori smugly raises her hands. "Well, it doesn't reflect well on either of you."

Insults crowd my mouth. It would take two seconds to call out her bullshit and level her fragile ego. But there's no point. I'm not that cruel, nor would I do anything to ruin Katy's big night. Tori is a nonentity in my life, and what will bother her most is seeing that she's lost all power over me. The app pings again, as if to punctuate my insight. I quickly up my bid before facing off with Tori.

"Actually, you couldn't be more wrong. Now, go support your stepson and let me enjoy my daughter tonight." I walk away before she gets another dig in, certain she won't make a scene in front of all these people.

The truth is she's the one who's most concerned with public opinion. If I'd been smarter at twelve—or even more recently—it would've spared me a lot of tears.

Katy glances over her shoulder at me and wiggles her eyebrows before her hand shoots up in the air again. "Dan! Over here!"

Tonight is living up to the gauntlet I expected. But I'm still standing. That's a win.

My gaze follows hers through a cluster of people to Dan. My heart fills until I see that he's here with an attractive woman about his age, maybe a few years older. The app pings again, but I'm too crushed by this unexpected reality to move. Dan's head swivels toward us. The hand covering my stomach doesn't stop the somersaults. There's no way to blow out my breath without everyone noticing, so it's trapped in my lungs.

He smiles at my daughter before excusing himself from his companion to come to greet us. "Hey, Katy." He glances at me. "Anne."

Richard extends his hand, surprising Dan and me. "You must be the contractor. I'm Richard, Katy's father."

"Nice to meet you. You've got a great kid." Dan then turns to the rest of us.

After quick introductions to everyone, Dan says to Katy, "I saw your collage. Looks like you're putting the shed to good use."

"We are." She gestures between herself and Tomás. "So is Mom."

"That's good." He then slides another look at me.

"I wasn't sure we'd see you tonight," I blurt.

His hands are clasped behind his back. "I never miss the big events in our small town."

I'm almost glad for the horde around us because my mind is blank, although half-formed thoughts race through my head—like how much I miss talking to him, and how sorry I am that I didn't realize that before he met someone new.

"Dan!" The woman he came with is waving him back.

"Well, you all enjoy your evening." He nods. "Great job, Katy."

And just like that, he's absorbed by the crowd and disappears.

Jealousy is unfair. I told him not to wait around. He deserves happiness, and that woman looks nice enough. Still, my chest feels bruised.

"Maybe we should look at some of the other students' work," I say, hoping no one can tell how hard I'm trying not to frown.

"Sure," Katy says. "There's some cool stuff in the atrium. This way."

We follow her like a ragtag band of groupies. Lauren is offering compliments but otherwise staying very much in the background. Someday we might coexist without my gut simmering with bitterness. I'm not quite there yet, but with time and determination, I will be. Striking a new balance with Katy and investing in my art is already helping.

Before I remember to update my bid, the auction closes.

"Oh no!" I gasp.

Richard turns, brows tight. "What's wrong?"

My shoulders drop. "Someone outbid me for Katy's piece."

A slow smile spreads across his face as he raises his phone. "Sorry, but you know how much I like to win. If you want, we can share it."

I bark a laugh because it is both absurd and perfect. Katy will beam when she learns that her father wanted her work enough to outmaneuver me. "Deal."

"Well, we'd best get home to relieve the babysitter," he says. He grabs Katy and murmurs something to her that makes her smile; then he and Lauren wave goodbye.

"I'm looking forward to your chestnut stuffing next week," Dad says. I'm grateful for the distraction because, despite my progress, a tiny part of me will always regret that my family is split in two.

"Yes. Can't believe Thanksgiving is almost here. You'll bring Gram?"

He nods.

Gram takes my arm, leaning close. "I'm glad you came back, Annie. Martin would be happy that you're in the house."

That makes my eyes mist, and I hug her. "I'm glad, too. Isn't it funny? You gave me a sanctuary when I was little, and once again your home is my haven."

"Life is strange." She makes a face, all her wrinkles gathering together.

"And wonderful." Even when it isn't perfect.

CHAPTER TWENTY-NINE

ANNE

"Why can't I have a glass of champagne?" Katy asks as another tray goes by. Finch Street Studio's lights are so bright tonight it feels like a Hollywood premiere, especially with the festivities and holiday lights all around town for its annual Holiday Stroll celebration. "You let me at home."

"We're not *at* home." Two weeks ago we celebrated Katy's show, and tonight it's my turn. I fiddle with my jacket sleeves while she sighs. Black velvet with bell sleeves and ribbon lacing running up the back, paired with flared black silk slacks and a scoop-neck camisole. I added silver and turquoise jewelry for flair. It's the most dressed I've been since before Richard announced our divorce.

It feels surprisingly good, even if a small part of me has to look great in case I run into Dan and his new girlfriend tonight. Between his friendship with Trudy and his sociable attitude about town events, chances are high we'll cross paths. I wonder if that woman at the school has become very important to him, or if she is still relegated to the casual zone. If he comes alone, I will find the nerve to test the waters between us.

"Are you mad at Pop-Pop for not coming?" Katy asks.

"No." I wipe the frown from my face. "I don't want him on the highway. It's supposed to snow a little this evening, and his night vision isn't great."

Outside the plate glass window of Trudy's gallery, silvery clouds move against the dark sky. The snow hasn't started yet, but a metallic tang hangs in the air.

Despite expecting to dread my first holiday season as a divorcée, I don't. Thanksgiving went well. Katy will be with me on Christmas Eve and morning, and then join her father for dinner Christmas night. When she leaves, I'll soak in my tub, treat Gram to a homemade dinner, and be grateful that my daughter and I are finding our way forward with less drama and more optimism. The new year will kick off nicely now that Jackie's invited me to her annual New Year's Eve party. She's determined to play matchmaker, but maybe Dan will be free.

"I still think you should've let me bring Gram," Katy says.

I put an arm around her. "I wanted us to be able to relax and enjoy the night without having to keep a close eye on her. The crowds overwhelm her, and I worry she could get jostled or worse at the stroll."

Katy nods just as Trudy stops by.

"Anne, I'm really excited about your piece." She touches my arm. "I thought you might show up with Dan, since he introduced us and is such a fan of yours."

Katy's brows rise even as she looks at her feet. When we got home from her school's art show, she'd asked me if I was upset about Dan being there with someone else. I'd brushed it off as a mild disappointment, but she's too perceptive to have believed me.

"Thank you, Trudy." I let the remark about Dan go. "I love where you placed it."

My painting is one of very few that hangs on its own short wall.

"It works. And it's deserving of extra attention. I'm sure it will sell quickly." She smiles and turns to Katy. "You must be Anne's daughter."

"Hi." Katy shakes her hand. "I'm Katy."

"Nice to meet you. I'm Trudy." She crosses her arms. "Do you share your mom's talent?"

Katy shakes her head. "I don't paint much, but I draw and take photographs."

"She's got great vision, especially with photography and collage." I can't help but brag. It's what mothers do, I suppose.

Katy blushes.

"Next year you should contribute something here. You see it's a mishmash in December, everything from photography to metalwork."

"It's cool," Katy says.

Trudy laughs. "Teens don't often accuse me of being cool, so I'll take the praise." Then she gives a little wave. "Well, I must mingle. Enjoy the night. When you leave, you should visit the other shops. The Holiday Stroll is lovely. Most shop owners serve hors d'oeuvres and beverages . . . Cocoa and salted chocolates are popular."

"Sounds delightful," I say.

"Have fun. Ciao!" Trudy moves on to the next small crowd, leaving us alone again.

"I'm not surprised she gave you your own wall. Yours is one of the better paintings, Mom." Katy points over her shoulder to a remarkably intricate and delicate paper sculpture of snowflakes. "But I like that piece, too."

"I can't imagine the tedious hours of cutting and layering it required." We walk closer to inspect it. The price tag reads $2,800.

"Buy it. It'd look great on that empty wall in your bathroom."

It would, although the moisture from the tub and shower might damage it over time. "That's pricey for bathroom art."

Katy wrinkles her nose. "Why'd you put such a low price on yours?"

Five hundred dollars doesn't seem low to me, considering I haven't painted in years and have no name to speak of. "I calculated a twenty-dollar-per-hour rate on top of the cost of materials, which seems fair. It's not about the money, though. Putting myself out there is a huge step for me. That's the win."

"Do you feel better seeing how good it is compared with most of the other art?"

My nose wrinkles. I won't get close to my best work until I regain my old confidence and take risks. But it is a competent step back into this world. I throw an arm around her shoulders and give a squeeze. "Thank you, but you are biased."

She cocks her head. "Dr. Grant says we should accept compliments instead of deflecting."

Katy isn't wearing any rubber bands tonight, so I will adhere to whatever Dr. Grant says. "You're right. Thank you. I'm glad you like my work."

Katy tips her head side to side, glancing around while tapping her toe against the floor. It's not a shock she's bored among all the adults. "Tomás is working at Sugar Momma's tonight. Can I go say hi?"

I glance at my watch. We've been here only fifteen minutes, but I remember being young and don't want to force her to hang out with me. "Okay. Keep your phone on. I'll text you when I decide to sneak out of here and catch up with you."

"Cool. See you later." She gives me a quick hug. "Good luck!"

Her smile and breezy joy are the best gifts I could receive this season.

When the champagne tray passes by, I take a flute and head to the back of the gallery to take a slow stroll past all the artwork. I'm standing in front of a pastel impressionist oil of the bay. It's a decent amateur attempt, though not particularly evocative. But with practice, this artist will improve.

"Anne?" Dan says from behind me.

I turn suddenly, nearly spilling my champagne. He looks even more handsome than he did at the high school show, dressed in nice jeans and a lightweight sweater, much like the night of our ill-fated date. "Dan. Hi!"

I'm too bright. I can tell because my cheeks hurt from holding my grin in place. The woman he was with at the high school is right behind him. My lungs deflate, but I extend my hand. "Hi, I'm Anne Sullivan. Dan did work on my house this summer."

When I say it like that, it sounds distant and impersonal. So unlike the truth.

"Hi, Anne. He's mentioned your project." She smiles. "I'm his sister, Melissa."

His *sister*. The relief that floods my system makes me feel faint.

"He did a great job," I reply before gulping down the rest of my drink.

"It's nice to have a handyman in the family." She slaps his shoulder; then her attention is pulled. "There's Trudy. Let me go catch up," she says to Dan. Then to me: "Nice to meet you."

"You too." I wave as she dashes over to hug Trudy.

Small towns.

The crowd around us fades into the background, almost like we are surrounded by a moat. My heart expands, pounding against my ribs for another chance.

"How are you?" A loaded question that can be either trivial or monumental depending on who is asking and how much they care.

"Busy. Joe has the flu, so I'm working overtime trying to finish up two projects by Christmas."

"Hopefully he'll recover quickly."

Dan nods. We're drowning in awkward silence while I muster the courage to ask if he's still interested in getting to know me on a deeper level.

"Katy seems better. Brave collage she put up at the school," Dan volleys.

"You were right about her. She's tougher than I thought." I draw a breath for courage. "I've wanted to call you, but I didn't know what to say or if it mattered . . . Then when I saw you at the high school, I thought you were on a date."

He smiles. "It's okay. You needed space. I get it."

"I did. Need space, I mean. But things are better." I look him fully in the eyes.

"I'm glad." He gestures toward my painting. "Looks like you're getting back into the swing of things."

"It's been a good way to channel my emotions."

"My house could use some new art," he says as he steps toward my painting.

I detect his approval from the hint of a smile and the way his eyes move across the canvas. With my hands clasped behind my back, still holding the empty flute, I say, "Maybe I could come over to see your house sometime . . . and help you find the right piece."

I hold my breath, flushing.

He turns his head to meet my gaze and touches my arm. "I'd love that."

"So would I." I'm about to ask when, but his sister returns.

"Sorry to interrupt, Dan, but we've got to run. Mom's already grabbed us a table at East Beach Café with my kids." She tugs at him. "Again, it was nice to meet you, Anne."

"Enjoy your dinner." I wave.

"Congratulations on the show." Dan leans in to give me a kiss on the cheek and murmurs, "I'll call you."

"I look forward to it."

He holds the door for his sister but glances over his shoulder and winks at me before they leave. I let out the breath I've been holding and spin on my heel to take it all in. Me, alone, looking good and at my first art show in more than a decade, with a handsome man interested in getting to know me better.

I'm no longer Anne Chase, nor am I Anne Sullivan the art student, or even Annie, who used to summer here. I'm a reincarnated version of those three women on the verge of a fresh new life. One that I will craft by myself, for myself. One that my daughter can look up to as we make our way into the future.

With a satisfied smile, I text Katy and make my way toward Sugar Momma's as the first snowflakes gently fall from the sky.

AN EXCERPT FROM

FOR ALL SHE KNOWS

A POTOMAC POINT NOVEL

EDITOR'S NOTE: THIS IS AN EARLY
EXCERPT AND MAY NOT REFLECT THE
FINISHED BOOK

CHAPTER ONE

GRACE

Sunday in late January, 12:15 a.m.
Shock Trauma Hospital near Baltimore

Everyone warned me that the day would come when I'd regret befriending Mimi Gillette. But despite our many differences, Mimi and I had clicked from the moment we first met in our sons' toddler playgroup years ago. Sure, she could be flamboyant, and I didn't agree with her stance on teen drinking, but she had a huge heart—even after her ex-husband ground it beneath his bootheel and left her to raise their son alone. And so I'd tuned out public opinion, blind to the fact that such neglect could lead to my own son's life-changing injuries.

I should've known, though. Kids often pay the price for their parents' mistakes.

Curling forward, I hugged my calves and drew deep breaths. *Do not panic before knowing all the facts.*

With my eyes closed, I recalled the scene in Mimi's basement and felt sick again. Since becoming a mother, it had been unlike me to be nonchalant about anything, including friends. This kind of tragedy had been my worst fear since becoming a mother, so I'd conscientiously managed my family to prevent one. We lived in a close-knit community with low crime rates. Encouraged nonviolent extracurriculars, such as theater and academic clubs. Sat down to family dinners on a nightly basis so that my husband, Sam, and I could keep connected to our kids and head off bad decisions. We even attended church most Sundays, where I regularly prayed to God to safeguard us against evil.

Whenever another incident of online bullying or a random school shooting sent me into a tailspin of worry about our kids' fates, Sam and Mimi would tell me to relax. Like many others, they relied on the odds to assure them that those awful things would never claim one of our own.

But I knew.

I always knew that someday the scales would be rebalanced, because it had never seemed fair that my life had been so easy while others endured endless struggles.

Mimi didn't sympathize with my sense of dread about that invisible "other shoe" dropping, probably because she'd been ducking them left and right for most of her life. Yet despite facing one catastrophe after another, she rallied in the face of the insurmountable. It was impossible not to admire a woman who rolled up her sleeves and worked her butt off to overcome whatever was thrown at her, which was why I'd never acquiesced to the gossips and naysayers.

In any case, most of us feared things we hadn't experienced, and I'd had very little experience with real pain before tonight. A shudder racked me at the memory of Carter's tears, then I swallowed another surge of bile.

"Excuse me." I reached out for the young nurse cutting through the waiting room on his way toward the nurses' station, despite his focus on the iPad in his hand. "My son, Carter Phillips, was rushed into MRIs a while ago, but I haven't heard any updates. It's been more than an hour."

"Let me check for you." Despite being harried, he flashed a sympathetic smile before continuing toward the nurses' station.

"Thank you," I called after him.

The thought that my firstborn might never walk again made my body prickle with heat and my vision blur. I pinched my cheek and blinked in a vain attempt to pull myself together.

The clock read twelve thirty. My God, every minute seemed an eternity.

Across the waiting room, our daughter, Kim, was half-asleep in her pink-and-black leopard-print pj's and slippers, her lanky ten-year-old body strewn across Sam's lap. When we'd gotten Mimi's phone call, I'd charged over to her house to catch up with the EMTs—still in my Ugg slippers and yoga pants—while Sam had stayed behind, waiting for the girls at Kim's birthday sleepover to be picked up by shocked parents. Now he was stroking Kim's hair, staring into space, probably praying like me.

Our eyes met, but I glanced away.

"Grace," came his deep voice.

"Not now." I crossed my arms and closed my eyes, wishing that when I opened them again, this would be nothing more than a terrible nightmare. Sweat seeped from every pore.

"You can't stay mad forever. We have to come together for Carter," he said.

"It's been three hours—hardly forever. If you'd only listened to me this morning, we wouldn't even be here." Until then, we'd always presented a united front to our kids.

His cheeks colored as if I'd slapped them. "Blame won't help anyone."

Of course he'd say that now, when his judgment had been as poor as Mimi's. Bad enough that Carter might lose the use of his legs. The possibility that I might never forgive Sam hollowed out my heart, because he'd been my everything since we'd met in college.

I tugged hard at the hair in my fists, but no self-inflicted pain would reverse time. Darkness wrapped around me, suffocating me in self-loathing because, deep down, I knew that everything would also be different if I hadn't lacked the courage of my convictions.

Every sound in the waiting room reverberated in my head, making me nauseated and twitchy. I sprang from my chair and paced, picturing my sweet boy in a wheelchair. *What's that like? How will we manage rehab and school? How do we make the house accessible?*

Answers were unlikely to help me accept whatever fate had in store. Impossible—just like forgiveness. I needed to find strength, because I couldn't help Carter accept paralysis with fortitude if I crumpled into a heap of bones on the floor. My thoughts and my body seemed disconnected and disjointed, as if I'd stepped through an invisible hole in the universe that made everything unfamiliar. Tonight's outcome remained a mystery, but I knew that—whatever happened next—I'd never be the same person I'd been mere hours ago.

This was too big. Too much. I covered my mouth with both hands to keep a scream from erupting, then bent forward again—hands on my knees—burdened by the history and decisions that had caused this catastrophe.

Looking back, the first big turn of the wheel that had led us here was when Mimi's ex, Dirk, left her four years ago. Her distraught expression that afternoon had pained me.

"This shouldn't hurt so much. It's nothing new, this nonsense with Miranda Wright. But now he's leaving me to follow her up to Annapolis. Rowan's upstairs crying. He needs a father, Grace. Even an average one like Dirk is better than an absent one. How will I get him through puberty on my own?" Mimi had blubbered while tossing used tissues around like a tornado.

Her son, Rowan, had a good heart but had always lacked impulse control and any interest in school. Nothing I'd ever suggested had helped motivate him to hit the books. He'd rather climb a tree or go for a sail or work out on the field. We all favored pastimes that played to our strengths. Rowan had gone on to become an all-star wide receiver for the high school football team at only fifteen. He was also as handsome as his mother was pretty.

"Honey, it'll be okay," I'd said. *"Sam and I will help. Sam can toss a football or talk about responsibility, and whatever else you need. Rowan can come home with Carter after school until he's old enough to be alone. Honestly, this could be the best thing for both of you. Once you get over the sting, you'll be better off. There are good men out there, Mimi. We'll find you someone who treats you with respect. Someone who you don't consider another child."*

That's how Mimi had referred to Dirk whenever he'd drunk too much or taken "mental health days" from work—which led him to getting fired. Still, she had a soft spot for bad boys like her ex, almost like she thought her love would reform them.

Personally, I'd always suspected that Dirk envied Mimi's successful career. Becoming a hairstylist had been a perfect fit for a chatterbox with an eye for making people look their best, especially after she opened her own salon. His getting fired had put a strain on their finances, which kept her from reinvesting her profits and expanding. Odds were that her complaints about doing all the work inside and outside the house made it easier for him to follow his wandering eye into another woman's bed.

In the end, he'd left Mimi alone to raise their son as the middle-school years hit. And as much as she adored Rowan, when she'd had a second glass of wine, she'd confide in me her worries that he'd turn out like his dad—a car salesman who wasn't keen on taking responsibility for much, including child support. But the kind of trouble that culminated tonight began when Mimi started overcompensating for Dirk's absence by letting Rowan run wild and call the shots. By the end of his freshman year of high school, her permissiveness was legendary.

Some of the other moms would question me or expect me to say something, as if it were my business to tell Mimi how to parent. I defended her right to raise her son as she saw fit, never dreaming her choices would end up hurting Carter. Another example of my own weakness—the legacy of my childhood conditioning.

My phone vibrated in my pocket. Mimi again. I couldn't deal with her now. Didn't care about her apologies or her distress. The cops might still have been at her house, for all I knew or cared. I'd demand justice for Carter eventually, but at the moment, all I wanted was for somebody to tell us that our son would recover and walk.

I collapsed back onto my seat.

Sam slid out from beneath Kim and stretched. "I'm going for coffee. Do you want one?"

"No thank you." I still wouldn't meet his gaze but crossed the room to sit with Kim while he was gone.

That my daughter could sleep in this brightly lit, hardly peaceful waiting room astounded me. I toyed with a curl of her blonde hair, wanting to cradle her to my chest and squeeze her tight, as if my arms would keep her safe in a way that I'd failed to do for Carter.

Oh God, how was this happening? A tear rolled down my cheek. I leaned forward to stop myself from throwing up, then rocked in my seat, desperate for positive thoughts. None came. Or if they did, they got crowded out by recriminations and the frustration of my own impotence.

The more I thought about it, tonight's skirmish had really heated up weeks ago, when parents started arguing over the superintendent's proposed capital expenditures to upgrade the school's sports facilities instead of its science labs. A boon to students like Rowan, an athlete with a spotty academic record. But Carter—an aspiring chemical engineer who never set foot on a field (and all the other students like him)—would see no benefit from that use of tax dollars.

In other words, I was vehemently opposed. Last month's PTC meeting got so contentious, the next day kids started taking sides, too. But for once in my life, I took a stand and spoke out at the public hearing this past Monday night.

To think that, when Mimi and I had bumped into each other in the produce aisle at Stewart's Grocery Mart on *that* afternoon, my biggest worry had been whether our friendship would survive if I won that debate.

"Mrs. Phillips?" A doctor whose name I couldn't remember how to pronounce looked down at Kim and me just as Sam returned to the waiting room. "I have an update."

ACKNOWLEDGMENTS

As always, I have many people to thank for helping me bring this book to all of you—not the least of whom are my family and friends for their continued love, encouragement, and support.

Thanks, also, to my agent, Jill Marsal, as well as to my patient editors, Chris Werner and Tiffany Yates Martin, whose keen eyes made this book so much stronger. And none of my work would find its way to readers without the entire Montlake family working so hard on my behalf.

Unlike many of my previous books, base elements of this story grew out of personal experiences with depression, anxiety, and the confusion otherwise known as motherhood. Most of the research undertaken for the teen cutting issue in this story was conducted online, without personal interviews. I suppose I should thank Google and YouTube for the copious amount of information one is able to uncover in an instant. Honestly, I am awed by authors who wrote books before the internet existed. The time and effort it must've taken to research anything is staggering. But I would like to thank Maddee James, a graphic designer with a keen eye for art, for pointing me toward some sources that helped me create Anne's character.

I also need to thank my critique partners, Linda Avellar, Barbara Josselsohn, and Ginger McKnight, for their guidance. Additionally, a big thanks to my beta reader, Katherine Ong, for her feedback on the early draft, as well as hugs for writers Tracy Brogan, Virginia Kantra, Sonali Dev, Priscilla Oliveras, Falguni Kothari, and Barbara O'Neal, for taking time to talk through plot knots or providing feedback on a chapter or two. It seems that every book I write is really a group project! I also offer a heartfelt second thank-you to Barbara O'Neal for the beautiful praise she bestowed on this book. Her approval means so much to me.

I couldn't produce any of my work without the MTBs, who help me plot and keep my spirits up when doubt grabs hold, or my Fiction From the Heart sisters, who inspire me on a daily basis.

And I can't leave out the wonderful members of my CTRWA chapter. Year after year, all the CTRWA members provide endless hours of support, feedback, and guidance. I love and thank them for that.

Finally, and most important, thank you, readers, for making my work worthwhile. Considering all your options, I'm honored by your choice to spend your time with me.

ABOUT THE AUTHOR

Wall Street Journal and *USA Today* bestselling author Jamie Beck's realistic and heartwarming stories have sold more than two million copies. She is a two-time Booksellers' Best Award finalist and a National Readers' Choice Award winner, and critics at *Kirkus, Publishers Weekly,* and *Booklist* have respectively called her work "smart," "uplifting," and "entertaining." In addition to writing novels, she enjoys hitting the slopes in Vermont and Utah and dancing around the kitchen while cooking. Above all, she is a grateful wife and mother to a very patient, supportive family. Fans can get exclusive excerpts and inside scoops and be eligible for birthday gift drawings by subscribing to her newsletter at http://eepurl.com/b7k7G5. She also loves interacting with everyone on Facebook at www.facebook.com/JamieBeckBooks.